Mike Lucas is the author of several picture books including CBCA Notable Book *Olivia's Voice*. He has also written and published several books of children's poetry, has had work highly commended in magazines and contributed to poetry anthologies. Mike is one of the main organisers of the Adelaide Festival of Children's Books and an Honorary Member of the CBCA (SA). He presents writing and poetry workshops at schools, owns a bookshop in Blackwood, South Australia, and works as a full-time engineer. He doesn't sleep much. In 2022, Mike's first YA novel *What We All Saw* was published and shortlisted for the Readings Book Prize – Young Adult 2022, CBCA Book of the Year – Older Readers 2023 and the Prime Minister's Literary Award – Young Adult Literature 2023.

ONE BY ONE THEY DISAPPEAR

MIKE LUCAS

PENGUIN BOOKS

Note: this story is set in Nazi Germany during World War II and as such contains content that some readers may find distressing.

PENGUIN BOOKS

UK | USA | Canada | Ireland | Australia
India | New Zealand | South Africa | China

Penguin Random House Australia is part of the Penguin Random House group of companies whose addresses can be found at global.penguinrandomhouse.com.

First published by Penguin Books, an imprint of
Penguin Random House Australia Pty Ltd, in 2024

Cover design by Christa Moffitt, Christabella Designs
Cover image: Angyalosi Beata/Shutterstock.com
Internal design and typesetting by Midland Typesetters, Australia

Printed and bound in Australia by Griffin Press, an accredited
ISO AS/NZS 14001 Environmental Management Systems printer

A catalogue record for this book is available from the National Library of Australia

ISBN 978 1 76104 9 866

penguin.com.au

We at Penguin Random House Australia acknowledge that Aboriginal and Torres Strait Islander peoples are the Traditional Custodians and the first storytellers of the lands on which we live and work. We honour Aboriginal and Torres Strait Islander peoples' continuous connection to Country, waters, skies and communities. We celebrate Aboriginal and Torres Strait Islander stories, traditions and living cultures; and we pay our respects to Elders past and present.

Dedicated to the children who have suffered,
and continue to suffer, under the barbarity of war.

ONE

The Black Forest
Confederation of the Rhine
Winter 1811

The small house, perched high on the side of the snowy mountain, groaned and shifted as the wind gusted against its wooden frame. Inside, three brothers stared up at the dark rafters while the old woman, unfazed by the rugged storm, finished telling her story.

The wind eased, and the brothers' eyes returned to the woman's wrinkled face. With every flicker of the candle it seemed to change, the contours of her skin rippling across her wizened features. Her pale lips were half smiling, half sneering, as though she were taking pleasure from the discomfort of her audience. Despite her age, her eyes were the clearest blue, like those of a newborn.

The eldest brother coughed and nervously fiddled with his cravat. Without moving his head, he glanced over at the next eldest, who laid his fountain pen down upon the table and rolled the blotter across the page to remove the excess ink. The youngest brother sat on a stool in the corner, arms crossed, lost in shadow.

It was the middle brother who spoke. His hair was fairer than that of his siblings, his profile less severe. 'Thank you, Frau Fischer. That is a very interesting tale.'

The old woman gave a toothless smile. 'I am just one in a long line of storytellers.'

The youngest leaned forward, out of the shadow. He held up his hands, inspecting his nails as though they were the only thing of importance in the room. 'It was tedious. Like all the others you have told us.'

'Magnus!' reprimanded the middle brother. 'I have told you before –'

'You have told me, and I have told you. These primitive people with their ludicrous stories. It is better they are lost to the depths of history.'

The old woman rubbed at the whiskers on her chin and chewed on nothing. There was something in the younger brother's eyes she didn't like. She read a troubled future in them. For those around him. For many.

The middle brother let his gaze linger on Magnus a while longer. 'I am sorry, Frau Fischer. Our brother, he is young and –'

'I am old enough to know that these tales are nonsense,' he retorted.

'We should be going,' said the eldest brother, standing up. 'We have a long journey ahead of us.'

As if to argue the point, the house shook with a blast of thunder.

'You won't be going down off the mountain this night,' said Frau Fischer. 'You can stay here.'

The elder brothers exchanged glances while Magnus scowled at the old woman.

'I am hungry,' he said.

She pointed to a door. 'There is milk in the larder, and bread less than three days old. I have one more tale I would like to tell your brothers. You have no interest and, besides, it is not for your ears.'

'I'm not a child. I shall be fourteen in a few months. I have travelled with my brothers and heard tales of terror far worse than yours.'

The old lady chuckled. 'Perhaps. But it is best for you that you do not hear this.'

'Go and eat, Magnus,' said the eldest brother. He had finally found his tongue. When the boy didn't move, he said, 'Magnus, leave the room.'

'But –'

'Do as I say!'

Magnus, with lips pursed and temper flared, stormed from the room. The middle brother stood up and closed the door behind him. 'Please, Frau Fischer, when you are ready.' He dipped his pen into the inkwell.

'You cannot write this down,' the old woman said.

'But that is what we do. We write the stories.'

She lowered herself into her chair. 'Not this one.'

'Why not?' His pen was poised above the paper.

The old woman laughed. 'Very well, you shall see.' And she began to tell her tale.

The middle brother scratched away at the paper, trying to catch every word the old woman said.

'A wonderful story, Frau Fischer,' said the eldest brother. 'But forgive me. There is nothing extraordinarily frightening in that tale that a child would not be able to hear.'

'I never said there was.'

'But you said . . .'

'I said the tale was not for the child's ears.'

'That's odd.' The middle brother, interrupting the exchange, put one hand up to cover his mouth while the other flicked back through the pages of his notebook.

'What is it, Wilhelm?' asked the elder brother.

'They're blank,' gasped Wilhelm. 'Though I have been writing upon them for the last half an hour.'

'You could not have been.'

'I have, Jacob. You have watched me. You have heard me. I have seen the words myself. Look!'

He pointed to the most recent page, and Jacob craned his neck to see.

Both brothers gasped. Jacob leaped back and Wilhelm pushed his chair away. Their faces were ghostly.

'How is that happening? What is this?' asked Jacob.

'I told you it could not be written down,' laughed the old woman.

As the two brothers watched, letter by letter, word by word, the final sentences of the tale disappeared from the paper until it was as clean and white as the snow outside the cottage.

Magnus stepped into the room with a sneer. 'My brother was correct. I am anything but startled.'

Jacob tore his eyes from the book. 'You heard?'

'Every word,' smirked Magnus.

'You should not have listened,' said the old woman, though there was no anger in her voice. 'I warned you.'

'But now I have, and I do not have the vapours, old woman.'

Frau Fischer didn't like this young man, which made it easier for her to deliver the message to him. 'There is nothing I can do for you now.'

The boy was still smirking, though his brothers were not. They had seen something they did not understand. And if that was real, then, perhaps, so were her warnings.

Frau Fischer pushed herself out of her chair for the last time that night. The wind outside was dying, as was the fire, as was the candle, as was she.

'You can sleep in here tonight,' she said to Jacob and Wilhelm. 'Leave in the morning.'

She hobbled towards the doorway and, without turning, added, 'And you should both say goodbye to your younger brother.'

Then she disappeared.

They woke to find the storm had passed and the old woman dead in her bed. Her expression carried a slight smile, as though she were happy to be rid of this world.

Jacob trekked to the village and returned with the priest in tow. It was too late for last rites, but a prayer was said over the old woman's body and her head was covered with a sheet. They left her there, alone in her room, and stepped back into the parlour.

'I shall inform the doctor,' said the priest.

The brothers nodded. 'If there is nothing else,' said Wilhelm, 'we should be going, while the skies remain calm.'

The priest eyed them with suspicion. 'Tell me ... what was it that brought you here, to see Frau Fischer?'

'We are collecting tales of folklore, for a book,' said Wilhelm, picking up the bag containing his notebook, pen and ink. 'We'd heard the village is famous for its stories.'

'That it is,' said the priest. 'We are home to a special type of storyteller that will not be found anywhere else in the world. Frau Fischer was one of our finest. I'm glad your trip hasn't been wasted. There were just the two of you?'

The brothers exchanged glances, hesitated, but then nodded.

'Very well. There should be no need,' said the priest, 'but just in case the doctor has any questions, who should I say to contact?'

Wilhelm reached into his pocket and brought out a card. He handed it to the priest. 'Grimm,' he said. 'Wilhelm and Jacob Grimm.'

TWO

Stuttgart
Germany
21st September 1942

It was the book that was responsible for all that happened to Hannah after the death of her parents. One book with so many tales. She gripped it tightly in her lap as she glanced out the train window. Desperate eyes stared back at her from a ragged hole in the boxcar boards opposite.

At first she thought it was a calf, or a lamb. But then a nose appeared, as if searching for fresh air, and she realised it was a person. A child, by the looks of it. Why would a child be inside a cattle car? Perhaps they were trapped. Or hiding. Like her.

She glanced away. Just for a second. But when she looked back, the face was gone. All that remained was that dark, splintered hole. As though the person had never existed.

The shrill blow of a whistle yanked her out of her thoughts. From somewhere ahead there was an explosive puff, a hiss of steam and a long, piercing toot. She had never been on a train before, but she had seen and heard them. She tensed as her carriage lurched forward, leaving behind the boxcar and whoever was inside it. The jagged teeth of a broken building beneath a smoky sky momentarily came into view, before being replaced by another boxcar with its wide door chained and bolted closed on the outside. The puffing and hissing and jolting increased in intensity and speed as her carriage sped past the livestock boxes. When she had counted twenty of them, she stopped.

Her train veered to the right, away from the boxcars, revealing a line of machine guns mounted on their roofs, barrels pointing at the sky, a soldier behind each one. Their uniforms were grey, not the black of the SS, but still she felt her teeth clench and her stomach tighten. Hannah had come to hate and fear soldiers – the stomp of their boots on the roads; the rumble of their trucks; the orders they barked as though the people were nothing more than dogs.

It hadn't happened overnight. There had been a slow, incremental descent. Hannah had been around five years old when she had first noticed it, but it had started long before that. A false narrative spread by the bigots in power, believed by the weak and ignorant. Arriving in her life as whispers from passing strangers, a nod in the direction of her and her family. Sometimes a pointed finger. Not just targeting them, but also their neighbours and friends. All of them with one thing in common. They were Jews.

And a year or so later, the whispers became unrepressed insults, then angry shouts of threat and abuse. That they were vermin, filthy dogs. That they weren't wanted here. Here in their home city, their own country. If they didn't leave of their own accord, they would be made to. They would be chased out. Eventually, Hannah, her mother, even her father began to fear going outside their door.

In the winter of 1938, six months after her eighth birthday

and a year before war broke out, those threats turned into violence.

Hannah was lying in bed, a book propped up on her pillow, fighting against sleep in order to finish the chapter, when the angry shouts and jeers made their way into her room from the street two floors below. Then the sounds of shattering glass, heavy footsteps, splintering wood. Hannah sat bolt upright, all her senses on high alert. More jeers and shouts. Smashes and crashes. The smell of burning. A scream.

She dropped the book and ran to her parents' room. Her mother was sitting up in bed, her father at the window. He let the curtains fall and turned when she came in. She could just make out their pained expressions. The ones that were becoming all too familiar. Lips tight, eyes wide and staring, nostrils flaring with each breath. He got back into bed, and Hannah squeezed between them. They wrapped their arms around her in the semi-darkness of their rented apartment, and together they huddled and listened.

CRASH!

That was closer. The nearby shattering of glass. The crunching of it beneath heavy feet. Menacing shouts. Cruel words. Frightened sobs. Pained cries.

The night's terror seemed to stretch for eternity. They remained in the room even after the shouts moved on, the sun rose and the sound of glass being swept up reached them through the closed window.

When her father deemed it safe enough to venture outside, he discovered it was more than windows that had been broken. Homes. Livelihoods. Families. Bodies. Their neighbours – the Goldbergs and Nudels – disappeared. The tobacconist shop below their apartment – looted. Herr Blau, the owner – beaten beyond recognition.

Hannah had always known her father to be confident and outspoken in his beliefs and virtues. But as the days passed, he seemed to shrink in character, burdened down by the fear and timidity he was forced to carry. Her mother, who had always worn a smile and could rid Hannah's mind of worry with her words, grew sullen and silent and refused to let Hannah out of her sight.

Less than a week later, Hannah's best friend Leah and her parents came bustling into the apartment from across the hall, holding up a newspaper that declared all Jewish children were forbidden from attending school with Germans. It was absurd. Hannah had been born a German. Why couldn't she be Jewish *and* German?

Her father had already been prohibited from teaching, and now she wasn't allowed to go to the same school as her friends. Why was this happening? Would all the hard work she had put in at her school be wasted? Surely, this couldn't last forever. All the people she would miss! Jewish, German – it had never mattered.

The girls were asked to go to Hannah's room so that the adults could talk. They tried to listen, but somebody kept ruffling the newspaper, and words were spoken in hushed tones. But the girls had seen and heard enough to know the way things were going. They had watched families in their neighbourhood pack up their belongings and leave. Others had just seemed to disappear. And she and Leah feared their parents announcing that they, too, would soon have to go somewhere. And the two friends would end up parting.

They made a pact. If they left, and went separate ways, they would find each other when it was all over.

In the living room was a wireless radio. Hannah's father said it was their window to the world, though he warned her to never believe everything that came out of it. Because the man talking (for it was usually a man) worked for the government; was controlled by the government. And so the man would only say what the government told him to say. *Question everything*, her father said. *Never ever blindly believe.*

The following year, Hannah and her parents sat and listened with ever-growing dread to the announcement that Germany had invaded Poland. That news was true, her father told her. The government gained nothing from lying about it. And he had heard it through other channels. Channels he would get into trouble for listening to.

Hannah didn't get it. She just couldn't comprehend how one country could assume the right to take over another. The unfairness made her blood boil. But that energy was soon sapped by the realities of living through a war. A war that was not only with Poland, but also Poland's allies, Britain and France. Hannah quickly discovered that war led to shortages, especially of food, and that hunger followed. It was bad enough in the early months of the war when her family had money coming in. But when her father, who had already been forced out of his job as a teacher, had his cleaning job taken away, it became almost impossible to find enough food to keep them going. But that was what the Nazis wanted. That was why Jews could only shop at certain times, usually at the end of the day after most of the produce had been sold to the *German* citizens. And that was why Jews always paid more for less of the same product.

A new decade arrived, though there were no celebrations for Hannah's family. She watched her parents getting thinner, and suspected they were giving her their share of the food. They denied it, and she was too hungry to give it back. They began to sell their furniture and jewellery – their memories – but when the law was introduced that all Jews had to wear the Star of David on their sleeves, it became impossible to bargain for a fair price. Being Jewish meant you took what you were given and didn't argue.

Hannah felt resentful and angry seeing her parents accept all this. She knew her anger should be directed at Hitler and the Nazis and the people out there who were following their despicable lead. But the only safe way to unleash that anger was at home, at her parents. And so she challenged them time and again over it. She wanted answers. She wanted reasons. But there were none. And it wasn't fair. It wasn't just. And after a while, even she lost the will to fight, the will to argue. And she accepted the way things were.

Then the news arrived that changed everything.

The soldiers had come for Leah and her family. Her friend had gone. Where, she didn't know. And, when she questioned her parents, no answer was forthcoming. Just pained, pale expressions, the shaking of heads and a silence that said everything and nothing. That was when she knew, without doubt, that all Jews, even the children, were considered the enemy. And that no soldier would ever show her kindness. If they came to their apartment . . . what? Hannah didn't know. She wasn't sure her parents did, either. Only that it wouldn't be good.

The next day, they ran.

THREE

October 1941

The cold bit into Hannah's face and the fear ate into her thoughts as they made their way through the dark streets. But her body remained warm from the layers of clothing her mother had told her to wear. It was the easiest way to carry them, she had said. And they would need as many clothes as they could take to get them through the winter.

It was past curfew. If they were caught . . . she wasn't sure. But they would be in big trouble. Sent away, like Leah and her family. At least, wherever they went, they would stay together.

Danger lurked in every shadow. It was as if the city itself had betrayed them; the bricks and timber, the cobbles and trees had turned against them. Her only comfort was her gloved hand holding on to her mother's. Every sound and movement arrested her already-alert eyes and ears. Her father was a step ahead, carrying a case packed with the rest of their clothes, a few photographs and the small number of valuables they had held onto. Her parents had argued about taking the case.

It makes our escape look obvious, argued her mother.

We are Jews out after curfew, responded her father. *We have removed our yellow stars. Discarded our Kenncartes. Carrying a case is hardly going to mean anything if we are caught. We will take the menorah. And the Tanakh. With all we are leaving behind, it is the least we can do to honour our culture, our identity.*

And her mother had conceded.

Hannah understood. But it hadn't made it any easier looking around her room for the final time, trying to choose just one thing to take. She had finally decided on a wooden pencil case given to her by Leah.

Along the dark pavements and treacherous alleyways they crept. Autumn had only just arrived, but the air was frigid, as though winter had been seconded by the ruling party to work against them.

This was a part of the city Hannah had never visited. She didn't know where they were going. Only that the people they would be staying with were kind to hide them in their home. Her father had told her he had never met them. But they had exchanged messages, passed through a mutual friend, and, once they were there, they would be safe for a time. The doubt, though, was there in his voice when he spoke. And in the way he tore his eyes away from her when he had finished.

They trod swiftly but lightly, eager to get to their place of refuge, but fearful that the sounds of their hurried footfalls would give them away. Sometimes, she could hear soldiers talking and laughing. Three times she saw them. And, in a very close call, they turned a corner to find a group warming their hands against a pyramid of burning furniture. From the way those soldiers were joking and the slurs they were using, Hannah knew it was a Jewish family's possessions they were burning. Before ducking back to safety, she was horrified to see a soldier casually throw a pile of books on the fire. Would her own books, too heavy to carry, suffer the same fate? She burned, too, but with hatred at the thought of their belongings being set alight.

They made their way down a narrow alley and stopped as equally light footsteps approached. The silhouette's features evolved out of the darkness and the man's hunched shoulders and ever-shifting eyes told Hannah that the person who was helping them was as terrified as they were.

'Herr Meyer?' asked her father, and the man nodded.

He gazed beyond them, and Hannah couldn't help but turn to look over her shoulder, half expecting to see a soldier, gun raised. But the alley was empty. Herr Meyer placed his hand gently on her father's shoulder, then smiled at Hannah and her mother. He led them to the end of the alley, leaned out and looked left and then right.

'Just across here,' he whispered, before running across the street. They followed him to a door that was hastily opened by a figure who retreated into the darkness.

Herr Meyer ushered each of them inside. Hannah first, feeling the warmth of a burning fire embrace but not comfort her. Her mother close behind, still holding tight to Hannah's hand. Then her father and finally Herr Meyer, who closed the door silently. Hannah, in unison with the grown-ups, released the breath she hadn't realised she'd been holding. She stood there trembling and trying to calm her hammering heart. Without a word yet spoken, they were led down the darkened hall to a fully furnished living room where Frau Meyer and two children stood like statues in front of a glowing fireplace, the fear and awkwardness that Hannah felt reflected in their eyes.

Compared to what Hannah's family had left behind after everything had been sold, this room was a palace. Matching furniture, a thick pile rug and heavy curtains that blocked light from escaping, as was the law, ensuring no help was given to enemy aircraft looking to drop their bombs. Hannah hadn't realised how much she had lost until now. Now that she could see a home, a family, that still had this much. And they were prepared to risk it all for them. Strangers. Her heart, sunk so low for so long, felt lifted to know there were still good people in the world.

Whispered introductions were quickly made. The girl was called Sofia, her brother Mikhail. Herr Meyer was Franz, his wife Margarete. Though Hannah could never envision herself addressing them as such.

Hannah glanced up at her mother, who was staring about the room as if she were trying to recall a lost memory. Her father removed his gloves, brought his hands up to his mouth and blew on them. Hannah, feeling the need to do something other than stare at the uneasy faces, pulled her hand free from her mother's and did the same. It seemed to bring her mother out of her reverie, and she followed suit. Frau Meyer excused herself, saying she had some milk heating on the stove.

Just the mention of warm milk made Hannah's mouth water and her stomach realise how empty it was. And she could suddenly smell it, if only in her mind.

Mikhail stepped forward and offered to take their overcoats. Hannah shrugged hers off and handed it to the boy, who had managed to find a smile to paste upon his face. Hannah tried to return it but wasn't sure she succeeded. Her parents removed their coats, and Mikhail left the room. Sofia stepped into the space vacated by him. It all seemed very rehearsed.

Sofia flicked a quick glance at her father, who replied with a nod. She brought her hands from behind her back and, smiling politely, held out a book to Hannah.

'This is for you. It's my favourite, but I know all the tales off by heart.'

Hannah, who had had to leave all her books behind, held out her own hands and let the volume fall into them. It was thick and heavy, comforting in its weight, leather-bound with gold embossed writing on the front and spine. The light reflecting off the letters hypnotised her for a second. None of her books at home had been this fine. And she had hated leaving them. So to have this, now …

She realised everybody was waiting for her to speak.

'Thank you,' she managed. 'I shall take good care of it.' She felt overwhelmed with gratitude, but worried that her words hadn't conveyed it. 'It's beautiful. I shall treasure it.'

Hannah registered the blush that erupted on Sofia's cheeks.

'A friend of your father's told me you're an avid reader, Hannah,' said Herr Meyer, shattering the unwarranted awkwardness.

Hannah glanced at her father, for a clue as to who this friend could be. But he just nodded for her to respond. She turned back to Herr Meyer. 'I have a lot of books,' she began, before realising her mistake. 'I used to …'

Her father must have felt a pang of guilt. 'We could only carry so much. And books are heavy.'

Another puddle of silence, and glances down at the carpet.

It was Sofia's turn to brush it away. 'I have more books you can borrow. Or I can bring you some from the city library if you've already read all the stories in that one.' She stumbled slightly as she raced to get the words out.

Hannah appreciated the sentiment. 'I've only read a few of the tales. Thank you,' she conceded.

She opened the book to the front page and there, in cursive script, was Sofia's name, and a message from her parents.

'You can cross that out if you like,' said Sofia quickly. 'And add your own name.'

Hannah shook her head. 'No. It can still be your book. And when we leave here, I will give it back.'

Sofia's eyes flicked to Herr Meyer, and Hannah looked at her own father. No one said anything, but the understanding was there. They wouldn't be leaving here for a long time. Not unless they were discovered by the Gestapo.

The sweet taste of warmed milk thawed the atmosphere as well as their bones, and the parents followed theirs with a small glass of clear liquid, which brought a smile to her mother's lips and a blush to her father's cheeks. Despite the room being well lit, Herr Meyer struck a match and lit a paraffin lamp. Then he ushered them back down the hallway to a door below the staircase, which he opened to reveal a small cloakroom. He swept aside the coats, disappeared inside with the lamp and, after a few seconds of clattering and clanking, stuck his head back out.

'I built this cloakroom myself,' he said. 'Just in case . . .' He didn't need to clarify. 'Before that, this door opened directly onto the stairs leading to the basement. If you'll follow me . . .'

The basement. Hannah's heart sank. She had been foolish enough to believe they would be staying in a bedroom on one of the upper floors. Perhaps even two separate rooms. She loved her parents, but the thought of spending every waking – and sleeping – hour in their company . . .

This isn't forever, she told herself. Just until things get better. They had to get better one day, didn't they?

Her father went first, and Hannah followed. She felt a soft hand reaching again for hers, and laced her fingers with her mother's, wondering if, perhaps, her mother needed that touch more than she did. Herr Meyer held the lamp aloft, while keeping the coats away from the flame with his other hand. Hannah could see enough to make out a wooden panel leaning beside a rectangle of darkness. A cold breeze blew out from that hole, frigid air that they would have to get used to, that would only become colder as winter approached and dug its teeth into the city and the ground below it. What had they escaped to? At least their home had been above ground, warm at times. Down here they could become trapped.

She tried to settle her panicked mind. Her parents knew what was best. And this was it.

'Mind your step,' warned Herr Meyer, as he trod through and began to descend. Hannah felt her mother's fingers tighten around hers as they followed, taking one slow step down at a time. Hannah counted them. Ten steps, each feeling colder than the one above it. The lamp did little to banish the shadows, and Hannah had no idea how big the basement was until Herr Meyer pulled at a cord and a single, bare bulb lit the room and all it contained.

Two mattresses – one large, one small. A simple table with a ceramic bowl and mirror on top and a plain wooden chair tucked in underneath. A couple of wine barrels, a tea chest and a set of drawers. Folded blankets. A bucket and mop. A broom. A makeshift curtain in an alcove, which Hannah feared was their only source of privacy. And, worst of all, she realised in despair, there was no sign of a toilet down here.

The walls were rough brick, the floor broken concrete. Thick beams ran from one end of the ceiling to the other, and thin slats of light flickered through the boards above, the unfelt warmth of the fire teasing them with its closeness. Their whole world, down here in the depths of the house, was no larger than their old sitting room.

'The light must stay off at night,' explained Herr Meyer. 'There are gaps in the floorboards where it may be noticed if someone were to enter the house. And it must be turned off during the day if you ever hear heavy footsteps above. My family and I always remove our shoes when we are in the house.'

Hannah scanned the room, taking in the dark corners where anybody and anything could hide. She reminded herself that the only dangers were outside and above these walls, and as long as they never came within, she and her family would remain safe. Terrified, cold, miserable. But safe.

'There is a bowl over there for washing. One of us will bring a fresh bucket of water each morning. We will take the pot and bring a clean one.'

Hannah couldn't help but gasp. A bucket! A pot! They had had their own toilet and running water in their apartment. The idea of doing her toilet in earshot of her parents was bad enough, but to leave it there. And for them to leave theirs. The smell would be atrocious in this small space. Herr Meyer paused in his instructions.

'It's all right,' said her father, placing his hand on her shoulder. 'We will get used to it. We have to.'

'There will be breakfast in the morning,' continued Herr Meyer, as Hannah tried to convince herself she didn't need to pee while really needing to pee. 'And a warm meal in the evening. I am afraid there is no heating down here, but there are plenty more blankets we can bring you . . .'

Hannah listened as Herr Meyer recited the instructions, and her parents nodded at every pause or change in tone. She wondered how this family could afford to feed an extra three people. Food was already in short supply, most of it going to the soldiers before civilians. Leah had told her that. And it was getting more expensive every day. Hannah and her parents were already used to eating very little, but even so, either the Meyers would need to halve their own meals or they would need to double their food purchases. Even if they somehow managed to buy extra ration stamps on the black market, Hannah knew there was a chance somebody might notice, and betray their secret.

While these thoughts tumbled through her mind, Hannah was overwhelmed with gratitude. She tried to embrace this feeling, rather than the rudimentary horror that surrounded her. Her father was right. They had to get used to it. Or they would end up like Leah and her family.

The thought of her best friend strengthened her resolve. She had to do this. Only then would she be able to fulfil her side of the promise that she'd made with Leah to find each other. Be thankful, she told herself, that there are people like the Meyers in this world. It was a welcome feeling after sitting so long with the deep emotions of unfairness and anger, sorrow and fear. She let it grow inside her, and hoped that, if the roles were reversed, she and her family would be able and willing to do the same. Gradually, despite her cold, hard surroundings, her body relaxed, warmed by the generosity of this man and his family. And, perhaps, by the multiple layers of clothes she was still wearing, too. She listened to her parents express their own gratitude with constant *thank yous* until, finally, her father laid his hand upon Herr Meyer's shoulder and hugged him.

When Herr Meyer had left, Hannah's mother began to unpack the case. She laid the few clothes they had brought in three piles, took the photograph of the three of them in happier times and placed it on a wine barrel, directly below the lamp. Then their Tanakh beside it. And finally, the menorah, which she set upon the table, graciously glistening in the meagre light. They didn't have one candle, let alone nine, but still it looked beautiful. And its presence gave Hannah hope.

'Come here,' said her mother, sitting down and patting the small mattress. Hannah's bed. Hannah walked over and sat beside her as her father lay down on the big mattress, closed his eyes and began to snore.

She felt her mother's gentle hands in her hair, unclasping her clips, felt her hair fall to her shoulders.

And then the brush. The one her mother had used on her hair since she was a baby. For the next half an hour they sat together as her mother brushed, smoothed and plaited her hair. Just like they did before.

They had left their home. Now this was their home. This cold, dark room in the bowels of a stranger's house. A friend of a friend of her father's, the two men having seemingly never met before. But Hannah was determined to do all she could to make it work, the knots in her shoulders lessening a little as those in her hair came loose with each gentle brush-stroke from her mother.

The next day she began to read the book that, on the cover, in gold embossed letters, bore the name of The Brothers Grimm. And, on the inside, in simple blue ink, that of the person she was soon to become.

FOUR

21st September 1942

The man opposite reached into his breast pocket and removed a pipe. He wriggled around in his seat as he tried to find his matches. With one hand, he retrieved the matchbox, took out a match and, with a brisk flick, a flame appeared. He dropped the box onto his lap, held the match to the bowl of his pipe, puffed and exhaled, puffed and exhaled. Hannah wondered why, with half the city smouldering away behind them, anybody would wish to breathe in more smoke. The sharp, acrid smell filled her nostrils and she tried to take shallow breaths. But the anxiety wouldn't let her. The small boy to her right wrinkled his face, pinched his nose, turned to his mother and voiced Hannah's thoughts.

'That stinks like our street. I don't like it.'

The mother, hair in pin-curls and cheeks the colour of the carnations Hannah's mother used to keep on the living room table, hushed him with a finger. Pin-curls. Her mother had once spoken of getting them put in. But it had never happened. Now it never would.

She breathed deep and glanced at the man, who furnished her with a look of annoyance. But the young boy's lack of tact had the desired effect. The man took one large suck on his pipe and then placed his thumb over the top of it. When it was out, he tapped it on the ashtray and stowed it back into his pocket. Hannah caught the boy's eye and smiled at him, thankful for his candour. He rumpled his nose at her.

Hannah began to relax as the city fell behind them. She was out, away from the only place she had ever called home. But it was no longer that. Parts of it were nothing more than piles of toppled bricks and twisted steel, the air above filled with choking smoke and dust. Let the soldiers who had spread terror throughout the streets have it.

A thick forest swallowed the train, spitting them out every now and then into a world of low hills and green fields. A few farms made brief appearances but, for the first hour or so, the view was mostly one of wood and fir, untouched by war. It helped to lift her spirits, knowing that places like this still existed. But for how long? Would the bombs eventually reach here? Would there be anything left at all by the end of the war?

The train rattled on, emerging from the forest into a small town, fortunate for now in its relative insignificance. They passed some sidings and open yards and the train pulled into a station. The man with the pipe stood and donned his hat, ready to alight the train. He caught her eye and nodded in simple acknowledgement. Or perhaps he had noticed something in Hannah's eyes. Something that gave her away. As if the star she had once worn on her sleeve was tattooed across her forehead. The thought momentarily terrified her and it was all she could do not to place her hand over her face.

Trust no one. That was what Marianne had said.

She gave as good a smile as she could muster, admonishing herself for her paranoia. When the man disappeared, the young boy hurriedly claimed the vacated position beside the window. An elderly couple shuffled into the carriage. The old man helped his wife into the seat next to the boy and then lowered himself down beside her.

The whistle, the puff, the hiss, the toot and the train was moving again.

Several minutes later, Hannah's heart leaped at the sound of the door snapping open, and she looked up to see a man in uniform standing there. Not a soldier, but a ticket inspector. Still, it was enough to resurface her panic and set her stomach churning. The old lady handed him two tickets from her purse, and the inspector stamped them with no more acknowledgement than a trawlerman would give to an individual fish trapped within his net. The young mother rummaged around in her bag with increasing panic. The inspector stared out the window with a look of disdain for everything passing. His gaze went to Hannah. *I'm coming for you next,* that look said, and Hannah forced herself not to swallow or do anything that would give her away. Instead, she opened her book to the front and removed the ticket that Marianne had folded in there.

Whatever you do, don't lose the ticket. They won't give you another one, and you'll be thrown off the train at the next station.

After a period of frantically shuffling through her bag, the woman found her tickets and held them out to the inspector. She swept her hair from her eyes and let out a sigh of relief. The inspector looked somewhat disappointed that the world had not provided him with a victim. He barely extended his hand and the woman had to shuffle along the seat, smiling at her son before the tickets were stamped and half-thrown back.

The inspector shifted his attention to Hannah, but she was already holding out her ticket, that strained smile upon her face.

The man didn't move. Hannah was aware of the eyes in the carriage going from her hand to the unforgiving face of the inspector. His eyes flicked to the cast on her leg, then the crutches leaning up against the window and back to Hannah's face. She kept his gaze and held onto her smile, even while the fear of being discovered and the anger at the man's expression rose inside her. Her leg itched inside the cast and she fought the urge to scratch it. With an audible huff, the inspector took that small step into the carriage and snatched the ticket from Hannah's fingers. She felt a sense of relief, but tried not to show it. *All is as it should be*, she told herself. *To everybody else, I am just a girl on a train. Nothing more, nothing less.*

The man went to stamp it but fumbled, dropping it to the floor. Hannah saw the smirks on her fellow passengers' faces as he bent to retrieve it, and she felt a little pride at her small victory over this petty man as he stamped the ticket and thrust it back at her.

'Thank you,' she said, maintaining the stiff smile upon her face. She would not stoop to his level of arrogance.

The inspector stomped back out through the door into a world he so obviously despised.

'What was the matter with that man?' asked the boy.

It was the old man who answered. 'He has the same affliction that plagues much of the world of late. The unwillingness to take that extra step to help others.' He gave Hannah a smile and his eyes twinkled. 'Well handled, young lady. Never let them take you down with them.'

She smiled back at him, feeling that something had just changed in her. She wasn't sure what. But she had just had a small victory, taken her own step forward. She had done it all by herself, and she felt stronger because of it.

The small boy frowned at her, as if trying to work out exactly what she had just done.

She pushed her fingers down inside her cast and scratched away at the itch. It felt so good.

FIVE

Hannah's eyelids began to droop. The rattle of the wheels and the gentle rocking of the carriage were lulling her thoughts and dulling her senses. She felt herself disconnecting, floating up, gazing around and then down at herself and the other four passengers.

You need to get off at Kalterfluss. If you're still on the train when it leaves, there's no telling where you'll end up. Do not fall asleep.

Hannah pulled herself back and forced her eyes open. She glanced around the carriage with an unwarranted sense of guilt, as if Marianne were there, watching her. The elderly couple had also succumbed to sleep, as had the boy opposite. His mother was leaning towards Hannah, staring out and up at the soaring peaks that now dominated the landscape. Hannah followed her gaze. The sky, populated with bovine clouds, pressed down upon the gargantuan mountains that were unworldly, almost terrifying in their enormity. She felt her stomach pitch and yaw.

The woman shuffled back. 'I'm sorry.'

'That's all right,' said Hannah. 'I shouldn't have fallen asleep.'

'They're breathtaking, aren't they? They give me hope. That no matter what we do to the cities across the world, no matter how we continue to destroy ourselves, we cannot touch them. We cannot change what they are. We are all so small.'

Hannah, who had felt small for so long, gazed back up at them, trying to find that hope the woman was talking about. If it was there, she was yet to see it.

'Do you live there?' asked the woman. Her voice was soft, her smile seemed genuine, her words compassionate. Still, Marianne's warning came back. *Don't trust anybody. Don't give away more information than you have to.*

Hannah nodded.

'The safest place to live,' continued the woman. 'Until it's all over. If it ever will be.'

Her words echoed Hannah's sentiments. When she had moved into the Meyers' basement with her parents, she had been able to imagine life returning to normal once the war was over. But now, on her own and on her way to an unknown place to live with a stranger, she wasn't even sure what to be hopeful for.

The woman took a deep breath and shook the melancholy from her voice. 'I'll leave you to your thoughts. And the mountains.'

Hannah returned to them both. Mountains high and thoughts low. And the train rattled on.

Shadows shifted, colours came and went. Places appeared and vanished. All so slowly, though, almost as if there were no movement at all. The mountains revolved. The sky shrank. Whenever Hannah thought they must be nearly there, a new landscape opened up before them, a fresh tapestry of forest and rock, with scatterings of pinprick houses.

The last time she had seen the mountains, it had been from a distance. Last spring, six months or so into the year that they had spent living in the Meyers' basement. They had, by then, fallen into a routine, and life had become – while not easy – acceptable. Cleaning chores had been diligently set out and shared between the three of them, and Hannah's mother had watched over their completion – that small sense of purpose, Hannah had seen, taking on a large air of importance in her mother's mind. They had their rituals of washing, eating, sleeping, and they kept track of the days and the outside world through the newspapers Herr Meyer brought them.

Hannah realised her father's sense of purpose was maintained through her study. He was, once more, a teacher. Unfortunately for them both, Hannah was often a reluctant and frustrated student. She used to enjoy school, but it wasn't the same. Paper was scarce, and it was hard to concentrate in the dim light of the frigid basement. She often wondered why she was bothering, if there was no life for her outside these walls anyway.

The Meyer children helped with the housekeeping by bringing fresh bowls of water and clean pots, and by taking away the old. At first, Hannah and her parents had been embarrassed and apologetic about Sofia and Mikhail having to remove the toilet pot. The children had been polite, but it was obvious by the way they would try to leave it to each other, and then carry it at arms' length with breaths held, how much of an unpleasant task they found it. But, eventually, it became as natural and automatic as sweeping the floor.

Keeping warm had been a problem. In the winter, especially. The only defence they had against the cold was the four walls around them, the layers of clothing they wore, the blankets supplied by the Meyers, and each other. And too soon, the clothes were being kept together by little more than holes. The darning was endless, and often the holes she and her mother repaired only served to delay the inevitable end to the garment. All they could do at these times was unravel it and use its thread to postpone the demise of other items of clothing. Hannah could remember getting dressed one morning in spring, trying to find a sleeve in her cardigan and putting her arm through a new hole in the stitching.

Later that day, there had been a knock on the panel at the top of the stairs leading from the cloakroom. A fast double tap followed by two slower ones – the agreed knock. Hannah, sitting in their only chair, a blanket wrapped around her shoulders, was pulled from the worlds of the Brothers Grimm. When she wasn't studying, she spent much of her time here in forests and small villages, palaces and castles, meeting princesses, kings and witches.

As always, she felt her heart speed up, despite knowing whose fist was gently knocking upon the door. That knock was quickly followed by Herr Meyer's placating voice, always sounding unnecessarily apologetic.

'Ilse, Benjamin, Hannah. It's me. May I come in?'

Hannah's father raised himself from the old wine cask he was perched upon, rubbed at his knees and climbed the stairs. Hannah heard the panel shift, and then her father's voice.

'Is there a problem?'

Herr Meyer's laugh. As though he had said the most stupid thing and suddenly realised. 'No, no, no. Everything is as it should be. I just thought . . . may I come in?'

'Yes, of course. I'm sorry.' The two men descended into the basement. Herr Meyer smiled and bowed his head to Hannah's mother. She did her best to respond, but it didn't come easy. Of the three of them, she seemed to be finding it the hardest. Hannah swung between feeling sorry for her and being frustrated at her inability to adapt. Herr Meyer turned his smile on Hannah. Wider, as if he thought he hadn't tried hard enough with her mother. Hannah made up for her mother's reticent response by forcing the corners of her own mouth up higher than necessary.

'It is a beautiful day today.' Herr Meyer cast his eyes up at the beams, as though the sky could be seen through them. 'Beautiful. As clear as I've ever seen it.'

Hannah's mother paused at her darning, and her father's face sank at the mention of the outside world. Hannah, however, allowed herself a tinge of excitement, daring to hope. Herr Meyer, ever the reader of other people's feelings, continued.

'I was thinking that maybe young Hannah here would like to see the mountains. From the attic.'

Hannah leaped to her feet, the wooden chair scraping back across the floor. But then she felt her mother's hand on her shoulder.

'I don't know. If somebody were to see . . .'

'Please, Mama. Just for a moment. I haven't seen them for such a long time.' And it was true. Trapped down here in the semi-darkness for the past few months, with only the occasional visit to the rooms above. And even then, it had been in darkness. The curtains had been drawn closed and the shadows had remained. Always talking in hushed tones.

There had been times when her father and Herr Meyer had enjoyed that clear liquid that seemed to warm them and make their words louder and braver. Warming Hannah's heart, too, to see her father as he used to be. The two women, half-heartedly telling the men to hush before their own voices broke out into barely suppressed laughter. Hannah loved these moments, though they were rare and over too soon.

Sometimes, she would disappear into the living room with Sofia and Mikhail to play Skat, or to listen to them talk about their day. She had endless questions about what they had seen, what they had heard, how they felt. And Sofia and Mikhail were happy to talk, so it worked well between them. Even when the two broke into a sibling argument over something trivial, Hannah enjoyed the sense of normality it brought, though that normality was short-lived.

There had been her birthday, when Frau Meyer had saved enough ingredients to bake a simple cake, and they had all joined together in whispered song. At Hanukkah, Herr and Frau Meyer had surprised them by bringing nine candles to the basement for the menorah. They had been saving them for a couple of months, and Herr Meyer apologised for cutting them in half to make up the number. His eyes had flicked up towards the ceiling as he handed them over, and Hannah's father, obviously reading his concerns, had promised not to light them after dark. Frau Meyer had baked challah, and the smell was deliciously overpowering, bringing back memories of happier days. Though she'd used too much flour, Hannah's mother had said, and it was too hard.

Hannah's father had invited the Meyers to stay and take part in their Hannukah rituals, but the Meyers had declined. They did not wish to impose, they'd said, at a time when there had already been too much imposed upon them. Hannah remembered her mother had closed her eyes and nodded her head slowly, which she had thought rude at the time. But thinking back now to the blessings they had whispered as they briefly lit the menorah candles, it was right that the Meyers had left.

And then there had been Christmas Day. Hannah had never celebrated Christmas before, and celebration wasn't exactly the right word. But it was a time of joy and being together, Herr Meyer had said, and nobody could argue that they had to find joy wherever and whenever they could.

But those visits had become less and less of late. And she could only guess that it was because the risk to them all was becoming greater. The newspapers passed on by Herr Meyer were filled with talk of German victories, but told them very little about the world directly above them. Hannah had begun to feel her own spirit closing in on her, just like the cold walls that surrounded them. To be able to rid herself of them, just for a moment, to see the world as she used to know it – the vast, open sky and the almost unimaginable mountains beyond – that would help to hold back those walls inside her mind a little longer.

'It will be safe,' promised Herr Meyer, his eyes shining as though he wanted this as much as Hannah. 'We shall keep a close watch outside.'

Hannah glanced from her father to her mother, trying to influence them with her eyes. But they were just staring at each other, straight-mouthed and sunken-eyed, neither wanting to make the decision that had no right answer. It was her mother who conceded, who gave permission with a barely perceptible nod beneath the single lamp.

'Very good.' Herr Meyer's gaze lingered on Hannah's father, as though the man's agreement was still necessary.

Her father tipped his head to nobody but himself and stared at nothing. The decision made, Hannah leaped up and clenched her fists.

'Ilse, are you coming?' asked her father.

Her mother shook her head – quick, short shakes, almost a tremble. 'You go with her. But be quick. And, Hannah, not a sound.'

'I promise, Mama,' replied Hannah. She felt that she would agree to almost anything, just to see the roof of the city and the sky.

'They will both be safe, Ilse. I give you my promise. We have plans in place, just in case ...'

But she had returned to her darning.

Hannah watched the two men exchange glances, as if they both understood. And then Herr Meyer led them back up the stairs, the comforting touch of her father's hand upon her back, but still her heart beginning to gallop and thrum in her ears, as it always did when she first left the sanctitude of the basement. They crept through the hole in the wall into darkness, Herr Meyer brushing coats and scarves aside and Hannah catching them and holding them back for her father.

There were three floors to the house. Hannah knew that from when they had arrived. It would be a long way back down if they had to return in a hurry. She imagined footsteps outside, a knock at the door, and these thoughts made her want to move faster. But Herr Meyer walked slow and steady, as if he were ambling through his house alone, without a care in the world. And this began to calm her, to slow her drumming heart.

The stairwell was narrow and dark, with wooden walls and electric lamps on each landing. Up and around they went to the top floor, and then they turned again. The last few steps led them to a small door that opened into a dingy room, filled with solid shapes that Hannah couldn't make head nor tail of. It smelled stale and musty, reminding Hannah of an old Jewish bookshop they used to visit. Herr Meyer led the way through, finding a secret path where there seemingly was none.

He stopped beside a rectangle of light set within the wall and inched the shutters apart, glancing left and right out the window. Then he opened them fully, flooding the room with a brightness that shrank the shadows and breathed life into cobwebs and dust.

Hannah closed her eyes against the unfamiliar glare, red circles dancing in the darkness of her lids. The warmth of the day fell upon her face, and she let her skin soak it up, turning the moment into a memory she would be able to relive in the darker days to come. She heard Herr Meyer step back, and she gradually opened her eyes, shielding them from the glare with a raised hand. Slowly, the world came into focus, and she was able to lower her arm. It brushed against her father's, next to her, as he did the same. There were no more words of assurance. Just the silent acknowledgement that the treacherous journey had been made and, though danger was still present, the treasure was in front of them.

'It's all still there,' she gasped. 'Just as it was.' She didn't know what she had expected. For the world to have been destroyed? For darkness to have been cast over it? But no. The beauty of the day was everywhere. From the pigeons on the roof opposite to the myriad of houses spread across the city, the jagged skyline in the distance and the wispy clouds floating overhead.

The range ran the length of the window and beyond. Hannah leaned as far forward as she was able. The peaks were of a different world, the teeth of a marvellous beast. Something that could surely not exist while she and her family remained locked up in a room of semi-darkness and closed walls. She felt her heart lift while her spirit sank. What she would give to be somewhere in those mountains, away from all the horror.

'I have a sister who lives there,' said Herr Meyer, pointing. 'High up on that peak.'

She followed his finger. 'Which one?'

'The one that looks like a shark facing upwards. She lives near the black spot that looks like its eye.'

Hannah could make it out clearly. Its twin peaks, one higher than the other, the eye that could be rock or forest.

'Do you ever visit?' asked Hannah.

'Alas, no. Maud and I have not been in touch for some time. We last saw her when Sofia was a baby.'

Hannah stared silently out as the sound of a horse's shoes clattered along the street below, drawing her attention to the people carrying provisions, cycling, sweeping, leading normal lives. But when she looked closer, she noticed smaller things. A bakery across the street, its window half empty even though it was only mid-morning. A barefoot child, too young to be sitting alone. Posters, all the same, pasted onto the walls of buildings. Soldiers in doorways. Watching. And now she saw how people walked faster, kept their arms to their sides, their heads down. She had been wrong. It wasn't the same.

'That's enough for now,' said her father. 'We should be getting back.'

She had known the moment would come, but so soon? 'A little longer?' she asked, trying to keep the sadness from her voice.

'Your mother will be worried.' So that was what her father was going to use to get her going. It was unfair, but it worked.

She raised her gaze back to the mountains for a few more seconds, etching every detail of the landscape into her memory for conjuring up in the coming days. To keep the walls from closing in. To imagine, one day, walking in those mountains.

She stood up.

'Thank you, Herr Meyer.' And she hoped he knew she didn't just mean for this short trip to the top of the house.

She had finally arrived at those mountains, away from the city that had imprisoned her and her family. But she had never wanted it to be like this. Now that she was here, she longed to be back in that basement with her parents. What had Death said to The Old Man in one of Aesop's fables? *Be careful what you wish for.* She understood that now.

After six hours on the train, the peaks now rose to unimaginable heights above her. She craned her neck to take in the summits, with the magical snow that never melted. She had to narrow her eyes against its brightness and tried to envisage the view in winter, when the white blankets would unroll to cover the world.

From along the corridor the inspector's voice, announcing the next stop. Kalterfluss. Her stop. The one that Marianne had drilled into her.

Tall houses with steep roofs and exposed beams rushed past. Smoking chimneys and white window frames, shutters thrown open above small stone planter boxes that bloomed with pinks and reds. As the train began to slow, her heart sped up. The squeal of the brakes caused a rush of panic that started at her stomach and rose to her chest. She quickly placed her book inside the string bag Marianne had given her and slung it over her shoulder.

Make sure you get off at Kalterfluss. If you don't, there's no telling where you'll end up. And there's no way of getting you back.

She pushed herself up off the seat, but after sitting for so long her legs had as good as fallen asleep. She fell back again.

Another jolt as the train continued to slow. And then the toot of the engine and the platform was alongside them. Hannah stamped her good foot to wake it up, and silently cursed herself for not preparing to alight earlier. She should have made her way out to the corridor before the houses appeared. She had forgotten that she wasn't able to jump up at a moment's notice to hurry for the door like she and her mother had used to do on the trams. Hannah glanced back out the window, wishing that Marianne had been able to tell her who to look out for. But she hadn't known. *It doesn't work that way,* she'd said. *The less everyone knows, the better.* Which was all very well, but if Hannah didn't know this person, and they didn't know her, how were they supposed to find each other?

The train halted with a shudder, a man and woman disembarked, and Hannah saw a young soldier board. This only increased her panic. She was sure the train was going to start to pull away before she'd even made it out of the carriage. One more push and she let her breath out in a grunt. She was up. She felt a hand on her back.

'Do you need some help getting off the train?' asked the pin-curled woman.

'Yes! Yes please!'

'Open the door, Robert,' said the woman to her son, but before the boy could get there, it slid across with such force that the glass should have shattered in the frame. A huge, bearded man took up the whole doorway, wearing a wool hat pulled down to his bushy eyebrows and fleece jacket fastened tight behind his curly beard. He looked terrifying. Or terrified, she couldn't be sure.

'Sofia,' he said, and it wasn't a question. This was her contact.

Hannah nodded, Marianne's words loud in her head. *Nobody must know. From now on, you are Sofia.*

The man glanced out the window, then reached down and placed his arm around her waist.

'Do you mind . . . ?' he said. She nodded. She did mind, but knew he was only doing what needed to be done. In a single movement he cupped her in his arms. She yelped as the feeling started to come back into her legs, dropping one of her crutches as she placed an arm around his neck, silently cursing for not being more useful in getting herself off the train.

The woman grabbed her son and fell back into her seat.

'Pass me the crutch,' said the man, calmly but firmly. The woman bent and picked it up, and he took it in his free hand, nodding his gratitude. Outside, the whistle blew, and Hannah used all of her concentration to wish them off the train.

The man spun around. The cast on Hannah's broken ankle knocked against the narrow doorframe. She cried out. The man shouted an apology as the train lurched forward. Hannah kept her bad leg tucked in as the man manoeuvred sideways into the corridor, crashing against the walls of the too-small space in the rush to reach the exit. Hannah was breathless with fear when she realised the train was already moving. But then they were at the door, Hannah holding the man's neck tightly as he used one arm to scramble for the handle. The door swung open. Hannah held her breath as he stepped out from the moving carriage. She was sure they were going to tumble below the train's wheels. But then the man's feet hit the platform, the force knocking the breath out of her. His strong legs took a few paces, and the two of them came to a standstill.

He gently put her down, handed her the crutch and gazed up at the heavens, then at her. His brown eyes grew to double their size as he raised his brows and exhaled, blowing out his cheeks. 'That was close.' He sucked in some more air. 'I'm Pieter. I'm here to take you to your aunt.'

'Hi Pieter,' said Hannah. 'I need to pee.'

SIX

15th September 1942

Hannah had, in the endless basement hours of terror and tedium, convinced herself that she and her family would inevitably be discovered by the Gestapo, whose only purpose was to find and remove those who Hitler deemed a threat to his master race. In particular, the Jewish people. But it wasn't so. Nearly a year after they arrived at the home of the Meyers, it was a bomb that found them.

The whine of the city's sirens was joined by the drone of planes' engines soaring through the night sky high above them. That evening, the Meyers had gone to the theatre, carrying on life as though there weren't a Jewish family hiding in their basement. And so it was just Hannah and her parents in the dark room at the bottom of the house when it happened.

Hannah had stopped reading as soon as the lights went out and moved with her parents to their bed. She lay on her back between them both, hugging Sofia's book to her chest, listening to her father's murmured prayers and feeling her mother's heartbeat as hard as her own.

Hannah had also always imagined that, when a bomb hit, it would be over within an instant. That it would be everything and then nothing. Light and then darkness. But that was not the case.

She had heard the whistle before, during previous air raids, had heard the pitch getting higher as the bomb fell. She knew well the terror that went hand in hand with that whistle, that started in the pit of her stomach, growing and growing to fill her entire being, as she wondered if this one was meant for them. And then the explosion. The sudden rush of relief, knowing it had missed them, followed by the guilty knowledge that somewhere not too far away, others were probably injured, or dying, or dead.

But on this night, the whistle stopped, as though the needle had been lifted from a gramophone mid-tune. Then the silence – for an instant and forever – before the explosion, sounding as if it were directly above them. Hannah tensed. Her mother screamed. Her father's prayers ceased.

This was it, she knew. This was the day they would die. There would be no more running or hiding.

She heard each floor collapsing, splintering, shattering. The stairway folding down onto itself like a giant, broken accordion; an orchestra of destruction, every note imaginable being played at once and rising to a deafening crescendo. Every piece of furniture in the house, every ornament, every memory falling together as one, down onto the floorboards that she and her family had hidden below for such a long time.

And as they, too, splintered and collapsed onto them, her thoughts surprised her by turning toward hope. Hope that whatever came next would be better than the place they were leaving behind. And thanks that the Meyers, who had risked everything for a family they barely knew, had avoided this fate.

It was a few days later that she found out otherwise.

SEVEN

'Sofia!'

A man's voice, deep and angry. With heavy boots clomping around on the floorboards above.

'Sofia!'

Where was Sofia? Perhaps Hannah should come out of hiding and help the man find her. But then, a memory. *My family and I always remove our shoes when we are in the house.* No, it must be a stranger. She needed to stay hidden. But everyone was a stranger now. Was it a good stranger or a bad stranger?

Where had her parents gone? She had been having a terrible dream. Of an explosion. Of being buried alive. She looked up, squinting at the slats of light falling upon her face. There was the flicker of fire, broken by the dark soles of those boots. She could smell the smoke, but there wasn't just wood burning. There were other things. The boots stopped directly above her. Hannah could hear her own breath and was certain that the owner of the boots could hear it, too.

More of the light disappeared as the man sank to all fours. A single eye appeared at the slat.

'Are you in there, Sofia?'

Hannah shook her head. Her body began to tremble, her gaze transfixed on that single eye as it wiggled around in its socket, trying to see Sofia. Hannah tried to shift back into the shadows, but the walls of the basement had closed in. She felt trapped. The eye smiled.

'Ah, there you are.' A thin finger, thinner than was possible, squeezed down through a gap in the boards. 'Sofia . . .'

I'm not Sofia!

The finger grew longer and longer, reaching towards her, almost touching.

The world tilted. Now she was the one in the room above, peeking down through the crack in the floorboards at herself looking back up. She saw the fear in her own eyes.

'Sofia.' A whisper.

The Hannah below the boards shook her head and closed her eyes.

'Sofia. Open your eyes. Sofia . . .' And then she was back below the floorboards, hearing the voice from above morphing into that of a woman.

'Sofia. Open your eyes.'

Was she dreaming? Had she and Sofia been discovered? Whatever was happening, she didn't want to be a part of it. She wanted her parents. Her home.

Her home.

She no longer had a home. The basement . . . the Meyers . . . the bomb . . . her parents?!!

The memory took over. Of the explosion. Of being crushed below the home of the Meyers. That feeling of being smothered came again. At the top of her chest, rising into her throat and sinking into her stomach. She was finding it hard to breathe.

'Sofia . . .' The finger brushed against her face. But it was soft. 'Sofia, it's all right. You're safe now.'

She opened her eyes. And closed them again. It was too bright. Too white.

'Give her a few seconds,' said a voice.

She tried again. Not so bad. She blinked and reached up to wipe away the blur.

A woman was looking down at her. Dark hair in curls, and eyes that shone. A nurse. Smiling.

'Hello, Sofia. You're back.'

Hannah twisted her head left and then right. A hospital ward. A row of beds. She wasn't in the basement. That had been a dream. But there was no sign of Sofia. Why did the woman keep saying her name? And why was she looking at her when she said it? Hannah hurt all over. But especially her leg, her head. The bright lights weren't helping.

'My parents . . . are they here?' she gasped. She searched beyond the nurse. A row of beds stretched out along the wall, each taken up by a patient, but she couldn't see either of her parents.

A smell in the air reminded her of the pharmacy she and her mother used to visit. And the butcher on the High Street near where they used to live. She reached out and grabbed the woman's arm.

'Where are my parents?' she pleaded once more, trying to take the breaths that weren't there. She went to push herself up, but the nurse leaned forward and stopped her.

'Not yet, darling, not yet. You've got some injuries. Wake up first.'

Another nurse appeared, but Hannah's angel waved her off.

The woman leaned over her and placed a hand on her cheek.

'Breathe slowly,' she said. 'It's going to be all right.'

'Let me make you comfortable.' The nurse reached over and piled up the pillows below Hannah's head.

Hannah's lungs were filling with air once more. She had her breathing back under control, though her thoughts were still brimming with that barely tamped-down panic. *Where are my parents?*

The nurse's heels echoed off the hard floor as she walked round to the opposite side of Hannah's bed. Hannah felt a sting at the back of her head as she turned to follow the nurse's movements. And her leg ached terribly.

She felt herself on the verge of losing control, the panic rising, threatening to take over her breathing again.

The nurse picked up the book from the metal bedside table, opened it to the first page and tipped it toward Hannah.

'Sofia. That's your name?' she asked, tapping her finger at the handwritten letters. But before Hannah could say otherwise, the nurse crouched down. 'I'm Marianne. You have to be brave for what I'm about to tell you.'

'Sofia? No, I'm ...' And then she realised. The nurse had got it wrong. Her parents were probably looking for her. 'I'm not Sofia.' A feeling of relief began to wash over her. But then ... the Meyers had been out, hadn't they? Maybe they had come back. But, if so, Sofia would have been with them, wouldn't she?

There was too much confusion.

'I'm Hannah. Hannah Ginsberg. Sofia ...' She pointed at the book. 'That's not me.'

Marianne bit at her bottom lip. Even in her dazed state, Hannah could see the woman's thoughts clicking away. 'You're not Sofia?'

Hannah shook her head. 'No, she went to the theatre. With her parents. Are they dead? Are the Meyers dead?'

Marianne took a deep breath. 'I don't know. You were found with two people. A man and a woman. They were . . .'

Hannah's panic was coming back with force. Her lungs didn't want to work. Her heart was pounding too hard and too loud, like a drum. One of them was going to give in, she was sure. Her head throbbed. Her hands were numb. She looked at them, trying to remember when she had lost her grip on her parents.

'We were in the basement,' she managed, her breath running out at the end of the sentence as silent sobs tore through her body.

The woman's gentle hand upon her shoulder. 'Hiding from the bombs?'

Hannah nodded, then shook her head, while her body convulsed with grief. 'Hiding from the . . . we were living . . . staying . . .' she managed to get out. And then she suddenly realised. There was no way out of this. The truth couldn't save her. The truth couldn't bring her parents back. She knew they were gone, but she still needed to hear the words out loud. 'They're dead?'

'I'm so sorry, darling, but yes.' Marianne leaned in closer and smoothed her arm. Hannah flinched. Her heart finally broke and began to slow as her tears flooded out. It couldn't work any harder. If it stopped altogether, she wouldn't care. She squeezed her eyes shut against the world. How could there be any world without her parents? She leaned over and vomited. A pair of shoes leaped back from the bed.

'Can you give us a moment, Doctor?' asked Marianne. 'Sofia has just received some very bad news.'

Hannah remained leaning over the side of the bed while her stomach decided whether it had finished ejecting its contents. She heard the man say, 'Of course. I'm so sorry.' Then his shoes stepped back out of sight.

She lay back and her body took deep breaths of its own accord, trying to get itself back under control. She hadn't died. She wasn't dying. She was in a hospital, in a world that had been irrevocably changed. If only she could be left alone now. If the sun could go down and she could curl up in the darkness and disappear. She squeezed her eyes shut, balled her fists against her cheeks and lay there, wishing it all away.

'I think I understand,' said Marianne from beside her. The nurse had quietened her voice, but her tone had become urgent. 'You've been through a lot and you're still going through it. But you need to listen. You will have plenty of time to mourn. I think I can guess why you and your parents were there. But you need to understand. You cannot trust anybody. From now on, you are Sofia. Do you understand?'

Hannah considered the woman's words. She understood all too well, and she hated the idea. She didn't want to be Sofia. She wanted to be herself, Hannah Ginsberg. And she was pretty sure Sofia would agree with her.

'Do you understand?' whispered Marianne, her eyes imploring her to.

Hannah gave in. 'Yes.'

'Good girl,' said Marianne. Hannah's grief broke loose once more. Tears flooded her pillow, and her body shuddered as it slowly exhausted itself. It didn't take long for her to fall into a deep, dreamless slumber, only waking when the pain in her leg cut into her consciousness.

A pain that had, up until then, been overshadowed by one that cut much deeper, and would take much, much longer to heal.

EIGHT

21st September 1942

Hannah had never seen the world from this height. Far below the mountain track they were travelling along, the village of Kalterfluss was a fragment of all she could see. Beyond it was a lake, sparkling and clean, low ridges rising from its far side. Dense forest made up the rest of the foreground, and beyond rose more peaks. She wondered in which direction her city lay. There was no smoke in the sky, no sign of destruction. Just soft white clouds that floated level with their carriage.

She sat beside Pieter as the wooden wheels of the carriage clunked and clattered over the loose stones of the beaten and barely used track. She had never ridden on a horse-drawn carriage before, had never been this close to a horse. She watched their flanks strain in front of her, one mottled grey and the other the colour of the chocolate treats she used to see in the window of the bakery.

It wasn't the most comfortable of rides. The seats weren't padded like those of the trams back in the city, and her feet didn't quite reach the boards. At first, she held on to the seat, fearing a rut in the track would throw her off the carriage. But Pieter told her to sit back, to let her body ride with the wagon, and eventually she relaxed and let the carriage rock her from side to side, relieved that there had been a working toilet at the station and not minding so much when she was jostled against Pieter.

The itch on her leg came now again, but somehow the rocking of the carriage seemed to alleviate it.

There was another way up, Pieter had told her; a smoother, more comfortable route. But this was the way the horses knew well. And it was a route along which they were guaranteed not to come across any soldiers. This last word came out of a mouth that looked as though it had swallowed something bitter, and Hannah wondered what he had experienced to make him feel the same way she did.

'You don't say much, do you?' Pieter commented.

She didn't respond. After all, he was right.

'Well, that's not a bad thing. Too many people with too much to say, these days. And it will please your aunt no end. She's of the opinion that children should be seen and not heard.'

That was hardly something to look forward to. 'You know her?' she asked.

'I know of her,' replied Pieter.

She wondered what kind of life she was heading towards, and a surge of grief swept over her for the life she had lost. Hannah stared out over the precipice and let the tears fall down her cheeks, a sob rising to the surface. She clenched her jaw to keep it inside, wiped at her eyes and took a deep breath of cool mountain air.

This was how she was now. A sad, broken wreck, lost at sea, riding the waves to survive another day until the grief whipped up once more and threatened to drown her.

'I'm sorry. I didn't mean to upset you. And it's not that your aunt doesn't care. She does. She wouldn't be taking you in if she didn't. Maud Meyer doesn't seem to be the kind of woman who would do anything she doesn't want to.'

She hoped Pieter was right about her newly adopted aunt. But what would happen if the woman ever found out she wasn't who she was pretending to be? That she had callously stolen her niece's identity?

The scene below disappeared behind trees and rocky rises, reappearing in an unexpected location, as though the mountain had rearranged itself.

It would be easy to get lost up here, thought Hannah. And wasn't that precisely what she was here to do? She wasn't sure she was ready for it. She definitely didn't want it. But what choice did she have?

She knew it was a risk, but she wanted one final acknowledgement of who she really was.

'Do you know?' she asked.

Pieter chewed at his bottom lip, staring straight ahead, as if considering how to answer. Hannah's gaze shifted beyond his profile to a sheer wall rising from a small copse of firs on the other side of the carriage. It gave her the impression that the mountain was trying to push them off.

'I know what I need to know. That's all. And that's the last time you ask that question. Do you understand?'

She did. And it would be.

She reached down and pulled the book from her bag, opening it and flicking through the pages to find a tale that would carry her thoughts away from the past and the present.

'You enjoy reading?' asked Pieter.

Hannah nodded.

'And what is it that you are reading today?'

'Just fairytales.'

'Ah. Just fairytales.'

There was silence between them for a while. Hannah stopped turning the pages when she came to *The King of the Golden Mountain*.

'You know,' said Pieter, as they entered a cluster of trees, 'there is no such thing as *just* fairytales.'

'What do you mean?'

'What I mean is there is truth in every tale.'

Hannah frowned. 'A frog never turned into a prince when he was kissed.'

'Perhaps not. But maybe that prince felt like a frog until the princess kissed him.'

She had never thought of it like that. It put a whole new meaning into the stories she had read.

'You realise those stories weren't meant for children?' asked Pieter.

'Why not?'

'Many of them were considered too frightening. And do you know the most amazing thing about them?'

The two locked eyes, and she noticed how one of his pupils was larger than the other, as though he were half in darkness. She shook her head.

'No matter how thick that book is, those brothers collected many more stories that aren't in there. And there are a whole lot more they never got to hear, that have by now been lost forever in the silent voices of those who are gone.'

He held her gaze a moment longer, then gave a crack of the reins. The world, having shifted around once more, opened up in front of them.

NINE

17th September 1942

Hannah's first night in the hospital had seemed endless. Despite her earlier feeling of wanting to curl up in a ball of darkness, she lay awake, willing the sun to rise and the shadows, both inside and out, to be cast away. She couldn't help wanting to know what had happened to her parents' bodies. The Jewish custom was to be buried within a day. But, to everybody else, they weren't Jews. Marianne had assured her that they'd be buried in marked graves alongside other Germans, but if nobody knew whose names to put on the headstones, how would she ever find them?

If there was anything she could count as a blessing, it was the fact that she had come away relatively unscathed. She had cuts and bruises in places from head to toe as well as a fractured ankle bone, and she had also suffered a concussion. Her right leg had been cast in plaster up to her knee while she was unconscious. She had no recollection of her journey to the hospital or of any treatment she had received until Marianne had brought her out of her troubled dreams.

The ward was a bustling world of hard sounds and sharp echoes during the day; of heels upon floors, wheels that squeaked and instruments dropped onto trolleys. Even the doctors' voices were harsh and abrupt.

By the end of the second day, Hannah could visualise every detail of the ward with her eyes closed. There were eight beds along her wall, six along the wall opposite, only two of them empty. A grey, stone floor and a white, high ceiling with floral cornices, supported by six columns along its length. Arched windows in the wall behind her and at both ends. A single doorway in the middle of the wall opposite.

Twelve children. Hannah guessed the youngest to be around four and the oldest, a boy of fifteen. It was hard to tell what injuries they had until the doctors or nurses came round. When that happened, sheets were pulled back to reveal broken limbs, dressed wounds and, on one occasion, a missing arm. Every now and again she would catch a pair of eyes staring back at her. There were few smiles exchanged and even fewer words. Hannah could understand that. She didn't feel like giving either away.

There was very little privacy in the ward. Nurses flitted. Doctors strode. Cleaners mopped. Sometimes, a parent or relative wandered in to sit beside a child, speaking low and slow, casting short glances at the other patients. But most, like Hannah, had no visitors.

Hannah's only jaunts outside the ward during the first few days were to the toilet. On the first day, she was wheeled there and 'helped' by a nurse who said very little and smiled even less. After that, she was offered a pair of crutches so she could take herself, but barely shown how to use them. At first it wasn't easy, and several times she nearly toppled over. Whenever she stood, the pain in her right ankle intensified before subsiding. Her headache had all but disappeared, but the raw lump behind her left ear smarted whenever she touched it. The corridor connected to her ward was long and narrow, with doors and other passageways leading off it. From somewhere down the far end, she heard the chatter of nurses and the clatter of a typewriter.

As the light outside fell, the lamps above came on, buzzing and sometimes flickering so fast that she had to close her eyes. When they were finally turned off, Hannah was once more able to curl up and be swallowed by the darkness. But that darkness ate into every corner of her mind, and the despair and loneliness left her longing for the swift return of daylight.

During the night, the usual nonstop groans and coughs were accompanied by barely suppressed whimpers, many of which came from Hannah. Every so often, footsteps echoed down the hallway and distant voices could be heard. Presumably from the hospital staff. From outside came the drone of motor vehicles, occasionally the wail of an ambulance but, thankfully, none of the low thrumming and high whistling from the skies.

Whenever doctors or nurses came around, Hannah answered to the name at the bottom of her bed. She trusted no one apart from Marianne. Not even the nurses who smiled and asked her how she was holding up. Marianne knew who and what she was. And it was Marianne who told her that God, with his unenviable talent of giving with one hand and taking with the other, had worked his magic with the name written inside the book. That she must take what she could from this tragedy and use it to stay alive.

Hannah had both beliefs and doubts about God. And, of late, the scales were tipping in favour of those doubts. She believed that there was some higher form looking down upon them all, watching their every move and making decisions. But she wondered how the God she believed in could stand by and watch the world destroy itself as it was doing. And what her parents would think of her doubting thoughts.

Her parents hadn't been strict in their worship. They had had neighbours and friends who had been pious in their belief, reading from their siddur three times daily. But the Ginsbergs had, until that terrible night in 1938, attended the synagogue for Shabbat most weeks, dressed in their best clothes. They took the tram to a synagogue that didn't have a mechitzah so that Hannah and her mother could sit with her father in prayer. They would stay together in all aspects of life, her father insisted. And they had.

Hannah realised that there were so many parts of her life that would now be forbidden. Even while in the basement, she and her parents had followed their usual daily rituals that had been part of their Jewish culture. But no longer would she begin Friday mealtimes with the Shabbat blessing and kiddush, or enjoy her mother's homemade challah on a Saturday. Her mother would never again light the Shabbat candles as she had done every week of Hannah's life. Her parents would never get to see her doing mitzvot in the world. She'd planned to do so much good. But how was she to do good in a world that was so very bad?

Hannah's cheeks burned with angry tears. What was so bad about all those things that were a part of being Jewish? Was it all gone forever for her now? All the things that she had taken for granted. It all seemed so important now.

On Hannah's third day in the hospital, Marianne gave her more news of the badness in the world. The theatre had been bombed on the same night as the Meyers' house. There had been multiple fatalities, many of the bodies unidentifiable. And there had been no record of the Meyers showing up at any of the makeshift camps set up across the city. Hannah didn't think she had any more room for grief, but it found a spot deep in her heart.

'The authorities will be trying to find relatives,' said Marianne. She placed a hand on Hannah's shoulder.

'I don't have any,' replied Hannah, raising her head. 'None that I have ever met.' It was true. Her parents had spoken of how they had travelled with their own families from shtetls in Poland after the Great War. The plan had been to go on to America, but they had found it hard to get work in Germany and save enough money to continue on. Her mother's parents had returned to Poland, her father's gone on to Berlin with the hope of better prospects. But before those decisions had been made, Hannah's parents had met and fallen in love. They had never seen their families again.

Marianne surreptitiously surveyed the ward. Hannah followed her gaze, wondering what she was looking for. Hannah could just see the usual hospital scenes; children lost in their own solitude, visitors in conversation, the staff buried in their tasks.

Marianne's fingers touched Hannah's chin and pulled her face back to hers, which was now a little too close for Hannah's comfort. 'You need to pay attention to me, Hannah. There are bad things happening around us. You, more than anybody, should know that.'

Hannah swallowed. Marianne was scaring her.

'Is there anybody who will take you in?' asked the nurse. Hannah let her silence speak for her. Marianne's whisper was so low that Hannah had to lean in to hear. 'God willing, I'd take you home with me...' The faint spark of hope ignited by those words was soon extinguished. '... but that would raise too many suspicions.'

Fear filled every part of her. 'I don't . . . I really don't have anybody. Not any more.'

'*Hannah* doesn't have anybody. Stop thinking like Hannah. You're Sofia, now. Think like Sofia. Did she or her parents ever mention any other family?'

The Meyers' family? What good would that do her? She may be able to take Sofia's name, but she didn't have her face. They would know. And anyway, she had never heard them talk about any relative, so it was useless. It wouldn't work. She would have to try to make it on her own. Go somewhere by herself. Her father had spoken of them escaping once. Leaving Germany altogether and heading for Switzerland. Across the mountains. The mountains she had last seen from the attic window. Herr Meyer had pointed to them and told her . . .

The memory flooded back. Almost his exact words, and an idea dropped into her head like an egg yolk into a bowl of flour.

'A sister! Herr Meyer had a sister who lived in the mountains. He said he hadn't seen her for years, not since Sofia was a baby.'

'A sister? Did he mention her name?'

It was there if she just concentrated. 'Maud! He said she lived on the mountain that looks like a shark. The village is close to the shark's eye.'

Marianne caught hold of Hannah's hand and squeezed it, her face beaming as though it were her in need of refuge. 'That's good. So good. She wouldn't know what Sofia, what you, looked like at all.'

Hannah still wasn't convinced. And the thought of going to live with a stranger, pretending to be somebody else, terrified her.

'We'll try to find her,' whispered Marianne.

'We?'

'There are people I know. They can go there. See if she will . . .'

A shadow appeared at the bottom of the bed. Hannah's heart leaped in her chest. She looked up, fearing the doctor had heard their conversation.

Marianne stood and turned to him, placing her hand on her heart and gasping. 'Doctor! I didn't see you there. What are you trying to do to us, creeping up like that?' She turned back to Hannah. 'You're all done, young lady.' As she folded Hannah's sheet down, she glanced up and gave her a nervous smile. Then, back at the man. 'Do you need me, Doctor?'

He nodded and led her away, muttering something about bad news and loss. Hannah didn't want to hear. She had had more than her fair share of both.

TEN

A short, severe woman with small round glasses and a bowl-shaped haircut came around the next day. She wore a starched grey jacket pulled in tight to her neck, and a skirt that hugged her calves. A doctor with greasy hair and an uneven moustache led her to a young boy who, like Hannah, hadn't received a single visitor. He was pale and quiet and seemed to be getting visibly thinner by the day. She had tried to smile at him once, but he had just turned away. Even Marianne had been unable to coax a word from him.

The woman shook her head and they moved along to a bed where an older boy lay. Hannah's heart echoed in her ears and her mind began to work on what she would say when they got to her. The woman asked the boy if he had ever held a rifle. He nodded and she wrote something down. The doctor strode over and pulled back the covers to reveal an empty space where his arm should have been. The woman crossed out whatever she had written and moved on to Hannah, who wished with all her heart that Marianne was here with her. Without looking up, the woman collected the clipboard and studied it. The doctor stood stiff and straight, eyes staring ahead, as if he knew better than to speak before being asked.

'You have a broken ankle.'

Hannah didn't answer. It hadn't been a question. And she was worried that, if she tried to speak, the woman would read something into her words and order her to be taken away immediately.

'Speak!' barked the woman, snapping her head up.

'Yes.'

The woman's eyes drilled into her, and Hannah was sure she could see right through to the lie being told by the name on the paper she was holding.

'And you have no family.'

She felt tears coming at the callousness of the woman's words. How dare she speak of them as if they had never existed. Hannah wanted to scream at her exactly what had happened, who they had been, who she was.

Stop thinking like Hannah. You're Sofia now. Think like Sofia. Be Sofia.

'I have an aunt.'

The doctor frowned. 'Is she here in the city?'

The woman pursed her lips and cast her dagger eyes at him. The doctor swallowed and hung his head, sufficiently admonished for his interruption.

'She lives in the mountains.' Hannah could feel the words coming easier now, as if her mouth and thoughts were finally working together, gaining momentum.

'And she has agreed to take on the burden of a child?' asked the woman.

Hannah felt herself shrink. Was that what she had become? She decided to take a risk. 'She has. She will be coming to collect me soon.'

The doctor's head shot back up. Another frown. Deeper.

The woman pondered Hannah's words. She wrote something down, placed the pen in her pocket and marched off. The doctor gave Hannah one last look.

He knows I'm lying, she thought. *But he's too afraid of her to speak up.*

Three beds down, the woman stopped. A girl whose face was half burned lay on her back, her single eye staring up at the ceiling. The doctor shuffled off to join them.

'We've found her,' said Marianne, as they made their way along a path at the rear of the hospital. Hannah was on crutches, still struggling to use them at times, especially on uneven surfaces like grass and gravel. She got out of breath too quickly and her hands hurt from holding her weight. But Marianne had made it clear that she needed to get her strength up and practise walking with them so she could leave this place. She told her she would need them for six weeks, maybe longer, depending how quickly her ankle healed.

'Sofia's aunt?'

Marianne nodded.

Thoughts whirled through Hannah's mind about what this would mean for her.

'She's exactly where you said she'd be. Near the eye of the shark. A small village called Felshoven.'

They stopped talking as two nurses strolled past. It was an early-autumn morning and the dew was sparkling on the ground. The sun was low, shining through the gaps in the tall spruce at the edge of the grounds. Between the trees, Hannah caught grey, tattered glimpses of her city and heard heavy vehicles moving about. The underlying stink of smoke and destruction lingered in the air, and Hannah wondered if this was the stench of the world all over now.

'Does she know about Herr Meyer? About Sofia?' Hannah stopped and corrected herself. 'Does she know about me?'

Marianne didn't answer. 'We have somebody on their way to see her. We're hoping she'll take you in.'

Hannah stopped still. 'Marianne, I'm frightened. I didn't really know Sofia. I don't know how to pretend to be her.' And she didn't. The thought saddened her. That she had been living under the girl's roof and the two of them had never got to know each other. Not really.

'Neither did her aunt, according to what you told me Herr Meyer said. You will just need to talk of the Meyers as though they were your family.'

Hannah stared up at the overhanging branches, trying to gather her thoughts about how she felt. Yes, her family were gone and she was still here. But to pretend that she was somebody else's daughter felt as if she were wiping her own parents from her past, like they had never existed. She already felt a deep guilt for surviving when they had perished. And now, Sofia? Wasn't it wrong to take her place in the world?

Marianne must have sensed her thoughts. 'Your parents will always be your parents, Hannah. Nothing will ever change that. And maybe someday, when this is all over, you can speak the truth to the world. But for now, you need to be Sofia to stay alive.'

She was right, of course. 'When will I know if she's said yes to taking me in?'

'I'm hoping to have an answer in the next few days.'

An image came into Hannah's head of the woman with the bowl of hair and the stiff grey suit, asking her if she had family willing to come and get her. As if she were an old bicycle left at the side of the road. A sob escaped.

Marianne placed her hand upon Hannah's shoulder. 'Everything will work out, Hannah. I promise you.'

If promises came true, thought Hannah, there would be no need for hope.

And hope was all she had left to cling on to.

ELEVEN

21st September 1942

The clouds were below them. They had stopped several times to give the horses water, and once for Pieter to disappear behind a bush. Most of the track was clear, but every now and then they came to a spatter of rocks that the horses had to be carefully manoeuvred around.

Hannah watched the world below melt into swathes of greens and browns. The temperature fell as the sun sank. Pieter reached behind and pulled out a blanket. He handed it to Hannah, and she draped it over her shoulders. There was no sound up here other than the clunk of their wheels and the panting of the horses. Every so often, a sweet, pleasant fragrance wafted towards her on a gentle breeze. Small fields sat dotted with yellow and pink flowers. Once she saw a mountain goat, speckled black and white, watching them with suspicion from a rocky outcrop. But as they got closer, and their sound and scent reached the animal, it turned and skipped away over a ridge.

'It isn't far now,' said Pieter, as they passed a low cave set into the wall of rock.

'What's that?' asked Hannah. It looked too smooth and symmetrical to be natural.

'It's an Erdstall. A tunnel that leads deep into the mountain.'

'Who built it?'

Pieter shrugged. 'Nobody really knows. But some believe they were built by elves or gnomes.'

It was hard to tell if he was joking. He had the kind of face that always appeared ready to break out into a smile but rarely got there. In the short time she had known him, since he had brusquely scooped her from the train, her perception of him had mellowed. There was something calm and reassuring about him.

The world once more opened up before them. A sheer drop of what must have been hundreds of metres. Pieter turned the horses so that the carriage wheeled along a narrow path with rising cliffs to their left and nothing to their right. Hannah felt her stomach lurch while, at the same time, she craned her neck to see over the edge. Neither Pieter nor the horses appeared at all concerned.

The path turned to the left, away from the precipice, and for the rest of the journey they travelled between field and forest. The daylight began to fall out of the sky, taking the temperature with it. Hannah pulled the blanket tightly around her. Eventually, they came over a small rise and she could see down into a valley where small cottages peppered the forest. Beyond that, the trees disappeared and the village took over.

The track zigzagged down, the village hidden again behind expanses of fir trees. The air took on a smoky aroma that conjured up images of wood ovens with cinnamon pastries or freshly stuffed sausages, baked by the old village wives in the tales she had read.

They passed a small cottage with a crooked chimney that exhaled thick smoke into the evening air; an unpainted, broken-tiled building with dirty, cracked windows and a door that opened directly onto the stony track. Despite the poor state of the house, well cared-for clay planters below each window boasted colourful flowers. The buildings in the city, before the war, had seemed so tidy and well maintained compared to these. But that city only existed in her memories now.

The track turned into a cobbled street, and an old lady attempted to hide her nosiness by sweeping an invisible cloud of dust out into their path. A chimney sweep, dressed from hat to boots in black, collapsed broom over his shoulder, trudged along the side of the road and nodded at them. Hannah was ready with a smile.

They passed a cheese shop, a butcher, a bakery. The buildings grew taller – two and then three storeys – and Hannah noticed the cables strung between these, and the tall wooden posts that carried them away from the village, further up the mountain.

The narrow road began to rise, houses on either side crowding in around them. More people, mostly women, but a few elderly men and children. There were no motor vehicles. No sound of engines at all. It seemed to Hannah that the village was lost somewhere in the past. In the old storybook that rested upon her lap. In a fairytale.

Up they went to the top of the village. For the first time, Hannah felt she had put a safe distance, both physically and emotionally, between her and the people she and her parents had hidden from. Surely no danger could come to her here in this world high in the sky, cushioned between the mountains. This village that seemed as insignificant to the outside world as a drop of rain to a stormy sea.

The road levelled out and Pieter pulled at the reins. The horses slowed to a trot and stopped beside a tall house overlooking the square. They harumphed and clomped their hooves on the spot, and Hannah wondered whether they knew they had arrived at their destination. Pieter answered them with, 'Here we are! Rest now!' and they seemed to understand. Their breathing slowed and their restless feet grew still. Their shanks relaxed and their heads dropped.

So this was it. Hannah's new home. Her stomach fluttered as she gazed up at its faded, white rendering and wooden beams, shutters thrown open and curtains pulled closed. There were pots either side of the front door, and baskets hanging above the lower windows, all boasting blooms of colourful flowers, like the houses on the road. Like most buildings in the village. There was colour here that she had never seen in the city.

It was a large house, perhaps the largest in the village. A lodge, Marianne had said. She just hoped there were no other lodgers staying or, if there were, that they kept themselves to themselves. She wasn't ready to live with lots of strangers.

Hannah stretched and poked her fingers down beneath the plaster. That itch! At least it was where she was able to get to it now. She hoped it wouldn't move further down where her fingers couldn't reach.

Pieter clambered down, the pain of the journey evident in the way he rubbed at his back and rotated his neck. He staggered around to her side. 'Let me help you down.'

She felt bad for adding her weight to his already aching body, but she wasn't sure how else she would get down without landing on her broken leg. Clutching her book in one hand, she gently lowered herself into his strong arms. Despite his apparent discomfort, he made her feel as light as a feather, just as her father had when she was younger. She shook her head in an effort to rid herself of that pang of sadness for her parents. She needed to be ready to meet Sofia's aunt, to start her new life. Her past couldn't help her now.

Pieter dropped her lightly to the ground and reached up for her crutches while she leaned against the carriage on one foot. She tried to take in more of the village square and the buildings. Darkness was falling, and lights shone in some of the windows. She suddenly felt so tired.

'Let me take that,' Pieter said, nodding to the book.

She exchanged it for the crutches.

'I won't be long,' Pieter said to the horses. And those words brought home the fact that Hannah would soon, once more, be saying goodbye to somebody she was just getting to know. And like.

At the door he raised his great fist and knocked, soft and gentle for such a strong man. They waited, the world around them seeming to hold its breath, the air still and silent.

He knocked again. This time a little harder. 'It's a big house, and your aunt could be lost somewhere within its depths.'

Hannah suddenly worried about how she appeared. She had bathed earlier that morning. Marianne had brought her clean clothes, brushed and plaited her hair. But that seemed a long time ago. She had travelled a fair way across the country and halfway up a mountain since then. What must she look like? She straightened her plaits. Smoothed down her hair at the front. Wiped at her cheeks. Checked the buttons on her coat.

'You look fine,' said Pieter. And then, as if that weren't enough, 'Very smart.'

The sound of steady, regimental steps approaching across a hard floor. Hannah felt her breath catch in her throat and swallowed it back down. There was the rattle of a lock being turned, and the door swung inward to reveal a tall, thin woman dressed in a long black skirt and stiff navy blouse buttoned up to the neck. Her dull, greying hair was pulled up into a bun, giving her a harshness that would put an Alpen winter to shame. She looked Hannah up and down with piercing, judgemental eyes, and pursed her already tight lips even tighter. Hannah, resting on her crutches and good leg, tried to force a smile, but wasn't sure it came through.

The woman flicked her eyes to Pieter. 'So, this is my niece.'

'This is Sofia,' said Pieter.

'Does she speak?'

Hannah felt her heart thumping away in her chest. For a moment she was back in her hospital bed, fumbling for the right thing to say as starch lady questioned her.

'I do,' she finally replied, summoning all the nerve she could.

Maud Meyer's head shrank back into her neck, as if she weren't used to being spoken to by a child. 'Well, I hope you don't talk too much. I've grown accustomed to a quiet life.'

Hannah got the impression that you couldn't win with this woman.

'I'm sure Sofia will allow you to continue living one,' cut in Pieter. 'Isn't that right, Sofia?'

His words gave her strength. She allowed a few seconds to pass, pretending to consider the idea before working up a reasonable smile. 'Of course. It's very nice to meet you, Aunt Maud.'

Aunt Maud nodded back and snorted. 'I'm sure it is. And I only wish I could say the same. I made it my business long ago not to raise any children, and I don't intend to start now. You will live here and earn your keep like I did when

I was young.' She glanced at Hannah's crutches and then at her plaster before adding, 'Injured or not.'

She left her words hanging there, and Hannah tried to find a similarity between her and Herr Meyer. There was something there, in the narrow nose and thin frame. But in character they couldn't have been more different.

Aunt Maud took a step back. 'Well, you'd better come in. The house doesn't heat itself, and winter is just around the corner.'

And with that, Hannah placed her crutches inside the doorway and swung her legs over the threshold into the warm entrance hall of the lodging house. Pieter removed his hat and followed behind.

TWELVE

19th September 1942

At first, she had thought it was a dream. How else could she explain what she was seeing? The ward below her was in darkness, silent except for the snores of the other children. There was no smell, none of the chemical odour that normally pervaded. She stared at the window, but all she could see was the reflection of the ward.

Though not of herself.

Was this real? The idea terrified her. She lowered her gaze to the bed, to the body asleep below its covers. Her eyes were closed, though she thought she could see a slight flickering of the lids as she slept. And then a thought far worse hit her. Was she dead? Was that really a flicker, or just her imagination? No, she could see the sheets rising and falling with every breath. So this had to be a dream. People couldn't just leave their bodies, could they?

She gazed around the ward, looking for any clue that could explain what was happening. It was too dark to be sure, but everything seemed to match what she remembered from her waking hours. Wouldn't a dream be more magical in some way? Or would it play with her memories to convince her that all was as it should be?

Could she move if she wanted to? Perhaps go outside?

Just the thought of this and she was at the window, looking through the glass at the hospital grounds. She could just make out the gardens where she and Marianne had walked earlier that day. And on the sill below, behind her sleeping body's headboard, a single dead flower.

She moved closer. It was a lily, once white, now a decaying brown. She wondered if it would still smell like a lily, even though it was dead. She'd check when she woke up . . .

Hannah focused her sight on a point across the ward. She rose up and over sleeping bodies in hospital beds. She reached the doorway, a warm rectangle of light, and headed down the bright corridor, floating just below the ceiling. There were voices somewhere up ahead. A doctor appeared from around a corner. She stopped moving, feeling both uneasy and potent as he passed below her and disappeared into a side room. She headed towards the voices, close enough now to recognise them.

The door was open, but she remained outside, not daring to enter in case she somehow interrupted the conversation. The woman in the grey suit was standing above the doctor with the greasy hair and uneven moustache. She had a folder open in her hands. The man's foot tapped nervously on the hard floor as the woman's eyes scanned a page.

'This one will be relocated tomorrow,' she said, holding the folder out to him.

He took it from her and studied it. 'But we said a week.'

'It is almost a week.'

'She says she has family.'

'She lied.'

He frowned. 'Lied? In what way?'

'In every way,' said the woman. 'Look.'

She handed him another sheet of paper. Hannah watched as he read. She knew it was her they were talking about, but she couldn't bring herself to get any closer to the woman to check. In case she reached up and snatched her out of the air.

'What am I looking at?' asked the doctor.

'The names of the dead that have been brought in,' replied the woman. 'The ones who can be identified, anyway.' She pointed to some words on the sheet. 'Here.'

'How do you know it's the same girl?' he asked. 'It's a common surname.'

'Look at the address.'

He still wasn't getting it. But Hannah was.

The woman snatched the paper back. 'It's the same place where the girl in there was found. There can't have been two Sofia Meyers living at that address.'

'But why would she lie?' asked the doctor.

The woman shook her head. 'Honestly, Doctor. Are you naïve or stupid? Why do you think she would lie?'

Hannah didn't need to wait around to hear his answer. She left, floating back down the corridor, through the ward and into her body where she woke, trying her best to convince herself it had all been no more than a dream.

She pushed the sheets off, sat up and twisted herself around to look behind her headboard.

The once white, now brown lily stared back. She leaned forward and breathed in. The smell was faint, but still there, as if its spirit were reluctant to let go.

She eventually fell asleep. This time she did dream. Of dead flowers above her nameless grave.

'Hannah! Wake up! You must come now!' Marianne was beside her, gently nudging her shoulder.

'What?'

'We have to get you out of here. They're planning to move you today.'

Hannah wiped at her eyes, trying to clear away the mist of sleep. There was something about Marianne's words . . . some memory that was connected to a dream. 'They're moving me? Where to?'

Not a dream! A memory! The lily!

She was wide awake, throwing off the sheets, lifting her broken leg first, then swinging her left. She winced at the pain as her injured leg dangled over the side of the bed, but managed to keep a cry inside. Where were her crutches?

Marianne pulled the wheelchair closer from the side of the neighbouring bed. 'Climb in!'

'My crutches.'

'We don't have time!' And the way she spat these words made Hannah realise just how quickly they had to move. She dropped onto her good leg and fell back into the chair, placing both feet on the rests. Before Marianne turned it, Hannah leaned forward to look behind her bed. It was there. The lily.

'What are you doing? Get in!'

Hannah grabbed her book and sat back down, trying to process what was happening to her.

Marianne began to push. Hannah's heart was racing, her fear rising. But she was learning how to deal with these feelings. She focused on the task at hand, not on the threat. They had to get out. Don't worry about why. She set her sights on the door and, just like the night before, she willed herself there. But then where . . .?

'Where are we going?'

'Somewhere safe.'

This wasn't the time to question Marianne. She had to trust the nurse.

Hannah's focus on the door wavered and she couldn't help but look at the faces of the other children. Some of them lay still, undisturbed, but others watched wide-eyed and confused as they flew past. A nurse tending to a small boy looked up and opened her mouth to call out.

Hannah shook her head, pleading with her eyes that she remain silent. The nurse's mouth fell shut and she shot a glance at the open doorway. Then she gave a flick of her wrist and silently mouthed the word, *Go!*

The corridor was long and bright. Closed doors and windows with lowered blinds. Yellowed walls and high, ornate ceilings. Black-and-white floor tiles and that sickly chemical smell. From somewhere ahead the *clack-clack-clack* of heels echoed off a hard surface.

A corridor led away to the left. Marianne turned. Hannah waited for the *clack-clack-clack* to speed up, but the rhythm remained the same. They hadn't been noticed.

Still, Marianne started to run, and Hannah had to fight the unhelpful urge to leap out and do the same. She couldn't, after all. Not with a broken ankle. It looked like they were heading for a dead end, that they would be trapped here, spotted and dragged back. The footsteps were still somewhere behind, and Hannah had no way of knowing if they had been seen. They reached the end of the corridor and Hannah was relieved to see they weren't trapped. The corridor turned right, and they followed it.

Marianne slowed and Hannah held her breath as the nurse tried to catch hers. The sound of those heels was fading. Hannah let out a long, slow, quiet breath. They had made it. For now. But how much further until they were home free? Hannah had never been this way before.

A doctor burst through a set of doors. He stopped and held one open, smiling at them as Marianne bustled them through.

'Thank you, Doctor,' said Marianne. She was trying to put breath she didn't have into words, Hannah could tell. She just hoped the doctor couldn't.

Now they were in a lobby with a lift and a stairwell. Hannah twisted and placed her hand upon the nurse's. 'Thank you,' she said.

Marianne gave a pained smile and pressed the button for the lift.

There were only three floors in the hospital, Hannah knew, but the wait seemed endless. She and Marianne took it in turns to glance behind them, and Hannah felt the fear burrowing further inside her.

The chime of a bell and the lift doors opened to reveal, thankfully, an empty compartment. Marianne wheeled her inside and pressed the '0' button again and again. Hannah had her back to the door and imagined feet running along the corridor, bursting into the lift and dragging them back to the ward.

But it didn't happen. The doors closed and Hannah felt the descent in her already sinking stomach. Again, her hand found Marianne's, and they stayed that way until the doors opened.

The ground floor was bustling with people. But that was good. Nobody took any notice of a nurse wheeling a girl with a broken leg down a hospital corridor.

'I need to leave you here for a moment,' said Marianne, stopping outside a door with a sign that read STAFF ONLY.

Hannah caught hold of her sleeve. 'Please don't be long.'

Marianne pulled her hand away. 'We have to act normal. Keep your eye out. If anybody asks, tell them you're being taken to radiology.'

Marianne disappeared through the door, and Hannah watched a flurry of activity around the main entrance. A man with bandages wrapped around his entire head was led by a nurse towards and past her. A woman wiped at her eyes as she spoke to a nurse behind a desk. Somewhere a baby cried, and somebody shrieked. Trolley wheels rattled, doors slammed, footsteps echoed.

The phone on the desk began to ring. The nurse glanced at it, but the woman was still speaking to her.

Hannah knew who the caller was. She knew it would be the doctor who followed starch lady around. That her bed had been found empty. That the woman had told him to call down to the entrance to stop them from leaving. That right now, she was on her way here with her *clack-clack-clack* heels scuttling along the corridor, gathering an army of doctors and nurses to catch Hannah and take her away. Her fear was beginning to turn to panic.

She placed her hands on the wheels and started to slowly roll herself forward just as Marianne came back out of the room carrying some crutches, a cloth bag and what Hannah first thought was a blanket.

'Put this on,' she said. The blanket unfolded into a long brown plaid coat, with mismatched buttons and a wide collar edged with fur.

Hannah, who was still wearing her hospital gown, didn't question her. She stood up on one leg and, with Marianne's help, pushed her arms through the sleeves. It was a little big, but who would care? A quick glance along the corridor told Hannah that nobody seemed to be taking any notice. She went to take the crutches.

'Not yet,' said Marianne. 'Let's get out of here first.'

Hannah sat back down. Marianne placed the crutches and the bag on her lap. 'There are shoes in there. Put one on your good foot. It's cold outside.'

She did as Marianne said. It fit perfectly. They began to move once more, slowly now. This was Marianne's way of trying to look casual, she guessed. The woman at the desk hung her head as they approached. The nurse took her chance and reached for the ringing phone. *Still ringing! It has to be her!* As the nurse held it to her ear and listened, her eyes found Hannah. Then Marianne. She stood up, and Hannah's eyes were silently yelling out, *Run, Marianne! They've found us!* when the nurse said, 'Thank you, Doctor. I'll let him know.'

They were past the desk. A soldier in grey uniform on his way in through the entrance doors took a step back and held them open. Hannah tried not to catch his eye, fearful that he was here for her. But he just stood there and smiled.

Then they were out into the day and onto the busy city street.

THIRTEEN

They ditched the wheelchair near the entrance to an alley. Marianne took the bag, and Hannah began to make her way on the crutches. She soon picked up the rhythm of swinging and stepping. At the other end of the alley, they emerged into a street that seemed, at first glance, undamaged. But, at the far end, high piles of broken brick and jutting towers revealed more evidence of where the city had been blown apart. To her amazement, people appeared to be getting on with their lives as if all were normal. Or were they? Is that what they thought of her when they looked? Who knew what grief was hidden behind each pair of eyes?

They joined a group of people waiting for a tram. Hannah couldn't help but glance back the way they had come, but a quick nudge and shake of the head from Marianne told her to stop. A couple of young soldiers ambled past, their eyes poring over the civilians. Hannah looked away, her heart beating in her ears. They weren't out of trouble yet, she knew.

With the ring of a bell, the tram arrived, and people stepped back to allow Hannah on first. She handed Marianne one of the crutches so that she could grab hold of the rail and pull herself on. A man stood to offer her a seat, but Marianne thanked him and said they were only going a couple of stops.

They began to move off. Marianne kept the crutch to allow Hannah to hold on to the rail.

After three stops, Hannah had begun to relax. If they had been followed, surely they would have been captured by now. The tram slowed, and Marianne said this was their stop. She passed back the crutch and they disembarked.

When Hannah was satisfied that nobody was within earshot, she asked, 'Are you going to tell me where we're going now? Am I going to stay with Frau Meyer?'

Still, she eyed anybody passing with a degree of suspicion. And she saw Marianne doing the same. Was this how it would be from now on? It was a terrible thought.

'I'm taking you to a safe house,' said Marianne, her lips barely moving.

'A safe house?' She didn't know there was such a thing. How could there be? If it had a door, it could be kicked in. And windows could be smashed. 'To be safe? Or to feel safe.'

Marianne hesitated. 'You'll only be there for a few hours.'

'And then?' Though she thought she knew.

'And then on to the mountains to stay with Frau Meyer.'

It made her feel like she was being sent to a different planet.

'It's for the best,' said Marianne. And Hannah knew she was right. But it still hurt. Far more than her leg, which was by now starting to throb with every step she took. The adrenaline of the escape was wearing off, and she could feel her body beginning to flag. Her arms ached from the exertion of supporting her every step, and her hands rubbed painfully against the wooden holds.

'Is it far now?' asked Hannah.

Marianne shook her head. 'No. Just at the end of this street. You're doing great. We're nearly there.'

Hannah was exhausted, but she was determined to get there without asking for help. There was a lot she would need to do by herself in the coming days. No matter what pain it caused.

The house was hidden. Not by walls or trees. There was no greenery here, like there was (or had been, Hannah corrected herself) in other parts of the city. It was hidden by its similarity to all the others along the terraced street. Off-white render, three storeys, an attic room with dormer windows. Hannah supposed it was important for a safe house to blend in, in much the same way she and Marianne had tried to remain unnoticed all the way here. A skill she would have to learn to perfect for the foreseeable future. To fit in. To hide in plain sight.

A narrow, uneven pavement ran along the front of the houses, and they passed tall wooden doorways with skylights set above them. Without stopping, without looking, as if they were doing no more than returning home, Marianne pushed open a door and ushered Hannah inside. The house smelled damp. The hallway was sparse. There were no pictures on the walls. Just a single, round table with a man's cap on it.

'Hugo,' called Marianne, softly.

It hadn't occurred to Hannah that somebody else would be here. But if Marianne knew them, it would be okay.

'In here,' came a man's voice.

Hannah followed Marianne down the hall.

There was a young, tall man waiting for them in the living room. He had a long, thin moustache that accentuated his genuine but nervous smile. He stood up when they entered and gestured for Hannah to take his deep, comfortable-looking armchair. She let him take her crutches and sank into it, gladly.

He placed his hand upon Marianne's arm, and Hannah wondered if they were a little more than friends.

'Hello, Sofia,' he said, once the door was safely shut upon the outside world. His hair was wavy, parted in the middle. A sprig of it fell over his face and he flicked it back. 'I'm Hugo. It's nice to meet you.'

So he didn't know her real name. Did that mean she could trust him or not?

Her look must have given away her concern. 'I don't need to know,' he said.

She felt a little embarrassed, and decided to move on. 'It's nice to meet you, too.'

The room was as sparse as the hall. The chair, a sofa and a simple table. Bare floorboards. No ornaments or pictures. No rug on the floor. But curtains. For obvious reasons, thought Hannah. And because it was the law.

'Here,' said Hugo, pouring her a glass of water from a jug.

Hannah drank it down. She hadn't realised how thirsty she was.

'I'll warm up a bath,' said Marianne. And Hannah, right then, couldn't think of anything her body would like better. She had rarely bathed at the Meyers', had had to share the water with her parents when she did. And the one bath she had had in the hospital had been tepid and rushed, and under the supervision of a nurse.

'Hugo will explain everything,' continued Marianne. 'You can trust him as much as you trust me. We're the same.'

It seemed they had everything sorted. As if they had done this before.

'There's a warm bath waiting for you down the hall. With soap and shampoo.' Marianne followed her voice into the room. 'Take your time. We have a few hours before you have to leave.'

Hannah felt a surge of panic once more. 'Only a few hours?'

Marianne smiled through pursed lips. 'It's for the best. The sooner you leave . . .' She left the words hanging there, and Hannah knew, once more, that she was right.

'Have you done this before?' she asked.

Marianne nodded as Hugo left the room. 'Too many times. But don't think you mean any less to me because of it. If anything, each time I do this, I feel a greater pain of letting go.' She shook Hannah's arm gently. 'But come on. This is a good thing. And who knows? Maybe, when this is all over, we'll see each other again, hey?'

Hannah couldn't see that happening. But she nodded anyway. For Marianne's sake.

Marianne opened the bag she had collected from the nurses' room. It contained clothes, she explained, from children who had been brought into the hospital. Hannah wondered where those children were and whether they would ever be needing them back. There was fresh underwear already in the house for her, but Hannah was thrilled to see the bag contained clean, white socks, a singlet and a blue-and-white dress. After living for so long in the same few clothes that had begun to grey and thin, and then the hospital gown, Hannah felt her spirits lift from just looking at them.

'I'll help you get yourself in,' said Marianne.

'That would be good.' She knew from her stay at the hospital how difficult it was to get into a bath with the cast on.

'And you don't want to get that cast wet.'

'I know.' But she would give anything to wash that leg. It was beginning to itch.

The bath was simple, but to Hannah it was luxurious. Nothing, though, compared to what she used to enjoy at their apartment. A warm, cosy bathroom with all the comforts of home, her mother's toiletries on the shelves, flowery scents in the steamy air and the knowledge that she was safe from harm. This bath wasn't like that. But it was everything when compared to her time in the basement. Marianne helped her lower herself down, emptying a little of the water once she was in. She kept her plastered leg on the side of the bath and lay there, feeling the dirt, the grime, the tension float away. Her bruises were still there, up and down her body, but they were beginning to yellow and fade. The cuts had scabbed over, some of them almost gone.

She dried and dressed, sitting on a chair in the corner of the room. There was a brush beside the sink, and she took her time to rid her hair of tangles, wincing when the brush got stuck and she had to force the bristles through the strands. When she was done, she pulled herself up at the sink, reached out and wiped the mist from the mirror. The face that stared back was both familiar and a stranger. She felt older than she looked, but looked older than she should. She watched as her features slowly faded back into the misty glass, then grabbed her crutches and headed back to the living room.

'You look beautiful,' said Marianne, as Hannah negotiated the doorway on her crutches.

'I feel . . .' She didn't know how to finish, so instead said, 'Thank you.'

Marianne closed her eyes. Like Hannah's mother used to when she was trying not to cry. She opened them again, swallowed and smiled. 'Would you like me to plait your hair?'

Hannah faltered as the memory of how her mother used to do this for her filled her mind. But she shook a smile onto her face and agreed, lowering herself down into the same chair that had welcomed her before her bath. Marianne began to twist and separate the strands of her hair. The feeling was pleasant and reassuring, but at the same time wistful. Marianne's fingers worked it into two plaits and, when she had finished, she fished a compact out of her bag and flipped it open to let Hannah stare in at herself.

Again, she studied her face, turned her head from side to side. Definitely older. Thinner, too. And sadder. No matter how much she forced a smile onto her face for Marianne, her eyes no longer shone. Marianne's did, though. When Hannah turned to face her, the woman was wiping at them.

Another goodbye. But at least she would get to say this one.

'Do you know what Aunt Maud's home is like?' asked Hannah, purposely addressing her new guardian as such to make Marianne understand. She would try to accept her new identity; to become, from this moment on, Sofia Meyer. 'Is it big?'

'I think so,' answered Marianne. 'It's a lodge.'

Hannah's confidence wavered. Would there be people coming and going? What if one of the guests suspected she wasn't who she claimed to be?

Marianne must have sensed her concerns. 'It's a small village. Winter is coming. The lodge will have few, if any, visitors. The authorities … those people at the hospital … they'll forget about you.'

That would be good. Perhaps, in return, she should forget them. But it would be hard.

'What will you do now?' she asked.

Marianne sighed. 'Disappear. For a while.'

'You can't go back?'

Marianne shook her head. 'No. But I can move on. There's somebody else out there right now who will need me.'

'And Hugo?'

'We stay together.'

Hannah was happy about that. In a world where there were too many lonely people, Marianne and Hugo had each other. And they were good people.

'They'll forget you, too,' said Hannah. It felt like a wise thing to say.

But Marianne shook her head. 'No. We will be put on a list. We probably already are, under different names.'

'Marianne isn't your real name?' That was a sad thought. It made her a little disappointed, too. That Marianne didn't trust her enough to share her real name.

'It is for now, and it will be for a little while longer.'

'Where will you go?'

'Wherever we're needed. We're good at disappearing.'

Hugo reappeared at that point, flicking the hair from his eyes. He carried a plate of bread, cheese and pickles. And a fresh jug of water.

'You should eat,' he said. 'You have a long journey ahead.'

And she suddenly realised how little she had eaten over the past few days. And how hungry she was.

'We have to go. The train leaves in half an hour,' said Hugo.

Marianne handed Hannah a ticket. 'Don't lose this.' Here, put it inside.' She picked up Hannah's book and opened it. 'I know your book means a lot to you. This ticket, for now, must mean more.'

Marianne told Hannah how she had to keep the ticket ready to show whoever wanted to see it, whenever they demanded, but she must always get it back. How Hugo would take her to the station and put her onto the correct train. But the most important thing that Hannah had to do was to stay awake, even though the journey would be more than six hours. She must not miss her stop. Kalterfluss. Marianne got her to repeat it several times.

And she should say as little as possible to anybody about anything.

But what about when she arrived there? 'Will somebody meet me?' She could feel panic beginning to return to her body, starting at her chest. She couldn't do this on her own. What were they thinking?

'Yes. Somebody will meet you. They know to look out for you. They will find you.'

'Who? Shouldn't I look out for *them*?'

But Marianne shook her head. 'It doesn't work like that. Hugo and I don't know. And it's best that way.'

She didn't understand. She wanted to ask more, but something in Marianne's expression told her to let it go.

'It will be okay,' said Marianne. 'If you do exactly as we say, it will all be okay.'

And then it was time to leave. Marianne placed a palm on each of Hannah's cheeks and kissed her forehead. 'You have to go now. Hugo will get you safely onto the train.'

'You can't come?'

Marianne shook her head. 'If they're out there, they'll be looking for the two of us together. It's safer this way.'

Hugo helped her up onto her crutches, and the three of them made their way to the front door. Hannah took one last look at Marianne.

Outside, the sky above was clear and beautiful. The world below didn't care.

FOURTEEN

21st September 1942

The lodge was dark and musty. They followed Aunt Maud down a long, wood-panelled corridor, where black-and-white photographs of people and places hung like windows to a colourless, yet somehow brighter, place. Hannah stopped a moment to study them – white, winter wonderlands, open fields and hills, a boy and a girl outside what looked to be this very lodge. Maud and Herr Meyer, perhaps?

Pieter stopped behind her.

'There will be time enough for that,' said Maud Meyer, turning. She glanced down at Hannah's crutches. 'Can you manage the stairs?'

Hannah gazed up at the staircase that led into the darkness. It looked steep, the treads narrow. She wasn't sure whether she could manage them or not, and it would be a long way down if she fell, but she nodded anyway. She didn't want to come across as needy.

'Very well,' said Aunt Maud, taking a lamp from a table and lighting it.

Hannah was confused. She had seen cables strung across the houses on her way in. And so why wasn't there electricity?

'Follow me.' Aunt Maud began to ascend.

Hannah stood there with one hand on the banister, considering whether to put her good foot or a crutch upon the first step. Such a simple task now made so difficult.

Aunt Maud went on without waiting. Crutches first, Hannah decided, and she and Pieter fell into darkness as the lamp got further away.

The staircase wound around and up again into darkness, but they left it at the first-floor landing. Another long, dark corridor. Aunt Maud trotted on, her long spindly shadow following behind. She passed three closed doors and stopped at the fourth and last. Hannah wondered if there was anybody currently residing behind the other three doors.

Aunt Maud entered. 'This will be your room,' she said.

Hannah stood in the doorway and peered through, but she could see very little. Apart from the circle of light cast by the woman's lamp, the shadows were dark and deep, and the air had a smell that brought back long-lost memories of old schoolrooms. She placed her crutches inside and followed behind.

As she got deeper into the room, Aunt Maud holding the lamp high, her eyes began to adjust. She could make out the outline of a huge, dark wooden bed. And the thick mattress with folded-down sheets embroidered along the edge with what could have been wildflowers. It looked comfortable. More comfortable than anything she had slept upon for a long time. She was tempted to drop down onto it there and then, but she fought the urge and cast her eyes around the rest of the room. *Her* room, she realised. Her very own room. Bigger than the whole cellar she and her parents had shared for nearly a year. She tried to feel pleased, but it was hard to be enthusiastic about anything.

Other furniture poked out from the shadows. Small chests of drawers sat either side of the bed. A wider, higher matching chest to her immediate left, and a tall wardrobe along the adjacent wall. There was a desk under the window, and a mirror to the right. The walls appeared to be mahogany, a carved architrave running along their centre. The carpet was a montage of faded shades which could have once been any colour under the sun. Somewhere in the darkness, a clock ticked.

She lowered herself onto the bed, feeling its softness. She felt so tired, but had a feeling sleep wouldn't come easily. Not here, alone. Not for a while.

Aunt Maud placed the lamp down on the dressing table. 'I believe there is everything here that a girl your age will need. Though I don't confess to be an expert on such things. I haven't been where you are for a very long time, and have as little to do with children as possible.'

Every time Aunt Maud spoke, Hannah felt less and less wanted. All the love she had once had in this world was gone. She had taken for granted the assumption that it would always be there. She was starting to feel sorry for herself, she knew. But she couldn't help it. Perhaps the woman would begin to soften as she got to know Hannah, but she couldn't envision words of love or comfort coming from her hard lips.

Maud Meyer turned to Pieter, who appeared lost and out of place, uncomfortable in his surroundings. 'I would like to thank you for bringing her to me. Though only time will tell if I truly mean that.'

Hannah, too, wondered what time would bring.

Pieter tipped his head, cast a glance at Hannah, and smiled. 'Goodbye, Sofia,' he said, and for a moment Hannah wondered who he was referring to. 'It's been a pleasure meeting you.'

'You aren't staying the night?' They had had a long journey. It was late. The man must be tired. Plus, she realised, she needed a constant in her life. Somebody who knew. Who had shown her some kindness. Just a little while longer.

'I cannot.' His eyes darted to Aunt Maud.

'But there are rooms here. Aren't there, Aunt Maud?'

Aunt Maud didn't respond.

'That's very kind of you, Sofia, but I have a friend who lives near the village. He has a place I can rest the horses for the night.'

Aunt Maud clasped her hands together. 'That will be all, then.'

'Thank you, Frau Meyer. Goodbye, Sofia.'

'Goodbye, Pieter. Thank you.' She couldn't help but keep the disappointment from her voice.

He went to leave, and then realised he was still carrying her book. He ducked into the room and lay it upon the bedside cabinet, nodded once more and left. Hannah felt a ball of panic in the pit of her stomach again. She was alone with a stranger once more. And, unlike Marianne and Pieter, she couldn't imagine this woman being any comfort to her if that ball unravelled and filled her whole being.

'Your father and I …' began Aunt Maud, seemingly unsure how to continue. 'We fell out of touch.'

The words surprised Hannah. Something about them made the ball shrink and tighten, until it was back under control.

'But family is family,' Aunt Maud continued. 'You've suffered a terrible loss. As have I. He was my brother.'

Aunt Maud reached down and smoothed out a crease in the bed cover. 'I take it you know how to use a needle and thread?'

'Yes, Aunt Maud.' Hannah was well practised in darning. Even before she and her family had entered the cellar, she had spent many hours fixing holes and sewing on buttons. Clothes couldn't just be replaced because of simple wear. Even when times had been better, her mother had drilled into her the importance of using what you had for as long as you could make it last. Clothes, food, water. There wasn't a bottomless pit of money, or goods. And, as time went on, that lesson had served them all well. She quite enjoyed it at times. It was something to focus on, away from what was happening outside her door.

'Very good.' Aunt Maud straightened a picture that was already level. 'Next year, all this madness will be over, you'll see. In the meantime, winter is on its way, and . . .' She didn't seem to know how to finish. Hannah wished she'd just leave. 'The bathroom is down the end of the hallway. My room is on the floor above. You will have no need to visit that part of the house. Try to move around quietly. The floors are hard, and the house makes enough sounds by itself without you adding to it.'

'Yes, Aunt Maud.' She *really* just wanted to be left alone now.

Aunt Maud pointed to the large set of drawers. 'There are some undergarments in there, and some dresses hanging up in the wardrobe. I had some time to collect things from the village, but not too much. It has all come as a bit of a surprise. If you need anything else, we shall see what we can do.' She caught sight of the book and picked it up. 'What is it that you are reading?'

'The Brothers Grimm.' Hannah half-expected a grunt of disapproval, but Aunt Maud placed it back down gently.

'Books are good for the mind and for the soul. I have some more in the study that you may borrow.'

That was encouraging. Something to do apart from darning and . . . and what? What else would there be for her to do here?

'I expect you're hungry,' said Aunt Maud.

She was. But she didn't feel like eating. Just sleeping. 'Thank you. I ate before I left.'

'Very well.' Maud Meyer walked back to the open door and placed her fingers on the handle. 'I shall leave you to wash and rest. You have had a long journey.'

Her eyes remained fixed upon Hannah's. She seemed to have an unmatched skill for commanding the silence. Hannah felt like she had to fill it. 'Thank you, Aunt Maud. For taking me in.'

The woman pursed her lips, took a breath and marched from the room, closing the door behind her.

Hannah fell back onto the bed. Within moments, she was asleep.

In what seemed like the middle of the night, heavy footsteps trying to sound lighter, and the turning of a key in a lock down the hall, woke her. The lamp had burned down and the room was cold. She removed her single shoe and coat, pulled back the covers and climbed beneath them.

The door along the hallway closed, the footsteps disappeared, and she drifted back to sleep.

FIFTEEN

Hannah slept well, probably better than she had in years, though the pain in her leg and that worsening itch brought her out of her slumber every so often. She thought she heard those footsteps leaving in the early hours, but might have dreamed it, waking to a scraping and grinding from out in the hall and, not long after, a knocking at the door.

'Come in,' she said, pulling herself up into a sitting position.

'Good morning, young lady,' said Aunt Maud, her tone no less severe than the night before. 'I see you approve of the bed. Well, it's time to get up and eat. There'll be no lounging around while you're under my roof.'

Hannah stretched and pulled back the covers. She still had her dress on from the day before.

Aunt Maud obviously wasn't impressed. 'Your first job after eating will be to change out of those clothes and have a good wash. Now, follow me.'

Hannah looked around for her crutches, eventually finding them on the floor at the end of her bed. She leaned over the side and lifted them onto the covers. Then, in one swift move, she placed her hands on the crossbars, dropped their ends to the carpet and swung herself upright.

She briskly made her way out into the hall, remembering Aunt Maud's warning about noise, and grimacing at the knocking her crutches made on the wooden floor. Aunt Maud was standing in the corridor beside a small, open door set halfway up the wall. When she saw Hannah, she reached in and pulled out a tray. On it was a plate of food, a glass of milk and some cutlery. Hannah could make out eggs and mushrooms and melted cheese, and her stomach grumbled as the scent drifted towards her.

'This is the first and the very last time I shall allow you to eat a meal in your room. You made your way up the stairs yesterday. You can make it down again later. I shall collect the dishes shortly. And I expect them to be empty. We live in a small village and there are ways around the rations. But food isn't as easy to come by as it used to be. I don't want any waste.'

Hannah limped up to stand beside her, staring into a small compartment that appeared to float in midair. Two vertical ropes ran from above to below. A dumb waiter. Hannah had seen one before, when she had gone with her father to visit one of his friends who ran a restaurant in the city. A long time ago.

'There won't be any,' promised Hannah. She was famished.

'Mind out of the way, then,' said Aunt Maud. She clomped back down the hall, Hannah following behind, her tongue almost lolling from her mouth for the food.

Aunt Maud put the tray on the dressing table, pulled out the chair and opened the curtains. By the time the room was bathed in fresh daylight, Hannah had plonked herself down, discarded the crutches and begun to fork the food into her mouth.

'Slow down, girl!' barked Aunt Maud, shaking out the curtain and opening a window. 'Those eggs aren't going anywhere soon.'

Yes, they are, thought Hannah. But she forced herself to slow and took a drink of milk. The chilly air blowing in was refreshing.

'I shall see you downstairs in a while,' said Aunt Maud. 'But take your time coming down. One broken leg is enough. And I don't want to spend all day scrubbing blood out of the floorboards.'

'Yes, Aunt Maud,' replied Hannah, and she continued to gulp down her breakfast.

Hannah tilted back her head to drain the last drop of milk, and had all intentions of going to the bathroom to wash, when her eyes caught sight of the view from her window.

Aunt Maud's lodge appeared to be the tallest house at the highest point of the village. Directly opposite was another house, its render cracked, its paint missing or maybe just dirty. Beyond the square, a jagged, snowy peak rose to a dizzying height. Below it, brown and grey crags of rock fell away to a thick green forest that almost made its way to the village. It was prevented from doing so by a carpet of green pastures, cut in two by a single road that led from the village to the forest.

Hannah placed her hand across the bridge of her nose, blocking out the village and the fields. Only the mountain and blue sky remained. She could almost believe that the world was without people. Would it be better this way?

The illusion was broken by a small swathe of light-brown straight lines amongst the ramble and tumble of tree and rock. Three turrets, one wall, that peeped out as if watching the village with an air of curiosity. A castle. Made small by distance and the gargantuan mountain upon which it nestled. But even from here, Hannah could tell it was bigger than any building she had ever seen. Even the cathedral back in Stuttgart.

She reached for her crutches and made her way over to the chest of drawers. After finding some underwear and tucking it under her arm, she went to the wardrobe.

There were three dresses hanging up that looked to be her size. Faded colours and stretched fabrics, but opulent compared to the threadbare clothes she'd worn in the basement. Hannah's opinion of Aunt Maud softened a little – she was grateful to her for taking the time to find them. She lifted a beige dress with black cuffs and collar off the hanger, added it to the underwear and made her way out into the hall. Her movements on the crutches were becoming smoother, more automatic – even since yesterday, she realised with a little pride.

She stopped at the dumb waiter. Now that Aunt Maud wasn't here she wanted a better look inside. There was something fascinating, almost magical, about a box that could travel from floor to floor through a hidden shaft. She opened the door. A cool breeze blew out, bringing with it a stale, damp smell. A thought came to her. She could fit in there. Legs tucked up, arms on her lap. It would be a squeeze. But she could.

She continued along the corridor, dark even now on the brightest of days. She glanced at the locked doors. She would ask Aunt Maud if anybody else was staying at the lodge. She remembered the footsteps from last night. Had they been Aunt Maud's? For some reason, she didn't think so.

An open door! Finally, the bathroom. Hannah navigated herself around the door as best she could on the crutches, and was surprised to find a spacious room furnished with a bath, sink and toilet. A warm bath. That's what she needed. She opened the hot tap and waited. She was suddenly aware of feeling grimy, and stripped off her clothes. She tested the water, hoping . . . it was a lodge, after all. But no, the water was freezing.

She sighed and took a face washer from the pile of towels on the shelf, soaked it in the sink, rubbed in the soap and washed herself all over. Except for her plastered leg. Which seemed to itch whenever she thought about it, as if it were pleading to be scrubbed, too. She bent down to clean her toes and caught the whiff of a stale, dull smell coming from inside the plaster. After living in the cellar with a shared chamber pot, it wasn't the worst thing she had ever smelled, but she wondered if it would get worse as the weeks went by. The plaster could come off after six weeks, Marianne had said. Hannah assumed there was a doctor or nurse in the village who would be able to do it when the time came. She scrubbed between her toes. It felt good.

She dried herself, dressed and stared in the mirror. She straightened the collar and gave a little nod of satisfaction. The dress was a little big, but it looked good on her. She unplaited her hair, feeling the freedom of it falling around her shoulders, and forced her mouth into a smile. It still looked out of place.

SIXTEEN

Going downstairs was surprisingly harder than going up. Mainly because she could see all the way down to where she would land if she fell. She could hear Aunt Maud (it was surprising how easily that title was coming to her each time she thought about the woman) pottering around on the ground floor.

She wondered what her parents would think about her situation now. They'd no doubt be happy for her, that she had made it up to a village in the mountains, far away from the city's troubles. But she didn't think they would like Aunt Maud. Could anybody? Though her parents had both been gentle, accepting souls. So, she supposed, they would have tried their hardest to get along with Maud. And so must she. She had a feeling it would be hard work at times. But she would do it for them.

It was a strange place to be ambushed by tears, halfway down the stairs. She didn't move, couldn't see clearly enough to. This was it. She had survived. She had escaped.

She had travelled. She had slept. Now, she must accept. This moment was the start of her new life.

There was no way back.

She didn't feel the same panic and fear that had struck her yesterday. It was simply sadness. She missed her parents. It was hugely unfair that they were gone and she was here, alone. She was sorry for them and angry that it had happened. That it had been allowed to happen.

Hannah was still there, leaning on one crutch, trying to wipe her eyes clear with her other arm, when she heard Aunt Maud's steps below. She brought her head up, waiting to be admonished for something, but the woman's face had momentarily lost its severity. She was wearing an apron and holding a mop.

'You're doing well, Sofia,' she said, and Hannah didn't know whether she was referring to how far she had come in her new life, or down the stairs.

But it helped. She sniffed, blinked away the tears, and carried on her descent.

'I ate it all,' said Hannah, as she reached the bottom.

Aunt Maud's features and tone sharpened once more until she was the same woman who had answered the door to her and Pieter the previous evening.

'I hope you did. Or I'll be sending you back up again to finish it off.'

And Hannah couldn't help but inwardly smile. Somewhere deep down, Aunt Maud had a heart.

Aunt Maud left Hannah to explore the ground floor while she busied herself around the lodge. When had she last been able to do this? To walk freely through a house, any house, without the fear of somebody breaking down the door. Always on alert.

She entered the kitchen first; a cool room of clean surfaces, closed cupboards and hanging pots. There was no smell of baking in here; none of the babka or lekach that Hannah remembered from long ago when her mother used to bake. Instead, there was the harsh scent of soap and vinegar and the impression that there was more cleaning than cooking being carried out.

She visited the dining room, with its large mahogany table, and chairs that may have once matched but had been reupholstered with a multitude of fabrics over the years. A chandelier hung from the high ceiling, and a glass cabinet leaned up against the far wall, showcasing sparkling glassware and ceramic ornaments. It appeared grand to Hannah, or at least as if it had been, once upon a time. But there was no indication that anybody had used it for a while. There was a sparsity of personality. It appeared wasted.

Back out in the hall, she noticed the black-and-white pictures she had seen when she had first arrived. They were mostly of mountain scenes, but there were some family photographs, too. Combinations of generations of what was so obviously the Meyers. On mountain tracks, around what she assumed was the village and one in front of the lodge. There was no doubting that the two children were Franz and Maud Meyer. Those gaunt faces, deep-set eyes, thin frames. The lodge hadn't seemed to have changed at all. There was some form of decoration around the door in the photo, but she couldn't make out much detail from the picture.

She moved on. There was a downstairs toilet at the end of the hall, and further along was a room that seemed to be a dumping ground for unwanted furniture and crates.

The parlour boasted three mustard armchairs and a green sofa on a faded, threadbare oriental rug. The room smelled of old woodsmoke and wine. A fireplace filled with charred wood was set into the wall adjacent to the doorway, and a sideboard ran along the opposite one. On it were decanters filled with amber liquids, the bust of some bald, old man and a radio with a black Bakelite front. Directly ahead of Hannah, looking out onto the square, was a window, its emerald-velvet curtains held back with gold ties.

Her leg ached. Her leg itched. She leaned her crutches against an armchair and lowered herself down into it. The pain eased but that itch remained. Deeper now. She tried to stretch her fingers to the source of discomfort but couldn't reach it.

'So you have seen all there is to see of this floor,' said Aunt Maud from the doorway. 'Which isn't much, I'm afraid. But it's enough for me . . . and for you now.'

But didn't a lodge have guests?

'Aunt Maud?'

'Hmm?' She lifted her head and stared down her nose at Hannah.

'Is there anybody else staying here, at the lodge? Where are the guests?'

'Guests,' replied Aunt Maud, as if trying to understand the word, 'I remember them.' And then, more abruptly, 'There's a war going on, young lady. You should know that better than anybody. Having a holiday is the last thing on people's minds.'

Hannah thought back to the footsteps she had heard in the middle of the night. Perhaps they had been Aunt Maud's, after all. 'So there isn't anybody staying here?'

Aunt Maud chewed over her words for a few seconds,

as if deciding how to answer. 'The lodge has one occasional guest.'

Hannah waited, but Aunt Maud seemed reluctant to say more. 'On my floor?' asked Hannah, and she realised her mistake as soon as she said it.

'It is not *your* floor. It is my floor. You are staying in a room on my floor. In my house. And before you say it, you are certainly not a guest. You are …'

'Family,' finished Hannah, before she even knew she was going to.

Aunt Maud huffed, and Hannah guessed that was the end of the conversation. Although she felt as if Aunt Maud were hiding something.

The itch was getting bad now. Hannah slipped a finger into the plaster below her knee, but it was no good.

'Here,' said Aunt Maud, walking over to the sideboard and pulling out a crochet needle.

Hannah's mouth fell open. What a great idea!

'Use this. But be careful, your skin has softened below that plaster. It will easily tear.'

Hannah didn't care. That itch was now so bad that she felt like ripping the plaster from her leg and digging her nails into her skin. She grabbed the needle and, ignoring Aunt Maud's warning, pushed it down inside the plaster. It did the trick. And it felt so good.

SEVENTEEN

Hannah heard Aunt Maud traipse up the stairs, followed by the rumble of the dumb waiter and the ring of a bell. She sat in the parlour, wishing she had brought her book down with her.

She stood up, hobbled over to the window and stared out. It was the same view as from her window upstairs, but from down here the fields and the road out of the village were obscured by the buildings on the far side of the square. But there was no hiding the mountain, nor the castle nesting in the forest.

A fountain stood at the square's centre. White and pink flowers sprouted from its high trough, and a small spout of water trickled from a brass pipe into the lower trough. An old lady walked into the scene with a basket over her arm and waved to someone out of Hannah's view. And two boys were kicking a ball to each other at the far end of the square. It was a Saturday, she remembered. No school today.

School.

A thought struck her. Now she was Sofia, would she be allowed to go? A flutter of excitement filled her stomach at the idea, but there was also a murmur of worry at her centre. If she went to school, she would have to pretend to everyone there. The more people she interacted with, the more she risked being found out and discovered. But it would be worth it. To be able to play and be friends with other children.

Hannah touched her face. She was smiling.

She was woken by a knock at her door. The room was darker than she expected, the world outside cast in a lilac hue.

'Come in,' she answered, for a moment trying to orientate herself. 'What time is it?' she asked, as Aunt Maud's head appeared around the door's edge.

'Gone six o'clock. There's food downstairs waiting for you.' Her footsteps disappeared along the hallway.

Gone six! Where had the day gone? Hannah's brain asked her stomach if it was hungry. The answer was yes. But she still felt so tired.

She was a bit shaky on her crutches and blamed it on the fatigue. She took her time on the stairs, the smell of burning wood rising up to meet her. As she passed the parlour she heard the pop and crackle of the fire. It smelled and sounded soothing. Perhaps she could feel at home here, after all. When she entered the kitchen, Aunt Maud had just finished stacking dishes beside the sink and was removing her apron. Hannah glanced at the bowl of baked potatoes, loaf of bread and slab of cheese upon the table. Her tummy gave a little appreciative rumble. But her face obviously didn't show the same level of enthusiasm.

'What were you expecting?' huffed Aunt Maud.

Hannah felt her cheeks grow warm. If only the woman knew what she and her family had survived on. The meal in front of her was so plentiful. And all this for just the two of them.

'No. It looks . . . We didn't eat well in the city. There's so much.'

'Mmm,' said Aunt Maud, in a tone of disbelief.

Aunt Maud sliced the loaf and cut the cheese, gesturing silently for Hannah to help herself. They sat and ate. Aunt Maud focused on her plate, and Hannah looked around the kitchen as she bit into the crusty bread, remembering her mother's kitchen and how, long ago, the two of them would spend hours in there, baking cakes and cooking pastries. Sometimes for special occasions like Hanukkah or Pesach, but often just for fun and feast. Hannah would love those moments, standing on a stool next to her mother, stirring and rolling and mixing and whisking. The sweet and spicy smells. Filling the pastries and layering the cakes and then licking the spoons clean. Her mother joking that they could put the spoons back in the drawer without washing them. Then impatiently waiting for the cakes to rise or the pastries to brown in the oven. The smell of baking teasing her. And having to wait for her father to come home from work before being able to take a bite. Sitting down together, her mother fibbing that Hannah had made these all by herself when really it had been mostly her. Choosing the biggest slice and sinking her teeth into it. Sighing with delight. Watching her father's face as he took his first bite . . .

The sound of metal against porcelain stole her back from her memories. She stared down through misted eyes at the dropped fork.

'It will get easier,' said Aunt Maud. And then, as if needing to balance out her words of kindness, 'But crying won't help.

We have to make do with what we are given. And what we are given right now is this meal, sorrowful as it may be. So eat up.'

Which she did.

Hannah's first full day at the lodge ended in the parlour with the fire blazing and the radio playing. They'd had a similar radio back in Stuttgart before they'd left to go to the Meyers'. A black square box with a cloth circle and dials. Theirs had had a number stamped on the front, just like Aunt Maud's. What it hadn't had was the eagle. Or the swastika. And unlike Aunt Maud's, theirs had had names of different cities that could be selected by the centre dial. Her father had told her that these cities were where the sound was broadcast from, sometimes hundreds of kilometres away. Hannah would sit with her parents in the living room and they'd listen to music, news, plays. Sometimes, comedies. She would laugh along with her parents, though she hadn't always understood the jokes.

If the same programmes were available here, Aunt Maud didn't listen to them. Her head nodded, almost imperceptibly, to a slow, orchestral beat. There was a shirt upon her lap, a tin of buttons open on the arm of her chair and a pile of clothes stacked beside her on the floor. An oil lamp on the dresser lit up her work and cast shadows onto Hannah's cast, which was propped on a stool in front of her.

'Whose shirt is that?' asked Hannah.

'Herr Richter's, the butcher,' replied Aunt Maud.

'Is he the one staying here?'

Aunt Maud didn't look up. 'Why would the butcher be staying here?'

Hannah had no idea. But then why would Aunt Maud be mending his shirt? She decided to ask.

'So that you and I can have sausages on Monday,' replied Aunt Maud, lifting the shirt and biting off the thread. 'And as we are going to need twice as many sausages every Monday, we are going to have to darn twice as many shirts. Starting next week.'

Hannah didn't mind. She quite enjoyed darning. She used to, anyway, back when . . .

'Do you mend shirts for anybody else?' she asked, stealing herself away from her memories.

'You ask a lot of questions.'

She didn't used to. Leah had always been the inquisitive one. But if Hannah had learned anything in the past few years, it was that information was important. The more you knew, the better equipped you were to make your own decisions.

'The lodge is a big place,' said Aunt Maud. 'Nothing comes for free. Not the wood on that fire or the bread in your belly. And it's the same for most people in the village. The war has made it hard to come by things. But not if you have a service to offer. If you have a skill and you know somebody who needs it, you can get enough to get by. We've all got something to offer, and I offer this.' She lifted the shirt. 'To anybody who needs it. And, as of next week, so will you.'

That was only fair, Hannah thought. She hadn't felt able to properly contribute before. Not to help her parents. Nor the Meyers. But if she did this, then perhaps she would be able to get on the good side of Aunt Maud, and then . . .

She tried to make her next words sound casual, as if what she was about to ask were a natural progression from the discussion they had been having.

'Aunt Maud?'

The woman looked up and flicked her eyebrows at Hannah. She felt her heart speed up. Whether it was because of the question she was going to ask or because of the answer she was hoping to get, she wasn't sure.

'Does the village have a school?'

Aunt Maud reached down and picked up a frock. 'All in good time, young lady. All in good time.'

EIGHTEEN

The next morning, Hannah woke feeling lost. She reluctantly opened one eye to see if it was light yet. It was. Very. She groaned.

Despite having slept like a log, she felt unrested. She forced herself to rise, but even the leg without the cast felt heavy. She heaved herself to an upright position and looked around the room. Her vision began to cloud, and a sob escaped. She sat on the edge of the high mattress and let more leave her body. It left her feeling even more exhausted, but calm. She wiped her eyes with a sleeve.

She reached for her crutches and hobbled to the bathroom. A determination to wash and dress before Aunt Maud came knocking on her door made her move swiftly through the morning routine.

Downstairs, there was no sign of Aunt Maud. But on the kitchen table she found some bread left over from the previous night, a slab of butter under a dish and even a jar of apricot jam. Hannah wondered how many shirts Aunt Maud had had to darn to get that. She sat and ate, feeling small and alone in this huge house. She decided to go in search of Aunt Maud, surprising herself with the thought that even her company was better than being alone right now.

She checked the dining room and parlour and followed the hallway to a back door. It opened onto a small courtyard surrounded by a high, grey stone wall, a wooden gate at its centre. Aunt Maud was there, busy stuffing fresh straw from a sack into the henhouse. A dozen or so chickens skittered around, pecking and clucking.

'Close the door, will you?' asked Aunt Maud, from inside the coop. 'I don't want these hens running havoc in the lodge.'

Hannah did as she was told and leaned against a pile of chopped logs, covered with tarpaulin. 'Thank you for breakfast,' she said.

'There would have been eggs.' Aunt Maud folded the sack closed and wiped her hands together. 'But they decided not to lay today.'

'It was good as it was,' said Hannah. And then, to continue in her attempts to get on Aunt Maud's good side, 'Can I help?'

'You can,' said Aunt Maud, exiting the coop. 'Help me get those hens back inside so that they can make up for their lack of laying. But don't you go falling over out here. Or you'll get pecked to death.'

Aunt Maud's attempt at humour again. Things were looking up.

Hannah picked out a hen and then began to limp towards it, waving one crutch, then the other. Aunt Maud did the same with her arms. The chickens ran and fluttered and squawked this way and that until Hannah and Aunt Maud decided, without speaking a word, to work together on one hen at a time. After five minutes or so, Aunt Maud, panting from the exertion, closed and latched the gate with all the hens safely behind it. Hannah took her place against the log pile once more, rubbing at her hands that were beginning to blister from the near-constant weight they were taking on the crutches.

'Always the same,' said Aunt Maud. 'I often wonder if chickens are worth their bother. But thank you. Believe it or not, that was easier than usual. Now for their feed.'

'I can do that,' said Hannah, 'if you have other things you want to do.'

'I've nothing that I want to do. Plenty I need to do. A handful for each hen. Scatter it around. Make them work for it,' explained Aunt Maud, gesturing towards a sack of grain. 'No more than a handful each, though. They're on rations, the same as the rest of us.'

Hannah watched her walk off, wiping herself down and shaking the dirt from her shoes. She had never fed chickens before. Couldn't ever remember seeing one alive. She rested one crutch against the coop, scooped a handful of grain from a sack, and proceeded to scatter it through the wire. The hens, who had begun to settle down, once more ran around pecking and squawking. Hannah watched in amusement and then scooped up a second handful. Then a third.

Why should the chickens suffer just because humans wanted to fight? This was going to be their lucky day.

She returned to her room, feeling better, thinking Aunt Maud may even have softened towards her this morning. When Hannah had come in from the chickens, Aunt Maud had offered to bandage her hands, to help stop the blisters becoming sores. Hannah was grateful, but didn't want more of her body itching below bandages. As a compromise, Aunt Maud suggested wrapping the crutches' wooden handholds with old scraps of fabric instead. It was a good idea, and Hannah could already feel the benefit.

Sunlight streamed through the bedroom window. She made her way over to it and sat down at the desk, enjoying the sun's warmth on her face.

Outside, a smudge of cloud spread itself along the village roofs. Shutters were thrown open and smoke trickled from chimneys into the bright, cool air. A black cat sauntered out onto a windowsill opposite and began to lick its paw. Superior in its position and attitude, it stopped for a moment to watch a man hobble by. He wore a long, grey trench coat held together with patches. One of his hands played with the fingers of the other, and his lips moved, as though he were thinking out loud. Hannah found herself leaning forward to follow his passage through the square. She glanced away when his head began to turn towards her. When she looked back, he was gone. There wouldn't be many men in the village. Those who could fight were away at war. And she wondered who he was and why he was still here.

Her eyes returned to the book upon her desk. Its gold lettering glimmered in the sunlight.

NINETEEN

Hannah woke the next day without the feeling of loss and emptiness overwhelming her. She was washed, dressed and downstairs before Aunt Maud had finished putting out the breakfast dishes. She ate while Aunt Maud pottered around, and then offered to feed the chickens again.

'That can be your job from now on,' said Aunt Maud, her voice lighter than usual. 'But remember . . .'

'. . . no more than a handful each,' finished Hannah. Maybe a little bit more.

'And when your leg's better, you can clean their cage out for me, too.'

'It's still quite sore,' said Hannah, and she thought she saw Aunt Maud's mouth curl up, ever so slightly.

Shortly after midday, Aunt Maud left the lodge, carrying two baskets filled with repaired clothes to return to their owners. Hannah remained in her room while she was gone. It was beginning to feel like a place of refuge. A hideaway that, despite what Aunt Maud had said, was hers and hers alone. But the village was beginning to beckon her more and more. Her fear of venturing outside was dissipating. She hadn't seen a single soldier since she'd arrived here, after all.

Hannah was sitting at her desk in front of the window. Her book was open in front of her, but every time there was movement outside she was snatched away from the story. Something moved, and she looked up again. A football appeared in the square. It was being chased by a boy with blond, wavy hair that fluttered across his face as he ran. He was dressed rather formally for kicking a ball around, Hannah thought, in a white shirt and flannel shorts held up with braces. Each time he caught up with the ball he would nudge it on further before taking aim at the fountain. It glanced off the target and rebounded towards the lodge. He ran after it and tried to flick it up into the air, but with little success – it just rolled further away. After a few more attempts, he bent down, picked it up and looked around to see if anybody had witnessed his poor soccer skills.

His eyes found Hannah. He instantly tucked the ball under one arm and gave her a wave with the other. Hannah slowly held her own palm up, but realised she was out of practice. She looked at her hand, as if it were someone else's. It had been too long since another child had greeted her with carefree friendliness. And it had been too long since she'd played outside. Suddenly, it was the only thing she wanted to do. Blast her broken ankle. She desperately wanted the boy to know that she would like to play but couldn't. She reached for a crutch and held it up.

The boy frowned. His mouth formed an O as he understood. He shrugged. Then he dropped the ball and went to kick it. It spun feebly to the side, and Hannah heard something smash. He glanced up at her, red-faced.

Hannah leaned on the sill to get a better view, but something else caught her eye. Aunt Maud, returning with two newly filled baskets. The boy turned to see what she was looking at and Hannah saw his whole body tense. He took a step away from the woman, who had by now sped up, the baskets bouncing up and down in her arms, threatening to spill the clothes across the square.

Crimson faces stared at each other, one in fear, the other anger.

Hannah bit her bottom lip, trying not to show the boy that she was laughing, feeling mean at doing so. But she couldn't help it. There was something comedic about the whole thing, and it was so long since anything had tickled her like this to make her want to laugh out loud – she was thoroughly enjoying the sensation.

Aunt Maud had now arrived at the terrified boy, dropping the baskets onto the ground. Her mouth was moving like a feeding fish, and she was pointing towards the lodge. Hannah couldn't see the boy's face, but by the way he was nodding and holding out his hands, she guessed he was apologising. She could hear Aunt Maud's shouty, angry voice, but couldn't make out what she was saying. Hannah wanted to open the window, but didn't dare, in case she was caught and somehow became implicated in the boy's crime.

Aunt Maud wagged her finger at the boy one final time, scooped up the baskets and marched towards the lodge's front door, out of sight. Hannah heard the door open below and instantly slam shut again. In the middle of the square, the boy stood alone, shoulders slumped. He plodded over to the guilty football, picked it up and then seemed to remember she was there.

He flashed a cheeky smirk towards her and gave her another wave, appearing to shake off his shame rather easily.

Her wave back was more enthusiastic than before. The two of them had shared something. They had both suffered under the tyranny of Aunt Maud. But while the boy was now free to return home, Hannah would probably be the target of her crankiness for the rest of the day.

She decided to stay in her room for as long as she could, and picked up Sofia's book to escape into the world of fairy-tales once more.

That night, she gazed down upon her body as she slept.

TWENTY

When Hannah came downstairs the next morning, she found a small, ornately engraved wooden box beside her plate of scrambled eggs.

'The hens have been busy during the night,' said Aunt Maud, as if it were them that had made the box and left it for her. Hannah lifted the lid. Inside were four different-coloured bobbins of thread, a darning mushroom and a small cushion with pins and needles sticking out of it. 'You did say you could darn?'

Hannah was proud of her darning skills – especially her blanket stitch. She had learned from her mother, and she used to enjoy it, like the baking. Being close to her mother, watching her as she placed the end of the thread in her mouth and then loaded the needle to start the stitch for her, before she was practised enough to do it herself.

But then later, in the Meyers' basement, it hadn't been enjoyable. The light had been dim, her fingers weak and cold. They had stitched out of necessity, not for pleasure or frugality. And stitches had been put upon stitches upon stitches. Clothes that were beyond repair were unravelled so the thread could be used on other items. Often the thread didn't match, in colour or thickness. But they only had what they had.

'I did,' said Hannah. 'I mean, I can.'

'Very good. There's a pile of socks in the parlour.'

Socks. The worst kind of darning there was. Especially strangers' socks.

'You can start with them. Rid them of holes. And then, when I'm satisfied, I'll let you work on the other, more delicate garments.'

She would be starting all over again. At the bottom. With socks. But she would show Aunt Maud what she could do.

She closed the box and began to tuck in to the hens' gifts.

Later that day, Hannah started on the darning. She hadn't felt useful to anybody for so long. But this would change all that. Hannah was going to earn her keep, and it felt good.

By mid-afternoon she had almost finished darning the socks. Her wrist was beginning to ache more than her ankle, and she was starting to squint due to the dimming light, but she was proud of the basket of finished darning at her feet. Her sewing box was on the desk in front of her, and she'd taken a cushion from the parlour to prop herself up in her chair. She had just started on the final sock when she heard the front door open and close. Had Aunt Maud gone out? No, that was her voice, although she was speaking in a tone Hannah had never heard her use before. It was friendly, welcoming – servile, even.

'Oberstleutnant,' she said.

Hannah jumped mid-stitch and the needle pierced her skin. She placed her darning on the desk, brought her finger to her mouth and tasted blood. *Oberstleutnant!* A soldier. A *high-ranking* soldier!

He's come for me! thought Hannah. *Starch lady has sent him.*

'Frau Meyer.' The man's words were sharp and succinct, as if he were used to giving orders.

She needed to hide! She reached for her crutches leaning against the desk, but in her frantic panic knocked one over. It hit the other one, and both crashed to the floor.

She froze. Too late to hide. Downstairs, there was silence.

Then, 'You have somebody staying with you?'

Hannah's heart echoed in her head. Her whole body was on high alert with that irrepressible need to hide.

'My niece,' explained Aunt Maud. 'I believe I mentioned . . .'

'Ah, yes, yes. Very unfortunate circumstances, I recall. The bombing. That is what we are fighting against.'

'And winning, I hear from the radio.'

'We will be triumphant. And soon.'

'That's good to hear. Anyway, how wonderful it is to see you again,' continued Aunt Maud. 'Will you be staying with us?'

Staying with us? Hannah glanced towards the hallway. Was this the occasional visitor? The absurdity of the situation! A Jewish girl living in a house with a German soldier.

'Not today,' replied the man. 'Perhaps later in the week. I just need to collect a few things from my room.' Then a lightening of his voice. 'Well, where is she? I would very much like to meet this young girl.'

'Of course,' replied Aunt Maud. But was there a hint of reluctance in her voice?

Footsteps on the stairs.

They were coming! What should she be doing? She didn't want either of them to see the panic that must be written all over her face. She leaned upon the desk and hopped to the mirror. The footsteps reached the top of the stairs as she studied herself. She looked too red in the face. She brushed down her hair, straightened her dress. Breathed in. Out.

Halfway along the hall now. She hobbled back and threw herself down into the chair. Why hadn't she just stayed there? Now she felt breathless, probably looked more flushed, too. She picked up the sock, the needle …

There was a knock at the door.

She cleared her throat, tried to get her voice steady, turned her head. 'Come in,' she managed to say.

The door opened and Aunt Maud walked in, clasping her hands in front of her.

'Sofia, I would like you to meet Oberstleutnant Kessler. Oberstleutnant, this is my niece, Sofia.' Her words carried the clarity of mountain air on a clear, sunny day. But there was definitely a slight tremor to it, Hannah thought. Was Aunt Maud scared of soldiers, too?

Hannah took a much-needed breath, put down the sock and needle, lifted her crutches and stood to face the door.

Aunt Maud was tall, but the man standing beside her, dressed impeccably in a grey uniform, was head and shoulders above her. His face was long and gaunt, and his black hair was shaved close at the sides and greased back on top. His skin was pallid, and his frame slightly hunched, as though he were preparing to pounce. His arms, like his legs, were spindly, spiderlike, even, and he held his grey cap in one of his skeletal hands.

Hannah may as well have had a yellow star stamped on her forehead. Here she was. Right in front of him. Caught. It was over. It had all been for nothing.

She couldn't speak. And the way Aunt Maud was staring at her, eyes threatening to pop out of her head, only made it worse.

The man's face softened. His pressed-together lips parted, his deep brow lost its shadow and his body straightened. And instead of marching over and dragging her away, he gave her a gentle smile. It almost seemed genuine, though she knew it couldn't be.

'Please sit, sit,' he said. 'Rest that poor leg of yours.'

Hannah looked to Aunt Maud, who relaxed slightly and nodded. She leaned the crutches against the desk and sat back down.

'Don't let this uniform concern you, Sofia.' The Oberstleutnant's words came out sounding warm and amicable. What was going on? He held out his arms and glanced down at himself. 'I am a soldier, but I am first and foremost a father. It is good to meet you. Your aunt has told me all about you. I am very sorry for your loss.' He bowed his head.

Hannah didn't respond. She couldn't respond. She didn't know how to talk to soldiers, even when she wasn't pretending to be someone else. Soldiers were always to be feared, never trusted. How was she meant to act in this situation? From behind the Oberstleutnant, Aunt Maud gave a single, prompting nod.

What was that supposed to mean? Hannah took a deep breath, gathered her thoughts and, in one full exhale, said, 'It's nice to meet you, too, Herr . . .'

'Oberstleutnant,' corrected Aunt Maud. 'This man is a high-ranking officer of the Wehrmacht.'

'Oberstleutnant Kessler,' repeated Hannah. She was beginning to get her breathing back under control.

'There is no need,' said the man. 'Herr Kessler will suffice.'

Hannah forced a smile which, to her, felt more like a grimace. The Oberstleutnant didn't appear to notice.

'I hope I have not woken you late at night or early in the morning with my comings and goings. I keep strange hours, as I must.'

So it was *him* she had heard that first night. Those heavy footsteps, different to Aunt Maud's gentle padding.

'No, *Herr* Kessler.'

Aunt Maud's pursed lips and sharp squint told Hannah just what she thought about her act of defiance.

The man took another step into the room and stared at the pile of socks beside her feet, the sewing box on the desk. 'I see your aunt is keeping you busy.' Another few steps, and he craned his neck to stare out the window. 'And you have a fine view whilst working.'

Hannah followed his gaze out the window to the village square and the mountain beyond.

The Oberstleutnant beckoned her towards him with a flick of his head. 'Let me show you something.'

Hannah glanced at Aunt Maud, who nodded again. She reached for her crutches.

'Here, let me help you,' said the man, gripping her elbow and lifting her from her seat. She winced, but not from pain. He was strong, and he smelled of musk and clean laundry. On anybody else it would have been pleasant.

He passed her one of the crutches, let go of her arm and offered her the other. She tried a smile again as he once more beckoned her to the window. Trembling, she stood beside him, staring out at the village.

'Do you see there?' he asked, pointing to the light-brown turrets that rose from the dense forest high in the mountain.

Hannah nodded.

'Speak up, Sofia,' barked Aunt Maud from the doorway.

'Yes, Herr Kessler.'

'That is where I work,' said the Oberstleutnant, ignoring her aunt, she noticed. 'It used to belong to a very rich man. A graf. But alas, no longer. It had, I'm afraid, fallen into a state of disrepair, inhabited by nothing more than bears and wolves when I arrived. I had to fight them off myself.'

Hannah knew better, but she raised her eyebrows anyway. The Oberstleutnant laughed. 'I'm joking. There are no bears. And though there are wolves that roam the forest, they rarely come close to the castle. That is where my men are based.'

'What do you do there?' She felt like he wanted her to ask. Otherwise, why would they be having this conversation?

'That's none of your business!' jabbed Aunt Maud.

'That's quite all right. An inquisitive mind is a growing mind,' said the Oberstleutnant, catching Hannah's eye and giving her a disarming wink. 'There's nothing special that we do. We train. We build. We look out for enemy aircraft.'

But you can't stop them, thought Hannah. *Otherwise I wouldn't be here, with you, in this village. And my parents would still be alive.*

The Oberstleutnant continued to speak, but Hannah's thoughts had taken her attention away from the conversation. She heard something about a visit and felt her confusion show on her face.

'. . . visit the castle?' he said again.

Hannah had no wish to. Not while it was occupied by soldiers. But she didn't feel as if she could say no to this man. 'I've never visited a castle before. But . . .' She lifted one of the crutches, pleased to have them as an excuse.

'When you are healed then.'

From behind them, Aunt Maud's feet shuffled and the doorhandle rattled. She obviously hadn't expected Hannah to garner so much attention from the man. Neither had

Hannah. And she was glad, for once, of the woman's bluntness. She and the Oberstleutnant turned away from the window.

'Well,' he said, 'I shall leave you both. It has been a pleasure meeting you, Sofia, and I'm sure we shall become the best of friends.'

She tried to read his face for any insinuation. But she saw none. Perhaps she had got this man all wrong. Not every soldier could be bad, could they? He was studying her, too, and she felt she should speak before he heard something in her silence. 'It was nice to meet you, too, Herr Kessler.' She made herself maintain his gaze. And, to her surprise, it was him who looked away.

'Ah,' said the Oberstleutnant, stepping over to the dresser and picking up her book. '*The Tales of the Brothers Grimm*. A fabulous book. I read it myself from cover to cover when I was a child.' He held it out in front of him. 'You know, it is the Führer's wish that every child in this great land of ours is given a copy of this book.'

Hannah shook her head. She didn't know that. But she wondered why. Why would a man who had invaded other countries, who had caused so much misery for others, care about what children read? She had read it so many times. Was there something about the stories she hadn't noticed? For a moment, the book in the Oberstleutnant's hand took on a different guise.

'And what is your favourite tale?' he was now asking.

Hannah's mind was trying to catch up. 'I'm sorry ... ?' she stumbled.

The Oberstleutnant laughed. 'I, too, have the same problem. So many to choose from. It is like asking the mountain in winter what its favourite snowflake is.'

He must have misread her lapse in concentration.

Another laugh and he turned to Aunt Maud, who quickly joined him, though with less enthusiasm and certainty. He returned the book to the dresser and looked Hannah in the eyes. 'I hope your aunt is taking good care of you. If not, be sure to let me know.' One more laugh from him, but not from Aunt Maud this time. Just her infamous scowl at Hannah, as if it had been her who had made the comment.

That night, Hannah found herself gazing down upon her body once more, this time from inside the window of her room. She'd left the curtains open, and the moonlight was bright tonight. Down in the square, the water in the fountain sparkled, and in the house opposite, the cat lay asleep on the windowsill, illuminated by the moon's cool glow.

She was getting used to the idea of being separate to her body. She couldn't help but scan the room, though, to check that all was in place, that everything was as it should be, that it wasn't a dream . . . She floated around the perimeter. *Next time,* she thought, *perhaps, I shall leave the door open. And maybe after that, the window.*

She saw the corners of her mouth curl upwards, ever so slightly, and then she was tugged back towards her sleeping body.

TWENTY-ONE

Hannah grabbed the crochet needle she'd kept from Aunt Maud. That itch! To be rid of it, if only for a few minutes! She dug it inside the plaster and scratched, scratched, scratched. She knew she should stop, take heed of Aunt Maud's warning about damaging the skin, but she couldn't.

When it came, the pain in her ankle was now more of a background ache. She rarely noticed it, but every now and then there'd be a twinge. The smell was getting worse, same as the itch, but there wasn't much she could do about that.

She leaned back and flicked her wet hair over her shoulders with her spare hand. There was no hot water in the lodge for washing, but Hannah had lived without it for so long that she had accepted it as normal now. Didn't even think about heating it on the stove. Not that she'd be able to carry a bowl of water anyway while she was on crutches. At least she could wash in private here.

A swift breeze blew in through her cracked-open window, sending a brief shiver through her body and bringing with it the perpetual smell of chimney smoke. She slowed the scratching and watched the trees throw leaves at the sky. Somewhere in the distance, somebody was chopping wood.

A new basket of darning, ready for her to start on Monday, was tucked under her desk. She was still enjoying her daily chores, and had secretly named each of the chickens.

Hannah placed the knitting needle inside the open book on her desk. She had just finished re-reading the tale of 'The Spider and the Flea', thinking how, just like the characters in the story, the world she had known had been washed away in an ever-growing stream of senselessness.

She caught sight of the footballer in the square. He was back, but without the ball. This time he had brought a friend – a younger boy who trailed behind him so close he was almost stepping on his heels. She felt a little jealous about how easily they walked across the cobbles. She had ventured into the square on her crutches after the Oberstleutnant's visit, and had almost toppled over when a crutch had slipped off one of the stones into the crack. She found herself missing the flat slabs that had paved Stuttgart.

The older boy looked up at her from the corner of his eye, but this time there was no wave. He appeared nervous as he made his way towards the lodge. Hannah wondered whether his parents had made him come back to apologise to Aunt Maud. That was the sort of thing hers would have done.

There was his knock on the front door and Aunt Maud's footsteps pattering along the wooden floor of the hall. The door opened. Hannah held her breath to listen.

'I'm here to –' began the boy.

'You're here because I asked you to be, Josef Kleftmann. Nothing more. Nothing less. I see you've brought some help.'

Josef. That was his name.

Hannah smiled to herself at Aunt Maud's gruffness. She wondered if she ever tired of being so grumpy. She picked up her crutches and went over to her door to better listen in without being seen.

'Good morning, Frau Meyer,' said another voice. Presumably from the younger boy.

'Good morning, Elias. I must say, I was expecting somebody a little stronger. Are you sure you two are up to it?'

Up to what? wondered Hannah. Were they here to do some chores? As compensation for the smashed pot? She felt a little annoyed that Aunt Maud had neglected to tell her that the boys were coming over, as she had obviously arranged it. Was she planning on at least introducing her?

Hannah's hand slipped off the crutch's loosening fabric. She was nervous, her hands sweaty. She hadn't made any friends or even spoken to any other children since the little boy on the train, and that had hardly been the start of a budding friendship, had it?

Thumping and banging started up from below, interspersed every now and again with shouted instructions and warnings from Aunt Maud. Hannah decided to make her way downstairs to find out what was going on. She lived here, after all.

'Where shall we put this?'

'Can we lay this down?'

'Is this worth a lot of money?'

Short, breathless interjections from the boys were answered with Aunt Maud's bristling replies of, 'Careful with that!' 'Not there!' 'Break that and your mother will be hearing from me!'

Hannah chuckled from halfway down the stairs. Thankfully her hands had stopped sweating, but she could feel butterflies flapping away in her tummy. Why did Aunt Maud have to invite boys over? The boys at her school had been really annoying. Although perhaps these boys knew some girls Hannah might become friends with.

'Ouch! My hand!'

'Never mind your hand, watch my lamp!'

Hannah reached the bottom of the stairs, hobbled along the hall and found Aunt Maud in the doorway of the junk room, overseeing the activity inside.

'Just in time,' Aunt Maud said.

'Just in time for what?' asked Hannah, trying to see around her.

The boys, red-faced and sweating, were leaning into a chest of drawers, straining to push it up against the far wall. In fact, everything had been pushed up against the walls, creating a path that reminded Hannah of Herr Meyer's attic.

'Move out of the way, boys. Let Sofia see what we've found. All she can see is you two awkward lumps.'

Hannah felt her face flush red, embarrassed for herself and the boys. The eldest boy – Josef, she remembered – rolled his eyes, and she instantly liked him. He flashed a grin and pulled the younger boy to the side, revealing the treasure at the end of the newly uncovered path. A full bookcase. A wondrous sight of blues, greens and reds, all lined up waiting to be opened and explored.

'I told you I had more books for you,' said Aunt Maud. She sounded truly pleased with herself, as though she had been the one doing all the hard work. 'They just needed a bit of finding. Josef and Elias here offered to help, didn't you, boys?'

'Yes, Frau Meyer,' they echoed.

And then, to Hannah's surprise, Josef looked directly at Aunt Maud and asked, 'Is that it? Are we even now?'

Hannah struggled to keep in a snigger. She would never think of talking to Aunt Maud like that. But, she had to admit, she admired his audacity.

'No, we are not even, Josef Kleftmann, and never shall be. No matter what you do, my flowerpot will remain forever broken. What you will be is forgiven, which is more than you deserve.'

'What have you done to your leg?' asked the younger boy with brown, greasy hair and ears that stuck out either side of his round, rosy face, like handles of a tankard.

'That's none of your business,' chided Aunt Maud, before Hannah could answer. Then, visibly shaking the animosity from her demeanour, 'Sofia, this is Josef. And Elias. Boys, this is my niece, Sofia.'

The two boys looked as awkward as Hannah felt, so she took it upon herself to play the dutiful, polite niece in front of Aunt Maud. 'It's nice to meet you, Josef, Elias.' She looked directly at each boy in turn as she said his name.

'It's nice to meet you, too, Sofia,' said Josef.

'Nice to meet you, Sofia,' said Elias, still studying her plaster.

'I broke it,' said Hannah, answering the question still posed by his gaze.

'As you broke my pot, Josef Kleftmann,' said Aunt Maud.

Just how special was this pot? And it wasn't at all the same, thought Hannah.

'It was an acci–' began Josef.

Aunt Maud clapped her hands and Elias jumped. 'Enough! I didn't ask you round here to chirp and chatter. If I wanted to hear nonsense, I'd get myself a chimpanzee. I have plenty to keep myself occupied with, and so I shall leave you all to get acquainted. I'm sure Sofia would welcome some good company. However, you two will have to do.'

That was a great quip, Hannah had to admit. Elias looked confused but, when she caught Josef's eye, she thought she could see a smile being harnessed in.

The woman strode off, leaving the three of them standing in silence.

'She doesn't mean it,' said Hannah, feeling sorry for them. Elias, in particular.

Josef finally released the smile. 'I know.'

Her eyes went to the books, and he followed her gaze. 'You owe us,' he said.

'And you owe me a pot!' shouted Aunt Maud from along the hallway. She really wasn't going to let this go. 'And I do mean it, young man! Have no doubt!'

Her hearing was good. Hannah made a note to keep this in mind for the future.

TWENTY-TWO

'I've never seen so many books,' said Josef, as Hannah edged her way closer to the bookcase, keen to find a novel after reading short stories for so long. But where to start?

She rested her right crutch against the shelf and leaned her weight on the left. With her head cocked to one side to help her better read the titles on the spines, she ran her fingers along each book in turn, wondering if they were in any order.

'Doesn't the village have a library?' Hannah asked, in acknowledgement of Josef's exclamation. She remembered the library in Stuttgart, where she used to visit every week with her mother when she was younger. Before everything that happened. The last time she saw this number of books in one place was in a big, burning pile on her way to the Meyers.

'Only at school. And that's not as big as this. And they're all old with ripped pages,' said Elias. 'Can we go now?' he asked, turning to Josef.

Hannah didn't want them to go, she realised. 'Do you like chickens? You could help me feed them, if you like.'

'I like chickens,' Josef said. 'Especially in a soup.'

The hens clucked and ruffled their feathers when the three of them entered the courtyard. And when Elias ran over to them, they became even more fractious.

'Can I feed them?' asked Elias.

The sack of grain was tucked into the corner, below a sheet of iron. Hannah remembered what Aunt Maud had said. About even the chickens' food having to be rationed. But they were making so much noise. And hadn't Hannah just promised . . .?

'Just a few handfuls, Elias,' said Aunt Maud from the doorway. There was no rigour in her voice now. She was more up and down than the mountain range on the other side of the lodge. 'They can have their evening feed early. It will save me a job. Sofia – make sure it's not too much. They need to be able to fit back into the henhouse tonight.'

She disappeared back inside. Hannah lay one crutch to the side, hobbled over and unfolded the sack. They each took a handful and spent the next few minutes scattering the seeds, watching as the chickens fluttered in a frenzy, searching for each and every one. Elias chuckled as he threw seeds first into one corner, then the opposite, the birds squawking and tripping over each other in their attempts to feed their beaks. His laugh was infectious, and Hannah found herself joining in.

When they'd had their fill, the chickens began to quiet and slow, but still the three of them laughed. It broke the ice between them, and Hannah felt comfortable enough to say, 'That's enough,' before Aunt Maud came out to do the same.

'Is it true that the cities are on fire?' asked Josef from beside her. The question took her by surprise. She hadn't really seen much of the city from the basement. And it wasn't fire she had seen when leaving the city, but smoke. But what was the saying? There's no smoke without it?

'There are fires. But not across the whole city. Not mine, anyway. It's more scarred. Broken.'

'Like your leg,' said Elias. 'And your aunt's pot.' He laughed and looked at Josef for a reaction. But Josef just nodded, as if he were picturing a burning city in his mind. She wondered whether he had ever visited one.

'We hear the explosions, sometimes. From here,' he said.

'Really?' said Hannah, surprised.

'They scare me,' said Elias, the tone of his voice as expressive as his words. He squinted against the bright sky as he stared up at her.

'We're safe up here,' she said. 'They can't fly this high.' She didn't know whether that was true or not. She just didn't want him to sound the way he did.

It didn't work. He continued in the same tremulous tone. 'But we hear them, and . . .' His eyes flicked towards Josef, as if asking permission to continue. Or perhaps he wanted the older boy to say it for him.

'One crashed into the mountain,' said Josef, and Hannah felt like she had let Elias down. That she had tried to deceive him. She made a mental note to only speak the truth from now on. Or, at least, a version of the truth . . . It was all so complicated. How was she ever going to make friends?

'It was quite a few weeks ago,' Josef continued. 'The soldiers came to the village to warn us to be on the lookout for someone who may have escaped. But we didn't see anybody. They must have all been killed.'

'*How* did you break your leg?' asked Elias. He blurted the words out fast, seemingly eager to change the subject. But, in his naïveté, he had failed to do so. The planes. Death. Her leg. They were all inexorably connected.

'Sofia might not want to talk about that, Elias,' said Josef, and Hannah wondered if he knew more than he was saying.

'Why not?' Elias pressed.

But the strange thing was, that naïveté, that directness of somebody approaching the subject with no preconceptions, no judgement, made it easier for her to feel like maybe she could talk about it. And she wanted to tell, if not all the truth, as much as she could.

'A house fell on it.'

It sounded ridiculous. Even to Hannah.

Elias's eyes widened and his mouth dropped open. 'A whole house?'

'Yes.' Hannah couldn't help but let out a small laugh at the younger boy's words. But it caught in her throat, and she swallowed. Was she going to cry now? Her emotions were all over the place. Mountains and valleys. 'An aeroplane dropped a bomb on it.'

'That must have hurt.'

Her mood rose again. Something about how he spoke. As if he had no filter to his thoughts. It was endearing.

'It did.'

'Does it hurt now?' He was staring at her plaster.

'It itches more than hurts.' And just thinking about it made it do just that. 'And it smells.'

He wrinkled his nose. 'Of what?'

'Strawberries and cream,' joked Josef. 'Have a sniff.'

Hannah shot him a smile and shook her head. 'Don't believe him, Elias. It smells worse than the chicken coop.'

'What happened to your family?' asked Elias. 'Were they hurt, too?'

Hannah's throat tightened. She hadn't had to say it yet. Not out loud. She took a breath, held it there. 'They were in the house with me. When it collapsed. They were killed.' A sob from deep inside her came out with that last word. Her face was hot, her eyes welled up. She wanted to sit down.

'Let's sit down.' Josef must have read her thoughts. 'Your leg must be aching.'

Hannah wiped at her eyes. Elias had turned away. She felt bad, although she wasn't sure why. She hadn't meant to upset him, but he had asked.

Josef dusted off a log and they all sat on it.

'Keep your smelly leg on your own side of the log, if you please,' Josef quipped. She was grateful for the diversion. Although, were those tears in Elias's eyes? Had he lost somebody, too?

She decided it was up to her to change the subject. 'Tell me about the village.'

'It's really quite boring here,' said Josef.

'Boring is good.'

'Sometimes. But not all the time.'

'Will you be going to our school?' asked Elias.

Another difficult question. Though it shouldn't have been. It should have been one of the easiest questions in the world to answer. She was a child, and children went to school. In a normal world.

Aunt Maud had told her to take one thing at a time, but she felt a degree of frustration about it. She had every right to an education. Everybody did. Her father had instilled that in her since she was little. He had been a teacher, after all.

Although, what if she'd fallen behind in some subjects? Would people guess that she hadn't been to school in a few years? And then, would they guess why?

'I'd like to,' she finally said. 'But I think Aunt Maud wants me to wait until my plaster comes off.'

'Does she scare you?' asked Elias.

'Does she scare *you*?'

He nodded.

'She scares me,' said Josef.

Elias frowned as if such a thing weren't possible.

'She scares everybody, I think,' said Hannah, wanting once more to make Elias feel better.

'Perhaps Hitler should use her to scare away the enemy,' laughed Josef, and Hannah pretended to join in. To her, Hitler *was* the enemy. But so were the Allies who had dropped the bomb that killed her parents.

'There must be *something* interesting about the village,' said Hannah. She was trying her hardest to force the conversation towards a lighter subject, but it kept returning to the war.

Because that's all there is now.

Elias jumped up and turned to face Hannah and Josef. 'We could show you around, couldn't we, Josef?'

Josef raised his eyebrows and nodded casually. 'We could. That would take ten minutes,' he laughed.

'I'm sure it would take longer than that,' said Hannah, to keep the conversation going. She'd like to explore the village with these boys.

'You're right,' said Josef. 'I forgot about your crutches. Fifteen minutes.'

He was funny. 'So, I've come to the most boring place in the world.'

'There's the castle,' said Elias, but there was no excitement in his words. Not like she imagined there should be with talk of castles.

'It's not really *in* the village,' explained Josef.

'Have you ever been there?' Hannah found herself leaning forward, anticipating a story of wolves and trapped princesses.

But Josef shook his head, and Hannah felt disappointed and a little naïve. After all, the Oberstleutnant had already told her he worked there. *I must start reading things other than fairytales.*

'There are soldiers there now,' Josef said, quietly, and Hannah could tell by the way his voice dropped that this worried him. 'They arrived at the beginning of summer.'

'I don't like them,' said Elias. 'They shouted at me.'

Hannah wasn't surprised. They were soldiers. 'What for?' she asked.

'I just asked them what they were doing. They told me to mind my own business.'

'Do they come to the village much?' she asked, thinking about the Oberstleutnant's visit to the lodge.

'They used to. They ran electricity from the castle to all the houses,' explained Josef.

'There isn't any electricity here,' said Hannah, nodding towards the lodge.

'It's just for the radios,' explained Elias.

'The soldiers came into our houses and connected the wires. They took away our old radios and gave us new ones,' said Josef.

'For free!' said Elias, excitedly. Apparently, he had forgiven the soldiers for shouting at him.

Hannah didn't believe that. Elias's parents probably didn't discuss money with him.

'They want us to know how well the war is going,' said Josef, and Elias's excitement fell away.

The radio certainly did that, thought Hannah. Whether or not it was true was another matter.

'But we haven't seen the soldiers recently,' continued Josef. 'We hear them shooting in the forest. Mama says they're practising for when they have to go to war.'

'Is your father up there?'

Josef shook his head. 'He's already gone.'

'Do you know where?'

Another shake of the head. 'We haven't heard from him for months.'

It must be terrible, thought Hannah, not to know where your father is. Or whether he was alive or dead. Was that worse than knowing for sure, though?

'All the men have gone. Except the old ones. One day soon, I'll probably go.' There was no emotion in his voice. Just the flat tone of acceptance. The propaganda she had seen on posters about the glories of fighting for a greater Germany obviously hadn't reached Felshoven yet. She was glad and hoped, for all their sakes, that it never would.

Hannah wondered about Elias's parents. But he had turned silent, staring at the hens who had finally settled down, two of them having returned to their nests. If he wanted to offer the information, Hannah was sure he would have done so by now. It was pretty obvious that he liked to talk.

They sat there a while longer. Josef did most of the talking. He was good at putting people at ease, she realised. He told Hannah how people in the village either worked on farms or in the small stores, and how they all did general chores to support each other. He lived with his mother and grandmother. Both grandfathers had died in the Great War.

'Do you think this war will be greater, Josef?' asked Elias.

Josef shrugged.

'I don't think *great* is the right word,' replied Hannah. 'I think terrible is better.'

'The Terrible War,' said Josef.

'That sounds more like it,' agreed Hannah.

'Will you be staying here for good now?' Elias asked her.

Yet another good question. She had no idea what was to become of her. But she did know one thing. 'I have nowhere else to go. So yes, Elias, I think I will.'

'That's good,' said Josef. He blushed and added, 'Isn't it, Elias?'

The smaller boy nodded.

Hannah felt a smile spread across her face, crinkling the cold skin around her eyes.

Elias grinned and was visibly shivering. 'Can we go back inside now?' he asked. 'I'm getting cold.'

'Me, too,' said Hannah, rubbing her hands up and down her arms – not that it did much good. She really should have put a coat on before coming outside.

They all stood up, although Hannah wobbled. Elias picked up the crutch that was laying down and held it for her while she steadied herself. She would be glad when she didn't need them to get around.

'So are we going to make our suggestion to the army?' asked Josef.

Hannah wasn't sure what he was referring to. 'Suggest what?'

'That they use your aunt to scare away the enemy.'

'Believe it or not, Josef Kleftmann, they have far more terrifying things than me in their arsenal,' came a familiar voice from behind them. 'Just pray you never get to see them.'

Great hearing *and* timing, thought Hannah. What other powers did this woman have?

'Aunt Maud,' Hannah ventured, as the three of them followed her inside. 'Josef and Elias have offered to show me around the village.'

'You can see the village from your room,' said Aunt Maud, immediately busying herself by brushing away a cobweb as she passed.

'I'd like to walk around it.'

Aunt Maud turned and folded her arms. Hannah stopped. The boys did, too. 'The last I heard, you had a broken ankle. And, from what I can see, it still hasn't mended itself.'

'We won't go far.' She needed backup here. If she waited until the boys left, she had the feeling Aunt Maud would refuse. She may refuse now, but with three pairs of eyes on her, all wanting her to say . . .

'Very well. But it will have to be tomorrow – it's too late now. And stay within the village. Wolves love a child who cannot run.'

She was joking. Wasn't she?

TWENTY-THREE

Hannah's earlier excitement about the books had started to wane. After immersing herself in magic and enchantment for the past year or more, she found the titles in Aunt Maud's library, or the few paragraphs she read, bland and uninviting. Some of them were also clearly written for adults, set in the backdrop of the last war, a place she didn't want to escape to. She finally settled on *Heidi*, a book she had heard of but never read, and she spent an hour or so lost in the mountains between the pages until the sky outside darkened and Aunt Maud called her for dinner.

Afterwards, Hannah and Aunt Maud did what they had started doing most evenings – they sat together in the parlour, each in their 'usual' chairs, and turned on the radio. The commanding voice of a man cut through the static, telling them how the army was making great advances each day. That the Allies were retreating, and victory would soon be theirs.

'Do you believe it?' asked Hannah. She felt she was taking a risk just by asking. Possibly opening herself up to Aunt Maud's own questions.

'You should be careful what you're saying,' replied Aunt Maud. 'There are discussions that should not take place when you don't know who is around the corner.'

Hannah assumed she meant the Oberstleutnant. But he wasn't here right now, was he?

'We need to listen,' said Aunt Maud. 'That is what they want, so that is what we shall do. And there will be no more said about it.'

The inexpressive way she spoke scared Hannah. More than her usual sardonic or cutting remarks. She was being serious. Deadly.

Hannah was being told to change the subject. So she did. 'When can I go to school?'

'I wondered when you would mention that again.' But she didn't answer the question.

'When, though? I'd like to.'

'Would you? Do you miss it?'

What was the woman getting at? Did she not want her to go? 'Yes, I would. And I do.' *It's been a long time*, she wanted to add.

'Perhaps when your plaster comes off.'

'But that's still weeks away,' Hannah said, trying and failing to keep the frustration from her voice. 'Can't we get a doctor to check it?'

'We don't have a doctor in the village,' continued Aunt Maud, ignoring Hannah's outburst, 'but I've done a fair share of caring for people.'

This surprised Hannah. She didn't think the woman was capable of caring. She caught herself in the thought and the guilt hit her. Aunt Maud had been caring enough to take her in, hadn't she?

'For who?'

'Your father, when he was younger. Your grandparents. Others in the village.'

Another pang of guilt. It hadn't been *her* father. Or her grandparents.

'So in four weeks, then I can go to school?'

'And then you can go to school. In the meantime, let me see if I can make some other arrangements.'

Hannah had an idea what that could be, and she hoped it wasn't the case. She didn't think Aunt Maud would make a very patient teacher.

TWENTY-FOUR

Josef and Elias arrived just after midday. Hannah was waiting for them in the parlour, her coat on, eager to be shown around the village. She had read a few pages of Heidi's adventures, but had found her heart elsewhere – outside, in the sun, across the village, at the base of the real mountains. Not the ones on the pages of her book.

She picked up her crutches and hopped to the door. She had tried putting weight on her broken ankle earlier, but it had hurt too much. Marianne had been correct. It was going to take six weeks. The two boys were standing side by side, rosy cheeked in the fresh autumn air. Josef was wearing a woollen sweater and Elias a navy-blue coat, with buttons the size of eyeballs. Before any of them had a chance to speak, Aunt Maud's harsh tones came from the far end of the hall.

'Rule one,' she said, 'no further than the edge of the village.'

Hannah didn't turn to look. Instead, she rolled her eyes and wrinkled her mouth. The boys remained earnest, Josef trying to keep a smile from his face, and Hannah guessed Aunt Maud was looking their way. She waited for rule two, but when it didn't come, she glanced behind her.

'She's gone,' said Josef, allowing the smile free reign.

'That's the only rule?' She couldn't quite believe it. Surely there had to be more.

'So you're allowed to climb trees?' joked Josef.

'She's not,' said Elias, sincere concern in his voice.

'Don't worry, Elias. I won't,' said Hannah.

She stepped outside into the crisp air.

'And be back before dark. Remember those wolves,' shouted Aunt Maud from the depths of the lodge.

There it was. Rule two.

'Yes, Aunt Maud!' she shouted. And then, to Josef, 'Close the door before she thinks up another one.'

He did as he was told.

'Where would you like to go, Hannah?' Elias asked.

Hannah had been confined in some way or other for so long that she didn't really care. Although she'd been staring at the fountain from her bedroom window for a week now, and she wanted to run her fingers through the water, and smell those flowers. 'To the fountain first. And we'll decide from there.'

She went, and the boys followed. This time she navigated the uneven cobbles with more ease and confidence. The air was fresh, the village quiet. Just the song of a lone bird and the trickle of water.

At the fountain, Hannah leaned on her crutch and dipped her hand into the clear, cool water. It felt wondrous, invigorating. Then under the spout, feeling it run between her fingers. She leaned over and smelled the flowers. Breathed deep and closed her eyes.

'Don't you have flowers in the city?'

'No,' she replied. 'We don't.' Because she hadn't. Not for a long time.

An image of the decaying lily on the hospital windowsill came into her mind. *Don't go there,* she thought. *Not now.*

She dipped her hand back into the water and turned to eye her new friends. They backed away from her.

'Splash Josef, not me,' said Elias. But his smile showed through.

'If she splashes me, I'll splash her back twice as much,' replied Josef, grinning.

Hannah removed her hand and watched as the water dripped onto the cobbles, revealing new, clearer colours. She felt like she was seeing it all for the first time.

'Let's go outside the village,' she said.

'But your Aunt said . . .'

'That's why I want to do it.' It would feel good to break a rule. She would truly feel free.

'But we will be back by dark, won't we?' asked Elias.

'Are you afraid of the wolves, Elias?' asked Josef.

Elias shook his head. 'No. The soldiers.'

'We'll be back before dark, Elias. Don't worry,' promised Hannah. But she decided to keep what she knew about soldiers to herself. That daylight couldn't protect you from them.

The smell of burning wood permeated the air, as much a part of the village as the bricks and timber of the houses.

The three friends ambled down the hill and turned right. Hannah was amazed by how quickly she'd got used to managing the cobbles on her crutches. Even when a crutch slipped, she was able to steady herself and keep going. The end of the village gave way to a field of grazing cows, the occasional clanging of a bell breaking through the silence of the day. The road led out of the village, turned to gravel and then rose steeply. If they followed it, it would lead them up to the castle, said Elias. The boys walked slow enough that Hannah didn't feel the need to rush. Which was good, because she was starting to get breathless and her arms were beginning to ache. The blisters on her palms had begun to dry and peel off. The fabric around the bars was helping to protect her hands to a degree, but she could feel a soreness in them returning.

When she was satisfied that they had left the invisible boundary of the village, her small rebellion achieved, she stopped. The forest was still a good distance from them, and she had no intention of entering it.

That is where my men are based.

They sat on the grass verge. Hannah gazed up towards the snowy peaks, many of them lost in cloud. Somewhere close by, a light hammering punctuated the silence. She bent her head to listen.

'That's a woodpecker,' said Josef.

She had never heard one before, but it sounded exactly as she imagined a woodpecker should sound.

'You can see the whole village from here,' she said.

'Nearly,' said Josef. 'Some houses are hidden by the trees.'

'Like mine.' Elias stared off to the right. 'You can't see mine.'

'Is that the school?' asked Hannah, pointing to a large, grey building with a fenced yard around it.

Both boys nodded.

'Is it nice?'

'Are schools supposed to be nice?' asked Josef.

'I like it,' said Elias.

'I liked it when I was your age. The teachers are kinder when you're younger. You wait.'

'Wait until what? What happens?' asked Hannah. And she realised she shouldn't have asked. Whatever Josef was referring to, Sofia would have known.

But he didn't pick up on it, just shrugged. 'I don't know. They just seem to have less patience. Herr Guttman doesn't live up to his name. He's the headmaster and is always punishing us for the smallest things. He's old and cranky.'

Hannah nodded along, relaxing into the conversation again after her hiccup of a mistake.

Elias ignored him. 'Frau Meinhardt's my teacher, Sofia. She's really nice. She tells us a new story every day.'

Hannah turned and glanced up at the castle. She shivered.

'Do you want to go back?' asked Elias. 'You look cold.'

'It's not that cold,' said Josef.

He was right. 'Yes. Let's head back to the village.'

'You can come to my house,' said Elias. 'My grandmother is baking. She'll have cakes for all of us.'

He still hasn't mentioned his parents, thought Hannah.

'I'd like that,' she said. 'Josef?'

'If there are cakes, I won't say no.' He pushed himself up.

The smaller boy grinned and leaped up. 'Come on, then.'

Elias lived with his grandmother in a cottage that stood on a gradual rise to the east of the village. They had to cross a small stone bridge to get there, over a stream that trundled and swirled around rocks and small grassy islands. They could smell his grandmother's baking long before they arrived – the sweet scents of cinnamon and marzipan. Hannah half-expected to see a house of candy canes and gingerbread when they arrived. But no, it was just a cottage of brick and wood, with roof tiles of every shade from where they had been replaced over the years. The garden was filled with cornflowers and forget-me-nots, with beds of roses running down one side. A faded white picket fence ran around it and a stone path led up to the front door, which opened before they reached it.

'Elias, my darling!' A grey head poked around the side of the door and smiled. 'You're just in time for some cakes.'

'I told you!' Elias beamed at Hannah and Josef.

His grandmother stepped fully into the doorway, wearing an apron embroidered with edelweiss over a plain, grey dress. She beckoned him to hurry to her and hugged him, as though he had returned from a long journey through the mountains.

'And hello, Josef.'

'Good afternoon, Frau Lister.'

'And who have we here?'

'Hi, I'm . . .' Hannah went to answer, but Elias beat her to it.

'This is Sofia. She has a broken leg,' as if it were the most important thing about her.

'I can see that,' said the old woman. 'Hello, Sofia. You must be Frau Meyer's niece. I heard you had come to stay in the village.' She stepped outside and gave Hannah a hug. It was the first time somebody had hugged her since Marianne. Hannah swallowed a lump.

'And we can't let you miss out, can we, Josef?' Josef wasn't so enchanted. Though he tried to be polite, he couldn't help but step back, facing away as the old woman embraced him.

'I know,' said Frau Lister. 'Nobody likes to be kissed by an old lady. But if you want a taste of fresh stollen, then that's the price you have to pay.'

'Did you say stollen?' Hannah asked, her tastebuds already salivating while Josef wiped his face.

Hannah savoured every bite of the stollen. She tasted cinnamon and marzipan, orange and sugar, but there was something else there, too. Aunt Maud had been right. It seemed the villagers had a way of getting around the rations.

'A house fell on Sofia,' said Elias through a fresh mouthful of stollen, as if this were a normal conversation starter.

'So I heard,' replied Frau Lister. 'But she's safe now. I'm sure Frau Meyer will take good care of her. It's nice to have another young face in the village. There are too many of us old, wrinkled ones around.'

'You're not wrinkled, Grandma,' said Elias.

Frau Lister leaned over and wrapped her arm around him. 'That's why I love you, my sweet boy.'

Elias looked down at his cake and took another bite. Hannah blinked away the tears that unexpectedly prickled her eyes, affected as she was by the simple exchange she had just witnessed. It showed such a deep bond. One that you could only get in families. One she would never experience again.

'What have you children been up to?' asked Frau Lister.

Hannah took a deep breath and fed on the air that filled her to answer Frau Lister. 'Josef and Elias have been showing me around. We went to the fields at the edge of the forest.' And then, just in case Frau Lister and Aunt Maud spoke, 'We weren't supposed to go that far. My aunt said . . .'

The old lady tapped her nose with a finger. 'I won't tell.'

'We didn't go in,' added Elias, quickly.

His grandmother nodded. 'Very wise indeed.'

'Yes, I've read the stories,' said Hannah. 'About wolves and witches.'

Despite Hannah's lighthearted intentions, Frau Lister took on a serious tone. 'Yes! There's that, too, and this part of the world has more than its fair share of both. But there are new dangers. It's best you all stay out of the forest.'

Hannah thought she knew what, or who, she was talking about. But Elias decided to be sure. 'The soldiers,' he explained.

'But they're on our side,' argued Josef. 'They wouldn't hurt us.'

Hannah kept her gaze steady, focusing on her fingers picking at the crumbs on her plate, trying not to betray her feelings about soldiers.

'There are many soldiers, away fighting, who are good men – like Elias's father, my son.'

Hannah's ears pricked up. So he *did* have a parent. She glanced around the room, wondering if there were any evidence of his mum living here. She saw none.

'And yours, Josef. And like many of the men from the village. Though I do question *why* they're fighting. But there are rumours of things going on here at home, bad things, and I worry for you young ones.'

'What bad things, Grandma?' asked Elias.

Frau Lister just sighed and shook her head. 'I don't really know. And I wouldn't like to guess. But when you get to my age, you get a feeling in your bones. It's like when a storm's coming. Before the skies darken, before the distant rumble of thunder. I've been getting that feeling a lot recently.'

Hannah glanced at Josef, who was picking at the last of the crumbs with a frown creasing his forehead. Elias, she could see, was trying to comprehend what his grandmother was saying. But how could he? He hadn't seen what Hannah had seen, been where she had been, lived like she had lived. And she was glad for him. But had his grandmother? Or was she just older and wiser?

'But,' said Frau Lister, clapping her hands, 'it could just be the arthritis in my bones. Let's not get all maudlin. You children should be making the most of your childhood. It doesn't last long. Just enjoy it here in the village.'

'We will, Grandma,' said Elias. He turned to Josef, who nodded, and then to Hannah, to make sure they were with him in agreement, Hannah guessed.

'Yes, we will,' she added, giving what she hoped was a reassuring smile to Elias, but catching Frau Lister watching her a little too closely.

Did Frau Lister believe her? After all, she had just admitted to lying to Aunt Maud. Thank goodness Frau Lister didn't know about all the other lies she was telling just by being here.

Josef and Hannah were slowly making their way downhill towards the stream. The shadows were deepening, the temperature dropping and, despite Hannah's assertion that she wanted to break the rules, she couldn't help but recall Aunt Maud's second rule. And worry, just a little, about wolves.

She had overdone it, she realised. Walked too far. Both legs were aching, both arms, and she could feel a tiredness creeping in that would only be overcome by a warm bed and a good night's sleep. Up ahead, at the crest of the bridge, a boy and girl stood throwing stones over the low wall. They were both dark haired and stocky. The family resemblance was obvious.

Josef, who was already dawdling, slowed even more. She heard a low groan escape him.

'What is it?' she asked.

'Not what. Who? And it's Boris.'

'Don't you like him?' Though the answer was obvious.

'It's him who doesn't like anybody.' She noticed how his eyes flicked down to her crutches. 'Stay beside me.'

'I wasn't planning on running ahead,' she joked.

The burble of water became louder. Loud enough, she hoped, that the boy and girl hadn't heard them talking. But they didn't even seem to have noticed Hannah and Josef approaching. They were a crutch swing away when the boy turned to face them, and Josef slowed some more. The boy smirked and tugged at his sister's sleeve. She followed his gaze, but her expression was more one of surprise. They all stood there, staring at each other. Then the boy stepped out into the centre of the bridge, blocking their path.

Hannah felt her heart speed up. But this was only a boy, she reminded herself. She had escaped far worse.

'Sorry,' he said, staring at her crutches, still smirking. 'No cripples on the bridge, Kleftmann.'

Hannah instantly felt the shame flare up inside her. The same shame that had been inflicted on her by the men in power and their supporters. She had nothing to be ashamed of, and yet there it was, and that was not okay. Hannah noticed how Boris's sister bit at her bottom lip and stared down at the floor. Somehow, that made it worse. Hannah couldn't let him get away with that. This was how it started. If only somebody had stood up to their so-called leaders when they had been younger ...

'NO BULLIES, either,' she said, moving in front of Josef on her crutches. 'There would be a sign, but most bullies can't read.'

The boy's smile faltered. Hannah guessed he hadn't been expecting that. Especially from her. His sister next to him peered at Hannah through her eyelashes. Was that a smirk on her face now?

'Out of our way, Boris,' said Josef, standing his ground.

But Boris, ignoring him, stepped up to Hannah. He was a head taller than her and now entirely focused on looking down at her. 'What's your name? I haven't seen you around here before.'

'Leave her,' said Josef. But he may as well have been talking to the bridge. Boris's eyes were locked with Hannah's.

For the first time since leaving the hospital, she nearly gave her real name. Despite her heart thumping away in her chest and her face feeling it had gone the colour of beetroot, she forced her voice to sound calm. 'Sofia. What's yours?'

The boy frowned. 'Why should I tell you, So-fi-a?' He spat each syllable of the name. She refused to be intimidated, although she was shaky on her crutches. She had an idea. Cruel as it may be, she didn't think the boy deserved anything less.

'I might recognise it.'

'How would you recognise my name?'

'From the list,' she replied, holding her nerve. She could feel her heart slowing, her face draining of colour, the scales of power tipping.

'What list?' He, on the other hand, was beginning to sound less confident.

'The list my father keeps. Oberstleutnant Kessler. We're staying at Frau Meyer's lodge. He works at the castle, and he has a list of all the boys in the nearby villages to be sent away to fight. I've seen it on his desk.'

She watched with satisfaction as the boy's smile dissolved. She could feel her will continue to strengthen.

'I'm not old enough to fight,' said the boy.

'You look old enough to me. That is what you want, isn't it? To fight?'

The girl stepped up beside her brother. 'He doesn't want to fight. He won't be on the list.'

'There is no list, Matilda,' scowled the boy, but neither his voice nor his expression appeared convinced.

'I think you may be,' continued Hannah. 'And if you fight well, I can let him know.' She was on a roll and had no intention of letting up.

'He's called Boris,' said Josef, as if he hadn't mentioned it a few minutes before. 'Boris Weber.'

'You should let them pass,' said Matilda in a quiet voice. Did Hannah detect a hint of concern?

The boy wrinkled his nose and flicked his sister a look of disgust.

'Boris Weber,' repeated Hannah. 'I did see that name on the list.'

The boy sneered, but not before taking a step back.

'But I can get it taken off. If I let him know you don't like fighting. My father will do anything I ask him to.'

Boris's mouth tightened but, to Hannah's relief, he stepped aside. It had worked. She had stolen his power.

He was Rumpelstiltskin, and she had guessed his name.

TWENTY-FIVE

Over breakfast the next morning, Aunt Maud told Hannah that the teacher from the village school was coming to see her and would arrive soon. Hannah felt excited about what that might mean, but also a little flustered.

'I would have told you last night, but getting home as late as you did, there wasn't the time,' said Aunt Maud.

'There was still some light in the sky,' Hannah offered, but Aunt Maud waved it away, and Hannah quickly packed up the breakfast things – she was getting quite good at doing things one-handed while balancing on one crutch and her good foot.

Hannah was waiting in the parlour, her book open on her lap, trying to look like a good student, when a lady accompanied Aunt Maud into the room. She wore an expression that reminded Hannah of her mother in happier times. It caught Hannah off guard, and she had to force her gaze away for just a moment. To blink away the tears and try to disassociate the two.

The lady's hair was neither dark nor blonde, her lips neither full nor thin. She had shiny cheeks and remarkably blue eyes that shone out through a pair of glasses sitting high upon her nose. They both waited for Aunt Maud to make the introductions.

'Sofia, this is Frau Meinhardt.'

'Hello, Sofia.'

'Good morning, Frau Meinhardt.' Hannah couldn't help but smile back. She realised she knew the name. Elias's teacher. Who, she remembered Elias saying, was very kind.

'Frau Meinhardt has offered to provide you with lessons, here, during the week,' said Aunt Maud.

So this was the compromise Aunt Maud had come up with. She wasn't going to try to teach Hannah herself, thank goodness. Still, Hannah's heart sank a little. She wasn't going to school for a while yet. The disappointment must have shown on her face.

'We discussed this, Sofia. You shall be taught here until . . .' She nodded towards Hannah's leg.

Hannah was considering telling her how far she had walked yesterday when Frau Meinhardt spoke up.

'Why don't we see how we go, Sofia? It will only be for a few weeks.' And the way she said it made it sound more like Hannah had a choice when she might go to school.

The woman had a way with words. And, despite Hannah's initial disappointment, she admitted to herself she was a little relieved. Hannah hadn't been to school for such a long time and she was sure she was at least a little behind in her studies. She'd always been top of her class when she'd been allowed to go to school. She didn't like the idea of being behind the other kids. Yes, it would be better for her to catch up here, with only this lady to judge her, rather than a whole class of children.

'All right,' she replied. 'That sounds good. For a few weeks. Until I can get rid of this.' She lifted her cast.

'Then that's settled,' said Aunt Maud, brushing down her apron. She stood there, as if waiting for Frau Meinhardt to follow, but the younger woman looked over and said, 'Could you give us a few minutes please, Frau Meyer?' When Aunt Maud didn't move, she added, 'Alone.'

'Very well. I shall be in the kitchen if you need me,' said Aunt Maud.

Hannah wondered what the teacher could want with her that Aunt Maud shouldn't hear. But she liked how Frau Meinhardt had firmly requested her to leave, and how Aunt Maud had done what was asked of her.

Frau Meinhardt closed the door behind Aunt Maud, then came back and sat opposite Hannah. Her smile faded slightly, but it was still there.

'Sofia, your aunt has told me what happened to your parents, to you. And I'm so sorry.'

Hannah slowly nodded while shifting her focus to those blue eyes. So piercing, but not in an intrusive way. More insightful, she decided, understanding.

'She is a formidable character, your aunt, and sometimes people like her can come across as harsh, uncaring. But she has welcomed you in . . .'

Hannah wasn't sure *welcomed* was the right word.

'. . . and I am sure she has your best interests at heart. Even though, at times, you may feel she doesn't have one.'

Wait. What? Did she just make a joke?

'So give her this,' Frau Meinhardt continued. 'Just for a few weeks. We can get to know each other. And then, when you're ready, and when your aunt agrees, you can come to the school.' She sat back.

Hannah's father had always impressed upon her the importance of *wanting* to learn. Not only arithmetic and literacy, science and history, but also learning about people – wanting to learn from others, about what made everybody different, what made everybody the same. Only then, he had said, could they hope to live in a world without war. How would she do that from Aunt Maud's house?

'But the bad news about that is that I won't get to be your teacher when you do.'

Hannah remembered Josef saying how the older children were taught by somebody else. Herr Guttman, who didn't live up to his name. Perhaps Aunt Maud's plan was a good one after all.

Hannah nodded her agreement.

'Good!' said Frau Meinhardt, clapping her hands. 'I'm going to very much enjoy getting to know you, Sofia. I'm free most weekdays, straight after school. How is that for you?'

'I think I'll be free,' joked Hannah. Something about the teacher was already bringing out a side of her she hadn't seen for such a long time. Frau Meinhardt was beaming, and Hannah felt herself doing the same.

'Very well. We shall start on Tuesday. You can begin by teaching me.'

'Teaching you?' What could Hannah teach her that she didn't already know?

'Yes. Where I should begin. I don't want to be teaching you things you've already learned. And I don't want to jump too far ahead.'

Hannah felt that fear of discovery creeping back into her. Would this woman be asking her questions about a school she hadn't been to for nearly four years? Would she be able to see through her lies?

'Sofia.'

'Yes?' Hannah had to stop getting lost in her thoughts like that.

Frau Meinhardt placed a hand upon her arm. 'I understand. The past can sometimes be painful. We'll try not to go there.' Still the smile remained upon her face, making it hard for Hannah to *not* go there. She stood back up. 'Tuesday, then, just after two.'

'Tuesday,' repeated Hannah, smiling up at her.

TWENTY-SIX

Hannah used one of her crutches as a foot to kick the ball back to Josef, casting a sharp look over her shoulder to check Aunt Maud wasn't watching. The ball bounced awkwardly, thanks to the edge of a cobblestone, and Josef compensated for his lack of control with a powerful kick that sent it careening into Hannah, nearly knocking her over.

'Oops! Sorry, Sofia!' Josef shouted, running over to check on her as the ball raced into the town square behind her.

'It's fine,' Hannah huffed, slightly out of breath, and sat herself down on a low wall. Josef plonked down next to her while Elias ran after the soccer ball.

Hannah's cheeks were warm from the exercise, but the cold was already eating into her, and she shivered. Autumn had begun to tighten its bite.

'Will you come with us to collect The Old Man's Bones, Hannah?' asked Elias, jogging back to them with the ball under his arm.

Hannah had no idea what he was talking about. 'The what?' She wasn't sure she had heard him right. Had he mentioned a man's bones? It sounded ominous, though somewhat intriguing.

'She won't know what that is,' said Josef. 'It's just our village that does it.'

Hannah needed to step back a few sentences. 'What did you call it, Elias?'

But it was Josef who answered. 'The Old Man's Bones. It's just a silly superstition.' He looked embarrassed.

Elias leaped up off the wall, ignoring Josef. 'It's to protect us from the Graf.'

'The Graf who has been dead for hundreds of years,' added Josef, rolling his eyes.

'How does collecting bones do that?' asked Hannah, ignoring Josef's comments.

'Well, first, all the children go around the village, and the people give us bones . . .' began Elias.

'Real bones?' Hannah scrunched up her nose at the idea of it, making both boys laugh, bringing them together again.

'The Old Man's Bones,' explained Elias. He said this like it was the most obvious thing.

'It sounds stupid, doesn't it?' said Josef.

Didn't most superstitions when you truly thought about them? 'It sounds a little bit creepy,' admitted Hannah.

Elias frowned, as though the thought had never entered his brain.

'They're not really an old man's bones,' explained Josef.

Hannah had assumed as much. 'I'm glad to hear that.'

'They're old animal bones.'

That still sounded odd. Her face must have said as much.

'It's just what happens. Every year,' said Elias.

'Why?' But did superstitions need to have any rationality?

'To protect us from the Graf, like Elias said,' smiled Josef.

'But how does that protect you from him?' They were going around in circles.

'We hang them around the doors to our houses,' said Elias, which didn't really explain anything.

Hannah tried to see it in her head. There was something familiar about this. Bare bones hanging from doorframes all over the village. But it still didn't make sense. 'But *why*?'

'So that he doesn't take away the children!' Josef leaped at Elias as he cackled the last word, arms raised in monster fashion, teeth bared.

Elias backed away from Josef. Hannah clocked him push his shoulders back in an effort at appearing brave, but his whimper gave him away. Hannah put her arm around him.

'The more bones you collect, the more likely he is to stay away.' Josef lowered his arms and swallowed his teeth.

'So has anybody ever been taken?' asked Hannah. 'By the Graf?'

Elias pulled away from Hannah. 'Has anybody, Josef?'

'Not that I know of. As I said, it's silly.'

Elias leaned his head to the side and closed one eye. 'So, will you come out with us, Sofia? To collect the bones?'

'I'll have to ask Aunt Maud,' she replied. But her hopes weren't high.

TWENTY-SEVEN

Two days later, Hannah found herself waiting impatiently for Frau Meinhardt's arrival. In the morning, she finished darning all the socks Aunt Maud could find, and her work even passed Aunt Maud's close inspection. Finally, she was allowed to work on the shirts, which allowed her to practise her fine darning on more delicate fabrics. Hannah felt a sense of achievement, but this soon gave way to boredom again, as darning shirt after shirt simply replaced the monotony of sock after sock.

When she'd finished all the darning before lunch, Aunt Maud gave her the afternoon to herself, and suggested she could relax with a book. But Hannah couldn't settle. It wasn't that she was excited about receiving lessons again. There was a nervous energy buzzing through her. She was concerned that Frau Meinhardt would see through her lies. That she would say something stupid, or fail some simple test she had been set, and that the teacher would see as clearly as the mountain air that Hannah hadn't been to school for such a long time. And from there, suspicions would grow until her true identity was revealed.

But she was also excited about learning again. About it being one step closer to returning to school.

Hannah had left her book in the parlour and retreated to her room, as her restlessness was annoying Aunt Maud. She sat down at her desk and decided she would prefer to have lessons here, away from Aunt Maud's prying eyes, nosy ears and interfering mouth. And so she spent the afternoon cleaning and tidying it.

Hannah heard the clip-clopping of hooves before she saw from her window the tawny mare appear around a corner. It trotted slowly and steadily and, like its rider, stood proud, staring straight ahead. Across the square they came, the only movement visible in the otherwise stationary scene. They passed the fountain, and Hannah watched as Frau Meinhardt dismounted and tied the horse to a post.

When Aunt Maud poked her head around the door to say that Frau Meinhardt had arrived and she had better come downstairs, Hannah replied, making sure she didn't inflect her voice into a question. 'I think I'd like to have my lessons in my room, Aunt Maud, if that's okay.'

Aunt Maud opened her mouth to speak, but the knock at the door downstairs stole her away, and so Hannah stayed where she was.

The nerves were back. She decided she should have a book in front of her, although *Heidi* was in the parlour, she remembered, and so she grabbed *The Tales of the Brothers Grimm*. She sat there, pretending to read, but then she worried she would appear disinterested in her lessons, and instead turned to face the door. She checked herself in the mirror. She looked fine, but felt a little awkward.

She decided to go to the door and wait, hobbling on one foot and a crutch.

Downstairs, the two ladies were speaking, and Hannah waited until she heard footsteps on the stairs before stepping out into the corridor to greet Frau Meinhardt. Even in the semi-darkness, Hannah could make out that smile and those bright blue eyes.

Any nerves she had felt immediately disappeared as the teacher approached her, carrying a leather satchel.

'Good afternoon, Sofia. How have you been?'

Hannah did as her father had taught her. She met politeness with politeness. 'Good afternoon, Frau Meinhardt. Very well, thank you. How are you?'

'I'm very well, too. Thank you for asking.'

The two of them stood facing each other. For a little too long. And Hannah realised she had been concentrating so hard on doing the right thing that she had forgotten to do the next right thing.

'Come in,' she said. 'This is my room.'

Frau Meinhardt followed her inside, and Aunt Maud trailed behind carrying a chair that matched Hannah's desk chair. There must be one in each of the guest rooms, she surmised.

'And what a lovely room it is.' Frau Meinhardt walked over to the window and stared out while Aunt Maud nodded at the comment and left the room.

When the teacher turned back, Hannah noticed that her smile had faded slightly. What had she seen? The smile was quickly replenished, and she glanced down at Hannah's desk. She picked up the book.

'The Brothers Grimm. Have you read all the tales?'

Hannah, who had by now read every story several times, nodded.

'And what do you think?'

Hannah had never been asked such an open question about the book. There were so many different stories, how could she answer? She should be able to answer, though. What *did* she think? Her mind went back to her discussion with Pieter on the way up the mountain.

'I think . . . it's not a book for children.'

Frau Meinhardt raised her eyebrows. 'Interesting. Why do you say that?'

She wished she hadn't. She and Pieter hadn't discussed it much further. She shrugged, but Frau Meinhardt still waited. So she opened her mouth and spoke the words that came. 'Because terrible things happen in it. And not always to the people who deserve it. I don't think that's a good lesson to learn.'

There. She had said it. But Frau Meinhardt wanted more.

'Why not? Do you think people in this world always get what they deserve?'

Had she answered the first question incorrectly? Hannah began to feel flustered, but Frau Meinhardt threw her a lifeline. 'There's no right or wrong answer here, Sofia. I'm not asking you if people do always get what they deserve. I'm asking you if you think they do.'

And now that she put it like that, the answer was clear. No, she didn't think they did. Had she got what she deserved? Had her parents?

'No,' she said. 'I don't think they do.'

'Neither do I,' replied Frau Meinhardt. 'But *I think* the world would be a far better place if they did. Don't you?'

Hannah did. But wishes only came true in fairytales.

She nodded.

Frau Meinhardt dropped the satchel to the floor and they both sat down.

'I have some paper and pencils in here. And some learning materials. But before we begin our work, I thought I would tell you a little about myself.'

The teacher took a few moments to gather herself, as if her past didn't immediately come to mind. Hannah knew that feeling.

'As you know, I teach at the school. A little bit of everything. To the younger children. But I haven't always lived here.' She paused. 'I was born in another mountain village a long way from here. But things happened that . . . there came a time when I had to leave.'

So they had something in common.

Frau Meinhardt went on to speak of her parents and her school years, her love of horses and her wish to one day return to her village. But she said little of her recent past, and Hannah didn't ask. She had her own secrets. Let Frau Meinhardt keep hers.

'So, that's me,' she finished, sitting upright and placing her hands on her lap. And then, catching Hannah off guard, 'Would you like to tell me a little more about yourself now? You don't have to.'

No, she wouldn't. Not about herself, or about Sofia. If she tried, she was sure it would all come out wrong. She would tie herself in circles. She was already tying herself in circles. She would contradict herself. She would give herself away.

But she took a deep breath and began to speak. And, despite her fears, she was surprised how well the lie had grown upon her and how easy it was to pick and choose which parts she told and which parts she left out. She was becoming quite the storyteller. Or liar. Either way, she was thankful her father had kept up her schooling, even during those dark times when she hadn't wanted to do anything. It lent some credence to the lie that she had attended school right up to the time the bomb had dropped.

There were some truths in what Hannah said, too – she was an orphan who had narrowly escaped death. And there was no lie in the tears that accompanied her telling of that part. Eventually, her words dried up, and there was no more of her, or Sofia, to give.

Frau Meinhardt leaned forward and gently rubbed Hannah's arm. 'I think we're going to get along just fine, Sofia. And, you never know, you may learn something, too,' she said, while reaching into her bag and pulling out paper, pencils and notebooks.

Hannah wiped at her eyes and let out a small snicker.

'Shall we do some work now? To keep your aunt happy?'

'I'm not sure that will keep her happy,' replied Hannah, glancing at the door.

Frau Meinhardt did the same, but there was nobody there. Hannah looked back to Frau Meinhardt, who caught her gaze with a mocking wide-eyed look, and the laughter that broke out between them told Hannah that Frau Meinhardt definitely had the measure of Aunt Maud.

TWENTY-EIGHT

The house was warm. Only the ticking of the clock and the distant drone of the radio could be heard. The scene outside her window could have been a still-life painting. A starlit sky. The black hole of a mountain, faint pinpricks of light from the castle. The dark, empty square, moonlight reflecting off the water in the fountain. Lamps burning in windows. The cat opposite stretched out on top of the wardrobe.

Her bedroom door stood open.

She drifted.

The corridor, void of any windows, was forever in semi-darkness. The only light that penetrated the space rose from the stairs at the far end of the corridor. She glanced back into her room, anxious of losing sight of her sleeping body. But she had done it in the hospital and managed to return safely.

Her curiosity got the better of her. She rose higher. Despite the darkness, she could see dust above doorways and webs in corners that would alarm and embarrass

Aunt Maud. She moved past the dust without disturbing it, and through the cobwebs without breaking them. She passed the door to the Oberstleutnant's room and reached the end of the corridor.

Hannah momentarily pondered which way to go. The floor above ended in shadow, an unknown place that she had been forbidden to visit. She decided to go instead with the familiar safety of the ground floor.

Down she went, expecting the floorboards to creak below her, still getting used to her weightlessness. The radio became louder. She expected the familiar smell of burning wood to hit her, but remembered that her sense of smell had disappeared along with her feeling of touch.

Hannah floated along the hall, passing the parlour where the radio played and, she assumed, Aunt Maud sat listening to it. The door to the dining room was open, and she entered. She circled the room up high, around the table and past the tall cupboards.

She passed back through the door, stopping suddenly as Aunt Maud walked past. What would have happened if they had collided? Would Aunt Maud have felt it? Hannah followed her into the kitchen and watched as she loaded a tray with bread, cheese, a boiled egg and jug of water.

Hannah and Aunt Maud had eaten supper together, and so who was it for? Perhaps the Oberstleutnant had returned without Hannah knowing.

She headed back up the stairs. At the first-floor landing, she made the decision to continue, following the course of the stairwell rather than rising straight through the centre. Even with her mind free to do as it wanted, she was still constrained by habit. The shadows deepened and the sound of the radio subsided to no more than a half-imagined burble.

A hallway identical to the one on her floor led away from the next landing. The stairwell continued up and around again into darkness, obviously leading to an attic. She drifted along the corridor, wondering which door would open to Aunt Maud's room, passing the hatch that hid the dumb waiter shaft.

A sound from above made her stop. So slight, she could have almost imagined it. But there it was again. Like a foot upon a floorboard.

But it was an old house, Hannah reasoned. It was bound to move, to creak and groan. In the basement of the Meyers', in the middle of the night, all kinds of noises had been born out of the silence.

Still, Hannah listened. A floorboard creaked, one foot down, then creaked again, one foot up. To her right. Then directly above. Then to her left. Softly. Gently. Slowly. She remembered her parents moving in the same way at times in the Meyers' cellar. At first with a concerted effort, but eventually by force of habit. She knew the sound well. It was that of somebody in hiding.

A rattle and groan to her right made her refocus her attention. Behind the small door, the ropes began to move as Aunt Maud sent the dumb waiter upwards. Hannah stayed and waited. Perhaps Aunt Maud would follow, and Hannah would be able to get a glimpse inside her room. From the shaft, the sound of the small compartment knocking against the brickwork came closer and closer. Up past the floor of her room, heading on to the one where she now floated.

She waited for the lift to arrive. It would stop, the bell would ring, and Aunt Maud would follow up the stairs. The bell rang. It was here. But it didn't stop. Up it went, past this floor and on to the loft above.

And that was where it stopped.

But there was no bell.

Another creak above. A door being opened. Something, perhaps a tray, being slid out.

One more creak, the door closed. And the lift began to descend.

TWENTY-NINE

Hannah was in the parlour, halfway through the latest pile of darning, when Aunt Maud marched in.

'Sofia, the Oberstleutnant would like to see you.'

Hannah stopped mid-stitch. Just when she was beginning to believe that things may be turning around, she had been discovered. She closed her eyes and tried to compose herself, wondering what would happen now. There was still a chance she could deny it. She had done so well in deceiving Aunt Maud and Frau Meinhardt. But this man would obviously be adept at knowing a liar when he saw one.

She put down the shirt and stuck the needle in a cushion. She stayed in her seat as one final act of defiance, and held on to the armrests for good measure.

The Oberstleutnant stepped in beside Aunt Maud. He was holding a pile of garments. And he was smiling.

'Good morning, young Sofia,' said the tall man cheerfully. His uniform was, as always, crisp and precise.

'Good morning, Herr Kessler,' Hannah replied, her nails digging deeper into the fabric of the chair.

Aunt Maud frowned. Despite the man telling Hannah she could address him as such, she obviously still felt uncomfortable.

'I trust she is behaving herself,' said the man.

'She is . . .' began Aunt Maud.

'I was speaking to Sofia,' quipped the Oberstleutnant, raising his eyebrows.

Aunt Maud visibly flinched and took a deep breath through her nose. Hannah was trying to make sense of what just happened.

'The Oberstleutnant has a gift for you,' said Aunt Maud.

The man stepped forward, holding out the pile of clothes.

He has darning that needs doing, realised Hannah. She held out her hands to take them, but he placed the pile on the table.

'I brought these for you, Sofia. They were my daughter's. She has grown out of them. I thought that, with winter coming, you could put them to use if you'd like to wear them.'

'That's very kind of the Oberstleutnant, isn't it, Sofia?'

Hannah was still playing catch-up. So her lies hadn't been uncovered?

Aunt Maud prodded her with a repetition of, 'Isn't it, Sofia . . . ?'

'It is. Very kind. Thank you.'

She could see some dresses in the pile, one a thick velvet. And a coat. Bright red with gold buttons and a black fur collar. And hidden below the coat she now noticed a pair of black, shiny shoes. She could still only wear one for now, but soon . . .

The man laughed. 'It is nothing. My daughter has far too many clothes. She wears them once and then she grows too big for them. I hope they fit you.'

'I'm sure they will,' replied Hannah, having no idea whether they would or not, and wondering who would only wear clothes once when there was already so little to go around.

The Oberstleutnant continued to smile. Maybe she had got him wrong. Maybe he wasn't like the other soldiers. The ones she had seen patrolling her streets, checking arms for yellow stars. After all, he had a daughter. Surely fathers didn't act that way.

He glanced to the side, and she followed his line of vision.

'Are you enjoying the Volksempfänger?'

She didn't see it as an object of enjoyment. Not the music, nor the voice that spoke on it. It wasn't like the radio she and her parents used to listen to back in their apartment in Stuttgart. There was no comedy, the music was slow and bombastic, and the voices were cold and severe. And there was only one station. But she wasn't going to say any of that. Not because of the clothes he had just given her. But because of Aunt Maud's words. *We are supposed to listen to it.*

'We listen to it every evening, don't we, Sofia?' For once, she was glad of Aunt Maud's prompting.

'Yes. Every evening.'

That seemed to please the Oberstleutnant. He spoke as though he had invented the radio himself. 'That is good. It is a gift. To the people. From our great leader.'

'And we appreciate it very much,' continued Aunt Maud.

What was she doing? Hannah couldn't tell whether she was frightened of the man or in league with him. But she decided to follow her lead.

'We do. Appreciate it.' Though she didn't think their great leader would give anything away without wanting more back in return.

'Well,' said the Oberstleutnant, springing to attention. 'I will leave you both and bid you a good day.'

'Will you be staying with us tonight, Oberstleutnant Kessler?' asked Aunt Maud.

'Not tonight. Perhaps tomorrow. By then I should be ready to escape.' He flicked his eyes towards Hannah on the last word, and she fought against the urge to glance away. Had he done that on purpose, or was it a coincidence?

He turned to go and then stopped. Aunt Maud stood up straighter, as if to attention, as he turned back.

'And Sofia . . .' he said.

This was it, she thought. It had all been a test, and somehow she had given herself away.

'I hope you are happy here in the village. If there is anything you need – anything at all – make sure to let your aunt know.'

She kept the breath inside of her, wanting to let it out, but afraid he would read something in it.

'Thank you. I will.'

She caught Aunt Maud's eye. The painted smile remained upon her face, but it was beginning to drop. She, like Hannah, was struggling to maintain it.

The Oberstleutnant spun around to face the woman. 'Good day, Frau Meyer.' He placed his cap upon his head, straightened it, marched down the corridor and exited the lodge.

THIRTY

A light wind was blowing across the square from the direction of the bakery, carrying the smell of rising yeast and warm spices. The clouds were low. The rise of forest disappeared into a grey, almost white, haze of nothingness. Hannah, wearing an olive dress and the red coat the Oberstleutnant had brought her, was in goal. It wasn't until she had put the dress on that she remembered her mother wearing one of a similar colour. The material had been thinner and a shade darker, its sleeves cut just above the elbow. But it was close enough to make this one Hannah's favourite. And despite what she thought of the Oberstleutnant, how could she not love the bright red coat that used to belong to his daughter? She could certainly never get lost whilst wearing it.

The goal itself was a high garden wall that Josef said belonged to the village undertaker. The post markers were Josef's jumper and Elias's hat.

They were out of view of the lodge and, more importantly, Aunt Maud, who no doubt would have scolded Hannah for hopping around on one crutch in her attempts to stop the shots that Josef and Elias were taking at the goal. Hannah was still only able to wear one shoe, her right foot dressed in two thick men's socks that stretched up and over the plaster.

'Why does the Oberstleutnant stay at the lodge?' asked Josef, passing the ball to Elias. 'If he's got a castle.'

'He says he needs to escape,' replied Hannah, remembering how his eyes had flicked towards her when he had said that word.

'Why? He's not a prisoner,' said Elias, lining up the ball and kicking a shot straight at her.

'I suppose he just wants some peace and quiet. Away from the soldiers,' she said, saving the ball easily.

'What does he do?' Elias persisted.

'Secret work,' said Josef.

There were a lot of secrets in the world at the moment, thought Hannah. She was one of them.

She knocked the ball back to Elias with her crutch.

Aunt Maud had a secret, too, didn't she? Up in the attic. She wondered who it was. Could it be a relative of Aunt Maud's? Or another guest? But who kept guests in the attic? Hannah sighed. She knew the answer to that.

Elias kicked the ball. It hit the wall to her left.

'You let that one in on purpose,' said Josef. But Hannah's mind was elsewhere.

'I think Aunt Maud has a secret,' she said. It came out of her mouth before she had time to stop it.

'What is it?' asked Elias.

'If Sofia knew, it wouldn't be a secret,' explained Josef. He flicked the ball up with his foot and caught it.

'Well, I sort of know.' What was she doing? She wanted to backtrack. Wished she'd kept her thoughts to herself. Wished she hadn't said anything at all.

'See?' said Elias, emboldened enough to ask again. 'What is it, Sofia?'

'I don't really know.' She wanted to tell them to forget it. After all, hadn't she and her family been living secretly in somebody's home? What would have happened if Sofia or Mikhail had shared their secret with a couple of friends?

Elias's faced dropped.

'Make up your mind,' said Josef. 'You either know or you don't.'

Josef was getting annoyed with her, she realised. She didn't want to argue with him or Elias. She should never have said anything. Why had she? They could still be playing soccer if she hadn't mentioned it.

'You have to promise not to tell,' she said.

'We promise, don't we, Josef?' pleaded Elias.

'I suppose so.' He picked up his jumper and put it on.

'No suppose so,' replied Hannah. 'Say you promise.'

'I promise,' said Elias, placing his cap upon his head.

'Josef?'

The older boy rolled his eyes. 'I promise.'

'Promise what?'

'Why are you making me say the words?' asked Josef. 'Why not Elias?'

'Because I can see that Elias means it.' And she could. The small boy's face was brimming with sincerity.

'I mean it.' Josef said. 'I might not believe you, but I mean it.'

'Say it.'

Josef sighed, sounding exasperated. 'I promise not to tell anybody about your aunt's secret.' He rocked his head from side to side with every syllable.

Hannah supposed that was as good as she was going to get. She flicked her eyes back towards the lodge to make sure Aunt Maud wasn't standing on the corner watching or, more importantly, listening. 'I think there's somebody hiding in Aunt Maud's attic.'

Josef straightened and Elias frowned. They exchanged quick glances.

'Who?' asked Josef.

'I don't know.'

She could almost see their brains ticking away.

'How do you know?' asked Elias.

'Yeah, how do you know?'

'I . . .' She hesitated, not wanting to lie to them. 'I went up to the second floor. I heard someone.'

Josef shrugged. 'It must have been your aunt.'

'She was downstairs. She made food and she sent the dumb waiter up there.'

'It was the Oberstleutnant then.'

'He wasn't staying that day.'

'Perhaps it was a ghost,' suggested Elias, looking as if he had just seen one.

'Perhaps it was,' agreed Josef, and the younger boy's eyes almost fell from their sockets.

'No. It was definitely somebody creeping around.'

She paused, and they stood around in silence.

'What do you know about my aunt?' Hannah asked.

'She's bossy,' said Josef.

'And scary,' added Elias.

'I mean, about her family.'

'You should know more than we do,' said Josef, eyeing her strangely. 'You're her family.'

Hannah attempted to recover from her mistake. 'My dad never spoke about her. They weren't close.' She was rushing her words and pushing the limits here, she knew. She could see Josef looking at her differently already. She didn't want him to think she was a liar. But that's exactly what she was.

'Sorry,' frowned Josef. 'It's just that the village is small. And the thought of not knowing your own family . . .'

Hannah swallowed a sob. If only he knew. But big cities were different, she told herself.

'Why would somebody live in the attic?' asked Elias.

Hannah had so much to say on this point, but was starting to struggle with what was the truth and what was a lie. She wanted to go back to before she'd said anything. 'It's probably nothing. Just my imagination.'

'We could send a note up,' suggested Josef, ignoring her now. 'In the lift.'

'Saying what?' Elias asked.

'Just *Hello*. We could send it up with a piece of your grandmother's cake.' And then, to Hannah's alarm, he added, 'I think we should.'

Elias nodded excitedly. 'I'll tell Grandma it's for us.'

'I'm not sure we should.' Hannah was trying to double back, to regain some control of the situation.

'When shall we do it?' asked Josef, continuing to ignore her.

'Frau Meyer goes out on Saturdays, doesn't she, Hannah? To collect clothes for darning, or for food? We could do it then?' Elias was excited.

Hannah nodded, wanting her reluctance to show through and somehow stop the boys.

It didn't.

'It's a plan!' said Josef.

'The fog is coming,' said Elias, and Hannah tore her thoughts away to look at where he was pointing.

'That's odd,' she said.

'That's normal,' replied Josef.

As Hannah watched, the little that remained of the mountain began to disappear. It unrolled itself down the mountain, metre by metre, eating whatever was in its path, as though the world were slowly closing its eyes.

Hannah felt a sense of foreboding as all that she could see shrank. She turned to face the mountains behind her, and they, too, were vanishing little by little.

'There's nothing normal about that,' she said, buttoning up her coat. Elias moved in between her and Josef.

'Maybe not in the city,' explained Josef. 'But it comes in like that around this time every year. And when it comes, it stays.'

The trees and houses on the edge of the village were beginning to fade. The church steeple had lost its red hue. Everything was turning grey and washed out.

Hannah had never seen anything like it. An irrational part of her feared that the world was being wiped out for good and that, when the fog reached them, they would be snuffed out like candles.

It swallowed the lower edges of the village and, now that it was closer, seemed to hurtle towards them. They were on an island in a sea of nothing. The wind had stopped, and Hannah could see now that it wasn't moving in a straight line, but puffing and billowing like the breath of an old man on a cold day. It washed over everything, filling every alley, every doorway, every space until finally it reached the square, lapping up the cobblestones, the fountain and them.

'Can we go inside?' asked Elias.

Hannah looked around, trying to shake off the fog's cold embrace. She felt disorientated. Even Josef looked a little concerned.

'Yes,' she replied. 'I don't think we should be out here.'

The three of them began to make their way back in what Hannah thought was the direction of the lodge.

They had only taken a few steps when a figure lurched out of the fog towards them. They stopped walking, startled by its sudden appearance. The figure did the same. Hannah recognised the ragged silhouette of the man in the long trench coat she had seen from her window when she'd first arrived.

She gave him a smile, but he had turned his head, looking over his shoulder as if searching for somebody.

'You made us jump, Herr Schundel,' said Josef.

The man turned back to them, coming closer, and Hannah could see that the left side of his face was hairless and shiny, as if he had been injured in a fire. The rest of his hair was long and curly, mostly black with ripples of grey at the edges. He wore a patch over his left eye, and she could only see the lobe of one ear. He stopped and stared at them.

'The same,' he replied. His voice was raspy, dry. A little out of breath. 'It's that time of year again.' He stared beyond them for a moment.

Hannah felt Elias shuffle up against her.

'It seems to get thicker every year.' The man's eye went to her. She reinforced her smile.

'Is that why you're carrying your gasmask?' joked Josef, and Hannah realised the man was holding a green, circular tin.

Herr Schundel stared down at the tin as if he were seeing it for the first time. He gave it a shake. 'Pebbles.' He didn't explain further. His eye went back to Hannah. 'You're staying at the lodge?'

He must have seen her at the window. She nodded. 'For a while. I'm Frau Meyer's niece, Sofia.'

'Heinz,' said Herr Schundel. 'I'm better with faces. Numbers, too. Not names.' He nodded at her crutches. 'What happened to your leg?'

'I was in an accident.' She didn't want to go into detail with this stranger.

'Me, too,' he said. 'A long time ago.'

'Are you off home?' asked Josef. Hannah was grateful for his intervention.

'Soon,' replied Herr Schundel. 'You should be going, too.' He lifted the hand holding the tin again, studied it, swallowed. Opened his mouth.

'Time to come in, you three,' said Aunt Maud, emerging out of the mist. 'There are new rules when the fog arrives. And you need to stop pestering Herr Schundel.'

'We're not pestering,' began Hannah, but the look on Aunt Maud's face told her that she wasn't going to take no for an answer. Hannah turned back to face Herr Schundel, wondering what he had been about to say.

'Get home safely,' he said. 'All of you. Try not to forget.'

But Aunt Maud was leading them away and, when Hannah turned back, all she could see was Heinz Schundel's silhouette disappearing back into the fog, like the memory of a fading dream.

THIRTY-ONE

It was Saturday, and Hannah was expecting Josef and Elias to arrive any minute now. With the thick fog blanketing the village and making walking around risky, the children had been told to go straight home after school, and so Hannah's only visitor this week had been Frau Meinhardt.

Downstairs, Aunt Maud was noisily wrapping herself up for her weekend outing to buy provisions. Hannah was watching for the boys at her window, wondering if they were waiting for Aunt Maud to leave before knocking on the door. The fog had well and truly curled itself around the village for winter. Hannah could see to the edge of the square from here, but no further. Still, the house remained warm. Aunt Maud seemed to have an endless supply of wood to throw upon the fire, and the walls of the house were thick enough to trap the heat within.

There was a knock at the front door, followed by the sound of Aunt Maud's footsteps. Hannah waited at her window for the boys to come and find her. She didn't want to go downstairs and look Aunt Maud in the eye while the boys were there, knowing what they were going to do. She still hadn't forgiven herself for telling Josef and Elias about Aunt Maud's secret. Although she was wondering now if she'd got it wrong, as she hadn't heard anything out of the ordinary since that day – not even the dumb waiter going up beyond her floor.

A few mumbled words from below reached her before she heard the door close again, and Aunt Maud trundled across the square and into the fog.

The boys' heavy footsteps were racing up the stairs. Hannah hobbled over to the door, now able to put some weight on her right leg, and opened it to a rich smell of almonds and spice.

'I hope you've brought more than one,' said Hannah, as Josef and Elias headed down the hall towards her.

'I asked for one each and another for Aunt Maud,' said Elias, laying a cloth parcel on her bed and hurriedly unwrapping it to reveal four small round cakes dotted with raisins. He picked one up and held it out to Hannah. Josef helped himself. Elias's grandmother had done it again. Hannah felt her tastebuds fight for each mouthful. Her mouth wanted to chew it until nothing was left. Her stomach wanted her to swallow it down straightaway. When she looked up from finishing, Josef's hand was empty and he was ogling the one remaining. Elias slipped the last bite of his into his mouth.

'How about if we only send half of Aunt Maud's up to the ghost?' asked Josef.

It was an enticing offer, even if half a cake between three of them would mean only a small bite each.

But Elias snatched the cake and shook his head, intent on following through with their plan. 'This is all for the guest upstairs,' he insisted, wrapping it back up in the cloth.

'It's okay for you,' groaned Josef. 'You get to eat them all the time.'

'Doesn't your grandmother bake?' asked Hannah.

Josef shook his head. 'Not like this.'

Elias stood in front of them holding the small cloth bundle in his hands. Josef grabbed a piece of paper and pencil from Hannah's desk. After a few seconds of sucking on the end of the pencil, he began to speak each word as he wrote it. '*Hello. We hope it is not too cold in the attic and that you enjoy this cake.* Do you think we should write our names?'

'If you want,' replied Hannah. Something about putting Sofia's name on paper felt wrong.

'I want to write mine,' said Elias. 'I'm very neat.'

The boys wrote their names. Hannah scribbled her lie.

'Perhaps we should send up a blanket with the cake,' suggested Elias. 'It's probably cold.'

'Ghosts don't feel the cold,' joked Josef.

'They don't eat cake, either,' said Hannah. 'And stop with the ghosts. You're scaring Elias.'

'I'm okay,' said the younger boy, but the pitch in his voice said otherwise.

'Come on, then,' said Josef, picking up the cake and the paper. 'The quicker we do this, the sooner we can all share this last one.'

Hannah hoped with all her heart that moment would come.

'We'll need to return the dumb waiter to the ground floor before Aunt Maud gets home. Otherwise, she'll know something's up,' said Hannah.

'So how long should we leave it up there for?' asked Elias.

They were all standing in the hallway, the cake and note inside the lift ready for the journey to the top of the house. Josef had one hand around the rope, ready to hoist it upward.

'The way that cake smells, if there's anybody up there, they'll already be waiting for it to arrive.'

'Two minutes,' said Hannah. Though Aunt Maud should be gone for a while, there was always the chance she would come back early.

'Elias, you start counting when I tell you.' Josef pulled on the rope. The lift began to rise. Hannah briefly considered reaching out her hand, taking the cake and stuffing it into her mouth. Would the boys be annoyed, or would they see the funny side of it? Either way, this nonsense would be over.

The cake, the paper, the lift all disappeared. The knocking at the sides of the shaft turned into an echo. From above they heard the ring of a bell. Josef stopped pulling.

'It's arrived at Aunt Maud's floor,' said Hannah. 'Keep going.'

She felt Elias's hand upon her arm and reached across to cup it in hers.

'It's getting harder,' said Josef. A few more pulls and his hands slipped. 'It won't go any further. Do you think it's reached the attic?'

'There wasn't a bell,' squeaked Elias.

No, there wasn't. She remembered that from last time.

'Perhaps it's been removed.' Josef was staring up at the ceiling as though he could see for himself. 'Start counting.'

The house was quieter than she had ever heard it. No boards moving, no Aunt Maud clattering in the kitchen, no distant radio.

And then Elias, whispering, 'One . . . two . . . three . . .'

Hannah began to count along with him in her head. Josef looked to be doing the same.

From far above, a click that could have been a door opening. A whisper of cold air, almost imagined, from the shaft. It carried a stale, damp smell.

Elias paused in his counting. 'Did you hear that?'

'Keep counting,' whispered Josef.

'Where was I?'

'Forty-two . . . forty-three . . . forty-four . . .'

The rope moved. Just a slight wobble. Josef placed a finger upon it.

Hannah hadn't realised she'd been holding her breath. She let it out in one long gasp. Her heart made heavy footsteps across her chest. They kept counting. Elias gripped Hannah's hand.

'Eighty-eight . . . eighty-nine . . .'

The ropes began to slide by themselves. Josef leaped back and all three of them screamed.

'You're doing that!' shrieked Elias.

Josef held up his hands. 'How am I . . .?' His eyes were trying to escape his skull.

The ropes continued to move, one up, one down. The bell above rang. The wooden box knocked against the shaft as it descended. Elias hid behind Hannah. They all watched and waited.

Finally, the bottom of the box came into view. Hannah heard Elias whimper. The bell rang as it arrived. Josef grabbed the rope, stopping it from continuing down to the ground floor. The whole house seemed to settle once more upon its foundations with creaks and groans.

They stared into the small wooden box. Its emptiness stared back.

THIRTY-TWO

The next day, Josef and Hannah made their way over the river to Elias's house. It was a lot colder outside than the last time they were here, and the fog had seemed to make the journey twice as long.

It was less than a week until the festival of The Old Man's Bones, and Elias wanted Hannah to hear from his grandmother the tale behind the superstition. But, he warned, it was scary. Hannah promised him she would be able to handle it.

Frau Lister ushered them into her cottage and through to the parlour before she let loose with the hugs. A fire crackled and popped, and a small ginger cat, which Hannah hadn't noticed last time, was curled up on a rug in front of it. Neither had she noticed the Volksempfänger, identical to Aunt Maud's, engraved with the eagle and the swastika, sitting on the sideboard.

Josef and Hannah shrugged off their coats and joined Elias on the sofa opposite the fire. Frau Lister, after hanging their coats out of sight, lowered herself down into her armchair on the left of the fireplace. Despite the woman's diminutive size, the chair groaned and sank.

'Now, to what do I owe the pleasure? I know you children wouldn't be in the company of an old lady unless you wanted something.'

Hannah was about to protest, but Frau Lister chuckled. 'Don't worry, my dear. I wouldn't have wanted to be when I was your age.'

'Can we have a sugar cube, Grandma?' asked Elias.

'Go on, then,' said Frau Lister. 'One each. Sugar's hard to come by these days, but too much of it doesn't do my old teeth, the few I have left, any good.'

Elias picked up the bowl and held it out for Hannah and Josef. 'Sofia said she'll come with us to collect The Old Man's Bones.'

'I said I might,' clarified Hannah, taking a cube from the bowl.

'Can you tell Sofia the story, Grandma? She's never heard it.'

'Oh, I don't know,' said the old woman, smiling. 'It's just a silly old fairytale.'

'I'd like to hear it,' said Hannah.

'Me, too,' added Josef. 'Though I already know it.'

'And what about you?' asked the woman, squinting at her grandson. 'You won't have nightmares?'

Elias shook his head, though Hannah wasn't convinced.

'Very well, young ones. I shall tell you the story behind The Old Man's Bones.' She cleared her throat and looked at Hannah. 'Have you seen the castle, my dear? High up on the mountain, hiding in the forest like a great stone bear ready to pounce upon the village?'

Hannah didn't think it matched the old lady's description. But she liked the idea, scary as it was. 'I can see it from my window. Or I could before the fog came.'

'Ah, the fog. The castle can't be seen from here, even on a clear day, but when I was a little girl, I used to imagine it creeping closer and closer to the village in that fog. I feared that one day I would wake up in this same house and the great stone walls would be right outside my window, staring in at me, ready to break right through and swallow me whole.' She sniffed and laughed. The fire popped, and Hannah jumped. The cat woke and stretched, rolled over and curled back up.

Frau Lister shuffled back into her well-worn armchair, placed her hands upon her flowery lap and began.

THIRTY-THREE

There once lived in the castle a very rich and powerful graf with his wife and their beautiful daughter. The daughter was given everything a young girl could desire but, despite this, or because of it, she grew up to be selfish and cruel-hearted.

Her beauty flourished and, as the years passed, she became even more mean-spirited. Soon, it was time for her to wed.

Messengers were sent across the kingdom to give notice of the Princess's intention to wed. There was no shortage of suitors, but only those considered worthy enough to take the hand of the Graf's precious, perfect daughter were summoned to the castle to prove their merit.

Through competition in combat, etiquette and worldly knowledge, these suitors were whittled down to three, and these three were each invited to spend a day with the Princess so that she could choose a husband deserving of her hand in marriage.

The first suitor was the son of a merchant. He was kind and gentle and walked beside the Princess through the fine gardens. When they came to the marshes, he placed his cloak down upon them so that she would not dirty her delicate feet, and took her hand to help her across. When a falcon swooped from the highest branches of the forest to steal her crown, he unsheathed his sword and fought it off, but was careful not to harm the bird. And when the Princess stumbled on some sharp rocks, he reached out and caught her in his arms, apologising for his forthrightness.

On returning to the castle, the Princess sat opposite the merchant's son and said, 'I shall ask you three questions. If you answer them to my satisfaction, you shall receive my hand in marriage.'

'I shall answer your questions with honesty and humility,' said the man, and the Princess began.

'What would be the first gift you bestow upon me?'

'That is easy, for you already have it. My first gift to you is my heart.'

The Princess smiled, but inside she thought, What use have I for his heart when I already have one that beats perfectly within my chest?

'And what would you do to keep me forever content?'

'I would write you a poem every day to show you how much I love and cherish you.'

What use have I for poems when they consist of nothing more than simple words? *thought the Princess.*

Finally, the Princess asked, 'And would you be mine forever?'

'Of course,' said the man. 'I would be yours until we die.'

The Princess leaped up and shouted, 'I shall never die! I shall not marry a man who believes such nonsense!' And she called for the guards to take the merchant's son and throw him over the wall of the castle.

The second man was the son of a nobleman. He was caring but flippant. When they came to the marshes, he placed his cloak down upon them, but joked about her falling in. When the falcon swooped from the trees, he fought it off, removing one of its feet with his sword. And when the Princess stumbled on the sharp rocks, he reached out and caught her roughly and unapologetically.

On returning to the castle, the Princess sat opposite the nobleman's son and told him what he must do to gain her hand in marriage.

'I shall answer your questions without fear of failure,' said the man, and the Princess began.

'What would be the first gift you bestow upon me?'

'I would give you a gold and jewelled ring to celebrate our wedded union.'

The Princess smiled, but inside she thought, What use have I for a single ring when I already own more jewels and gold than anybody in the kingdom?

'And what would you do to keep me forever content?'

'I would provide you with a fine home filled with laughing children.'

What use have I for his home or his children? *thought the Princess.* I shall soon inherit the castle, the finest home in all the kingdom, and would not wish to share it with such distractions.

Finally, the Princess asked, 'And would you be mine forever?'

'Of course,' said the man. 'I would be yours long after your sumptuous hair turns grey, lines carve up your beautiful face and your sparkling eyes begin to dull and fade.'

The Princess once more leaped up and shouted, 'I shall never grow old and grey! I shall not marry a man who believes such nonsense!' And so the nobleman's son was thrown over the wall of the castle.

The third man was a prince. He was angry and miserable, and though his face was handsome, he was ugly on the inside. He led the Princess through the fine gardens, pulling her along as if he were a horse and she were a cart. At the marshes, he didn't help her, but admonished her for losing her shoe in the thick mud. When the falcon swooped, he unsheathed his sword and killed it, brandishing its body above her. And when the Princess stumbled on the sharp rocks, he stood aside in case she should take him with her and watched impatiently as she dragged herself back up to the path.

On returning to the castle, the Princess asked the same three questions.

But, unbeknown to all, the Prince had sent spies out to listen to the questions posed to the two suitors before him. He knew that the Princess's hand relied only on telling her what she wished to hear.

'What would be the first gift you bestow upon me?'

'What would you like?'

The Princess thought. 'I would like a promise. That I will never grow old.'

'That,' said the Prince, 'you shall have.'

'And what would you do to keep me forever content?'

'Why, I would keep my promise.'

Finally, the Princess asked, 'And would you be mine forever?'

'Of course,' said the Prince. 'For you will forever remain young and beautiful.'

The Princess could not be happier. And so she took his hand and offered him hers in return, and soon they were wed.

Not long after, the Graf died, and his wife soon followed. The Princess gave herself the title of queen, and her husband took over the position of graf. They ruled the village with anger and hate, stole land from the peasants and left them with little food to live by.

The Queen remained young-looking and beautiful until one day she gazed in the mirror and noticed a small crease in her skin running outwards from each eye. And, when she looked closer, two grey hairs at the parting in her scalp. The Queen erupted in anger. She summoned the Graf, who was now used to her fits of temper, though he had never seen her quite like this.

'You promised me I would never grow old!' she screamed. 'That I would never lose my beauty!'

The Graf tried to calm her, but to no avail. The Queen threw him from her chambers and told him not to return until he had found a way to return her to perfection.

The Graf summoned a physician, but was told that time cannot be reversed; that ageing cannot be held back. And so he turned to magic.

There was a wise old woman who lived in the forest, and the Graf sent one of his knights to bring her to the castle, where he told her of his wife's predicament.

The old woman scratched at her hairy chin, sucked at her withered lip and shook her balding head. 'Being young is no fun. No fun at all. Better to be old like me.' Then she held up a thin, crooked finger. 'But there is a way . . .'

She took hold of his chin in her dry, warty hands, moving his head from left to right and back again, following his eyes with hers. 'I see you have no children of your own. You will have to use somebody else's.'

The Graf didn't like the way she said this, but he asked her to continue.

'You must find twenty-one spinning wheels, twenty-one spinners, twenty-one weavers and twenty-one seamstresses. The spinners must spin the silk into fine threads. The weavers must weave those threads into a rich fabric. The seamstresses must sew the fabric into an exquisite dress. And all this must take place under the light of the Hunter's Moon.'

The Graf nodded. 'But what has this to do with children?'

'You must have twenty-one bobbins, and each bobbin must be made from the bone of a child taken by you from their home on that same night.'

The Graf gasped in horror, but at the same time a scream of anger came from the Queen's chambers as she found more lines and grey hairs. He agreed, thanked the old woman and waited for the night of the Hunter's Moon.

Finally, it arrived. Under its light, the Graf rode to the village, crept in through a window and stole a young child away from its home. Wrapped in a blanket, the child was carried back up the mountain, through the snowy forest to the castle, where the Graf threw it into a pot of boiling water. He turned his face away so that he did not have to look into the child's eyes, and covered his ears so that he did not have to listen to its screams. Soon, all that was left of the child was a steaming pot of broth and, bobbing up and down in the thick soup, a mass of clean white bones.

Twenty-one bones were removed from the broth and passed to the twenty-one spinners who fitted them to twenty-one spinning wheels. Under the light of the Hunter's Moon, the spinners spun, the weavers wove and the seamstresses sewed. And by the morning a fine silk dress had been made. The fabric sparkled with gold, emerald and ruby colours.

When the Queen put it on, she was instantly young and beautiful again, her skin flawless and her hair a dark auburn throughout. She was, for a time, as happy as she could ever be.

But as the months passed, the lines and grey hairs reappeared, and the Queen demanded another dress to be made for her. And so, on the night of the Hunter's Moon, the Graf rode to the village, stole a sleeping child and returned to the castle, where he threw it into a pot of boiling water without looking or listening. Twenty-one bones were placed on twenty-one spinning wheels. The spinners, weavers and seamstresses worked under the light of the Hunter's Moon. And, by morning, a second fine silk dress was made for the Queen, who put it on, looked in the mirror at her younger face and was, for the time being, happy.

And so it went on. Each year the Graf stole away a child, and each year a fine silk dress was made using thread spun around the bones of that child.

Until one year.

An old gardener who worked at the castle had become wise to what was going on. He had heard talk from the village of a child disappearing every year on the night of the Hunter's Moon. And he had seen how the Queen emerged the morning after, looking young and replenished. This old man was living his last days. He knew he would not make it through the winter.

When the Graf rode back into the castle gardens with the child wrapped in the blanket, the old man stopped him and told him to beware, for a wolf had entered the grounds. Knowing that the Graf would value the beast's fur as a trophy in his hunting room, he promised to watch the package while the Graf rode off in pursuit.

No sooner had the Graf disappeared than the old man unwrapped the blanket and told the young, terrified child to hurry home without stopping, and tell the village of the Graf's misdeeds. Then he lay down on the blanket and wrapped himself up in it.

When the Graf returned, angry that he had not caught the wolf and annoyed that the old gardener had disappeared, he picked up the blanket and rode into the castle. The old man remained silent, even as his body was dropped into the boiling pot. The Graf turned his face away so that he did not have to look into his victim's eyes and covered his ears so that he did not have to listen to the screams, and very soon the bones were floating amongst the broth.

They were yellower than usual. And some appeared cracked and crooked. But the Graf did not stop to worry, and very soon twenty-one spinners were turning twenty-one wheels with twenty-one bobbins made from the old man's bones under the light of the Hunter's Moon.

This dress was not as bright and shiny as the others, but the Queen was waiting and she tore the dress from the Graf's hands and placed it over her head.

No sooner had she done so than the lines at her eyes spread and the few grey strands of hair multiplied to cover her whole head. Her skin sagged, her nose drooped and her teeth fell from her puckered lips. Liver spots appeared on her hands and face, her eyes clouded over and her legs grew bony and crooked. She fell to the floor screaming, clutching at her hair which came away in thick clumps.

The Graf looked on in horror as the Queen aged beyond recognition.

It was then that the Graf realised what had happened, but it was too late. The Hunter's Moon had disappeared, and the Queen, whose heart had always been old and bitter, took to her bed and died.

The Graf lived for many more years, and the thought often crossed his mind that perhaps he could steal a child from the village, boil it up and give its bones to twenty-one spinners so a fine suit might be made for himself on the night of the Hunter's Moon. But if he could not bring himself to look at the child or listen to the screams, how would he know if it truly was a child's bones or those of an old man?

And to this day, the village children hang The Old Man's Bones from their doorways. Just in case the Graf is still up there in the castle and the thought enters his mind. They hang them as a warning to him. That they know . . .

'. . . that we all know. And we will be ready.'

'I've never heard the tale told that well,' said Josef, his voice carrying a hint of amazement.

Hannah felt Elias staring at her, as if he were waiting for her to say something. She couldn't let him down.

'Thank you, Frau Lister. That was . . . wonderful. Elias was right.'

The smaller boy grinned. 'I told you.'

'It comes with practice,' said Frau Lister. 'I must have told that story a hundred times. Ninety-nine of them to Elias here.' She rose from her chair with a groan and glanced out the window. 'The fog seems to get thicker every year.'

Herr Schundel had said the same. Was it true?

Hannah followed her gaze. 'We should be going,' she said.

Elias groaned. 'Can't you stay a little longer?'

'You have school tomorrow, young man,' said his grandmother. 'And the wolves will be out soon.'

Aunt Maud had said as much about that once or twice. Hannah had taken her words as nothing more than scaremongering. A way to ensure she returned home before dark. But Frau Lister wasn't like that. And there was no humour in her voice. A grandmother with a warning about wolves. She glanced down at the red coat the Oberstleutnant had given her.

Surely, wolves wouldn't come into the village. But despite her attempts at self-assurance, she needed more.

'They wouldn't approach us, would they?'

Frau Lister rubbed at her chin. 'I'm sure they wouldn't. And besides, it's not the true wolves you need to fear.'

'It's not?'

The old woman shook her head. 'It's the ones who disguise themselves as sheep. They're the most dangerous.'

For some reason, an image of the Oberstleutnant appeared in Hannah's mind.

THIRTY-FOUR

The day of the Hunter's Moon arrived. Three days earlier, the first snow of the season had fallen. Hannah had watched in wonder from her window as, piece by piece, any colour that had not been claimed by the fog was slowly erased. It was mesmerising. Unlike in the city, where the fallen snow immediately turned to sludge beneath the trampling of feet and the turning of wheels, here the ground remained hidden below a uniform layer of healing whiteness. Part of her wanted it to stay like this forever, to cover the world outside like a spell within a fairytale, to send the village to sleep for a hundred years and for them all to wake up in a world without war. How could anybody be dragging people from their homes, shooting bullets at soldiers, dropping bombs on cities in a world that looked so peaceful and beautiful?

Despite Hannah's initial scepticism about the festivities, she was excited that Aunt Maud had given her permission to go with the boys. To be out in the snow, with other children, out of sight and out of earshot. It was all a bit macabre, she had to admit, but something about that made it even more appealing.

Aunt Maud said she could go on the proviso that they stayed together, did not do anything that would leave one of them flat on the ice and that they were back by dark. And, also, on the condition that they cut Hannah's plaster from her leg.

'It's close to six weeks,' said Aunt Maud. 'I've seen you walking on it when you think I haven't been looking. And it will be easier, and safer for you in the snow, if you lose those crutches.'

At last! Hannah had been waiting for this for so long. She would be able to scratch her leg. She would be able to wash it, rid herself of that terrible smell. And go to school? Hannah decided she would wait until tomorrow to ask. She had already been granted the freedom to take part in The Old Man's Bones.

'No running, mind you!' cautioned Aunt Maud.

'What about somersaults?' joked Hannah.

But Aunt Maud didn't find it funny. She told Hannah to put her leg up on the sofa while she went and found some scissors. She returned carrying the biggest pair Hannah had ever seen, the blades bent at the end.

'Now stay still. It would be a shame if we'd taken such good care of your leg only to cut it off now.'

Hannah did as she was told. Aunt Maud placed her fingers below the plaster and pulled it away from her leg. She inserted the scissors and began to work downwards, every now and then stopping to pull at the cut edges. As the plaster came away, the smell made them both wrinkle their noses. Hannah felt the welcome coolness of air upon her skin. It was so refreshing. The scissors cut, Aunt Maud pulled and ripped and then her foot was free.

She went to scratch at her skin and Aunt Maud's hand slapped her away. 'Be careful. Your skin will be tender. You could tear it.'

It looked pale and sickly, crinkled, as if it had been sitting in a hot bath for six weeks. She gently rubbed at it. Though she was still tempted to use her nails.

'That feels so good.'

'Wiggle your toes,' said Aunt Maud.

Hannah did. Aunt Maud put a hand below her calf and lifted it.

'Now, swivel your ankle.'

She did.

'Is there any pain?'

There wasn't. Just that stiffness. She shook her head. Then Aunt Maud got her to stand up and put her weight on it. Gently. And walk up and down. Slowly. And then, wrinkling her nose once more, Aunt Maud told her to go and wash it. Immediately.

She didn't need to be told twice.

The snow continued to fall and the fog lifted slightly as Hannah, Josef and Elias trudged along the streets and knocked on doors, each holding out their chosen receptacle to be filled by whoever answered. Ghosts of other children padded up and down the street, and their cries of delight brought out a groan from Elias as he worried others were getting the best bones, especially when they passed a house where an old man placed a huge, clean, cow skull into the arms of a small boy.

Hannah felt foolish and a little embarrassed when they'd knocked on their first door. But after being warned with winks and smiles to watch out for the Graf, she began to enjoy herself and promised to take heed. She soon became as competitive as the boys when it came to the bone collecting, and was buzzing with the freedom that being without crutches afforded her arm, swinging the basket Aunt Maud had given her until it was too heavy to do so. Old bones were heavier than she'd expected!

They made a stop at Josef's house to warm their hands by the fire. Josef's mother brought them each a glass of milk and his grandmother looked through the bones they had collected, recounting her own childhood tales of The Old Man's Bones.

They were crossing the square to Aunt Maud's when Hannah noticed a group of five children outside the lodge.

'Look,' said Hannah, as they passed the fountain. 'I know this is all about magic. But there isn't a spell strong enough to get Aunt Maud to –'

She didn't have time to finish her sentence. The door opened and Aunt Maud appeared with her hand dipped into a pot. She brought out bundles of old bones and shared them amongst the tree of hands sprouting up towards her.

'Miracles do happen,' said Hannah, noticing how Josef and Elias looked as astonished as she felt.

'Perhaps it's because you're living with her,' suggested Elias.

'What do you mean?'

The smaller boy shrugged. 'Maybe you've made her happier.'

It was a nice thought. But then Aunt Maud glanced over at them and closed the door on the idea.

Back at the lodge, they placed their wares on the table to see who had the most. Aunt Maud busied herself in the background but, Hannah noticed, didn't complain.

'People are more generous than when I was a child,' she said, making no mention of her own earlier generosity. 'And what with the war going on, too.'

That was something Hannah hadn't thought about until now. Meat had become such a rare and rationed commodity for anyone who wasn't a soldier, and so bones were boiled up for broth once they'd been stripped of meat and, after that, thrown upon the fire as fuel. Back in the city, she had even heard of families adding the charred bone remains to water for whatever extra nutrition they could get. No one would be giving away bones to honour a superstition.

'We did well,' agreed Josef. He glanced at Hannah's pile. 'I think you may have got more than me and Elias.'

Aunt Maud picked up a thick, grey bone from Elias's pile that had cracks running along its length. 'I expect some of these were around when I was a young girl.'

Of course! The picture in the hall of Aunt Maud and her brother. That must have been taken after the night of The Old Man's Bones.

'They're that old?' asked Elias.

'That old, yes,' half-joked Aunt Maud. 'There's a belief that the older the bones, the more powerful they are against the Graf. Now, I shall leave you to pick through your spoils of the day. You may place some around the doorway, but not too many. I don't want this place looking like an animal's graveyard.'

They hung the bones Hannah had collected from Aunt Maud's doorframe using twine that she had left out for them on the hall table. Josef tied some of the smaller bones together with bows. They looked like grim versions of the Christmas decorations the Meyers had hung around their house. Other, larger bones were hung either side of the doorway, and Josef lifted Elias up so that he could place what looked like a large femur above the doorframe.

'I hope it doesn't fall on Aunt Maud's head,' joked Hannah, and the boys laughed.

'I hope it doesn't, either,' said Aunt Maud. Her eyes found Josef. 'Or on my plant pots.' She gazed out across the foggy square. 'It's nearly dark. You boys should be getting home.'

'Come on,' said Josef to the younger boy. 'I'll walk you home. We still need to decorate our own doors.'

'Thank you,' replied Elias.

'Thank you from me as well. Both of you,' Hannah said, feeling a rush of gratitude for these two new friends.

'For what?' asked Elias.

Hannah felt a little embarrassed all of a sudden. She didn't usually give out compliments that weren't embedded in a joke. But Josef's cock of the head gave her courage to continue. 'For being you, Elias.'

Elias flashed her a grin. 'That's easy. And Josef, too? For being him?'

'That, too,' she replied, feeling a warmth creep into her cheeks that matched Josef's blush.

'Come on, Elias,' he said, grabbing the younger boy's sleeve and beginning to walk off.

'Make sure you walk, you two,' said Aunt Maud. 'No running, you hear? You don't want to slip and break a leg tonight. It feels like the temperature is dropping fast, and if you get stuck somewhere, you're likely to be found first by wolves.'

The wolves again.

'Yes, Frau Meyer,' they chorused, as a snowball found Josef's back from a front yard bordering the square.

Then another and, despite Aunt Maud's warning, the two boys sped off into the fog as a hurricane of white came at them from the arms of giggling children outside bone-decorated houses.

THIRTY-FIVE

Hannah packed away the game of Chutes and Ladders and glanced over at Aunt Maud, who was fast asleep and snoring in her chair. The radio played out the same message as it did every evening. Of how well the war was going. And how everybody had to pull together for the greater good. How they could contribute in many ways – rationing food, reporting dissidence, listening to the radio. The voice couldn't overemphasise how important, imperative even, it was that they listen to the nightly broadcast.

Hannah sat back in her chair in front of the crackling fire and wondered about this greater good the voice kept referring to. The only good she could recall was from so long ago, she felt it must have come from a story rather than a memory.

The words from the radio droned on. Great nation ... defeat ... armies ... responsibility ... Hannah felt herself drifting off, too. The fire was almost out, she noticed ...

A noise woke her. Or rather, it woke her soul. She somehow felt more separate from her sleeping body this time, as though it were submerged deeper below the surface of consciousness. It sounded like the closing of the front door. Hannah rose and floated out of the parlour, nervously glancing back at her sleeping self before leaving the room. The fear she had first felt after leaving her body had all but disappeared. Each time she had travelled, she had, without anything more than impulse, safely and successfully returned to her sleeping body. But there was always the possibility . . .

Down the hallway, the voice on the radio and Aunt Maud's snoring mingled and faded, replaced with the gentle *clack-clack-clacking* of bone against bone from outside. The front door was closed, but the creak of a floorboard above told her that somebody had stepped from the stairwell to the landing. Fear edged its way into her mind and, despite knowing that she could not be seen nor heard, she moved slowly and steadily, mindful of a surreal sense of trepidation. She made her way up the stairs, the footsteps above creeping along the corridor. Perhaps it was the Oberstleutnant, though it didn't sound like him. He couldn't creep anywhere.

She got halfway up the stairs and heard the opening of a door on dry hinges from somewhere above. She continued on, turning at the top to see nothing but a dark, empty corridor. There could have been anybody hiding at the far end, in the deepest shadows. And for the first time she wondered, no matter how irrational it sounded, if the Graf were in the house, come to take her body away and boil her up.

From her room came the sound of somebody creeping around. And now a faint light. Hannah floated forward, past the Oberstleutnant's door and the dumb waiter. On to her own doorway, half open. She peered in.

The light was coming from behind her door. Along with the sound of a drawer being gently closed.

Every element of her mind screamed at her to leave immediately, but curiosity won out. She was, after all, invisible, and could watch without the fear of being seen. She entered and glanced to her left, behind the door. A shadow unfolded itself, growing out of the darkness. The person turned to face her.

But it wasn't a person.

The light it held half-blinded Hannah and hid any detail of its features. All that she could make out was a bald and shiny head from which protruded a stubby, blunt snout, like that of a pig. It had two large, black eyes that reminded her of a magnified picture of a fly she had once seen in one of her father's books. It stared nowhere and everywhere at the same time and, before Hannah had time to realise what it was doing, it walked into her, the bluster of movement somehow pushing her further into the room.

The creature stepped outside, pulling the door behind itself.

Panic swallowed her. She threw herself at the door, willing it to open so that she could return to her body. But there was nothing she could do. She couldn't move past it.

She was trapped.

Terrified, she turned to the window, but that, too, was closed.

Hannah hung there in the darkness feeling lost and, once more, alone.

THIRTY-SIX

Hannah woke feeling groggy, with memories of the previous night ghosting in and out of her consciousness like the village houses on a foggy day. The memories of her out-of-body experiences were usually clear, and stayed with her for a long time. But this one seemed to be sinking further into the murky depths of forgetfulness with every waking second.

An image of the creature in her room flashed into her mind. She sat upright, fully awake now, and looked around for clues, anything, to indicate someone or something had been there.

Nothing.

Hannah wondered if, this time, her memory was in fact a dream. And, as the day dragged on, the image faded until it was no more than a half-imagined story from a book.

Aunt Maud sauntered around in a mild stupor for most of the day. Hannah almost commented, but couldn't quite muster up either the words or the energy. After lunch, she was surprised to pass the Oberstleutnant on the way to the bathroom. He greeted her with his usual cheer, which sent shivers down her spine even while she pasted a smile on her face, and informed her that he had decided to take a break from his work at the castle and had arrived at the lodge late the previous night. Hannah considered asking him if he had noticed anything strange, but decided not to start a conversation that could lead to questions she wouldn't be able to answer.

'I hope you didn't mind me carrying you to bed last night. I found you in the parlour alone and thought it best not to wake you.'

Hannah's smile dropped. She didn't want this man carrying her anywhere.

'Should I have left you?' asked the Oberstleutnant, his face suddenly a mix of mock concern and bemusement.

She pasted that smile back onto her face and forced her eyes to meet his. 'No, no. I'm glad you didn't. I'm still tired. That's all.'

'Perhaps it was the excitement of the day. I noticed you took part in the village tradition.'

For a moment she didn't catch on.

'Oh, The Old Man's Bones. Yes, with my friends. Josef and Elias.'

It was obvious by his face what he thought of it all. This time, it was his smile that disappeared. But only momentarily.

'Your . . . friends?'

'Yes. Is something wrong?' That wasn't the part of her sentence that she expected him to take issue with.

The Oberstleutnant shook off his look of puzzlement. 'Nothing is wrong. I was just surprised that your aunt allowed you to take part. She doesn't strike me as the type to condone such things. But that is good. I'm glad you have found some friends.' Though something in his eyes told her otherwise. 'Good day, Sofia.'

'Good day, Herr Kessler,' she replied, before dashing into the bathroom to stop her bladder from exploding.

The rest of the day carried on in much the same way, with Aunt Maud absent and Hannah herself feeling exhausted. She didn't think she'd ever dozed so much in her life, and today she was making up for it. Josef and Elias didn't come to see her at all, which was unusual for a Sunday. One of the boys not coming to see her was understandable, but both of them? They would have got home safely last night, wouldn't they?

The wolves . . .

The fog hung around like a soldier on duty, its presence felt everywhere, watching, waiting.

The following day, Hannah clock-watched until mid-afternoon and then waited at her window for the spectres of Josef and Elias to grow out of the fog after finishing school. She was looking forward to seeing them, to be shaken out of her melancholy by Josef's jokes and Elias's chatter. But today, Josef trod a lonely path through the melting snow like a clockwork toy whose spring had almost wound down. Confused, Hannah rushed downstairs and got to the door just as he knocked. But standing on the doorstep wasn't the Josef she knew. He looked like Josef, but it was as if the light had gone from inside him.

'How was school?' she asked, unsure how to speak to this Josef.

'It was okay.' He shivered and trudged inside. 'I think the fog has got into my bones.'

'Where's Elias?' she asked, closing the door behind him.

He turned. 'Sorry, what?'

'Was he at school?'

'Who?'

Was he playing a trick on her? Hannah wasn't in a joking mood. She took a deep breath to try to calm her irritation. Why was he being deliberately difficult? 'Elias,' she said. 'Why hasn't he come with you?'

Josef remained silent, staring blankly ahead with his fingers to his lips. Her friend really wasn't being himself.

Hannah felt something other than the fog creeping into her body. She felt a little woozy and wondered if they had both caught something. Part of her felt elsewhere, distant.

'Josef!' She hadn't meant to shout, and it caught Hannah off guard as much as Josef. 'Where's Elias?' she repeated.

'Elias?'

She had had enough. 'Elias! Small boy. About this high.' She held her hand out, palm down, at shoulder height. 'Never stops talking. Follows you everywhere you go. Stop being so annoying.'

'I . . . I don't . . .' Josef frowned and shook his head. 'Who?'

Hannah studied his face. There was nothing there to tell her why he was being like this. 'Have you fallen out?'

'With who?'

'With Elias!'

'What are you talking about?'

'Elias!' Her annoyance was edging towards anger. 'Josef! Where is Elias?'

Josef threw his hands in the air and took a step towards her. The indignation of his next words stole away her anger and replaced it with more than a drop of fear. She immediately felt it spreading through her body like ink in a glass of water.

'I don't know anybody called Elias!'

He wasn't joking. Hannah could see that now. The way he was looking at her, trying to read her the same way she was trying to read him. He narrowed his eyes and shook his head. She went to speak but swallowed her words. All she could do was stare back and try to make sense of what was going on.

'What is with all the shouting?' Aunt Maud appeared at the kitchen doorway, her face the colour of wild berries, hands on her hips. 'Well? Speak up, somebody!'

Hannah felt her own words stick in the back of her throat. It was Josef who spoke.

'It's Sofia. She's talking nonsense.'

Hannah gasped. 'It is not me. It's you who's acting weird.'

'Tell me what has happened!' When neither of them did, Aunt Maud barked, 'Sofia! Tell me!'

Josef raised his eyebrows at Hannah, and she leaped in. 'Josef says he doesn't know who Elias is.'

Aunt Maud's eyes flicked to the boy. 'Josef?'

'Well, I don't.'

'At least you both agree on what the problem is.' Back to Hannah. 'Now, young lady, will you please tell us both who this *Elias* is, and why he is so important that I have to be called away from my housework?'

Everything stopped. Hannah's breath seemed to catch in her throat. She sank into a chair and placed her head in her hands.

'Fetch some water,' whispered Aunt Maud. 'Josef! Water, now!'

Hannah's head was spinning. What was going on? Where was Elias?

She felt Aunt Maud's hand upon hers, gentle, and slowly got her breath back under control.

Josef appeared with a glass of water. Aunt Maud took it and passed it to Hannah.

'Drink slowly.'

Hannah took a sip, its coolness washing away some of the panic.

'He's been coming around here most days,' she said. 'For almost as long as I've been here.'

'Who has?'

'Elias.'

She glanced up to see Aunt Maud and Josef exchanging a look of concern.

'He has been! He came to collect The Old Man's Bones with us.' She could feel herself becoming angry again and took another sip of water. What was wrong with them?

Josef shook his head.

'The study. You and Elias cleared it so that I could get to the books.'

Josef shrugged. 'I don't . . . I helped your aunt.'

Aunt Maud rubbed at her pointed chin. Then, when that didn't wield an explanation, at the back of her neck. 'Yes, Josef's right. Sofia . . .'

'No! No! No!' She slammed the glass down onto the table. Water slopped out over her hand and sleeve.

Aunt Maud snapped back into herself. 'You need to get a grip of yourself, Sofia! There is not and there never has been any small boy called Elias in this house.'

'There is! There has been! He's my friend! He's your friend, too, Josef.' But Josef just lowered his eyes and stared at the floor.

Her mind in turmoil and her face awash with tears, Hannah marched up the stairs to her room and threw herself into bed, her thoughts ricocheting around her head, trying to come up with some logical explanation as to why neither Josef nor Aunt Maud could remember Elias. But there was none.

She lay there all evening and let the darkness come, praying she was asleep and would open her eyes to a bright new day spent with her friends. She tossed and turned for most of the night, but must have fallen asleep at some point, as she woke from a frantic dream where Elias toppled from a mountain ledge into a murky lake while Aunt Maud wiped down the cliff face and Josef practised his footballing skills.

THIRTY-SEVEN

The next morning, Hannah stayed in bed, even when the smell of melted butter and eggs wafted into her room from a distant corner of the house. She drifted in and out of a tormented sleep until, around midday, Aunt Maud brought some food to her, imploring Hannah to eat with the reminder that people could ill afford to waste food these days.

Hannah picked at the eggs, but it made little impact on what was on her plate. She pushed it to one side and shuffled down under the covers. There she remained until mid-afternoon when there was a knock at the door.

Hannah guessed it was Aunt Maud again, come to chastise her for not getting out of bed. But when the door opened, she was surprised to see Frau Meinhardt standing there. Was it that time already?

Hannah sat up, partly embarrassed to be seen like this by her teacher.

'Your aunt told me you were upset,' said Frau Meinhardt.

Hannah shook her head. Was that how Aunt Maud saw it? As her being upset?

'Shall I open the window?' Frau Meinhardt asked.

'If you like.'

Frau Meinhardt walked over to the window and opened it up. Cold air wafted in.

'You know,' said Frau Meinhardt, looking at the barely touched plate of eggs, 'you're very lucky to live in a village that still has so much good food. And an aunt that is willing to cook for you. There are too many people who have too little.'

Hannah lay back down. She didn't want to have this conversation.

The woman stood at the foot of the bed. 'Do you want to tell me what's wrong?'

'Didn't my aunt tell you?'

Frau Meinhardt shook her head. 'Only that you were confused.'

Hannah sat back up. 'I'm not confused.'

'So, what is it?'

She studied the woman's face. That smile was still there, as if waiting to make everything right. Could she? 'You know all the children in your class, don't you?'

'Of course.'

'And you wouldn't forget one, would you?'

She was expecting the woman to laugh. Instead, her smile faltered.

'Sofia, what's happened?'

'Elias.' She studied Frau Meinhardt's face for a hint of recognition. There was none.

'Elias?'

'Elias Lister. You don't remember him?'

Frau Meinhardt picked up a chair and set it down beside her. 'No, Sofia, I don't. Who is he?'

Hannah squeezed her eyes shut. The tears were coming again. 'He's my friend. He's in your class at school. But now ... now he's gone missing, and nobody can remember him but me.'

The colour fell from Frau Meinhardt's face. 'Do you remember him now?' asked Hannah, hoping something had suddenly jolted the teacher's memory. But Frau Meinhardt shook her head.

'He's real,' said Hannah quietly. 'I didn't imagine him. He was here. And now he's not. And something's happened to him. And I'm worried!'

Frau Meinhardt gripped Hannah's hand in both of hers. 'Tell me about Elias.'

At least she wanted to know. Hannah hadn't been shut down as she had been with Josef and Aunt Maud. Perhaps Frau Meinhardt could help in some way. She told the teacher as much as she could remember. How they had met after Josef had broken Aunt Maud's pot. How he had helped Josef tidy the study. How they had gone to visit his grandmother. 'Do you know Frau Lister?' she asked.

The teacher shook her head. She gently relinquished hold of Hannah's hand. 'But we can go and see her, if you like.'

'We can? Together?' That would be good. Just to know he was safe. And to prove what she was saying was true. She wiped at her eyes with the end of the bedsheet.

'If it means so much.'

Hannah nodded. 'I'd like that. I mean, his grandmother can't have forgotten him, can she?'

'I'm sure she can't,' replied Frau Meinhardt. But her eyes were looking elsewhere, and that smile was struggling to stay on her face. 'Would you like to go and see her now?'

'Yes.'

Frau Meinhardt stood up 'You can ride with me on Gretel.'

'Gretel?'

'My horse. She's outside. Let me go and talk to your aunt. In the meantime, eat your food. Even if it's just for your aunt's sake. And mine.'

She passed Hannah the plate.

The eggs were cold, but Hannah began to eat. Her appetite was back, if only partly.

THIRTY-EIGHT

Hannah could feel the cold eating into her, despite all the layers she was wearing. The snow hadn't fallen since the day of the Hunter's Moon, but it was still deep in places, and the thick fog persisted.

Aunt Maud stood behind her in the doorway, arms crossed and tight-lipped. 'I'm not sure how this is going to help,' she said.

'It will help Sofia,' explained Frau Meinhardt.

'Hopefully to come to her senses.'

Hannah ignored the two women and walked slowly up to Gretel. The horse stared straight ahead, every few seconds lifting a leg and clopping it down onto the cobblestones. Hannah placed a hand upon Gretel's flank. She had never ridden a horse before.

'Can you reach the stirrup?' asked Frau Meinhardt.

Hannah tried with her good leg, thankful that she no longer wore the plaster. Gretel was tall, and Hannah couldn't quite stretch her leg to reach the stirrup by herself. Frau

Meinhardt bent her knee and signalled for Hannah to stand on it to give her a boost. Between the two of them, Hannah managed to get a foot in the stirrup and swing her other leg over to settle herself in the saddle. She felt a little wobbly, but managed to keep enough balance to give Gretel a pat with one hand, while tightly holding the pommel with the other.

'Now it's my turn,' said Frau Meinhardt, who gently removed Hannah's foot from the stirrup, replaced it with her own and expertly pushed herself up behind Hannah, reaching around her to take the reins before digging her heels into Gretel's flanks. The horse trotted over the snowy cobblestones and into the fog, leaving Aunt Maud and the rest of the village behind.

There were times when Hannah felt she would slip off, but Frau Meinhardt's arms kept her upright and she held on tightly to the pommel. They crossed the bridge and climbed the pathway until they reached the fence surrounding Frau Lister's cottage.

The front door was closed. There was no sweet or spicy aroma coming from inside. Instead, the smell of smoke wafted towards them, and Hannah could see dark grey billows escaping the chimney, mixing with the fog. A light was on in one of the windows, but still the house looked a little lost and sad. There was none of the warm, welcoming feeling of her previous visits. She tried to tell herself it was because winter had arrived; because snow covered the ground and a fog had eaten the sky.

Still she held out hope as they made their way along the gravel path, as the door remained closed and the window failed to reveal a young face staring out at them.

Frau Meinhardt halted and dismounted Gretel, tied her to a post and helped Hannah to climb down. She knocked on the door . . .

Nothing.

Hannah started to worry that something had happened to Frau Lister as well as Elias, but her teacher's second, louder knock resulted in footsteps from inside.

The door opened and there was the old lady who Hannah had visited with Josef and Elias. The old lady who loved to bake and who had worn a sunbeam upon her face throughout those visits. But that sunbeam wasn't there now. Instead, there was a cloud of worry and confusion as she stared into Frau Meinhardt's blue eyes.

'Can I help you?'

'Good afternoon, Frau Lister. I'm Frau Meinhardt, a teacher at the school.'

Hannah, who was trying to look beyond Frau Lister, leaned into the doorway so that the old lady had to take a step back. Frau Lister clapped her hands to her mouth, returning to the warm old woman she had been before. 'Oh, Sofia, it's so good to see you again. Won't you both come in?'

Hannah couldn't wait. 'Is Elias here?'

Frau Lister tilted her head to the side 'Elias?'

'Elias. Your grandson.' And then she was barging past Frau Lister. 'Elias! Elias!'

She entered the living room, where Frau Lister had told them the story of The Old Man's Bones. The boy wasn't here. 'Elias, where are you? It's me –' In her panic she had nearly said her real name. She would check his room. He had to be somewhere.

'Sofia!'

She turned to see Frau Meinhardt staring at her, eyes wide and, for once, unsmiling. Behind her was Elias's grandmother, her hands over her mouth. *She looks scared,* thought Hannah, feeling slightly ashamed.

'He's not here,' said Frau Meinhardt, quieter now.

But if he wasn't here, in his home, where was he? Ever since he had disappeared, she had believed that he would be here. That there would be some sign of him, at least. But there was nothing.

'Who are you looking for, my darling?' asked Frau Lister.

But what was the point in trying to explain? His grandmother had no more memory of him than anybody else.

It was Frau Meinhardt who answered.

'She's looking for a boy, Frau Meinhardt. Elias. She thought he was your grandson.'

Frau Lister frowned at Hannah. 'My grandson? Whatever gave you that idea, my dear?'

'We came here,' she said. But her voice lacked conviction. Even to her. 'Josef and me, with Elias. You gave us stollen and you told us the story about the Queen and the Graf and The Old Man's Bones and . . .'

She didn't know how to continue, what more to say. Frau Lister was shaking her head.

'So, you have no grandson?' asked Frau Meinhardt.

'No grandson, no granddaughter. Being a teacher at the school, surely you would know. And that's why it's always nice to see the young ones. If it wasn't for Klaus – that's my cat – and that radio, I'd have no company at all.' She glanced over at the black box on the sideboard. 'I remember you coming, Sofia, with Josef. But I don't know what made you think there was somebody else here – a grandson . . .'

'Can we go?' asked Hannah. She didn't want to be here, didn't want to look at Frau Lister any longer. Not unless she could see the memory of Elias shining in her eyes.

'I don't know what to say,' sighed Frau Lister, and Hannah could hear genuine concern in her voice. That didn't make it any better, though. 'She has been through so much, poor girl. Only time will heal her.'

Hannah was beyond words. She didn't want to open her mouth, fearful that her despair would turn to anger. But at who? At the old woman who surely couldn't be intentionally misleading her? At Frau Meinhardt, who was trying to get to the bottom of the mystery? Or at herself?

'I want to go,' repeated Hannah. She stormed past Frau Meinhardt. Frau Lister moved to the side, and then Hannah was back in the kitchen and out into the front yard. She heard Frau Meinhardt speaking quietly to Frau Lister, and then a mumbled reply, but she had no interest in what they were saying. She barely registered being helped back onto the horse, and sat silently as Frau Meinhardt steered them away, welcoming the fog that blocked out the world around her. All that existed were the clip-clop of Gretel's hooves and her troubled memories.

And in those memories, one small boy shone brighter than everything else.

THIRTY-NINE

The lodge was quiet when Hannah got back. Aunt Maud must be out on an errand, she reasoned with herself. Even so, she felt a little abandoned.

Frau Meinhardt had tried to talk to Hannah on their way back, even hinting towards Elias being her imaginary friend, but Hannah didn't want to hear it. She was confused and completely certain all at the same time. She wanted nothing more than to go up to her room, climb into bed and let the darkness once more swallow her up.

She closed the door on Frau Meinhardt and Gretel, removed her coat and shoes and then made her way up the stairs, trying to order her thoughts and make sense of whatever was happening. If she searched her room, would she be able to find some proof of Elias's existence? Could he have left something that belonged to him? The only thing she could remember him bringing were the cakes, and they had eaten those. All except the one that had been sent up to the attic for whoever lived there. Along with the note.

The note on which Elias had signed his name.

The note that had never come back down.

Would it still be up there? It would be proof, to her at least, that Elias was real. But to get it, she would have to speak with the person living up there. And she wasn't sure she was brave enough.

Still, she could at least go up there and try the door. Then she could decide.

She went back down the hall and rested her hand on the banister. She had made this journey once before as her weightless, invisible self. This time, she placed one foot in front of the other and walked up the stairs, heart pounding for fear of being caught out by Aunt Maud as much as from what was behind the door at the very top of the house.

Here it was. She leaned forward and rested her ear against the wood. There were sounds – groans and creaks – but there were always sounds coming from the house when she listened. She stood back and stared down at the handle. Should she do this? Could she?

She slowly turned it. Locked. Why was she surprised by that?

She waited. Listened. She couldn't hear anybody moving around. But had anyone heard her? Would they be on their way now to throw open the door and pull her inside? Suddenly spooked, she turned and headed back downstairs.

There was no way into the loft to retrieve the note. She was disappointed, but also a little relieved.

Except there was, wasn't there? The cake and note had made the journey.

She stopped again on the second floor, weighing up whether to give up and return to her room, or . . .

The hallway looked darker than the one on her floor. She crept to the small door and pulled it open. Again, that cold breeze. She poked her head inside, gazed down the shaft and then up. A shiver ran through her.

She pulled at the rope and heard the lift rise from below, scraping and bumping against the shaft, the ringing of a bell as it passed her floor and, finally, another ring as it arrived.

She could fit in there, she was sure. She hoisted herself in, one rope either side of her legs. Then, before she changed her mind, she swiftly pulled the door closed. The darkness was complete. Her breathing was loud in the confined space, and she kept her hand against the door, ready to push it open if she lost her nerve. But then she began to make out a light rectangle around the wood, a gap between the door and the wall, and the two ropes. It was now or never. She grasped one and began to pull. The lift jolted, the compartment rocked from side to side. She pulled again with her other hand, this time a little further. Now she could see the mortar between the bricks falling away as she travelled upwards.

The temperature fell. She felt her breath heavy in her chest, her heart beating hard enough to rock the small lift against the walls. She kept pulling on the rope, one hand over the other. There was a groan from above and a clatter on the roof of the compartment, as if some small stones had fallen upon it. She instinctively ducked. Was she too heavy? Would the rope snap and plummet her to the ground floor? Her heart was drumming away and, despite the cold, her hands felt hot and clammy.

She slowed in her pulling, thinking she had heard movement from the room above. Slowly, finally, the brickwork at the top was replaced by another wooden panel. If there was a gap around the door, it was too dark to see out. And there was no bell. Hannah wondered whether, as Josef had suggested, it had been removed on purpose.

She took a deep breath and pushed at the door. It didn't budge. Had it been locked on the outside? Another shove, then the latch clicked and the door opened a fraction. The stale smell of dust and closed spaces drifted in towards her. But there was something else. The scent of a candle extinguished, maybe. And underneath all that, something familiar. Something that brought back memories of being in hiding.

She leaned forward and peeped through. It took her eyes a moment to decide where they should focus. All she could see were haphazard shapes, black against black. Hannah pushed the door open all the way, folding it back against the wall.

'Sofia?' said a voice from the darkness.

Hannah froze. She gulped and squinted into the black depths. Her breath felt laboured. 'Hello? Who's there?' Just get the note, she told herself. Get the note, then you can leave.

'Hello?' There was no malice in the voice. It carried more fear than threat.

'Who's there?' asked Hannah again. 'Why are you up here?'

From behind a curtain at the rear of the room stepped a man. Hannah instinctively leaned back, her hand keeping hold of the lift door, just in case.

She couldn't make out any of his features. He coughed and limped over to what Hannah now saw was a bed. After some fumbling around, there was the strike of a match and his face lit up. She guessed him to be in his mid-twenties. He was thin and pale. And frightened. Hannah could see that. He picked up a candle and lit it. He smiled and held up a hand in a wave.

She raised her hand back. His smile widened.

He pointed to himself. 'I'm Georg.' He spoke in an unfamiliar accent. It wasn't from her city, nor was it the same as that of the villagers here in Felshoven.

Georg stepped closer with the candle. His features, his clothes, his surroundings became clearer. His hair was brown, grown long enough to curl down his neck and around his ears. He had a sharp nose, and a slight chin covered with more than a few days of stubble.

Hannah felt her body relax, deciding she wasn't at risk. She agreed with it. The man looked harmless, almost ready to collapse. She swung her legs out and faced him.

'How do you know my name?' she asked.

'Your aunt told me. You are her niece.' He paused. 'She lets me stay here, too. She brings me food.'

Hannah had been right. Her estimation of Aunt Maud had just gone up. 'She hides you,' Hannah insisted.

The man looked down at the floor. 'She lets me stay here.'

'Why?'

She could see the man struggling to answer. He scratched at his head, then cupped his hand over his mouth and nose. Finally, he put down the candle and took a deep breath. 'I lied. I'm English. My name is George.'

The tension in Hannah's body was back. He was English. The enemy that had killed her parents. What was he doing here? Why was Aunt Maud bringing him food? Didn't that make Aunt Maud the enemy, too? She folded her legs back into the compartment and tried to focus her thoughts. She was here for the note. That was all. She didn't need anything else from this person.

'I'm not your enemy,' he said, stepping closer. She must have flinched in some way as he immediately stepped back again, holding up his hands.

'Why are you here?' she repeated.

'I was in a plane. It crashed.'

Hannah remembered what Josef and Elias had told her just after she had arrived. How a British plane had flown into the mountain. Nobody had survived, they'd said. But they had been wrong.

'I'm not your enemy, Sofia.'

The similarities between George's situation and hers, both now and at the Meyers', weren't lost on Hannah. Weren't they both hiding from the same people?

'You speak German well,' she said.

He laughed – a little nervously, she thought. 'My grandmother was German. My grandfather was English. When the last war began, they had to make a choice. They chose England.'

He could just as easily have been on Germany's side. She wondered about the decisions her own grandparents had made. How their choices had affected her parents. How two separate families had moved from Poland to Stuttgart and so enabled her parents to meet. To have a child.

She and George stared at each other in the semi-darkness. She took her hand from the rope. She needed to think about everything. And there was a lot now to think about. But first she needed what she came for.

'Did you enjoy the cake?' she asked.

He nodded. 'It was delicious. You should have sent two.'

Hannah smiled back. 'And did you get the note?'

'Yes, I got the note.'

'Can I see it?'

'You don't believe me?'

'I'd just like to see it.'

'I'm sorry,' said George. 'I don't have it.'

'You don't?' She felt the little hope she had allowed herself vanish.

'I am sorry. I don't understand. I burned it. If they ever found me, you would be in trouble. Just for knowing I was here. I shouldn't really have eaten the cake. I thought it was from your aunt. Until I read the note.'

'It doesn't matter.' Hannah hung her head. 'It's not important. It was nice to meet you, George. I need to go now.'

He nodded. 'You shouldn't come again. It isn't safe.'

She knew that. But they had something in common, and it wasn't just Aunt Maud.

She pulled the door closed and began to descend, though her heart was way ahead of the rest of her.

Aunt Maud knocked on her door a little while later.

Hannah was sitting on her chair, staring out at the fog, picturing Elias materialising out of it.

'Come in,' she said, without turning. What did Aunt Maud want now? Was she going to tell her to buck up and stop playing silly games?

But she surprised Hannah by asking, 'Did you and Frau Meinhardt sort out the confusion? At Frau Lister's?'

Confusion. There was so much of it inside her at the moment. Where was Elias? Surely, he had to be somewhere, didn't he? Was he safe? Was he scared? Was he hurt? She didn't want to think about that. And why him? Why hadn't anybody else gone missing? And why was she the only one who could remember him, when others were closer and had known him for longer? What made her so different?

Hannah remained looking out the window and shook her head at Aunt Maud's question. If she thought hard enough, could she make Elias appear? Was that any more magical than being able to leave her body and float around outside of it? Could her ability to leave her body have anything to do with it? Hadn't Elias disappeared on the night she had done just that? When she had seen that creature in her room?

'Well, I'm sure it will get sorted one way or the other,' Aunt Maud's voice cut into her thoughts.

Hannah barely nodded. She wasn't sure she believed it would.

'I'll see you downstairs for dinner.'

Hannah heard the door gently close, and Aunt Maud's footsteps retreating.

FORTY

'Your aunt's acting strange,' said Josef. He closed the door behind him.

'She always acts strange,' replied Hannah. Although she looked at Aunt Maud differently now, after meeting George, trying to find a hint of the person who would hold such a dangerous secret.

'Stranger than usual. She smiled at me.'

Hannah allowed herself a small smile, too. Josef ambled over and slumped down on the bed next to her. It was good to see him again. She had missed him. She hadn't seen him since their altercation here, in her room, the previous weekend. Since then, she had barely left the house. Frau Meinhardt hadn't come, either, since their trip to Frau Lister's. Aunt Maud had received a message that she wasn't well. Hannah had spent much of her time thinking, trying to come up with an explanation for Elias's disappearance. And worrying. Because, whatever had happened to him, wherever he was, it couldn't be good.

'How's school?' asked Hannah, more to break the awkward silence than anything.

'It's okay.' He sat down on the bed opposite her and clasped his hands tight on his lap. He chewed at his bottom lip. 'I'm sorry. For not remembering.'

Her heart lifted. Now it was her turn. 'That's okay. I can't blame you. Nobody remembers him. Not even his grandmother.'

His nod was barely perceptible. 'I wish I could. He sounds nice.'

'He was.' She corrected herself. 'He is.' She rubbed at her eyes. Just thinking about him made her stomach lurch. 'I'm so worried about him.'

'So, how do we explain it?' asked Josef.

He was trying, she could see.

'I can't. The memory of him, of us all together, is so strong in my mind . . .'

'And he's not there at all in mine,' said Josef.

'Or anybody else's.'

'The first day I came to the house,' said Josef, 'you asked me to tell you about the village. And I told you it was boring.'

Of course, Elias had been there, too, but she could only repeat herself so many times. 'I remember.'

'Well, it is. So we could do with an adventure. I'll help you.'

'Help me?' Could she hope to believe what she was hearing?

'To find Elias.'

She felt a grin break out on her face. 'You will?'

'I will. What do you need me to do?'

The grin faded. She hadn't thought this far ahead. 'I don't know.'

'You've been to his home?'

She nodded.

'And checked the school?'

This was encouraging. He was asking all the right questions.

'Frau Meinhardt doesn't know him. And she was his teacher. But I haven't checked inside the school. Is there somewhere in the school that somebody could hide?'

Josef frowned, shook his head. 'Not for this long.' He didn't seem to have any other ideas. 'Why Elias? Why hasn't anybody else gone missing?'

Hannah had been asking herself the exact same thing for days. 'Maybe they have,' she said, shrugging.

'I don't know of anybody else. Do you?'

'We wouldn't, would we? If we couldn't remember them?'

Josef screwed his mouth to the side and nodded. 'But *you* can remember him. What makes you so special?'

This was it. She had to open up now, had to trust Josef with her secret.

'Perhaps he was a ghost,' continued Josef.

'What? A ghost?'

'Elias. A ghost that only you could see.'

Hannah shook her head, thrown off course by Josef's change in direction. 'He wasn't a ghost, Josef. You spoke to him. Played football with him. Tidied Aunt Maud's study with him.'

He stared down at his lap, and she suddenly felt sorry. He was trying. But the mention of a ghost brought back a memory.

'That was what Elias said about the person in the attic.'

'What?'

'That it was a ghost.'

'Ghosts don't eat cake.'

Should she tell him about George? She wanted to, but telling Josef could put George at risk, as well as Aunt Maud. And her. And Josef. Had Sofia, the real Sofia, or any of the Meyers, ever revealed *their* secret to anybody? But this was different. Elias had disappeared. There was something strange going on in the village, she knew it, and Hannah couldn't help but wonder whether, somehow, George was connected to it.

'I went up there,' she said, before she had any more time to consider it. And once the words were out, it was too late to take them back. If she wanted Josef to help her find Elias, she had to tell him everything about what she knew.

Josef's face lit up. 'You did? Did you see anybody?'

He listened as she quietly told him about George. How he had been in the plane that had crashed and that, for some reason, Aunt Maud was hiding him. There was an underlying feeling of guilt as she spoke. A betrayal of George's trust.

'Do you think he's dangerous?'

Hannah shook her head. 'I don't think so. He looks sad. Scared.'

'I suppose it must be frightening. Locked up in a room for months, not knowing how you're ever going to get home.'

Hannah could attest to this.

'Are you going to visit him again?'

Hannah shrugged.

'Are you sure your aunt hasn't locked him up there? She doesn't seem the kind of person to . . .'

'. . . to risk her own safety for a stranger? I know. I thought the same.'

'Have you asked her?'

Hannah shook her head. 'She'd get in a lot of trouble. I mean, he's the enemy. And I don't think she'd be happy if she knew I'd found out.' She lowered her voice. 'We have to keep this between us, Josef. I trust you.'

'I like that you trust me.'

Hannah took her chance. 'Now I need you to trust *me*. I think I know why I'm the only one who can remember Elias.'

Josef sat perfectly still, his eyes alight. 'You do?'

Hannah nodded.

'Go on then. Tell me.'

'Do you trust me?'

'You're my best friend,' said Josef. 'Of course I trust you.'

And that was all Hannah needed to hear. 'The night Elias disappeared, I was here in my room.'

'So?'

'But my body was downstairs in the parlour. Fast asleep.'

FORTY-ONE

Josef sat and listened as Hannah told him about her first experience at the hospital, then her journey to the second floor and how she had wandered from her body on the night of The Old Man's Bones. She didn't mention the strange creature she had seen in her room. The passage of time and the fact that it hadn't reappeared had gone a long way to convincing her that that part, at least, had been nothing more than a dream.

'What does it feel like?' he asked her. 'How do you do it? Are you scared when you do it?' He asked lots of questions, but he didn't believe her, she could tell.

So she promised to prove it to him that night. Or to try to. She had never fallen asleep with the intention of leaving her body before. And she had never travelled outside. She didn't know how far from her body she could go. She couldn't move through walls or closed doors and windows, she told him. He would have to allow her a way in.

With more than a hint of scepticism in his voice, Josef agreed.

That night, she fell asleep with the sole intention of leaving her body, carrying this thought at the forefront of her mind into the realms of slumber. Some time later, she gazed down upon herself sleeping, tucked deep under the covers, trying to keep warm while the cold air wafted in through the open window.

With nothing but thought for an engine, she propelled herself over to the window and out. She hovered high above the snow, a ghost in the fog, with the exciting yet disconcerting realisation that she could travel anywhere. She didn't know whether there was a limit to how far she could go, but she was about to test it, and she tried to shake off the worry of somebody closing the window and preventing her from returning to her body.

Across the snowy square she soared. There were no lights on in the houses. The whole village was asleep.

She took a left down Dorfstrasse and counted the houses.

The third along. And there!

She saw the open window and slowed her travel, floating over and lingering for a moment outside.

Then she was in.

Josef was huddled deep inside thick sheets, just like she had been. *And still am*, she reminded herself. He was breathing heavily, lost in sleep.

A dog barked from outside and her heart skipped a beat. She quickly scoured the room and found what she was looking for, though it did nothing to calm her. Hannah had been right. Josef hadn't really believed that she could leave her body. If he had, he wouldn't have written what he did on the note she had asked him to leave on his bedside table.

I am very glad that Sofia Meyer has come to live in the village. One day, when the war is over, I will ask her to marry me.

Our next conversation, thought Hannah, is going to be an awkward one.

FORTY-TWO

'So, what's the plan to find Elias?' asked Josef after school a few days later.

Hannah shrugged. 'I know what isn't the plan.'

Josef flicked his eyebrows at her as he went to sit down.

'To get married.'

He didn't get it at first. Then, as he lowered himself down, his face reddened.

'I am also very glad that I have come to live in the village, Josef. One day, when the war is over . . .'

His cheeks turned crimson. 'What? How did you . . .?'

Hannah rocked back on her chair and burst out laughing. 'Your face, Josef Kleftmann!'

Josef was just staring at her, and for a minute Hannah thought he was going to storm out of her room. But then a smile broke free on his face and he fell backwards onto her bed and the two of them were roaring with laughter.

'This is so embarrassing,' said Josef, when he had got his laughter under control. He rubbed at his eyes and sat up. 'And amazing. How do you do it?'

She shrugged. 'I don't know. It just started happening like I told you, after the bomb.'

'What's it like?'

She described it the best she could. The feeling of weightlessness, the lack of touch and smell, the ability to still see and hear.

'I wish I could do it,' said Josef. 'So, what is the plan? If getting married isn't an option.'

It was Hannah's turn to feel her face heat up.

'We need to step through everything we've done together since we met,' said Hannah. 'Maybe something will trigger your memory of Elias. Or remind me of something he said.' Everything left a trace in the world. That was what it came down to.

'That makes sense.'

Hannah let him speak. She wanted to know what he knew.

'I saw you first at that window.' He glanced behind Hannah. 'I broke your aunt's pot.'

'She hasn't forgotten.'

'I know. And she made me come back and do some chores. To pay for it.'

'But you don't remember Elias coming with you to help?'

Josef thought for a few seconds. He shook his head. 'It's all a bit hazy. I remember working hard. Your aunt telling me what to do. I think she helped. Then you came down and we met. And we went around the house and out into the backyard and fed the chickens.'

'But no Elias?'

Just a shake of the head.

They stepped through their memories. They were the same except, of course, Elias was missing from Josef's, even when they went to visit Frau Lister.

'I often visit her,' he said. 'She bakes fresh stollen. She went to school with my grandmother and she's a close friend of my family.'

And on through the memories. Until they got to the day the fog came.

'It always comes like that at this time of year,' said Josef.

'You told me that on the day,' said Hannah. 'It was after we were talking about The Old Man's Bones.'

'And before Herr Schundel startled us, waving around that tin of pebbles.'

They stared at each other, silent and wide-eyed.

'*Try not to forget . . .*' said Hannah. 'That was what he said. Before Aunt Maud dragged us away. But I had the feeling he wanted to say something else.'

'Do you think he knows something?' asked Josef.

She wasn't sure, but for the first time since Elias had gone missing, she had something to focus on.

'Where does he live?' asked Hannah.

'A small cottage outside the village.'

'How well do you know him?'

'Not well. I don't know why he hasn't been sent away to fight like all the other men. But he comes to the school some days.'

'The school?' She had wanted to go there herself not long ago. Now she wasn't sure she could face it. She would be forever looking out for Elias. 'Why?'

'He fixes things around the village. And at the school. Sometimes he sits in the playground and watches us play.'

'That's weird. Just watches you?'

Josef nodded. 'He mumbles to himself and points, like this.' He jabbed his finger around the room from left to right. 'When he's finished, he starts all over again.'

'Why does he do that?'

Josef shrugged. 'It's like when we go for trips into the forest in the summer. When we get back, the teachers do the same thing. Like . . .'

I'm better with faces. Numbers, too. Not names.

'Like he's counting you. Like he's making sure nobody's missing,' said Hannah, a slight hope beginning to dawn.

A light seemed to come on in Josef's eyes. 'Yes, but also – it's as if he's trying to memorise each of us, one by one.'

FORTY-THREE

The following Saturday, Hannah met Josef at the agreed spot – on the bridge that led out of the village. The snow had all but melted now, but it was still there in places, dirty drifts lingering at street verges, like tufts of hair on the sides of a bald man's head. The fog hung still and thick, attenuating any sounds coming from its hidden depths. She heard Josef's footsteps well before she saw him.

'You're the only thing that cuts through this fog,' he quipped as he appeared out of it. 'There's no chance of getting lost wearing that.'

She glanced down at her red coat. The one that the Oberstleutnant had given her. That used to belong to his daughter.

'You, on the other hand,' she replied, looking back up at his mostly grey outfit, 'do not. You'd better stay close.'

Together, they continued over the bridge and into the forest, where the cobbles gave way to a snowy track with just a few sets of footprints travelling each way. Then they, too, disappeared. If Aunt Maud had known where they were going, the journey would have ended at the front door. But Hannah had waited for her to go out with her basket of darned clothing before she left.

The smell of smoke subsided. The cottages became less frequent, the forest closer. A few houses appeared empty, almost derelict, though Hannah couldn't get rid of the feeling that she and Josef were being watched from their cracked and dusty windows.

'That's it,' said Josef, as a small cottage grew out of the mist.

Hannah could see a smart and tidy house that was certainly in better condition than those she'd seen on the outskirts of the village. The render was smooth and clean, the roof tiles intact. And the wooden window frames and door looked freshly painted.

Herr Schundel was a man who took care of his home.

So why were three of the four windows broken, glass shards jutting out of those perfectly painted frames? And why was the door ajar, the jamb splintered, a dark boot print stamped upon one of its light-green panels. It reminded Hannah a little too much of scenes from back home . . .

'This is definitely Herr Schundel's house?' asked Hannah.

Josef nodded, concern etched into his forehead. 'I'll take a look inside,' he said.

Hannah was feeling spooked. 'I'll come with you.' The thought of being out here by herself seemed worse than going inside.

Josef shook his head. 'Somebody needs to keep a lookout. And if we have to get out quickly . . . your leg.'

He had a point. She was fine walking. It had barely ached on the way here. But they had taken it slow. If they had to make a fast escape, she wasn't sure she'd be able to run.

'Okay. But be quick.'

'It's only a small house.' He made his way through the opening in the low stone wall and up the ramshackle path. The sharp crunch of dry snow beneath his feet receded with every steady step.

'Herr Schundel!' Josef's voice sounded clamorous in the encroaching mist. 'Herr Schundel, it's Josef Kleftmann! Are you here?' He reached out and pushed away a thin branch. It snapped and fell to the ground. The fog intensified, the house disappeared. Josef began to fade. Then he, too, was gone.

Hannah craned her neck. She glanced left, then right, then up at the barely visible cable strung out above her. The world was nothing but a memory.

A minute or so passed.

'Josef.' Not a shout. It didn't need to be.

No reply.

Hannah stepped forward. She felt lost here in the empty forever. Lost and cold.

'Josef.' A little louder this time.

Nothing.

What if he had fallen and injured himself?

A sound from behind made her spin round. But there was nothing. She turned back.

And there he was.

'Josef?' He was creeping backwards, growing out of the fog. She couldn't see beyond him. The path, the bushes, the house were still lost.

Josef turned his head slowly and brought an index finger to his lips. His eyes were imploring. *Quiet.* The fog beyond him parted like curtains at the beginning of a performance, revealing the stage decorated with bushes and the house as a backdrop.

Josef stepped to the side.

A lone wolf stood there. Its head was down, though its eyes remained fixed on Josef, as though nothing else mattered. He took another step back. The wolf took one forward. It drew back its lips to reveal a mass of ravenous teeth. A low growl grew from within.

A second wolf appeared out of the fog behind it.

Another step back for Josef.

A third wolf. All eyes were on Josef.

And then the first wolf's gaze shifted. It had spotted her.

Hannah was no longer feeling the cold, only those hungry eyes upon her.

'Stay still, Sofia,' pleaded Josef.

'What?' Every piece of her wanted to run.

'Trust me. We get taught. In school.'

Josef slowly bent and dug his hand into the snow. Keeping his gaze straight ahead, he gouged a rock out of the ground.

The closest wolf leaned back on its haunches, ready to pounce. It was all teeth and snarls.

Josef's scream shattered the stillness. He raised his arm to throw the rock, but he was too slow. By the time he had launched it, the leader of the pack had begun its attack. Pulling its lips all the way back from its teeth, it let out a growl and leaped towards Josef.

Hannah turned to escape.

An explosion from the trees changed everything in an instant.

FORTY-FOUR

Hannah opened her eyes. The wolves were gone. Josef was folded in a heap on the ground. Had he been shot? No, he gradually lifted his head and stared at a point beyond her.

Breathless and freezing, she turned and followed his gaze.

The soldier stared back, his gun now pointing at them.

'Back away!' shouted the soldier. 'Slowly!' His face was ruddy, his cheeks the colour of rhubarb stalks. Puffs of mist billowed from his mouth, dissipating into the fog. He spat the words between heavy breaths, his eyes darting from Josef to Hannah and back again.

'Back away!'

She did as she was told, careful not to trip, until she was up against the wall.

The soldier stepped forward, thrusting the barrel of the gun out of the fog. 'You!' His focus was now entirely on Josef.

Her friend pushed himself up onto his knees and went to brush off his coat.

'Hands! In the air!' Every word the soldier spoke was an interjection. His knuckles were white and Hannah feared he was on the verge of pressing that trigger. She was beginning to see dark pulses every time her heart beat inside her chest.

Josef raised his arms and struggled to his feet. First one leg, then the other. His eyes glistened. His hands shook. 'We were just –'

'Turn around!'

Josef did nothing but stare and shake.

'Turn around!'

'Josef, do as he says.' Hannah knew what soldiers were capable of. He could shoot them both here and now.

The soldier pointed the gun at Hannah, and she instinctively turned her face away. But it was soon back on Josef, who shuffled himself around like an old man who has forgotten where he is, his trembling hands reaching for the hidden sky. The soldier marched up to him, lowered his gun and began to frisk him through his thick clothes. Hannah watched in horror, too frightened to speak.

When the soldier was satisfied that Josef wasn't armed, he turned to Hannah. 'You! Turn!'

She did so, her hands above her head, as the soldier swept over her back, her sides, down her legs. Then he swung her back around, stepped away and pointed the rifle at Josef's head.

He flicked the gun to his left. 'Walk!'

Josef obeyed.

Then the gun was at her. Another flick. 'Walk!'

She heard the soldier following behind, and when she turned to look, all she could see was the barrel of that gun.

'Don't look at me. Look at your friend.'

Once more, Hannah was filled with fear. For herself and her friend.

They headed away from the village.

FORTY-FIVE

The fog thinned as they climbed up through the forest. The snow became deeper, and the ache in Hannah's leg returned, then grew to a point where she worried about putting weight on it. She didn't know what damage she was doing but feared that, if she and Josef got through this, she would be back in plaster. And in a lot of trouble with Aunt Maud. Her breathing became more laboured, her body weaker. Josef was puffing and panting, staggering. Each step was hard and slow.

In a small clearing, her toes caught against a jutting rock and she stumbled onto her knees, crying out.

Josef turned. The soldier raised his gun.

'She has an injured leg! At least let me help her.' His teeth were clenched. His fists, too.

The soldier lowered the gun and flicked his head. Josef trudged back and helped her to her feet. He put his arm around her waist, she put hers around his shoulders, and together they traipsed on.

Eventually, the forest opened up and, beyond a gently rising field of virgin snow, a tall sepia-coloured wall ascended into the blinding fog. Three deer, grazing at the edge of the clearing, snapped their heads up. After no more than a second or two they vanished as one into the nearby trees.

'It's the castle,' she whispered. A ripple of fear ran through her. It looked ominous, threatening. But there was also a flutter of hope. The Oberstleutnant. He could make things right, couldn't he?

Three storeys of arched windows, then four, grew out of the fog. As they got closer still, she could see battlements at the top of the wall, though the upper reaches of the turrets remained hidden.

They arrived at a set of steps leading up to a large wooden door. The soldier told them to stop at the base of the stairs. He marched past them, up the steps, and knocked. The door swung open. A guard stepped out, and words were exchanged. The soldier turned and waved his rifle at them. Together, Hannah and Josef climbed the steps and walked past the two men, through the door and into a short, dark tunnel. The air was immediately warmer, with a musty, wooden smell. She and Josef were both shaking. They stumbled over the now-cobbled ground, past closed doors and below wooden beams.

And emerged into a different world.

They were back outside, but there was no sign of snow. On the opposite side of the courtyard, more steps led up to the main building and, though the three turrets and multitude of smaller ones were far higher than those behind them, they were fully exposed, framed against a bright blue sky. They had risen above the fog.

Lights burned in windows, and cables were strung around the structure, disappearing over the wall and into the forest below. From somewhere around the side of the castle came a low hum. The sheer size of the castle took Hannah's breath away. But that wasn't what made her gasp for air and almost collapse to her knees. Suspended and draped down over three storeys were two huge red and white flags, each emblazoned with that insidious, crooked black cross.

After running from the soldiers for so long, she had finally ended up in their lair. How foolish she had been to think the Oberstleutnant would save her. This was his home, and she was now his prisoner.

Half-a-dozen army trucks were parked against the wall to their left. She hadn't seen a motor vehicle since arriving at the village, hadn't thought it possible to bring them up here, especially in the middle of winter. But Pieter had spoken of an easier way up the mountain, she remembered. That the route they had taken was harder, but they were guaranteed not to come across any soldiers.

An entrance gate to their right swung open and the sound of an engine joined with the hum of machinery. A large, shiny black automobile entered, twin flags flying from its front, and Hannah had time to see that the road outside was also cleared of snow.

The soldier had stopped to watch the vehicle's path. It slowed to a halt at the base of the stairs leading up to the main building. Hannah held on tight to Josef, who was beginning to teeter.

The front door of the vehicle opened. A soldier stepped out and pulled open the car's rear door in one swift movement. A man dressed from head to foot in black commanded the attention of everyone in the courtyard. Around the top of his arm was a band that matched the giant flags hanging above them. The uniform of the SS. Hannah felt all the air leave her lungs as she gasped. The SS soldier straightened his collar and pulled at the cuffs of his coat as the driver saluted him, and Hannah recognised him. The Oberstleutnant.

Something made the Oberstleutnant turn in their direction. Hannah noticed the soldier who had brought them here tense. He straightened his uniform and adjusted his helmet, unslung his rifle, held it diagonally across his chest and stamped his feet. Finally, he gave a salute. Arm straight, angled towards the sky.

The Oberstleutnant's eyes flicked from the soldier to Hannah, then back again. The charm he normally exuded was gone. With pursed lips and daggers for eyes, he marched up so close that the two men's shoes were almost touching. He looked terrifying, murderous.

'What is this?'

It gave Hannah some satisfaction to hear the quiver in the soldier's voice. 'Sir, I found them at . . .' He glanced down at Hannah.

'Don't look at her! Look at me!'

His head snapped back up. 'Sir!'

'Why are they here?'

The solder flinched as some spittle flew from the Oberstleutnant's mouth.

'Sir, they were on the property.'

'What? Never mind! You can explain later!' He pushed past the soldier to Hannah, the wickedness dropping from his face like a hawk from the sky. It was replaced by his usual look of concern and sincerity. 'I am so sorry, Sofia. You must be frozen. But it is good to see you in that coat. It fits well.'

She was too tired, too scared, to respond.

'Let me get you inside, where it's warm. Find you something to eat.' He took hold of her hand and began to lead her away. She did all she could not to pull away from him, remembering the tale of 'The Runaway Pancake', who had climbed onto the back of the fox to escape, only to be eaten.

'Josef ...' she said, turning back. He looked ready to collapse, barely aware of his surroundings.

'Help the boy!' exclaimed the Oberstleutnant, and, to Hannah's surprise, the soldier slung his rifle onto his back, bent and hoisted Josef over his other shoulder. Josef couldn't have been that light, but Hannah thought his weight was nothing compared to the burden the soldier would soon be bearing.

FORTY-SIX

Hannah fought to keep the terror from bubbling up and out of control as they entered the castle. There were soldiers everywhere, some carrying guns, others with clipboards; some dressed in grey, others in that maleficent black. She could sense a trembling in her limbs, and hoped it wasn't being felt by the Oberstleutnant through the hand he was holding. Josef was now steady upon his feet and, the one time she turned to face him, he gave her a nod to say he was okay. But he looked as petrified as she felt.

They entered a hall that boasted high cathedral ceilings suspended upon golden arched beams, its walls decorated with dramatic hunting scenes – bloodied bears speared by men on horseback, wolves baring their teeth at soldiers wielding swords and daggers. Hannah thought back to how the Oberstleutnant had joked about the castle being abandoned and disused, occupied by nothing but wolves and bears. He could not have been more misleading. The great windows were alive with sunlit stories that cast a myriad of colours upon the chequered floor. Every sound became an echo.

The Oberstleutnant's voice boomed at the soldier to take Josef to the medical unit. Hannah didn't want to leave him and, from the look on Josef's face, he felt the same. But the Oberstleutnant assured them both that they were in good hands. A message would be sent to her aunt and to Josef's mother to let them know they were both safe, he said.

Hannah followed the Oberstleutnant up another staircase, past portraits of noblemen and women whose eyes seemed to follow her up and around to the balcony. He led her down a long, bright corridor and into a room that was bigger than a whole floor of the lodge. It led into a bathroom, and the Oberstleutnant told her he would leave her to remove her wet clothes and warm up with a hot bath. There were clean towels in the room, but somebody would be sent along with dry clothes.

'I see your plaster has been removed. How does your ankle feel?'

'It aches. But I can move it.'

'We shall get it checked out by a medic once you are warmed up. I wouldn't want to get on the wrong side of your aunt.' Despite the black uniform, the soldier had all but disappeared from his personality.

He left her there, in the most sumptuous room she had ever visited, promising to return her and Josef to their homes after a warm meal.

Hannah lay in the spacious tub, relishing the water that was actually warm. She closed her eyes, the treacherous journey to the castle gradually fading into the background of her mind.

The sound of light footsteps from the adjacent room pulled her from her restful state and made her remember where she was. In a castle, surrounded by Nazi soldiers. She tensed and suddenly wanted to check on Josef.

She climbed from the bath, wrapped a towel around herself and made her way to the door. The girl standing there was around the same age as Hannah, but a little taller. Her hair was cut short, and her clothes were plain and worn. There was something familiar about her.

She held out a bundle of purple and orange, which Hannah realised was a dress. On top, neatly folded, were some undergarments and a pair of shoes.

'I was asked to bring you a change of clothes,' said the girl. She smiled, but Hannah could see there was no happiness there. The girl's eyes flicked away. When they came back to her, she held an index finger to her mouth.

'Do I know you?' asked Hannah, but the girl's widening eyes told her not to continue. Hannah was sure they had met, but couldn't quite place her.

'Yes, just leave the wet towels here. I'll collect them later.'

The way she stared at Hannah, imploring her not to ask the question that was on her mind, convinced Hannah to play along. Someone must be listening in.

'All right,' said Hannah. 'Thank you.'

A soldier appeared in the doorway out to the hallway. The girl lowered her head and turned away.

'The Oberstleutnant says you are to stay for dinner, Fraulein Meyer. He will see you there at six, with the boy.' Then, to the girl. 'You, come with me.'

Without another look, the girl crept off, shoulders hunched and head down. When she reached the doorway, the soldier wrapped his hand around the top of her arm and roughly pulled her through, all the time keeping his eyes on Hannah.

Hannah maintained his gaze until the door was closed. The memory was hazy, but she was sure she recognised the girl. But how? From where?

She got dressed, all the time wondering about the girl. Was she a servant? She was young, but Hannah knew that some children were put to work at that age. She put on the dress, underwear, socks. And then the shoes.

The left one went on okay, but the toes of her right wouldn't go all the way in. There was something in the shoe. She pulled it back off her foot and poked her fingers inside.

A piece of paper. She pulled it out and unfolded it.

Please help me. My name is Matilda Weber. My brother is Boris. You met us on the bridge when you were with Josef Kleftmann. I know now that the Oberstleutnant is not your father. You were playing a trick on us. And we deserved it.

The soldiers came and took us from our house in Schulstrasse. They keep me here to serve, but I don't know where Boris is. Please let my parents know where I am and help them to find my brother. He can be a bully sometimes, I know. But I love him.

Don't let the Oberstleutnant find this letter. Destroy it, or he'll hurt you.

I'm sorry.

Matilda Weber

Bits of memories came tumbling back into Hannah's mind. She *did* know the girl. But something was stopping the full memory from unveiling itself. There was an altercation, she thought, but the details wouldn't reveal themselves. She'd still had her crutches. And yes, Josef was with her. But she couldn't remember anyone called Boris.

Hannah's heart was thumping away in her ears. Matilda Weber. A girl from the village. Taken from her house with her brother and kept here against her will. And, up until a few minutes ago, until Hannah saw her face, she had forgotten all about the girl.

Had Boris and Matilda disappeared from her memory, just like Elias had from everybody else's?

Destroy the letter, Matilda had written. But shouldn't Hannah keep it? Tuck it back inside her shoe to show Josef and Aunt Maud? The Oberstleutnant had told her a medic would be sent to check her leg. They would need to remove her shoe, maybe both of them. No, it was best to get rid of it. She glanced at the toilet bowl. But before she did, she would read it again. And memorise it.

FORTY-SEVEN

'This castle has been rebuilt and added to several times,' said the Oberstleutnant. He was out of uniform, dressed in a blue suit, white shirt and blue tie. His black shoes were polished to a bright sheen and his hair, usually oiled and swept back, fell in feathery strands across his forehead. Josef was looking better, the colour having returned to his cheeks and his mood restored. Hannah's leg had been checked, as promised, by a medic. She would be sore for a few days, he'd said, but there didn't appear to be any permanent damage.

The three of them were seated at a large table in a room off the side of the main hall. Occasional gunshots could be heard from the land behind the castle, which the Oberstleutnant told them were just from soldiers on training exercises. They had enjoyed a hearty meal of roast lamb in gravy, potatoes and parsnips. Hannah couldn't remember the last time she had eaten so well and, by the look on Josef's face as he shovelled it into his mouth, he felt the same.

A fire blazed in the centre of the far wall, and every so often somebody would silently and discreetly enter the room and add some more wood. Along the opposite wall, glass cabinets displayed goblets, medals and artefacts. Beams of light from the high windows warmed wintry scenes of the forest and castle. It seemed that, despite the village being hidden below dense and dreary fog, the castle was forever in sunlight. Above the fireplace, a longsword and battleaxe were crossed in combat beneath a stag's head.

Hannah had to wonder why the Oberstleutnant spent any time at all at the lodge when all the comforts he could desire were here.

'I expect you've heard many stories about the castle, most of which hold no truth whatsoever. But what is a castle without a fairytale attached to it?' He wiped at his mouth with a napkin.

Josef was busy scraping invisible streaks of gravy from his plate and licking them from his knife. The Oberstleutnant shot him a look of disapproval. The boy removed the knife from his mouth and gently laid it down onto his plate.

The man continued. 'The rear part of the castle, however, is thought to be the original, dating back to the fourteenth century. Have you ever visited a castle, Sofia?'

Hannah shook her head. 'No, Herr Kessler.'

'And, young man, I'm assuming the same goes for you?'

'Never.'

'I thought not. I'm sure the only times the village children came here were if they had done something wrong. And there's probably a very good chance they never went home again.' He took a long drink, while Hannah tried to hide her unease at his words.

'Who lives here now?' asked Hannah, trying to feign interest.

He cast his arms wide. 'Everybody you see lives here. It's not so much a home to them, I'll give you that. More of a . . . base. One of many across the Fatherland.'

'Doesn't the Graf live here?' frowned Josef.

'No, no, no,' chuckled the Oberstleutnant. 'Despite the stories you may have heard, there hasn't been a graf in the castle for a hundred years or more.'

'What happened to the last one?' asked Hannah.

'Like so many around the country, he became too rich and greedy, and the villagers decided they'd had enough.'

Hannah glanced at Josef, who was eyeing the remaining streaks of gravy on his plate. 'Did you know that, Josef?'

Josef shook his head. 'I only know the story Frau Lister told us. My grandmother told me the same story.'

The Oberstleutnant leaned back in his chair. 'Ah yes, "The Old Man's Bones".'

'You don't believe it?' asked Hannah.

'Do you?'

Hannah felt stupid. Of course she didn't. It was no more true than 'Cinderella' or 'Rumpelstiltskin'. Though she remembered what Pieter had told her on the way up the mountain. 'Not all of it. But it's probably based in truth,' she replied.

'I agree,' the Oberstleutnant said, nodding thoughtfully. 'Some of it has to be true. Something in every story has to be true, even if it's just the fact that some people are good and some people are not. Tell me, have either of you heard the tale of Edgar and Otto?'

Hannah and Josef shook their heads.

'No,' said the Oberstleutnant. 'I didn't think so.' Another sip from the goblet. 'It is a tale from another village, another castle. The Castle of Schwarzberg, to be precise, which is older than the village it overlooks. Some say it is older than the forest. The same family lived there for centuries, handing it down as each generation passed on. The village grew around it, as people sought protection from invading armies and uprisings.

'The peasants farmed the land, paid whatever taxes were owed, and the two existed side by side for centuries. Even the peasant uprising of four hundred years ago could do nothing to upset the balance that existed there.'

'Uprising?' asked Hannah.

'Yes, all over a snail's shell,' laughed the Oberstleutnant. 'But that is another story.'

'Did the peasants win?' Josef was leaning forward, mirroring the Oberstleutnant's stance.

'I'm afraid not. They were slaughtered in their thousands.'

Josef collapsed back. Hannah couldn't help but notice a glint of satisfaction in the Oberstleutnant's eyes. Was it because of the defeat of the peasants, or because he had disappointed Josef?

She wasn't sure that she wanted to hear this tale, but didn't think she should say so. Something had shifted again in the Oberstleutnant's manner. He looked at Josef in a way that sent shivers down Hannah's spine as he began telling his tale.

'This story starts with two young boys, not much older than you are, young man. The castle was, and still is, a grand place, built high onto the edge of the mountain, with a view out over the world below. There was much to do to keep it working – rooms to be cleaned and swept, candles to be kept burning, rats to be poisoned – to name but a few. And many of the villagers were kept busy there, providing luxury to one man and his two sons.

'The two sons were twins named Edgar and Otto. Their mother had died in childbirth while the Graf was away on business. In the ensuing panic nobody knew, or at the time really cared, which son was the eldest. However, as was the way, only one of them could inherit the title of graf, and all the riches that came with it …'

By now, Josef had settled silently back into his chair. And, as the Oberstleutnant continued the tale, Hannah found herself transfixed by his voice, almost as though the story were happening around her right there and then.

FORTY-EIGHT

One winter's day, the Graf and his two sons were out hunting. In the valley on the far side of the mountain, they spotted a lone wolf asleep in the middle of a frozen lake. It was an odd sight – wolves were rarely seen out in the open, and never alone.

The three of them rode their horses to the edge of the lake. The wolf raised its head and stared at them. Still, it did not stand up and run. It did not appear at all concerned.

'Shall we take it?' asked Edgar.

'It hardly seems fair,' replied the Graf. 'It's such an easy target.'

'I want to.' Edgar dismounted and stepped upon the ice, took the bow from his side and an arrow from his back. The wolf seemed to smile at Edgar, daring him to take the shot.

'It's too far away,' said Edgar. 'I can get closer.' He began to creep towards the lone wolf, preparing himself to take the shot if the animal stood up to leave. But it did not move. A few more steps and he was close enough. He raised the bow and stared down the arrow at the grey and white beast.

'Hold it steady,' said his father from close behind him.

Edgar did just that before he heard his father's shriek and felt the ice below his feet tilt. He reached out for his father's hand as the man sank below the freezing water. He caught it, but his father's weight was too much. He wouldn't be able to hold him. He was going to be dragged down with him if he didn't let go.

And then Otto was there, reaching down into the water and grabbing the man's hair. And between them both, with all the strength they had, they lifted their shivering father back onto the ice and helped him back to the edge of the frozen lake.

When they turned to look, the wolf was gone.

Several years later, an old travelling magician arrived in the village. Word quickly spread of the tricks he could perform – that they were truly magic – and so the Graf summoned the magician to the castle to give a performance for him and his sons. He invited the nobility from nearby villages and put on a great feast. The magician entertained them by pulling animals from his hat, turning walls into water and making people act like donkeys. There was one trick he performed that particularly intrigued Edgar and, when the magician had finished, the boy found the courage to go up and talk to him.

'How did you do that?' he asked.

'Do what?' asked the magician. His shoulders were hunched and his skin pallid but, despite his advanced years, his eyes were the colour of the summer sky.

'How did you make the rabbit disappear?'

'And the bear,' said the old man. 'Remember how I made the bear disappear, as if it had never existed.'

'There was no bear,' said Edgar, scratching his head.

'Precisely,' replied the magician. He rubbed his hands together and placed his arm around the boy's shoulder, guiding him away from everybody else. 'Why are you asking? Is there somebody you would like me to make disappear?' He turned his head and looked directly at Edgar's twin brother. As he did so, Otto raised his hand in acknowledgement.

'I want my brother to disappear,' whispered Edgar. The magician raised his eyebrows, tempting one more word out of the boy. 'Forever,' finished Edgar, and the magician smiled and stood back, though one arm remained upon the boy's shoulder.

After a few seconds of silence, the old man leaned in closer and sharpened the end of his beard between his fingers. 'If I do this for you, then I ask a favour in return.'

'What is it that you want?'

'I wish, simply, to never be forgotten.'

The boy thought about this. Edgar was sure he could remember him for the remainder of his days. 'Okay. I shall never forget you.'

The magician gripped the back of Edgar's neck and pulled him close. 'That is not good enough. I want never to be forgotten. Not by you, not by your children . . . nor by the village and theirs.'

'The whole village?'

The man placed a finger to his upper lip and nodded. 'Now you must say it.'

'Say what?'

'One name is all I need.'

Edgar hesitated. Something in those blue eyes told him that once spoken, there was no going back. But like a carriage with two wheels over the edge of a ravine, he had already gone too far. 'Prince Otto.'

'There. Now I have the name. It shall be done.'

The next morning, with the magician's last words unusually fresh in his mind, Prince Edgar dressed and made his way to the Great Hall where his father was sitting at the table, his head down, enjoying a lavish meal. Edgar sat down opposite the Graf. A servant placed in front of him a plate piled with meat and fruit, but he pushed it away.

'I am not hungry,' he said, glancing at the empty chair beside him.

'You must eat,' said the Graf, without looking up.

'Do as your father says,' came a voice from behind him. A tall woman dressed in the finest silks with hair in golden ringlets was gliding across the floor. She kissed him on the forehead.

Edgar flinched and pulled away.

'That's no way to say good morning to your mother,' she scolded.

'Who . . .?' began Edgar. But, though he had never met her, he knew who she was by the picture that hung in the Great Hall. The woman who had died giving birth to him and his brother was now seemingly alive and well.

'Lost your tongue as well as your appetite?' asked the Graf, licking at his fingers and raising his head. But the man staring at him was not his father. There was no mistaking those eyes of blue. All hints of grey within the hair and beard had disappeared. The lines in the face had become shallower and fewer. The man was no longer hunched over, but sat straight and tall. And his pallor was no longer sallow, but rosy and fresh.

'You're not my father,' scowled Edgar, leaping up out of his chair.

His mother placed her slender hand on his shoulder. 'Edgar, we have spoken of this many times.'

'He is not my father!' Edgar felt the heat rising to his cheeks, the anger pitted in his stomach, the fear cradled in his heart. 'He is . . . he is a wizard!'

The magician stood and held out his hand, his face now showing nothing but remorse. 'Edgar, I know I can never be your true father. He unfortunately sank that day to the depths below the ice. I know you were unable to save him. You were but a child, alone. I am only glad I came upon you in the forest and was able to bring you home.'

The instant Edgar's mother turned away, the magician exchanged his look of sorrow for a sneer.

And at that moment, Edgar's memories split in two. He remembered growing up motherless with his twin brother, Otto; but he also remembered being the only child of the woman who now stood before him. He remembered his father falling through the ice, he and Otto struggling, and eventually pulling him to safety; but he also remembered his father slipping from his hand and sinking down below the water's surface. He remembered being on the bank of the lake, exhausted, with his father and Otto, and seeing the wolf gone; but also of sitting there alone, weeping, as the man before him appeared from nowhere to take him home.

He remembered the world where Otto was his brother, and the world where Otto had never existed.

'And since that day,' said Edgar's mother, 'he has earned the title of father and, more importantly, that of graf.'

'And he has stolen this castle and all that is rightfully mine!' sobbed Edgar, placing his head in his hands and sinking to his knees.

A few months later, Edgar's mother died. Edgar waited for the magician to follow, but years passed and the man seemed to get younger.

Edgar married. His hair turned grey. The years took their toll on all that was around him. The castle servants grew old and infirm and, one by one, they died. As did his wife. The castle fell into a state of disrepair. Bushes and brambles flourished in the courtyard. Branches grew through windows, and roots broke through floors. Wolves roamed the halls at night and slept in the chambers during the day, and only old Edgar and the young yet ancient magician were left to live amongst them.

One day, an infirm Edgar woke to the magician sitting in a chair opposite him, the wolves at his feet.

'Have you never wondered why the world turns, people die, walls crumble, yet I remain as I am?' the magician asked.

Edgar coughed. 'Sorcery,' he croaked. 'You took the youth of my brother and made it your own.'

'Yes, your brother took away my years. But a child's soul will only last so long.'

'You have taken others?' asked Edgar. 'Children from the village?'

'Have you never had children of your own?' asked the magician, sneering.

'You know that to be true. You have lived here all this time . . .'

'Are you sure about that?'

And Edgar realised. He remembered. Children running around the castle. His children, playing. But also, of never having any children. 'You took away my children . . . my future . . . my heirs!' He coughed again. 'What did you do to them?'

'The same as I did to your brother,' said the magician. 'Before they left childhood and their ability to blindly believe, I told them a very special story. One that has to be told in exactly the right way.'

'But how? What happened to them?'

The magician threw back his head and laughed. 'I was waiting for you to ask that.' His mouth straightened and he stared into Edgar's eyes. 'I ate them. But not just me. I couldn't manage a whole child. I stopped after I had consumed their souls. My own children ate the rest.'

Wolves now flocked in through the door and stood around the magician, howling. And, as Edgar watched, the magician changed back to how he had been on that day, all those years ago, at the frozen lake.

Edgar wept. His soul was filled with regret. The wolves set upon him, ripping his flesh and fighting over his organs. As for his spirit, the magician had no need for such an old, tainted soul.

It is said that the magician lived in the castle for a very long time, passing the secret tale down to his own children who, like him, were part wolf, part human. And those children are still out there, telling their tales to any child who will believe.

And we all know what happens when they do.

'They disappear,' whispered Hannah. 'As if they had never existed.' A lump rose in her throat. She felt weak and sick. She glanced over at Josef, who stared back, his eyes asking the same question.

The Oberstleutnant fixed his eyes on Hannah, as if waiting for something to happen. Then he breathed deep, drained his goblet and sat back. 'Imagine having that power. To be able to make somebody disappear. As if they had never existed. And the beauty of it is – nobody would ever know.'

The bottle of wine was empty.

'Well,' said the Oberstleutnant, pushing down on the table and rising to his feet. 'We should get you two wanderers back to the village.' He stayed there, staring down at the polished surface of the table, then looked up at Hannah. 'Tell me, what were you two doing at Heinz Schundel's house?'

The question caught Hannah off guard. She felt her own words catch in her throat and swallowed. The fact that he even knew Herr Schundel and where he lived came as a surprise.

'Collecting clothes for my aunt to repair,' she lied, immediately regretting her answer. He could easily check with Aunt Maud.

'Of course, of course.'

He held Hannah's gaze until she turned away. She knew he didn't believe her. But his question had given rise to some of her own.

What was the soldier doing there? And where was Herr Schundel?

She didn't think she would believe his answers, either.

FORTY-NINE

Hannah woke the next morning in her own bed, prepared for an orchestra of condemnation. Aunt Maud had been asleep in the parlour when the Oberstleutnant had brought Hannah home last night, and they had agreed it best not to wake her.

Hannah put on some fresh clothes and headed towards the smell of breakfast and the sharp clatter of pots and crockery. Outside the kitchen, she paused, took a deep breath and tried to find the right voice.

'Good morning,' she said, as she entered. Perhaps a little too jovial.

Aunt Maud didn't look up, or even turn around. Her hands moved a pan from here to there and back again, brushed down her apron and then crumpled it, opened a cupboard and closed it without taking anything out.

Hannah decided it would be best to sit at the table and wait. She wondered if Josef was receiving a similar treatment from his mother.

Finally, the woman turned and marched over, dropping a plate of eggs in front of her. 'You and that boy were very lucky.' She didn't wait for Hannah to reply, but stomped over to the stove, banging the pans, smoothing her apron. Then back again, a cloth clenched in her hand. 'What were you both thinking going that far out of the village in this fog and snow? People have become lost far closer to home.' She folded her arms and stared at Hannah. 'Well?'

Hannah found it impossible to remain silent under her gaze. 'We were just . . .'

'You were just what?'

'If you let me finish . . .' Though she didn't even know what she was going to say.

'Well? Go on!'

Hannah went to open her mouth.

'You and that boy!'

'Josef.'

'That boy!'

Her eyes dared Hannah to interrupt her once more. She was on a tirade, and it was best for all concerned if Hannah just kept her mouth shut until it was over. 'There are wolves out there, Sofia. Wolves!'

So, she didn't know about the wolves. This probably wasn't a good time to tell her.

'You could have frozen to death. Thank goodness that soldier found you. And took you both back to the castle!'

That soldier had very nearly shot her and Josef, and then almost marched them to their deaths. 'We were trying to find out what happened to Elias.' She let the sentence hang there.

'That nonsense again.' Aunt Maud turned away from her and started to wipe down the hob.

'It's not nonsense, Aunt Maud, I swear. There was a girl there. Matilda Weber. She was terrified. She gave me a letter. It said the soldiers had come to her house on Schulstrasse and taken her and her brother.'

'Weber?' asked Aunt Maud. 'A young girl?'

Hannah nodded, feeling a faint glimmer of hope. Had she said something to pique Aunt Maud's interest?

'The girl's mistaken. I know the Webers on Schulstrasse. There are no children living there.'

This was so infuriating. How could you be mistaken about where you lived? 'Maybe there were. Maybe you just don't remember them.'

'Stop talking such gibberish. People don't just get forgotten. And where is this letter?'

'I flushed it down the toilet.'

'Hmmph!'

'Did you know the Oberstleutnant is SS?'

Aunt Maud crossed her arms. 'It doesn't surprise me.'

She was so annoying. 'Does it worry you?'

'You worry me, young girl.'

Hannah could see she wasn't going to get through to her. Aunt Maud was just being obstinate now. She decided to take a different tack.

'Josef believes me.' She wasn't sure he did, but for the sake of this argument …

'A boy will believe anything a girl tells him at his age.'

Hannah rolled her eyes again, though Aunt Maud was facing away. 'And Herr Schundel knew. He was trying to tell us …'

Aunt Maud threw down the cloth and spun around. 'Heinz Schundel wasn't trying to tell you anything. You just heard what you wanted to hear. That poor man has been through enough without you getting him mixed up in whatever it is you and that boy imagine has happened.'

'We haven't imagined anything. And there's no risk of us mixing him up in anything now.' She promised herself not to look away from Aunt Maud, not even to blink.

Eventually, the woman broke the silence. 'Well? What do you mean by that?'

'He's gone missing.'

'Like your imaginary friend, I suppose.'

Hannah shook her head. 'No, because you remember Herr Schundel. I remember Herr Schundel. The whole village can probably remember Herr Schundel.'

Aunt Maud suddenly caught on. 'So that's where you two were going.'

'He knows something.'

Aunt Maud slammed both hands down on the table and leaned in towards her.

Hannah locked eyes with her.

'What does he know?'

'He knows what's going on in the village,' said Hannah.

'He doesn't know everything,' replied Aunt Maud. For the briefest of moments, her eyes flicked up towards the top of the house.

And for once, Hannah had to agree. They all had their secrets.

'You can't come in,' said Hannah. 'Aunt Maud's not happy. With either of us.'

Josef craned his neck to see behind her.

'She's not here,' said Hannah.

But she could come back at any moment and, though she hadn't explicitly been told to stay away from Josef for the time being, that was the message she had come away with.

'So, come outside.'

Hannah had a better idea. 'Come through to the courtyard. If she comes back, we'll hear her. You can leave through the back gate.'

She glanced left, then right. No sign of Aunt Maud. Josef went to step inside.

'Take your shoes off,' said Hannah.

Aunt Maud could spot a dirty footprint at thirty metres. Especially when it belonged to a young boy.

'It's not a true story,' said Josef. He had put his shoes back on the moment they had stepped out into the courtyard. 'Things like that can't really happen.'

They had folded back some tarpaulin and found a dry length of the woodpile to sit on.

'I know they can't,' replied Hannah. She had spent most of the afternoon thinking about the Oberstleutnant's story and how a tale being told could mean the difference between growing old, and never having existed. 'But the Oberstleutnant seemed to like the idea of children disappearing, which is a coincidence, don't you think? With what happened to Elias.'

'I suppose so. Assuming Elias is real.'

Hannah swallowed her annoyance. The fact that Josef was willing to even discuss it was good enough.

'Josef, do you know anybody called Matilda Weber?'

She guessed what his answer would be. He poked out his bottom lip and shook his head.

'Boris Weber?' she added.

'No. Who are they?'

'I met Matilda yesterday. At the castle. She brought me clothes. There was a letter tucked inside the shoe. It said she and her brother had been taken by the soldiers. From their house on Schulstrasse. She was petrified.'

Josef sat upright. 'That could be the proof we need. Where is it?'

'I got rid of it.'

He collapsed back, his face sank. 'You did what?'

'It was too dangerous to keep!'

'I suppose so. But if they lived here, they would have gone to the school. How old are they?'

'Matilda was around my age. She said her brother was older. I didn't meet him. She doesn't know where he is.'

'What are you saying?'

'Do you remember the second time we went to Frau Lister's? When she told us the story of The Old Man's Bones?'

Hannah could see his mind working. He nodded. 'But I don't remember Elias.'

'I know. But do you remember our walk back home? Going over the bridge?'

Josef clamped his mouth shut and shook his head. 'Not really. I mean, we must have, but it's just a bridge. I've crossed it lots of times.'

'I couldn't remember anything special, either. But in the letter, Matilda said she and her brother were there. And when I saw her, something came back. Some memory of her being there. Just her, not her brother. It's all a bit hazy.'

'So, you're saying Matilda and Boris have been forgotten? Like Elias? And they're up at the castle?'

She was, and being here now, working through it with Josef, some of the pieces were beginning to fall into place. 'I think so.'

'But why have we forgotten them? How?'

She didn't know. But the Oberstleutnant was responsible, she was certain. 'He's done something to us.'

'The Oberstleutnant?'

She nodded.

'But what?'

'I don't know. But seeing Matilda ... it jogged my memory. Brought her back into it.'

'But why would he let you meet her?'

Of course! 'Maybe as a test? To see if I recognised her when I saw her. She was told not to talk, and she didn't. But she was clever and brave enough to warn me and to write me a letter.'

'We should let her parents know,' said Josef.

They should. But she had a feeling they would be just like Frau Lister when she had visited with Frau Meinhardt.

'Not yet,' she said. 'They won't remember. But we do need to find Herr Schundel.' She thought back to the broken windows and the boot print. 'What did you see? In his house?' she asked, even though she could guess.

'It was ransacked. Everything was smashed.'

They sat in silence.

'Do you think he's hiding somewhere?' asked Josef. 'If he knows something, and the Oberstleutnant knows he knows, he'll need to hide.'

Hannah hoped he was hiding. But they had to be careful, too. The Oberstleutnant was already suspicious. And an SS soldier was not a man to be messed with.

From the front of the house, the sound of a door being closed. Aunt Maud was back.

'You have to go,' said Hannah. But Josef didn't need to be told. He was up and at the gate before she had time to get to her feet.

FIFTY

'Have you ever heard the tale of Edgar and Otto, Frau Meinhardt?'

The teacher was sitting beside Hannah, checking through her answers to arithmetical problems. Her head remained down, the pencil hovering above the paper, before she added a few more ticks and then looked up.

'I'm sorry?'

'The tale of Edgar and Otto. Have you ever heard it?'

Frau Meinhardt placed the end of her pencil in her mouth and shook her head. 'I don't recall. Is it a book?'

'Oberstleutnant Kessler told it to me and Josef when we were at the castle.'

She took the pencil from her mouth. 'You were at the castle?'

'Aunt Maud didn't tell you?'

'You know your aunt better than anybody. Do you think she tells me anything she doesn't need to?'

'I suppose not.'

Frau Meinhardt placed the pencil and paper on the writing desk and turned her chair towards Hannah. 'Tell me about it.'

'The castle or the tale?'

'Both.'

How far back should she go? All the way, she decided. If there was anybody she could trust, who would not admonish her or Josef for their recklessness, it was Frau Meinhardt.

'Josef and I went to find Herr Schundel . . .'

'Herr Schundel? He works at the school.'

'I know. He fixes things. He lives outside the village. We thought he might know something about Elias's disappearance.'

And she went on to tell Frau Meinhardt about their journey to the castle. The teacher remained still and silent for the first few sentences and she gasped, wide-eyed, when Hannah told her about the wolves and the soldier. She covered her mouth when Hannah got to the part where the Oberstleutnant arrived dressed in black and she and Josef were taken into the castle. And she stared up at the ceiling when Hannah recounted how Matilda had sneaked the letter to her inside her shoe.

And then Hannah told her about the story of Edgar and Otto. The teacher continued to listen, leaning forward in concentration, not saying a word. When Hannah had finished, she sat up straight and placed her hands upon her lap.

'And all this is true?'

Hannah was a touch disappointed she had asked. But, she supposed, it did sound a little far-fetched.

'All of it.'

'I don't know any Matilda or Boris Weber. They'd be too old for my class, but I know most of the children in the school and I can look into it for you,' said Frau Meinhardt.

Hannah couldn't help but smile. 'You will?'

She nodded. 'So, the Oberstleutnant told you that tale? Of Edgar and –'

'Otto. I may not have got it completely right word for word, but yes.'

Frau Meinhardt sighed. 'He doesn't look the kind to tell stories.'

'You've met him?' asked Hannah. This conversation was throwing up a lot of surprises.

'I've seen him in the village at times.'

'He has two children,' said Hannah, returning to Frau Meinhardt's previous remark.

'Lots of people have children. They're not all storytellers.'

'So have you heard it before?'

The woman chewed at her upper lip. 'I don't believe so. I'm sure I would have remembered.'

Why had the Oberstleutnant told her and Josef that tale? Hannah couldn't help but think that he must have had his reasons beyond just entertaining or informing them.

'Do you think the Oberstleutnant took Elias? And that he knows I can remember him? Was he trying to tell me something with that story?'

Frau Meinhardt considered this for a moment. 'I don't know.'

Hannah's face must have shown her disappointment, because Frau Meinhardt reached for her hand and clasped it between hers.

'But you need to be careful, Hannah. You must not speak of your suspicions to anyone else. Do you understand? Men like him . . . they don't care. About anything that isn't in their best interest. Or anybody but their own. And that includes children.'

The way she spoke made Hannah wonder if she were talking from experience. Frau Meinhardt stood up.

'I have to go.'

Hannah glanced at the clock on the wall. The lesson was over. There hadn't been much studying.

'Thank you,' said Hannah.

Frau Meinhardt packed her things into her satchel. 'Remember what I said. Be careful.'

Hannah stood. 'You, too.'

The teacher nodded and left her there alone. She turned and stared out the window. The cat was curled up asleep opposite, totally oblivious to the world outside. The fog had thinned, and Hannah could see all the way to the far side of the square.

Somewhere out there, she knew, Elias was waiting to be found.

FIFTY-ONE

The following Friday, Hannah was determined to finish her homework before the weekend arrived. She was working through a series of fraction problems that Frau Meinhardt had set her, trying to, for a short time, put some semblance of normality back into her life, when she heard a low rumble that instantly set her on edge. The sound came up through the floorboards and into her bones. She knew what it was before she looked out the window. It was the sound of soldiers arriving. The sound that was usually followed by the shattering of windows, the thumps of heavy boots against doors, the screams of people being dragged outside.

She sat frozen to the chair, just like the last time she'd heard them. She closed her eyes and heard the shots and screams that would follow. But that was in the city. It wouldn't happen here, would it?

Hannah fought the urge to hide. She used her sleeve to wipe away the condensation on the window, her breath hot in her throat, her stomach churning. Grey shapes rolled across the white world, throwing spumes of smoke into the never-ending fog.

Curtains twitched in the houses opposite, and the cat leaped from the windowsill. An old man hobbling away from the square, bag of provisions in hand, cast a quick glance behind and then quickened his step. Three trucks, the same ones she had seen at the castle, circled the fountain and came to an abrupt stop. Soldiers in grey hurled themselves from their rears as though they were on fire. They spread out across the village, knocking on doors. Nobody was dragged outside, though. Instead, Hannah saw the soldiers handing out leaflets.

She heard an angry rap on the lodge door, and crept out into the hallway. Aunt Maud's footsteps echoed along the floor below and Hannah arrived at the top of the stairs just as the front door was opened. A soldier's abrasive voice ordered Aunt Maud to read the leaflet. She said nothing in reply, just closed the door as Hannah began to descend.

Hannah followed her into the parlour, where she was sitting at the table, staring at the piece of paper. She glanced up when Hannah entered, a look of concern on her face that she quickly tried to hide.

'What is it, Aunt Maud? What are the soldiers doing?'

'Whatever their leaders ask of them.'

'What's on the note?'

Aunt Maud picked up the paper and held it out. 'You can read it yourself. It concerns you as much as it does me.'

Hannah stepped over to the table and took the leaflet.

Germany will be victorious!

To the citizens of Felshoven.

The Führer has graciously supplied you with a quality, German-manufactured Volksempfänger. His loyal

soldiers have worked hard to supply electrical power to every house in the village. This is for the good of the people, for the good of the country, for the good of the world. The Führer wishes you to be a part of his victory.

There will be an important announcement broadcast at midday tomorrow, Saturday 7th November. It is imperative that every citizen of Felshoven – man, woman and child – turns on their radio and listens to it.

Action will be taken against anybody who fails to comply.

Oberstleutnant Erwin Kessler

'What do you think they're going to say?' Her throat felt dry, and she struggled to swallow.

Aunt Maud snatched the leaflet from her hand. 'I know as much as you do. Which is as much as it says here.'

'Can't you ask the Oberstleutnant?'

Aunt Maud shook her head. 'If he wanted us to know beforehand, he would have told us. We shall find out soon enough.'

They found out, as promised, the following day. For the first time since she had arrived, Hannah was interested in what the voice on the radio had to say.

She and Aunt Maud had been sitting in the parlour since half-past eleven. There had been no sewing. No reading. No games. There had been very little talking. The radio played the usual melodramatic music, interspersed with brief periods of static.

As the minute hand of the wall clock headed towards its shorter brother, a sense of foreboding came over Hannah. Aunt Maud's hands fidgeted in her lap.

The broadcast began exactly as the three hands aligned. Hannah was expecting the voice to belong to the Oberstleutnant, but felt relief when she heard a younger, warmer voice coming across the airwaves.

There was no immediate grand announcement. Most of the talk was an extension of what had been written on the leaflets. Germany was winning. Every citizen should be proud of the soldiers who were fighting on all fronts, and grateful to be alive in Germany at such a pivotal time in the history of the world. The Führer was pulling together all the might of his forces to make one final push. The war would soon be over.

Hannah didn't believe a word of it. The black box was an instrument of lies.

Both she and Aunt Maud stared at the radio, as though the owner of the voice could be seen as well as heard. Then the voice changed. It began to sound less like the voice of optimism, more of menace and threat.

'By the order of Oberstleutnant Kessler of the Schutzstaffel, every citizen of Felshoven is commanded *to be in the village square at midday on Sunday 8th November.'*

'That's tomorrow,' said Hannah. Aunt Maud held up her hand.

'Children are not to be excused. Every person over the age of 15 must bring their papers. Anybody who fails to comply will be dealt with accordingly.'

Hannah felt her heart thumping away in her chest. Her hands were too warm upon her lap. Felshoven was explicitly mentioned. Did that mean they were the only ones in Germany receiving this broadcast? Aunt Maud's cheeks had turned blotchy. She sat upright and closed her eyes as the voice was replaced by an orchestra.

'What will they want?'

Aunt Maud stood up. 'I don't know. But we have no choice. We have to go.'

She brushed invisible crumbs from her apron and walked slowly from the room.

She's right, thought Hannah, closing her eyes and collapsing into the cushion. *We have to go. But we may not be coming back*.

FIFTY-TWO

The soldier who wrote down their names didn't look much older than Josef. His uniform hung off his small frame and his hands shook – possibly from the cold, possibly not. He held Aunt Maud's papers up and glanced from them to Aunt Maud and back again several times. Hannah's heart kept up a steady rhythm in her ears while Aunt Maud studied the crowd as if searching for someone.

Finally, the soldier waved them through, and she followed Aunt Maud into the throng of people. Everybody was wrapped in grey layers, and nobody spoke. They moved as one, in ebbs and flows, heads down, feet shuffling, towards the wooden platform that had been erected overnight.

Hannah stood beside Aunt Maud, hidden from view of the platform by the crowd around her. That was good. She had no wish to be seen. Or to see the Oberstleutnant's long, pallid face with its counterfeit smile.

Time ticked on. Five minutes passed. Ten minutes. Fifteen. Nothing happened.

People rubbed their hands together and blew upon exposed fingers. Feet shuffled and a low murmur began to surface. An air of anxiety hung over the crowd, evident in the hunched stances and downcast eyes, the way children were held close and old people hung their heads.

From Hannah's right came the sound of heavy footsteps. And of something being dragged along. A man staggered against her, and people stepped to their left as somebody pushed their way through. Murmurs became gasps and whispered exclamations as the footsteps and dragging made their way towards the platform.

Hannah looked up at Aunt Maud who, tall as she was, was craning her neck to see.

'What's happening? Who is it?'

But before Aunt Maud could answer, the Oberstleutnant's voice, no longer smooth and friendly, carried across the crowd. The murmurs and exclamations subsided.

'Citizens of Felshoven, I thank all who have arrived *on time* for coming out here on such a cold day. But what choice did you have? It seems that every day is cold at this time of year.' He laughed. Nobody joined him. 'And, of course, you were commanded to come. Were you not?' Silence. 'Every one of you from the village, and a few from beyond, were commanded to come.'

He paused for several seconds. 'So why . . .' another pause, '. . . Gustav Dittmar . . .' pause, '. . . Ingrid Dittmar . . .' pause, and Hannah realised he was reading these names, '. . . and Esther Dittmar, did you not come?'

'We . . . we didn't know, sir.' The voice of a man. Trembling. Speaking too fast.

'You didn't know. So why were you all hiding when my men came to your house?'

A small sob escaped the man, and everyone around Hannah was now craning to see.

'Please, sir, truly. We didn't . . . we didn't know.'

'You did not hear the command on the radio telling you to be here?'

'No, sir. We did not.'

'And why is that?'

Silence from the man. A tiny whimper from the platform.

'Why is that?'

'We weren't aware, sir.'

'You weren't aware.'

'No, sir.'

'You didn't receive the note?'

'Note, sir? No, sir.'

'You didn't receive the note that one of my men is holding up? That was found at your home?'

Then a small voice. 'Papa?'

'Shall I read the note to you?'

'No, sir, no.'

'Is there no need?

'No, sir.'

'Why is there no need?'

'Because your soldier, he showed it to me. I read it. But, sir, my wife, my daughter – they didn't see it. My daughter can't read, sir.'

'You didn't read it to them?'

Silence.

'Speak up. Your fellow citizens can't hear you.'

'No, sir. I didn't.'

'Well, perhaps, Herr Dittmar, you would like to read it to them now. Hand Herr Dittmar the note, would you?'

'Yes, sir!' Marching boots upon the platform.

'There you go. Now, Esther, darling . . . Ingrid . . . come and stand here at the front. Your father, your husband, has something to read to you.'

After a few seconds, Gustav Dittmar's trembling voice sounded out across the crowd. It was nowhere near the same bombastic level as the Oberstleutnant's, and Hannah couldn't hear many of the words. But she had read the note herself. She knew what it said. His voice broke as he finished reading, the name of the man standing with him on the platform leaving his lips like the last drip from a rusty bucket.

'There, that wasn't too hard, was it?'

A loud explosion. A woman's scream. Hannah's heart leaped in her chest. Shouts from the crowd and everybody around her turning away, looking down, looking anywhere but at the stage.

Bang! Bang!

She jumped again. The nails of her right hand dug into the palm of her right, but she couldn't release her grip.

No more screams from the stage. But plenty from the crowd.

She looked at Aunt Maud, who was stood with her eyes closed and lips moving, as if in prayer. A cold sweat broke out upon Hannah's skin. Her heart pummelled away.

'Silence!' shouted the Oberstleutnant in a voice that Hannah had never heard him use before, not even when he had reprimanded the soldier. But something told her this was the real man. The one who had been sent to Felshoven to carry out his job. Whatever that was. Even if it meant shooting a family in front of the whole village.

Hannah felt Aunt Maud squeeze her hand, heard her sob as cries bubbled up out of the crowd. She squeezed her hand back and studied the cobbles at her feet. One of the stones was missing, its shape imprinted in the mortar where it should have been. The cobbles started to swim, but she blinked the tears away.

'Silence.' Softer now. The monster was once more in hiding. But what was the point? Everybody knew it was there. More gasps and stifled cries as something, some things, were dragged across the platform and then, *thump, thump, thump,* down the steps. Hannah squeezed her eyes shut.

'The instructions in the letter were quite clear, were they not? Very simple, were they not? Now, where is Sofia Meyer?'

Hannah's eyes shot open and her body flooded with panic. Aunt Maud roughly pulled Hannah into her. Hannah bit her lip. She tasted blood. That was good, something to concentrate on.

'Sofia, where are you?'

People began to look around for her. But it only took a few glances her way for everybody else to follow suit.

'Ah, you are hidden, Sofia? Please, everybody, clear a path so that I may see her.'

Hannah didn't want that to happen. She wanted to remain hidden. She pushed herself further into Aunt Maud's side, and felt the woman's grip tighten around her as the whole crowd parted. And then there was just the two of them standing as an island apart from everybody else.

'Will you come forward, Sofia?'

She had to go. There was no choice. Still, Aunt Maud pulled her closer and tighter, away from those red smears in the snow that led around the rear of the platform.

'What do you want with her?' asked the woman who had taken Hannah into her home.

But the Oberstleutnant ignored her and instead spoke directly to Hannah. 'Come here, Sofia. You will be safe, I assure you.'

Said the fox to the Gingerbread Man, thought Hannah.

'It's all right, Aunt Maud.' She tried to pull away, but Aunt Maud wouldn't let her.

'Frau Meyer . . .' warned the Oberstleutnant.

Aunt Maud's arm loosened. 'Come right back,' she whispered, and though it was a ludicrous thing to say, it was exactly what she needed to hear.

Hannah began to walk slowly past the villagers. Blank faces with blank eyes and turned-down mouths. Noses dripping with cold tears. Each one thankful they were not her. She heard the dirty sludge beneath her feet, felt the unevenness of the cobbles. The Oberstleutnant was waiting. Standing there on the platform, arms behind his back, chin up, revolver at his side. There was no smile. No expression at all.

Footsteps to her right, a low shout of, 'Come back, Josef.' And there he was beside her, taking her hand. He forced a smile, and she returned it.

They approached the platform, that insincere smile back upon the Oberstleutnant's face. Two soldiers stood beside him. There were no smiles upon theirs.

Hannah and Josef mounted the steps, side by side. One . . . two . . . three. Their footsteps so loud upon the boards.

Three distinct pools of red on the platform. Drips at the edge of the wood already beginning to freeze.

A few more steps and they were standing beside him.

'Turn and face the crowd, Sofia.'

She was shaking so badly, but forced herself to do as commanded.

Josef turned, too. He could have been trembling. She couldn't tell.

The Oberstleutnant either didn't notice or, more likely, didn't care. 'Sofia, here, has recently suffered a great loss. Isn't that right, Sofia?'

She gave a single nod at the dismayed crowd. Was this where he revealed her true identity in front of everybody? And then what?

'She has witnessed the evil we are up against.' He began to pace up and down. 'She has seen what will happen to all of you if we let this enemy win.'

She closed her eyes, trying to remain upright. Felt Josef's hand in hers. Concentrated on it.

'Now, understand this. I am here to protect you.'

Her eyes flicked once more to the red pools. Blood red . . .

'There is no excuse for my commands not to be met. When I tell you to do something, you do it. Is that clear?'

Hannah thought she might vomit as she realised what she was looking at.

Silence.

'IS THAT CLEAR?!'

A cacophony of affirmation. Exaggerated nods.

'Take a look around you. Study the faces. Take your time.' The Oberstleutnant surveyed the whole audience. Heads craned above the crowd. Eyes looking at eyes.

'Is there anybody missing? Is there anybody who has failed to follow my simple command?'

A few seconds passed. A woman's voice from the crowd. 'Hans Grosse is not here!'

'I am here! I am here with all my family!'

'An easy mistake to make,' said the Oberstleutnant. 'Is there anybody else?'

'Traudel Holzneckt!'

And just like that, the villagers turned upon each other. As names were shouted out, soldiers were sent down to gather more details and then dispatched to find the missing villagers. When no more names were called, the Oberstleutnant addressed the crowd once more.

'Now that each and every one of you understands the importance of following my commands, and the consequences to you and your families if you do not, let me explain what I need each and every one of you to do. And, believe me when I say this – I will know if you do not.'

The villagers' faces made it quite clear. They believed him.

Once more, Hannah closed her eyes, wishing she, and Josef, were anywhere but here.

'Every house in Felshoven has been issued with a Volksempfänger . . .'

From somewhere in the village, more shots. This time, Hannah didn't jump. But Josef did. It was her turn to squeeze his hand.

FIFTY-THREE

'That poor family! And for what?'

Aunt Maud was pacing the kitchen. Up and down, tugging at her clothes, clutching at her heart, looking up to the ceiling for answers.

Hannah had finally got her trembling under control. 'For not listening to the radio.' She was sitting at the table, trying to understand what had just happened.

'No, no, no! It can't have been for that. Nobody gets shot for not listening to a radio. It makes no sense! Turn on the radio or get shot! Listen every night at six or get shot!'

Aunt Maud was scaring her, and Hannah had already been scared enough today.

But why? Why was their listening to the radio so important? Hannah thought back to the nights she and Aunt Maud had sat there with it playing. Most evenings there had been nothing but news of the war, or seething orchestral music, and Hannah had asked why they couldn't listen to something else – to lighter, happier music, like she and her family had enjoyed in their old apartment. But her aunt had told her they had no choice. Their Volksempfänger had but one frequency.

And that one time, on the evening when Elias had gone missing, she and Aunt Maud had been listening. Aunt Maud had fallen asleep, and she had soon followed. But then she had drifted out and up the stairs, away from the sound of the radio. Had Aunt Maud continued to listen, even after she had fallen asleep? Had the radio done something to her mind? To everybody's minds in the village? Yes, they had been told to listen. Many probably wanted to listen. It was their window to the world. Many of them had loved ones away fighting. They would want to know that all was well. And the radio told them that, didn't it? Even if it was a lie.

But Hannah still couldn't make the logic work. Elias being forgotten by everybody except her. Every sign that he had ever existed disappearing. A half-imagined memory of a strange creature in her room. The radio couldn't do that, could it?

'It wasn't just because of the radio,' mumbled Aunt Maud.

Hannah had never seen her like this. But war hadn't truly come to the village until now. Apart from the occasional sound of bombs being dropped on distant cities, and the plane that had crashed into the mountain.

Hannah caught Aunt Maud casting another glance upwards.

'I know about George.' The words were out of Hannah's mouth before she had the chance to catch them.

Aunt Maud stopped dead. Her hands, which had been clasped over her eyes as if trying to rid her mind of the world, slowly fell away. Her face, a twisted ball of disbelief, gradually straightened itself out. She squeezed her eyes shut and leaned back against a cabinet.

'I would try to deny it. But you know his name. How do you know?'

Hannah didn't tell her how she had floated just below the ceiling of the second floor. 'I took the dumb waiter up. Out of curiosity.'

'The dumb waiter! Sofia!' And then, softer. 'You cannot tell anybody. Not even Josef.'

It was Hannah's turn to close her eyes. George had also told her not to let anybody else know. Who had she betrayed? Both of them?

'Oh, Sofia. No. You haven't?'

'Aunt Maud, I'm sorry.' And she truly was. The events of the day had proven that one slip of the tongue could mean the end for all of them. They stared at each other. She could see Aunt Maud's chest breathing in and out. Was conscious of her own doing the same. 'Can you tell me?' she asked.

'Tell you?'

'About George. Why he's here.'

Aunt Maud chewed at her bottom lip, looking like a nervous schoolgirl. Then she disappeared from the kitchen, and Hannah heard the front door being bolted. On her return, Aunt Maud opened a cabinet, found a bottle of clear liquid, then a glass, and sat down opposite Hannah.

'This stays between the two of us,' said Aunt Maud, removing the stopper of the bottle. 'You need to promise me.' She sat there, bottle in one hand, plug in the other.

Hannah swallowed. 'I promise.'

Aunt Maud began to pour.

'They brought him to me. Some of the village women. They had been herding the cows down the mountain ready for winter, not long before you arrived. But the rain had come in fast and hard, and they had taken shelter below rocks on the northern side. The storm lasted for several hours.

'As they were getting ready to move again, a young man came limping towards them, breathless, looking terrified. It was strange, they said, to see a male face that wasn't that of a young boy or an old man.

'He was waving at them, trying to catch up. But he was struggling with something heavy strapped to his back. As he came closer, they could see that he was wearing a uniform, but not one of ours.'

'And that was George?' Hannah had never heard Aunt Maud talk for so long. Her outbursts were usually short and sharp.

'That was George. The women began to herd the cows faster to get away. And it was working. Eventually, he sank to his knees and fell forward. It was a radio he had strapped to his back.'

'A Volksempfänger? Like yours?'

Aunt Maud took a drink, swallowed and shook her head.

'No, that one just receives. The one George has can send signals, too.' She paused to take another sip. 'The women didn't know what to do. They had never been faced with anything like this. An enemy on their doorstep. But a young man, all the same. One of the women went back as the others watched. She tried to lift George to his feet, but he was too heavy. The other two ran over to help and, as cows do, they all followed. Very soon, George was surrounded by cold, noisy cows. Then the soldiers arrived.'

'His friends?'

Aunt Maud shook her head again. 'Our soldiers. The ones from the castle.'

Was that better or worse? Which ones were the enemy? German soldiers had taken away Hannah's friends and neighbours. The Allies had killed her family.

'A British plane had crashed into the mountain a few days earlier, they said. They believed one of the airmen had survived the crash and was somewhere in the vicinity. The women didn't know what to say. It was obvious to them that if they gave George up, he would be killed. So, they lied. And, I suppose, there was no reason to doubt them. The cows had destroyed George's footprints, and so the soldiers left them and continued their search.

'The women came down the mountain with the cows, and with George hidden in their midst. And then they brought him back here. To me. And this is where he has stayed ever since.'

That all made sense. Except for one thing. 'But why here, Aunt Maud? Why you?'

Aunt Maud, who had been topping up her glass with the clear liquid throughout the story, emptied the last few drops from the bottle.

'Why here?' She gave a quick laugh. 'You should know that better than anybody.'

Hannah shrugged. 'How should I know?'

'Because that's what I do, Sofia. Or whatever your name is. I hide people who are in need. And I'm very good at it.'

'I knew the moment I opened the door to you.'

Hannah was dumbstruck. All this time, she had thought she was fooling Aunt Maud. But it was her who had been fooled.

'I met Sofia once,' continued Aunt Maud. 'When she was just a baby. In better times. When I still spoke to Franz, my brother.'

Hannah wasn't going to speak, but Aunt Maud waved her away anyway. Her words were becoming a little slurred.

'It's not important. Water under the bridge. Families fall out. And it was probably my fault. No, it was my fault.'

Hannah had no intention of judging. Not now.

'I knew you weren't my niece. That Sofia was probably gone, just like her brother, her parents. All the family I had.'

'How did you know?' asked Hannah. She had done everything right. Just like Marianne had told her.

Aunt Maud leaned in closer and stared into Hannah's eyes. She smiled and nodded. 'Sofia had had her father's eyes, olive green. Yours are brown.'

'So you know,' said Hannah. 'What I am. Why I'm here. Why I was staying at . . .' She struggled to say it. 'At Sofia's house.'

Aunt Maud nodded and smiled. 'I can guess. I did guess. And that's why I took you in. You may not have been Franz's daughter, but you were somebody's. And you needed help.'

Hannah's heart was filling with pure gratitude for this woman who had, just like her brother, risked all for a stranger. She studied Aunt Maud's face. Tried to see through that hard exterior to the heart of the real woman who so obviously cared deeply about people. Was the whole thing an act, a way to avoid suspicion, even from those she was protecting?

'And, fortunately for you,' said Aunt Maud, draining an already empty glass, 'I'm good at hiding people.' She laughed. 'I should be. I've done it before.'

'Why did George come here?' asked Hannah.

'I make it a point never to ask,' said Aunt Maud. 'The less I know, the better. Have I ever asked you?'

Hannah shook her head. 'But the Oberstleutnant staying here, too . . .'

'Oh, him,' scowled Aunt Maud. 'I had no choice in that. He just turned up one day and demanded a room. But I doubt he'll be back here to stay. Not after this afternoon.'

She screwed up her mouth. Hannah tried not to go back there. 'If he does,' said Aunt Maud, 'I may have to put something in his food.'

'I thought you liked him,' said Hannah.

'Good,' said Aunt Maud. 'That was what I wanted everybody to think. He took a shine to you. That concerned me. Why do you think I was so angry when you ended up at the castle? After all you've been through . . .'

'Was that why you were against me going to school?' asked Hannah. 'Because you knew?'

Aunt Maud swallowed. 'I had to make sure you were ready. That you wouldn't be found out.'

Hannah's life was split between fear and guilt. The latter flooded her now.

Aunt Maud continued. 'George was the biggest problem. His German wouldn't fool many people. He arrived here with a broken leg. Like yours, but worse. I treated him the best I could, and he healed well. But there was no way he would have been able to make it down off the mountain until spring. And he couldn't be given a room in the lodge like you. So he's had to live in the attic and stay quiet.'

'I know what that feels like,' said Hannah.

Aunt Maud nodded. 'I know.'

'So, the only people in the village who know about George are you, me, Josef and the women who brought you to him?'

'That was up until today,' answered Aunt Maud, standing up and placing the palms of her hands flat upon the table.

Hannah hadn't told anybody else. And she was sure Josef hadn't. 'Who else knows?'

'Nobody else knows. But now it's just me, you and Josef.'

'Where are the women?'

Aunt Maud closed her eyes. 'One of them was Ingrid Dittmar. The other two . . . I think they were the families who didn't turn up today. The Oberstleutnant, the soldiers . . . shot them.'

So that was it. That was why Aunt Maud had panicked earlier. Did the Oberstleutnant know about George? Had he fixed it so that the three women and their families would turn up late, or not at all? If so, why was the person responsible for hiding the airman still standing here now?

FIFTY-FOUR

Hannah let her fingers trace the rough brickwork as she thought about what she was going to say. She had only met George once, but, if what Aunt Maud had told her was true, he could possibly help her. Or help them. The village. Despite all the truths that had come out that afternoon, Aunt Maud still couldn't bring herself to believe Hannah when it came to Elias and Matilda and her theory about children being hidden at the castle. She believed that Hannah believed, she said, but grief could do terrible things to the mind. And it was best that she kept away from George. His existence had to remain hidden. For all their sakes.

But Aunt Maud had gone out.

The lift reached its highest point, and Hannah knocked and called out his name.

She heard rummaging around inside. Eventually, he pulled open the door and she was met by his warm, slightly breathless smile and the stale smell of his closed-off existence. She screwed up her nose.

He shrugged. 'I know. I mean, I can imagine. I can't smell it anymore.'

'It's not good. I'm surprised they can't smell it at the castle.' She swung her legs over the side. 'Aunt Maud knows I know. About you.'

George raised his hand. 'I know. She came to see me. She isn't happy. Sofia, you must not tell *anyone* else. You and Josef must keep this a secret. Nobody else can know.'

'Why did you come here? To drop bombs on us?'

He stepped forward. 'No, no. I promise. Not on people like you.'

People like her. What did he mean by that?

'On who, then?'

He shook his head. 'I cannot say.'

Hannah had an idea. 'Was it on the castle?'

He didn't respond.

'The Oberstleutnant shot the families of the women who brought you here.' She let it sink in while trying not to think about those pools of red . . . 'I think the Oberstleutnant already knows about you.'

George's mouth fell open. He shook his head. 'No. He would come for me. For your aunt.'

And that was what she didn't understand. 'Tell me why you're here,' said Hannah. There was too much going on in this small village. There had to be connections. Perhaps if she knew what George knew, she would be able to connect the dots.

'I shouldn't,' said George. But it wasn't a can't.

'I think it may have something to do with my friend's disappearance.'

His eyes narrowed. 'Your friend? What has happened?'

She told him. About Elias. And how he had vanished from everybody's memory but hers. He stared down at the floor as she spoke, grasping his mouth between thumb and forefinger.

'And there are other children who have disappeared,' she finished. 'I think the Oberstleutnant is taking them.'

'You do? Why do you think that?'

She wasn't prepared to tell him that yet. She needed to be able to trust him first.

'Tell me why you're here,' she said. 'Then I'll tell you what I know.'

He finished rubbing at his chin and sat upright. 'Very well. I'll tell you.'

Hannah felt a little surprised, but she hopped down from the lift and sat beside him.

'A few months ago, British Intelligence received news of heavy shipments being moved up the mountain. They knew something was going on. But not what. Our job was to gather intelligence. There were five of us in total – pilot, navigator and three troopers. The idea was to drop us at the higher reaches of the mountain, where we would make camp. It was important the mission was carried out before the snow set in.

'We were to infiltrate the castle. Hence the need to speak German.' He laughed. 'But I don't think I fooled you, so I doubt I could have fooled the Oberstleutnant.'

He was right. He spoke German well, but something about his accent gave him away.

'What were you going to do when you got inside?'

'Just watch. Listen. Find out what it was being used for.'

'And then?'

He shrugged. 'That depended on what we discovered. But we hit low cloud and crashed into the mountain before we made it that far. I was in the rear, so avoided the worst of the impact. Everybody else was killed. I escaped with a broken leg. I hid in the forest for two days, but I could hear the soldiers getting closer. And I was out of food and water. I had to move. Fortunately for me, I ran straight into the village herders. And they brought me here. To hide and recover.'

Hannah didn't say anything. She was too busy thinking. Was he telling the truth? His story matched up with what Aunt Maud had told her. But what was he *not* telling her? And again, that thought: Who was the enemy here? This man whose country had killed her parents and many others? Or the Oberstleutnant and the soldiers in the castle who had shot three families and were possibly abducting children?

'And now they're dead,' she said, surprised at herself for how easy those words had fallen from her lips.

'I'm so sorry. Perhaps it's a coincidence. It doesn't make any sense.'

'Do your people know you're here? That you're safe? Can you talk to them on your radio?'

'I can and they do.'

'And so, if I told you something that might help, you could pass it on to them?' asked Hannah.

'Something?'

'Information. From inside the castle.'

He laughed. 'You can't get into the castle.'

'I've already been.'

He sat upright. 'You have? What did you see?'

What did she see? Not much that was of any use.

'I met a girl who had been abducted. She said her brother was taken, too. I think there are others.'

'From the village?' His voice rose a pitch.

She nodded.

'But you don't know for sure?'

Did she? She couldn't prove it, but . . .

'Sofia, I can't just –'

'What if I could get some proof?'

'Proof? Like what?'

She didn't know. She was grasping at straws. But she could try.

'Sofia, you're hardly going to be allowed into the castle after what happened today.'

He was assuming she'd be seen. That wouldn't happen.

'But say I did get into the castle? What was the plan if you found out the castle was being used for something terrible?'

Silence. She'd hit a nerve, she could tell. Which meant he *did* think something terrible was being done at the castle. She bit her lip to stop herself talking through the unsaid thoughts she could tell were running through his mind.

'If . . .' he finally said, leaning forward and lowering his voice even further. 'If we had to, if it was so terrible and important enough for us to put a stop to it, we would call in help.'

'Help?'

'On the radio. We'd call in the bombers. And that castle would be wiped from the side of the mountain.'

FIFTY-FIVE

The following night, Hannah left her window open, determined to get some answers. Not from the castle. Not yet. Hannah and Josef's visit to Herr Schundel's house had shown, to her at least, that she and Josef had been on the correct trail. If not, then why had the soldier been there? She wanted to check his house for herself.

She wrapped herself in a few extra blankets. The temperature outside dropped below zero every night now, and she didn't want her body freezing to death while her mind was out searching for answers.

The fog was thinner tonight. But it was still there, hanging like a veil over the village. The sleeping cat ignored her, and she floated out across the square, trying not to look at the platform, left there from the day before as a menacing reminder.

The silence was enormous. Mixed with the snow below and the fog around her, it gave her the sensation of being separate from the world and all that was going on in it.

She flew. There was no need to follow the lines of the village anymore. She knew where she was going. Houses became trees, then a gap in the trees revealed a snowy roof. Herr Schundel's house.

She dived towards it and hovered a couple of metres above the ground. It appeared smaller in the darkness. Yet more sinister, a trap waiting to spring closed.

The door was no longer open. Had it blown closed, or had somebody been here? She chose one of the broken windows, scoffing at herself for being wary of the remaining shards as she floated through.

Josef was right. Everything had been destroyed. Drawers were pulled out, cabinet doors ripped off their hinges, the table and chairs thrown aside. Broken glass and scattered paper were everywhere as she moved through the house. The bed was upside down. A wardrobe leaning against a wall. A basin in pieces. Everything except the Volksempfänger, Hannah realised, which sat untouched on an upright stool.

It was obvious no one could live here anymore. Which made what happened next all the more startling.

'Hello again,' said a nearby voice.

She spun around, searching every corner of the room she was in. But there was nobody there.

'You must forgive me, but I'm not good with names. Better with faces. Numbers, too.'

FIFTY-SIX

Herr Schundel? she wondered.

'Don't be frightened. And please, call me Heinz.'

'Wait! Can you see me? Hear me?' Hannah shifted her attention around the room, still unable to pick up where the voice was coming from.

'No more than you can see and hear me,' replied Heinz.

She stopped looking around and closed her eyes, focusing on her thoughts and his voice in her head. 'You can do this, too?'

'I can.'

This was good news. Not only had she found him, but she was not alone in her ability.

'I only started being able to do this after I was in an accident . . .' she began, as if he had asked.

'I think it must have been more than just an accident. I think that, like me, you were so close to death that you could reach out and shake its hand.'

Hannah wondered about that. If it were true, then her parents had truly saved her life with theirs.

'How did you know I was here?' she asked.

'I sensed you,' replied Heinz. 'You'll learn to do that one day. When you meet others like us.'

'There are others?' It was a naïve thing to say, she knew as soon as she said it. How could they be the only two?

'Of course.'

'Where are you?'

'It doesn't matter. What are you doing here?'

'I was looking for you. I thought you might be able to help. My friend, Elias. He –'

'He vanished.'

He knew something! She had been right. 'Yes.'

'And nobody can remember him.'

'Do you remember him?' she asked.

'I told you. I'm not good with names. What did he look like?'

'He was eight years old, dark hair … He was with me. That day at the square.'

'I remember him.'

Hannah's spirit soared. 'You do?'

'I do. You were with two boys that day.'

At last! She had somebody to back up her story.

'But he isn't the only one who's vanished,' Heinz said.

'I know. I met a girl at the castle. Matilda. She had a brother. They were taken …'

'Before you go any further, let me tell you what I know. And there's plenty I don't. But maybe you can fill in some of the blanks. Maybe you can find out what's going on and warn people. Because nobody seems to know. Or even care.'

She remained silent and let him talk.

'I built this house after the last war, with help from a friend. I had had enough of civilisation, of progress. And of war. Luckily for me, my injuries, the ones you can see and the ones you can't, meant I wouldn't be sent back into it. But I've always been good with my hands. I earn money from building things, fixing things around the village.

'A few months ago, the soldiers arrived. Lots of soldiers. I count things, all the time. In my head. It can be tiring, sometimes. But it can be useful, too.'

She remembered what Josef had told her. About Heinz pointing at each of the children in turn.

'I counted forty-two soldiers. But there are probably more I haven't seen. I couldn't work out why so many were here, in a small, insignificant village in the mountains. I didn't like it.'

Hannah was beginning to catch on. To understand why Heinz had started to suspect.

'And I remember faces. Every detail. One day, five or six weeks ago, the number of children at the school went down by one, and it didn't go back up again. I didn't think much of it. Perhaps they were ill. But it bothered me that I couldn't think who it was. I couldn't picture the person who wasn't there. I kept on counting. And the number went down by one again.

'I asked the headmaster, Herr Guttman, but he was adamant that no children had left the school for the past few months. That made me think there was something wrong with my mind.'

'But you weren't wrong.'

'No, I wasn't. Children were going missing.'

'How did you find out?'

'I like to draw. Portraits. It's something I've always done, and I'm good at it. I've drawn many of the villagers over the years.'

Hannah drifted down towards the floor. The scattered paper. Portraits. They were good. Very good. As good as any photograph.

'You sat in the playground and drew the children?' Josef hadn't mentioned that.

'No. I came back here and did it from memory. Fast, before too many others vanished from my mind. I told you, I'm good with faces, which was why I found it so hard to believe I couldn't remember the missing children. I drew every night and I continued to count every day. And when the number went down again, I checked my drawings.'

'You remembered somebody?'

'I did. A girl of about eight. With dark pigtails in purple bows. She had vanished from my memory. But when I looked at her face, it was like there were pages stuck together in my mind. With glue. And not just the glue of time. But something else. Something stronger. You know how, say, you forget the name of somebody, or what you had for dinner one night? And you only remember when somebody mentions that name, or you have that meal again?'

Hannah knew. Things were never really forgotten. Just hidden away somewhere in your mind. Like when she had met Matilda at the castle.

'Those drawings were like that. They helped me pull at the corners of those pages in my mind to reveal the memory of that girl.'

'How many more are missing? What did you do?'

'I don't know how many. But now I had proof. I was planning on taking the drawings to the school. To show the headmaster. Hoping it would do the same to him. Unstick the pages in his mind. But before I could show him, I saw a soldier outside here – well hidden, but I'd spent many hours keeping my eyes peeled for hidden soldiers during the last war. I knew he was there. And it made me suspicious. And frightened. Not just for me. I was even more sure that I was onto something, and that the soldiers from the castle were behind whatever was going on.

'That was when I decided I had to hide the portraits somewhere. Of the children.'

Back at the pages on the floor. There were no children on them, just adults.

'So I took my gasmask tin and some stones . . .'

'That was what you were carrying. On the day you ran into us. When the fog came.'

'The fog may have helped. I wasn't sure if I was being followed. Either way, the soldiers were waiting for me when I got back. They took me to the castle . . .'

There was a silence unlike any Hannah had ever heard. No wind outside, no whisper of her breath, no beating of her heart.

'They made us all forget,' said Heinz. 'The whole village. But I don't know how.'

'I think it has something to do with the radios,' Hannah said.

'The Volksempfänger?'

'I think it does something to our minds.' Hannah told him about the night Elias had disappeared, how she had left her body and drifted away from the radio, unable to hear it. 'I think they're using the radio to hypnotise people. So that they don't notice the children are gone.'

Silence again. Hannah assumed he was considering this.

'I'm not sure that's possible. But, at the same time, I have no other theory. It would explain why the soldiers ran cables to every house . . .'

'... and gave everyone radios that they *have* to listen to.' She continued the line of thought that she had already been down.

She could almost hear him rubbing his chin. 'Mmm-hmm. It does start to make a strange kind of sense. It would explain why the soldiers are at the castle.'

'It would?' Hannah had assumed it was just because of the space available. And the Oberstleutnant's comfort.

'They would need somewhere high to transmit. Somewhere in sight of the whole village.'

'I hadn't thought of that.'

'I don't really know how a radio works. But, if they can send voices through the air to a wooden box and then into our heads, I suppose it's not a big step to believe those voices can control us. Tell us what to do. What to think. Wipe out whole parts of our memories.'

Hannah recalled the nights when Aunt Maud had lay asleep in her armchair, listening to the voice on the radio. And her, too – hadn't she succumbed to sleep on some occasions because of the Volksempfänger?

'But why are they doing it? Here in the village? Why are they taking the children?' Hannah wanted to know.

'Maybe to prove that they can. If they can make parents, grandparents, friends forget a child, just think how easy it would be to make the world forget.'

'To forget what? Who?'

'Anybody. They could make a whole race disappear if they wanted to. And nobody would ever know they had existed.'

Surely that wasn't possible. It was a horrendous thought. But did that mean people like the Oberstleutnant wouldn't try? She felt her anger rising and pushed it back down. Was this what her parents had been hiding from? She felt more determined than ever to stop whatever was going on in the village.

'Are you still being held at the castle? Are you . . . are you okay?'

'I escaped. I'm somewhere they'll never find me. Don't worry about me. But the drawings. They're somewhere safe.'

'They are?' Hope. More than she had felt for a long time. 'Where?'

'In the fountain in the square. They've been there since the day you saw me. Find them, Sofia. Pull at that corner. Tell the village. Get those children back.'

FIFTY-SEVEN

Hannah was freezing. She opened her eyes, a dream whispering at the edges of her consciousness. The curtains fluttered in the breeze coming through the window. The open window.

It wasn't a dream.

Hannah leaped out of bed. She needed to get those drawings. A chill ran through her. She spied the dress she had worn yesterday on the back of her chair and threw it on over her nightdress. Yesterday's socks, too. She stumbled. Far too noisy.

'What on Earth are you doing up at this time?' Aunt Maud shouted from downstairs.

Hannah ran out of her room and down the stairs, past Aunt Maud to the closet. She needed shoes. There they were. She managed to get one on standing on one foot, but doing up the buckle was too difficult. She plonked herself down on the bottom step and hurriedly fastened them both. She needed to be quick. No soldiers could get to the pictures before her.

She glanced at Aunt Maud, who was standing with her hands on her hips waiting for a response to her question.

'You'll see,' Hannah said, one arm in her coat. The other arm finding its way in as she pulled the door open.

'See?' replied Aunt Maud. 'The only thing I see is you hopping about like a flea with an itch. Where are you –?'

'I'll only be a minute.'

'But you haven't got . . .'

Hannah never found out what she hadn't got. She slammed the door. She'd be in trouble for that.

It was cold. The fog was thick again. Snowflakes drifted and fluttered through the still air. The bones still hung around the door. She grabbed the biggest one she could reach.

The fountain grew out of the fog, a lone, grey structure in a world of white. Thick, icy necklaces decorated the trough's edges. And beyond it, the ghost of the wooden platform. She tried not to look at it.

She reached the fountain and pushed her hand down onto the frozen surface of the trough. The ice, as she had feared, was too thick to break. She was conscious of the door to the lodge opening as she raised the bone and brought it down hard onto the surface. The impact was loud and sharp and ricocheted through the village, but it worked! Hannah plunged her hand down into the icy depths. But she could only reach so far.

'Lord help us,' came Aunt Maud's voice from behind her. 'The girl's gone mad.'

Hannah didn't take any notice. She had to get those drawings. She leaned her body on the stone edge and stretched deep into the agonisingly cold water. She groped around, but couldn't find anything. Had somebody already found the tin? Could it have somehow gone down the drain? What if –

Her fingers brushed something. She stretched a little further. There! She had it in her fingers. She stood upright, pulling the tin with her, along with water and ice and an excruciating pain that was quickly creeping up her arm and into her shoulder.

But she didn't care. If this tin contained what Heinz claimed he had hidden in it, everything could be about to change. She remembered how, just by seeing Matilda's face, a vague memory had come back. And then, slowly, more. It had taken a while, and Matilda's letter had helped, but she had only met the girl once. If relatives and friends of the missing children saw their faces, they'd remember, wouldn't they? They would believe what she had to say. Which meant they would do something to get Elias and the other children back. And that was worth a lot of pain.

She turned, waving the tin high above her head, relieved and exhilarated. 'Aunt Maud, I've found it! I've –'

She clamped her mouth shut. What was she doing? Sound travelled in this fog, she remembered. She lowered her arm, turned a full circle to stare into the grey. The feeling of being watched overwhelmed her. Not just by Aunt Maud.

Hannah tucked the tin into her armpit and started back. She couldn't walk fast enough. The lodge, Aunt Maud, seemed too far away. A pair of hands was going to reach out of the fog and grab her any second. But now Aunt Maud was stepping out of the doorway in only her house shoes, her dress and apron, glancing left and right and beyond Hannah, stretching out her arm so that Hannah could grasp it, and then pulling her inside and closing the door behind them both.

They didn't speak until they were in the kitchen. Aunt Maud grabbed a towel and began to rub at Hannah's frozen arm. Hannah hugged the tin as the blood flowed to the surface of her skin and the pain began to recede.

'Aunt Maud, I –'

'What have you got?'

Hannah stared at the tin, as if seeing it for the first time. It felt too heavy to contain just drawings. Oh no! She hoped the water hadn't got in. She gave it a shake. Pebbles. Of course, she remembered.

'Proof,' she said, placing the tin upright on the table.

'Proof?' Now Aunt Maud was staring at the tin, as if she were expecting it to give up a secret there and then.

'Inside the tin,' said Hannah. She pulled out a chair and sat down.

Aunt Maud did the same. 'Proof of what?'

'You'll see.' *I really do hope.*

'Go on, then,' said Aunt Maud. 'Open it. Show me what all this fuss is about.'

Hannah placed the tin on the table. She held it with one hand, and pushed up on the catch with the thumb of the other. It wouldn't budge. Both hands around it. Both thumbs pushing. Teeth clenched. But no. The top was on tight. That was good, she reminded herself in her frustration. That meant there was a good seal.

'Here, let me,' said Aunt Maud.

Hannah, defeated, passed it to Aunt Maud, who wiped her hands in her apron and tried. Still nothing. Then she wrapped both hands in her apron, picked up the tin and brought the catch down on the side of the table, hard. There was a pop, and the lid flipped up, pebbles spilling out onto Aunt Maud's lap and the floor.

'You did it!' said Hannah, jumping from foot to foot, unable to stand still.

Aunt Maud unwrapped the tin from her apron. She didn't look inside, but placed it on the table in front of Hannah. 'Show me,' she said.

Hannah turned the tin upside down to empty the pebbles onto the table. Dry pebbles. She stared into the open end of the tin. And there they were. A stack of drawings, rolled up to fit inside, but looking clean and dry. She pulled them out and spread them across the table.

There were fifty or so, on paper the size of postcards. And they were good. Really good. *Almost like photographs.* Many of them of children she didn't recognise. But wait!

She picked one up. A picture of a boy. About thirteen, she guessed. He looked familiar. His expression. Almost a sneer.

'Boris,' she said. The whole memory came back to her like water filling a dry gully. Of being on the bridge with Josef and Matilda. Of Boris's taunting. Of her sharp retort about the Oberstleutnant being her father. The glue that held the pages of her mind together was coming away. The corner had been pulled.

She went to show Aunt Maud, but Aunt Maud's hand was reaching out and taking another drawing from the pile. Hannah watched as she lifted it and, her hand beginning to tremble, held it up in front of her slowly collapsing face.

Hannah saw what was on it. She held her breath and waited.

Aunt Maud's other hand went to her mouth. Another corner being pulled. She pressed her palm harder. The pages were becoming unstuck. She shook her head and squeezed her eyes shut.

'How could I forget?' she sobbed. 'How could I?'

There he was. Elias. His hair cut short around his ears, a cheeky smile, a mouth half open. Probably asking a question.

'It was the radio,' explained Hannah, but Aunt Maud didn't appear to have heard her. She was rifling through the other drawings, picking them up, studying them.

'Are there others?' she asked.

'Yes, but I don't know how many.' Hannah had found a drawing of Matilda in happier times, a sparkle in her eye, her hair braided. She passed it to Aunt Maud, along with the picture of Boris.

It took a couple of seconds, but the glue finally melted away. 'The Weber children. I don't know their names.'

'Matilda,' said Hannah. 'And Boris.'

Aunt Maud nodded, as if she had known all along. 'You said you met this girl at the castle? She gave you a letter?'

'She was taken,' said Hannah. 'With Boris.'

'So they're all at the castle? The missing children?'

'I don't know, Aunt Maud.' She would like to think they were. At least, that way, they knew where they were and there was a chance they could be brought back.

'But why? In God's name, why?'

Hannah didn't know how to reply. What was the reason for any of it?

'Those poor, poor children.' Aunt Maud placed the drawings back on the table and held her hand against Hannah's cheek. It was warm and comforting. As if this were the woman she really was. Or had been, once. 'I am so sorry.'

'It's not your fault,' said Hannah, tears stinging her eyes. 'The Oberstleutnant fooled everybody.'

The mention of the Oberstleutnant had an immediate effect on Aunt Maud. She scooped the drawings up into a pile, folded them back into the tin and resealed it.

'I believe his days of staying here are over. But I can't be certain. We need to be careful with these.'

Hannah fought the urge to run to the end of the hallway and lock the door.

'What should we do about the radio?' she asked.

This time, Aunt Maud heard her. 'The radio?'

'That's how he's doing it.' She realised she didn't have any proof of this. 'I think so, anyway.'

'The radio?' Aunt Maud repeated.

'I think it does something to our minds. Makes us forget.'

Aunt Maud tittered. Then her mouth straightened. Her gaze appeared to turn inwards. 'I visited a travelling fair once, when I was a little girl. With your . . . with my brother and parents. There was a hypnotist there. You could watch him, then just drop a coin in the hat. I saw what he could do with his words. Make people behave in the most foolish ways and then, with the snap of his fingers, make them forget.'

Hannah waited for her to say some more. But she didn't. Instead, she glanced up at the clock.

'Nearly half past eight. Too late.'

'Too late for what?' asked Hannah.

'For you to catch Josef before school.'

'That boy?' asked Hannah, allowing a smirk to spread across her face.

'You've had one apology from me already this morning, young lady. Don't push it.' There was a lightness to her voice, but the old Aunt Maud was on her way back. 'You should go there after school today. Bring him back here. He deserves to see these. After all the help he's given you.'

FIFTY-EIGHT

Hannah was exhausted. The nervous energy and emotional relief from this morning had wiped her out. Aunt Maud had said they needed to keep acting as if everything were normal, and so Hannah had gone to her room to finish her darning, but she couldn't concentrate. She looked out her window to the castle. Was Elias there? And the other missing children? Her eyes were heavy. A snap decision and she was in bed, letting sleep wash over her . . .

The castle rose up at her, the turrets lost in the heavy fog above. Up and over the walls she travelled. And into the courtyard where the Oberstleutnant had admonished the soldier.

She took a moment to calm herself. To remind herself that she was untouchable. Still, it was difficult when, hanging from the balconies above, were those red, white and black symbols of hatred.

Last time it had been almost empty, but now the courtyard was filled with black, shiny cars. What was going on?

She slowed her travel and floated over the tops of them. Soldiers milled around, smoking cigarettes and talking, rifles slung across their backs. She made her way up the steps and across the balcony. A guard opened the main door to let a man in SS uniform inside. Hannah followed him in.

'General,' said another SS soldier appearing from a room to their left. He raised his arm out straight. 'Heil Hitler!'

The General returned the gesture silently.

'If you would follow me,' said the man.

Hannah floated behind, down a long corridor that boasted grand pictures and shallow alcoves that contained rich artefacts, through a door that led into the great hallway.

The room was filled with people. Hannah had been expecting to see the men in black uniforms. What she hadn't expected were the women in frocks and heels. Or the children running around.

She forced herself to enter.

Drinks were being handed out. Platters of fine food adorned the tables. There were smiles and laughter. Light-hearted banter. It was more like a birthday party than a meeting of military personnel. A young girl carried a plate up to an old man who wore an eyepiece. He removed it to study what was on offer, took a pastry and waved her away, replacing his monocle.

Hannah hovered beside the group of three men, and the girl turned to face her. Matilda! She was thinner and there was a fresh bruise upon her cheek. Hannah felt her misery.

'Oberstleutnant Kessler is proving a valuable asset to the Third Reich,' said the man with the monocle.

A thin man with a weasel's face and a mouth too wide gave a single nod. 'He will be rewarded for his hard work, Hermann. It is such a genius idea.'

'No more genius than your idea of handing out the Volksempfänger to everybody in the country, Joseph.' This man was short, his hair shaved close at the side. He had a thin moustache and rimless spectacles.

Joseph gave that single nod again. Not a smile. His face didn't appear to be made for smiles. 'I will take the credit for that. But they weren't handed out, Heinrich. Every German citizen paid for them.'

Hannah drifted across the room to another table, where a group of children were helping themselves to cake.

'Your father's castle is enormous, Fredrik,' said a dark-haired boy of around ten. His eyes looked like saucers through his thick glasses. 'I nearly got lost.'

The blond boy spoke with his mouth full of cake. 'My father says Ursula and I are going to move here soon, with Mama. When he's finished his work.'

'I don't want to move here,' said Ursula with a pout. 'I like having friends, but Papa says there aren't any children in the village.'

'There are still some,' said Fredrik. 'But not for long.'

'Where are they going?' asked Ursula.

'Away, to be locked up. Like the Jews,' sneered Fredrik.

What did he mean, locked up? Locked up where? How would he know, anyway? He was only a child. Like her.

'Jews have to be locked up,' said a pony-tailed girl a little older than Hannah. 'Or they spread diseases.'

Hannah screamed inside. This was worse than the conversation between the men. These were children.

'If they have diseases,' said Ursula, 'shouldn't we try to cure them?'

'We are curing them,' replied Fredrik, and he and the older girl laughed. But it was the laughs of foxes in a henhouse. The boy with the glasses didn't join in. He looked defiant, as though their words worried him.

'It's in their blood,' said the brown-haired boy. 'It's not the same as ours.'

'Is it a different colour?' asked the older girl.

He shook his head. 'If it was, they would be easier to spot. They're very good at hiding.'

We've had to be, thought Hannah. *Because of people like you*.

Two men strolled up to the children. The Oberstleutnant's tall, wiry frame was instantly recognisable. The other man had dark hair combed forward and to the side. He wore black trousers, but his jacket was grey. The children immediately raised their arms in a straight salute. The Oberstleutnant returned the gesture.

'These are your children, Oberstleutnant?' asked the man.

The Oberstleutnant nodded. 'Yes, this is Fredrik and Ursula,' the Oberstleutnant said.

The Oberstleutnant's children! But that couldn't be his daughter. Hannah had been wearing her hand-me-downs. This girl looked barely eight.

But if the clothes didn't belong to his daughter, where would they have come from?

'It is very nice to meet you, Fredrik and Ursula,' said the man. 'Your father is doing very important work for the Fatherland.'

They both stood there, the sweetest smiles upon their faces.

The Oberstleutnant stared nervously from the man, to his children, and back again. Hannah had never seen him like this.

'Well, what do you say, children?'

They both shot their arms out, straight, palms down.

'Heil Hitler!'

Hannah floated over, up and behind the children, facing the two men.

There was no mistaking that moustache. Those cold eyes.

She fell back with terror. The picture of that face refused to dissipate from her mind. She wanted to shut it out, but she had no eyes to close. She focused upon the high ceiling, the chandeliers, the windows. Anything but him. Gradually, coherent thoughts returned, her reason for being here, and she began to pull herself together.

Without any announcement, the men began to drift towards a door that Hannah hadn't noticed before. She followed them into a small room with vermilion walls and a long, polished table that ran down the centre. Servants ushered the men over to ornately carved mahogany chairs where they stood, stiff and solid, waiting.

Adolf Hitler stopped at the doorway. They all turned and raised their hands. 'Heil Hitler!'

A single, stoic nod of acknowledgement, and he lowered himself into his seat at the head of the table. The rest of the men followed suit. At the opposite end of the table sat the Oberstleutnant. Water was poured and papers were shuffled and Hannah waited, anxious and afraid, above it all.

'Mein Führer, gentlemen, I welcome you all to castle Felshoven. And I look forward, very soon, to providing you with a remarkable demonstration of Operation Schwarzberg.'

Schwarzberg! The castle where the tale of Edgar and Otto had originated. Dread flooded her.

'As you can see, the castle is now fully equipped with electricity, provided by twelve generators on the land to the south. The first task I set my men when we arrived was to connect electricity throughout the castle and to every house in the village that lies below us, four kilometres to the north-east. As counted six weeks ago, it had precisely four hundred and forty-three inhabitants.'

He waited for the information to sink in.

'There are now four hundred and twenty-five inhabitants due to eight children having been removed, and an unfortunate incident a few days ago.'

A low murmur went around the table.

'Removed?' asked a grey-haired skeletal man sitting beside the Führer. 'To where?'

'All but one are in the castle dungeons. The one who is not was serving your food earlier under close watch.'

So Elias and the others were here! But in the dungeons. The bowels of the castle. Behind too many locked doors. Hannah wouldn't be able to get there today.

'But they will be moved to the camps when we have taken the rest,' said the Oberstleutnant. 'Tomorrow night we shall take the population of Felshoven down to three hundred and sixty-one by removing all remaining children. Sixty-four in total.'

Hannah was starting to panic. Every child! Including her.

'Jews, I assume,' someone said from the table. 'You've brought us all up here to show us that?'

'Please continue,' said their leader, ignoring him.

'Thank you, Mein Führer. They are not Jews. They are German citizens.'

How many times had she heard that? Why was it illegal to be both?

Another murmur.

'You are removing German children? For what purpose?' asked a huge, bald man.

'To show you all what *can* be done to the Jews. They are, how should I put it, necessary losses.'

What did he mean? *What* can be done? There was something terrible being revealed here. Far worse than anything Hannah had thought possible. But she still didn't understand. Didn't want to believe . . .

A thin man with sharp shoulders and a patch over one eye laughed. 'We all know what can be done to the Jews. Every man here is doing his best to rid Germany of them. It is not a secret.'

The Oberstleutnant slammed the table. 'Precisely! Everybody knows!'

The murmuring stopped.

'The world does not have the wisdom of our great leader. They do not understand. They refuse to understand.'

'Then we shall make them understand!'

'No, gentlemen. We shall not. What we shall do is make them forget.'

The table was now silent.

'Let me put this to you, gentlemen. We have removed eight children from the village in the past six weeks. Eight children from their homes in the middle of the night. What do you think the village is doing about this? What do you think the parents, grandparents of these children are feeling?'

'Despair!'

'Anger!'

'Fear!'

'No,' replied the Oberstleutnant. 'Because, gentlemen, they do not know they are gone. Those children are, as far as the world is concerned, forgotten.'

'Do you mean to say,' asked the man with the eyepatch, 'that even the parents of those children have no memories of them?'

'None whatsoever. To the people in the village, those children never existed.'

'Nonsense.'

'Impossible!'

'And, very soon, we shall remove the rest. We shall bring them here from the village. You will talk to them, ask them their names, where they live. Whatever you like. And the day after, we shall take a tour of the village. And I assure you that not one of the parents or grandparents will remember them at all.'

'But how?'

'Do you inject them?'

'Remove a part of their brain?'

The Oberstleutnant motioned to a servant, who wheeled over a trolley holding something covered in black cloth.

'There is no medical procedure. All we use is this.' He pulled at the cloth, passing it to the servant. The men around the table stared and shook their heads, scratched their chins and whispered to themselves.

This was the confirmation that Hannah had been looking for. She had been right. But there was no satisfaction at being right, just a regretful acceptance that she was.

'The Volksempfänger. A marvellous, some say magical, box that can take a voice from a hundred kilometres away and repeat it as though it were in the same room as the listener. A box which, thanks to General Joseph Goebbels here, is in every citizen's home across the Fatherland.'

'You mean this ... radio ... is all that it takes to make them forget?'

'Perhaps not all. But is it so difficult to comprehend? We are all aware of the power of hypnosis. One voice being able to control another's mind. All I have done is to extend this to the masses.'

Hannah surveyed the faces, grotesque in their malice.

A single clap from the far end of the table made everybody turn. Another clap. And another, and then everybody was joining in.

When the applause finally subsided, somebody said, 'That is all very well, Oberstleutnant, but how can you be sure they will all be listening to the radio?'

'Let me just say they have been convinced.'

Hannah tried not to see those pools of red.

'You mentioned that the Volksempfänger is not the only tool you use. What else is there?'

The Oberstleutnant laughed. 'Come, gentlemen. Like a magician, I cannot expose all the tricks I have up my sleeve. All will be revealed tomorrow night.'

Tomorrow night!

'Astounding,' said one of the men. 'And you say there is not one person in the village who has any idea of what is going on.'

The Oberstleutnant seemed to ponder this. 'There is one. But we are looking into it. That person will be dealt with.'

Heinz! They must mean Heinz!

'But back to the demonstration,' said the Oberstleutnant. 'At six o'clock tomorrow evening, every radio in the village will be on and every villager will be listening. These radios have been modified so that they broadcast only on one frequency. A frequency that I have full control over. At eight o'clock my troops will enter the village from the south. The houses containing the children are identified by animal bones hanging from the doorways.'

'Animal bones?'

'Some strange superstition that exists in the village. Why do you think we chose Felshoven? For the purpose of this experiment, think of the children as Jews and think of the bones as yellow stars painted on their doors. The soldiers will enter the houses without resistance. They will find everybody sleeping soundly. They will remove the children to the waiting trucks and move on. A second team will go in after them. They will search the houses for any signs of the children's existence – toys, books, drawings. School records will be removed by a third team. Any other houses these children may have visited will also be searched. Everything found will be taken and thrown into the trucks for disposal. There are sixty-four children left to locate and remove. The operation should be over in less than six hours. We start at eight, finish at two.'

'And the purpose of this demonstration?' asked a fair-haired man sitting next to the Führer.

'Isn't it obvious?' asked the Oberstleutnant, silently taking in every face around the room.

'Tomorrow, you shall witness the success of Operation Schwarzberg. After that, with the Führer's blessing, we shall roll it out across the whole of Germany ... France ... Poland ... Belgium ... We shall rid the world of every Jew, every person of colour, everybody who is not as we are. We shall purify our race. And nobody shall know. Nobody shall remember. They will all, every one of them, be forgotten.'

Hannah finally understood. Not only what the Oberstleutnant was planning, but also what was happening all across the country. She fled, leaving behind the sound of scraping chairs, the stamping of boots and the terrifying chants of 'Heil Hitler!'.

FIFTY-NINE

The first thing Hannah did when she woke was to strip herself of the clothes the Oberstleutnant had brought her. She didn't know where they had come from, didn't dare to think. But they hadn't belonged to his daughter. Instead, she changed into those given to her by Aunt Maud.

Aunt Maud. Hannah needed to tell her about what she had just seen and heard! Straightaway!

But she couldn't. Not yet. Aunt Maud finally believed her about Elias. But how would Hannah explain this? What would she say? That she had floated out of the village and up the mountain to the castle in her sleep?

She had been able to convince Josef. She just might need some help convincing Aunt Maud.

'Straight there and straight back,' said Aunt Maud. She was standing in the kitchen doorway, rubbing her hands together as if she were washing them under a tap. Hannah got the impression she had just surfaced from deep thought.

Hannah tried not to give anything away with her voice, and kept looking down at her shoes as she buckled them up. 'But Josef has to let his mother know first.'

'Yes, yes, of course.'

Hannah pulled her coat off the hook.

'And don't run.'

Hannah nodded. She wouldn't run. But she wouldn't dawdle either. There was a lot to do. She just wasn't sure what it was yet.

Hannah stood in the playground where Heinz had counted and memorised the children before he had gone home to capture their images on paper. Some of the younger ones came out laughing and skipping. Others, mostly the older children, carried looks of worry behind the playful banter and friendly smiles. She eventually spotted Josef amongst them. He was no longer the same happy-go-lucky boy who had broken one of Aunt Maud's pots with a ball shortly after she had arrived. Now, he shuffled along in the shallow snow, hands in pockets, head down.

She walked over to him. He would have passed right by if she hadn't reached out and grabbed his sleeve.

He looked up, fear in his eyes. He must have read the same, or worse, in hers.

'What are you doing here? What's happened?'

'You need to come back to the lodge,' said Hannah.

'Why?'

Hannah glanced around the playground. Imagined eyes around every corner, peering out of the fog. 'Not here. Back at the lodge. But go home and tell your mum where you're going first.'

A couple of quick nods. 'All right.' He turned to go, but she grabbed his sleeve again.

'Josef?'

'What?'

'Frau Meinhardt? Is she still here?'

He nodded towards the entrance. 'She's inside. The room down the end on the right.'

'Okay. I'll find her. You go.'

She thought of telling him not to run, but he was already off.

The smell brought back memories from long ago. What was it? Chalk had no smell. Did pencils? Perhaps paper, ink. Wooden desks and chairs. Chalkboards. Children.

She hadn't been inside a school for such a long time. She hurried down the corridor, past the stragglers, glancing through doorways at rows of desks, pots of pencils, colourful drawings stuck to walls, burying her own memories as she fought to stay focused on the task at hand.

'Sofia!' Frau Meinhardt had stepped out of the room at the end.

'Frau Meinhardt.' She hadn't thought this through. 'Umm. Aunt Maud wants to see you.'

The teacher frowned. 'Your aunt? Is everything all right?'

No. No, it isn't. Not at all. She needed to get her to the safety of the lodge first. Not here, beside open doors and echoing walls.

'She would like to see you. About me starting school.'

'That is good news,' smiled Frau Meinhardt. 'But can't it wait until –?'

Hannah shook her head.

'I'll get my bag,' said the teacher. 'You can tell me on the way.'

It was too much. Hannah had given something away. But it didn't matter. Frau Meinhardt was coming to the lodge.

'Thank you for coming,' said Aunt Maud. She closed the door behind them and swept the bolt across to lock it.

Frau Meinhardt raised her eyebrows.

'Make your way through to the kitchen,' said Aunt Maud. She and Hannah exchanged nervous glances. 'Josef is already here.'

Hannah felt her breath catch in her throat. The normally automatic task of taking in air suddenly felt like a labour.

Josef was sitting at the kitchen table. It was empty, apart from the tin sitting at its centre. He flashed a quick smile. She flashed one back.

The room was filled with the smell of freshly brewed coffee.

Frau Meinhardt pulled up a chair.

Aunt Maud closed the kitchen door.

'What's this all about?' asked Frau Meinhardt.

'It's not about me going to school,' replied Hannah. She needed to say something before the reveal. Just to get herself breathing naturally again.

Aunt Maud poured coffee into cups. She hadn't asked who wanted one, her mind obviously elsewhere.

When they were all sitting, Aunt Maud took a sip of coffee before saying, 'Sofia, open the tin. Show them.'

Hannah reached for it, feeling all eyes upon her.

The lid came off easily this time. Hannah didn't tip the drawings out onto the table, but instead pulled them out carefully, as if they were the children themselves. The drawing of Elias was on top. It was only fair that Josef should see it first. She handed it to him.

'What's this? Oh, that's a good drawing. Who . . .?'

'Heinz Schundel drew them, Josef,' said Hannah.

His face lost all expression. 'That's . . . Where did you . . .?'

'What is it?' asked Frau Meinhardt, leaning over to take a look.

'I don't . . .' Josef scratched his forehead. 'Is that . . .? It is, isn't it?' He looked up at her. Like he had just seen a ghost. Which, in a way, he had. 'It's Elias.'

Frau Meinhardt snatched the drawing from him. After a few seconds, her hand went to her mouth, much like Aunt Maud's had.

Hannah didn't know whether to smile or cry. In the end, she did a little of both.

'You were right,' said Josef. The corner of the page was being pulled away. The glue was starting to come off. 'I remember . . . we . . . we sat in the courtyard, and we fed the chickens.' Hannah kept nodding and smiling. 'We went to Frau Lister's. She's . . . she's his grandmother.'

Hannah could almost hear the pages separating.

'He was in my class,' said Frau Meinhardt. 'Elias Lister.'

'We sent the cake up in the lift,' continued Josef. Hannah flicked her eyes to Aunt Maud, but the words seemed to have bypassed her. Either that, or she didn't care. 'And The Old Man's Bones. We went together. The three of us. We hung them on your door, Frau Meyer.'

'You did, Josef, you did.'

Frau Meinhardt was shuffling through the other drawings. Her usual smiling face seemed a long way off. Apart from those bright blue eyes, her whole face had lost colour.

'I walked him home,' said Josef. 'And then he disappeared.'

Hannah nodded once more, and a tear fell out and rolled down her cheek. This moment had been such a long time coming, but it had finally arrived. Aunt Maud placed her hand upon hers. She looked like she was about to cry, too.

Frau Meinhardt was still going through the drawings, dropping each one onto the table without speaking.

Josef picked them up one at a time. 'There's Ingrid . . .' He held up a picture of a girl whose hair was in bows. The one Heinz had spoken of. 'That's Karl . . . Boris . . . and Matilda. I'd forgotten. But how . . . where are they?' asked Josef, when he had gone through them all.

'They're in the castle dungeons. Except, maybe, Matilda.'

Hannah glanced at Frau Meinhardt. She was just staring ahead, silent. Hardly breathing, it seemed. Hannah hadn't expected that response from her. She had expected tears, maybe questions. But they were coming from Josef.

'It's the Oberstleutnant,' said Hannah. 'He takes the children, then uses the radios to wipe the memory of them from our minds.'

Frau Meinhardt seemed to wake up. 'The radios? Are you sure?'

'I am.'

'We have to get them out,' said Josef.

SIXTY

'The Oberstleutnant is planning to take us all,' said Hannah, scanning each of the faces around the table.

'All?' asked Aunt Maud. 'What do you mean, all?'

'Me, Josef, every child in Felshoven. And he plans to do it tomorrow night.'

'Where would he take them? asked Frau Meinhardt.

Hannah didn't know. She could only repeat what she had heard. 'Away. To be locked up.'

Frau Meinhardt frowned. 'Where did you hear this?'

To Hannah's surprise, it was Aunt Maud who said, 'Does that matter? We've doubted Sofia on too many things, and look where that has got us. So let's not doubt her today. Let's act and ask questions later.'

Hannah could have kissed her.

'There are people at the castle right now. The worst people. The Oberstleutnant wants to show them what he's doing. What he can do. And that's what is happening tomorrow night.'

'What people?' asked Aunt Maud.

Was there any other way to tell them? Would any of them believe this? Even Josef?

'The Führer,' she said.

Frau Meinhardt's blue eyes turned to saucers. She shook her head in disbelief. Aunt Maud closed hers tight. Neither of them saw Josef's mouth drop open and his silent mouthing of *No way!*

'And all his SS cronies,' added Hannah. 'With their wives. Even their children. Eating and drinking and laughing about it.' She stopped talking, realising she was speaking as if she were there while all this was happening . . .

'You went to the castle again?' Aunt Maud asked.

Hannah nodded.

'When? How? Does the Oberstleutnant know that you know?' Josef asked.

Hannah locked eyes with him to answer his question, saw the realisation settle in his raised eyebrows.

'Tomorrow night, the Oberstleutnant is going to send his soldiers for us. He'll take us away and nobody will ever know.'

'Because of the radios,' said Josef. She wasn't sure if this was a question.

'So we destroy the radios,' said Frau Meinhardt.

'But that won't stop him trying,' said Aunt Maud. 'And you've seen what he can do when he doesn't get his way.'

They had.

Silence.

Aunt Maud, who had dared to hide a Jew *and* a British soldier under the same roof as an SS soldier, looked defeated. But why? When both the Jew and the British soldier were still unknown to the Oberstleutnant . . .

'We hide the children,' said Hannah.

'Hide them?' Frau Meinhardt asked. 'Where? And for how long? I don't see how –'

'How many children are there in the village?' asked Aunt Maud, ignoring the teacher's questions.

'There are sixty-four children left in the village,' said Hannah, remembering what the Oberstleutnant had said. Nobody asked how she knew. Whatever she said, it seemed, was now being taken as fact. She glared at Aunt Maud. 'And you have to hide them.'

Aunt Maud sat back. 'Me? Hide sixty or so children? How am I supposed to do that?'

Hannah leaned on the table, trying to keep her frustration in check and annoyance from her voice. 'That is what you do. Remember?'

Aunt Maud held her gaze. A look of disappointment flickered across her face.

Hannah looked away. She was sorry for that – she hadn't meant to betray her trust. Aunt Maud had the power to betray hers now. Would she?

'You hide people?' Frau Meinhardt sat back, her eyes flicking between Hannah and Aunt Maud. 'Who do you hide?'

This was it. Hannah kept her head down, cast a glance at Aunt Maud through her eyelashes. Aunt Maud's eyes hadn't moved from Hannah's face.

'George,' said Aunt Maud, sheepishly. As if she were a child being forced to own up to something.

Frau Meinhardt held her hands up. 'Who is George?'

Aunt Maud paused. Hannah could see the options of what to say and what not to say running through her mind.

'He's a British soldier,' she finally said.

'And where's he hiding?'

'In the attic.'

Frau Meinhardt put her face in her hands and shook her head. 'This is all so –'

'I think he can help,' Hannah interrupted.

'Help?' asked Aunt Maud. 'How can George help?'

Josef rubbed the back of his head. 'Yeah, Sofia, how can George help?'

'He has a radio. He can make contact with –'

'Actually, I don't think you should tell me any more,' said Frau Meinhardt. 'Just do what you have to do. Josef and I will arrange to get the children out. You're right, I think that's the only way to stop this from happening. But we haven't got time to explain this to every household and get them to agree. Let's face it, who would agree to that?'

'We could take them from the school,' said Josef. 'Tomorrow.'

It sounded absurd. But it would be the easiest option. The quickest. They would all be in one place.

'We steal the children without their parents knowing?' Frau Meinhardt's voice wavered.

Aunt Maud threw up her hands. 'What choice do we have? Either we do it, or the Oberstleutnant does.'

'But how do I convince the headmaster? We'd need his help.'

Josef held up one of the drawings. 'You show him this.'

They all stared at the perfect replication of a young boy's face.

'Who is it?' asked Hannah.

'It's Felix Guttman,' said Josef. 'The headmaster's grandson. He's another one of the children who were taken.'

Frau Meinhardt took the drawing from him and studied it. 'Of course it is.'

'But where do we go?' asked Josef. 'Where is safe from the Oberstleutnant and his soldiers?'

'There is nowhere safe. Not in the village. And we can't just head into the forest. Everyone would freeze to death,' said Frau Meinhardt, still looking at the picture.

Hannah was starting to deflate. There must be somewhere they could hide. They couldn't stumble now.

'There are tunnels,' said Aunt Maud. 'To the north.'

Hannah smiled her relief at Aunt Maud. Of course! *Some say they were built by elves or gnomes.* 'Erdställe. I saw one. When Pieter brought me up the mountain. Can so many children hide in there?'

'I think so,' said her aunt. 'They're narrow, but deep. Josef, do you know the way?'

He nodded. 'I've been there a few times. But don't tell my mum. She says I shouldn't wander that far.'

Aunt Maud winked. Actually winked. 'Your secret's safe with us.'

'We leave the school early in the afternoon,' said Frau Meinhardt.

'But when they don't return home . . .' said Aunt Maud. 'We need to let the parents know. They'll worry. They'll call on each other. When they realise all the children are missing, they'll panic.'

'They'll go to the school,' said Hannah. 'We need somebody there to explain. Not before, or the parents would try to stop them. But afterwards, when they would already be on their way to the Erdställe.'

'I can do that,' said Aunt Maud.

Hannah stared at the papers scattered across the table. The village children. Six of the eight missing captured here.

'No,' she said. 'I have a better idea.'

She ruffled through the drawings and pulled out the portraits of Elias, Boris, Matilda, Ingrid and Karl, and lined them up on the table.

'Their parents. Their grandparents. They'll be more convincing. They can tell everybody what the Oberstleutnant has done.'

But first, those parents and grandparents had to be reminded of what had been taken from them.

SIXTY-ONE

It was still light when Frau Meinhardt took the drawing of Felix Guttman, and offered to walk Josef home safely. They could finesse the details of what they'd need for the next day along the way, she'd said. Josef had already been thinking aloud about packing some of his old toys for the younger children.

Aunt Maud had insisted that she should be the one to speak to the parents and grandparents of the missing children tomorrow. It was her village, she'd said, and no one argued.

Once Josef and Frau Meinhardt had left, Hannah felt the coldness from Aunt Maud come back.

'I'm sorry, Aunt Maud,' she whispered.

'What's done is done. Now, let's find out how George can help us.'

Hannah could smell George before she saw him. He entered the kitchen behind Aunt Maud in a half-stagger, his eyes squinting against the late afternoon glare coming through the window.

'Take a seat, George,' said Aunt Maud.

He smiled at Hannah.

'Hello, George.'

He glanced back at the door. 'Are you sure this is safe?'

'It's safe, George,' said Hannah. 'Nobody is coming here today.'

'How do you know?'

In this light, Hannah could see just how pale he had become, living in near darkness for so long. Thin, too. And hairy.

'That's what we need to talk to you about,' said Aunt Maud. 'Sit down. I'll bring you some coffee.'

George rubbed his hands together and sat down. 'That would be good.' He took in the surroundings, his eyes still narrowed. 'It is good to be out.' His German, Hannah realised, was too stiff. Too formal. As if he were trying too hard.

Aunt Maud brought over the coffee. He took a long sip, closed his eyes and swallowed.

Enough time had been wasted. They shouldn't waste any more on small talk. 'George, we need your help,' Hannah said.

He lowered the cup and looked at Aunt Maud. 'My help? Why? What has happened?'

Aunt Maud's eyes went to Hannah, surrendering the situation to her.

'George, remember what you said? About what you could do if something terrible was happening at the castle?' Hannah pressed.

'Yes . . .'

'Well, something terrible is happening. Tomorrow night.'

He sat forward and clasped his hands together. 'Tomorrow night? How do you –? What's going to happen?'

Hannah glanced at Aunt Maud, who gave her a nod to continue. Hannah was the only person who had all the pieces to hand. She just had to figure out how to put them together to save the village children. This was the first piece of the puzzle. Possibly the only bit she was confident about.

'The Oberstleutnant has been taking children.'

'Such as your friend?'

'Yes, and other children, too.'

George turned to Aunt Maud. 'And you believe her now?'

'I believe her.'

He rocked his head, his shoulders, back and forth, considering this. 'And tomorrow night?'

'He's going to take the rest,' said Hannah.

'You know this for sure?'

She nodded.

'But how?'

'It was from a trusted source, George,' said Aunt Maud.

Good old Aunt Maud.

'The Oberstleutnant and his soldiers are going to take the rest of them. Of us. Tomorrow night at eight o'clock. It's some kind of experiment. He's been using the radios to make the whole village forget their children.'

A snicker from George, as if he were doubting her.

'George, this is serious!'

He held up a palm. 'I know. I'm sorry. But this is so … unbelievable.'

'Believe it, George,' said Aunt Maud.

'We're going to take the children out of the village,' said Hannah. 'Hide them until it's safe.'

'Hide them? Hide them where?'

'Somewhere safe. It doesn't matter. But far enough away from the Oberstleutnant and from your people.'

His eyes, which had begun to adjust to the light, once more narrowed as he considered what she was asking. 'No, no, I can't.'

‘Can’t what?’ asked Aunt Maud. Hannah wasn’t sure who she was asking.

‘You can’t or you won’t?’ Hannah pressed him.

‘Can’t what?’ Aunt Maud’s voice cracked.

Hannah’s eyes remained on the airman. ‘George’s mission was to find out what was happening at the castle. And if it was bad, he was going to call in his planes to bomb it.’

‘It’s bad,’ said Aunt Maud. ‘Call them in, George.’

‘I’ll need more than what you’ve told me.’

Hannah was beginning to lose her patience. Why was he being so difficult?

Something seemed to overflow inside her. She leaped to her feet. The chair flew back, toppling over. ‘How about Adolf Hitler up there in the castle right now? How about the SS generals up there right now? All the big men in their fancy black uniforms with their medals and their plans to rid this country of every Jew? To make them disappear forever? To make the world forget they ever existed? How about that, George? Is that enough for you?’

George closed his eyes. He placed his palms upon the table and hung his head. His body heaved in time to his breathing. Hannah waited, her eyes drilling into the top of his head, willing him to agree.

‘Are there children up there?’ he asked. She still couldn’t see his face, but she guessed he was mulling it over.

‘They’re in the dungeons,’ said Hannah.

‘Then they should be safe.’

Matilda! She had forgotten about her. She just had to hope and pray that the girl, when she wasn’t serving the Oberstleutnant, was kept in the dungeons like the others. She realised she’d forgotten to mention the children she had seen, including the Oberstleutnant’s . . . Hannah felt sad to think how little she cared. She chewed her cheek. Did that make her as bad as them?

George finally looked up. One deep breath. 'All right. I'll do it.'

She closed her eyes, felt the tears welling up. 'Thank you.'

'There is a chance they won't come,' said George. 'Or they will come too late. But I will do my best.'

That was better than him saying no. It was a chance. A good chance.

'But I ask one thing in return.'

'What do you want?' asked Hannah.

'A warm bath,' replied George, pulling at his beard. 'And a shave.'

'I think we all want you to have that,' said Hannah.

That night, after finally falling asleep, Hannah visited Heinz's house. But no matter how much she called his name, there was no response.

She returned to the lodge and to a deep, dreamless slumber.

SIXTY-TWO

Their first stop in the morning was a small house with a thatched roof on the main road into the village. The woman who opened the door and invited them inside was about the same age as Hannah's mother would have been, but her hair was grey. Aunt Maud didn't waste any time in showing her the drawing of a child forgotten. Ingrid. At first her face opened up. Then the creases reappeared. Her hand went to her mouth and her features rolled themselves up into a wet ball. She folded her thin frame in on herself and wept. Aunt Maud took her hand, waited, then told her what had to be done. The mother nodded, determination shining through her tears.

Next was a tall house, leaning forward as if tempted to topple over on a steep lane. When Aunt Maud knocked, a dog barked, and a middle-aged man opened the door. He was on crutches, and Hannah could see that, beneath his thick trousers, one leg was missing. He seemed pleased to see Aunt Maud and invited them in, calling out to somebody inside. A woman came into the lounge and offered them tea. Aunt Maud took out two drawings. Matilda and Boris . . .

Then the plan explained. Then a goodbye.

Next, a mother and baby. A house that was little more than a barn. A picture of a small boy. Karl. An exposed memory, a collapsed face. A broken person. A plan. A goodbye.

And the final house. A house Hannah had visited several times. Across a bridge. A white picket fence. The smell of baking. A warm welcome from Frau Lister. Into the parlour. The cat asleep at the fire. The drawing came out. Of Elias. Smiling. The glue softened. The corner of the page came away in Frau Lister's mind. She clutched at her chest. She fought for breath. Another look at the drawing. *But why? Where is he? Sofia tried to tell me. How could I forget?*

And this time, they all cried.

SIXTY-THREE

The first thought Hannah had as she and Aunt Maud left the square and headed towards their meeting place was: *Those children shouldn't be coming home.*

Josef emerged out of the fog, running as though his life depended on it.

Aunt Maud stopped. 'God help us, what's happened?'

Hannah gripped the woman's hand. Something had gone terribly wrong. That much was obvious. She could hear one small boy's sobs. Uncontrolled and desperate. Josef hurtled towards them, slipped on the cobbles, regained his feet and continued.

'What is it, Josef? What's happened?'

The small boy ran past them. Hannah watched him go. Home, to where he thought it was safe. But nowhere was. Not if their plan had been discovered.

Josef was struggling to catch his breath. 'The Oberst . . . the Oberstleutnant . . . he was there . . . the soldiers . . . they knew.'

There was nearly a dozen children on the street now. All in some state of distress or panic. Hannah watched as they ran in all directions, two girls crashing through doors and slamming them closed behind them.

Josef was struggling to speak. From somewhere in the distance, lost in the fog, came a scream.

'Don't talk now,' said Aunt Maud. 'We need to get back. Then you can tell us.'

Hannah grabbed Josef's hand and began to pull at him. He let himself be led like an obedient dog, back across the square and in through the door of the lodge. Down the hallway into the parlour. The fire was still glowing but Josef was shivering.

Aunt Maud led him over to an armchair and sat him down. Eventually he got his breathing under control.

'Tell us what happened, Josef,' she said.

Hannah had never seen him like this. Not even when the soldier had searched him at Heinz's house. His terror was slowly becoming hers.

Josef took a breath. 'They were there. The Oberstleutnant and the soldiers. They knew. I don't know how.'

Another deep breath. Hannah held his hand.

'All the children were in pairs. We followed Herr Guttman, towards the track that leads to the forest. They were hiding. In the fog. The soldiers. Six of them. Like . . . like ghosts. And then we saw the Oberstleutnant. He asked us where we were going.'

Josef was beginning to sweat. Aunt Maud removed his hat.

'Herr Guttman said we were just taking a stroll. Finding our way in the fog. In case the children ever got lost. But the Oberstleutnant didn't believe him. He walked over to Gisela and bent down. He asked her where we were going. *To the caves*, she said. *To meet our parents. We're going on an adventure.*

I tried to get her to be quiet. I told the Oberstleutnant she was only small. She was confused. We were doing what Herr Guttman said. Taking a walk round the village. That was when he hit me.'

Aunt Maud unwrapped his scarf. Blood was mashed all around his mouth. His top lip was blue and swollen.

'Dear Lord,' she said. She disappeared outside.

'It's okay, Josef, you did well,' said Hannah. He nodded, but his eyes weren't convinced.

When Aunt Maud returned, she was carrying a damp cloth. There was fresh snow on her boots. 'Put this on your lip.'

Josef took it and placed it against his mouth. His words became muffled, but Hannah could still make them out.

'Herr Guttman started shouting. He rushed at the Oberstleutnant and told him he wanted his grandson back. But the soldiers grabbed him. They pushed him down on the ground and one of them stepped on his face until he stopped shouting. Or he kept shouting but with no words. I'm not sure.

'Then they lifted him to his feet. They separated us. Boys on the right. Girls on the left. And they asked . . .'

Josef began to sob. Hannah wiped at her own eyes. Aunt Maud did the same and then took a corner of the cloth and wiped at Josef's. 'Go on,' she said.

Josef took hold of his sobs. He looked up, such pain in his eyes. 'He told Herr Guttman to choose. The boys or the girls. Who should the soldiers shoot?'

Aunt Maud raised her head and stared at the ceiling. Hannah reached for Josef's hand. It was cold and limp, not even aware that it was being held. He swallowed. Again. And again. Then he folded in half.

'I wanted him to say the girls. I just wanted him to. I'm sorry, Sofia. I'm so sorry.'

Aunt Maud wrapped both hands around Hannah's and Josef's and squeezed.

'But he didn't,' said Hannah, remembering how boys *and* girls had run down the street towards them. 'He didn't do it.'

Josef shook his head and looked up. 'Herr Guttman refused to choose. The Oberstleutnant, he said that was why men like him could never lead this country to victory, why he was here spending his days teaching children while braver men were out there fighting.' Josef stared straight ahead. 'Then he shot him.'

Hannah placed her hands behind her head and squeezed her eyes shut.

'That man fought in the last war. Came back a hero.'

'Then he let you all go home,' said Hannah, knowing full well what that meant.

But Josef shook his head. 'First he told us to take a message back to our families. To remind them. Turn on the radio tonight at six. Listen. Don't leave the room for an instant. Tonight, something special would happen. And he told me to give you a message, Sofia.'

Hannah felt her bones go cold.

'What message, Josef?' demanded Aunt Maud.

'He said to tell you he would see you at the castle. And the wolves were waiting.'

Aunt Maud clenched her fists and leaped up. 'That man! That Devil! And to think I offered him my hospitality. Well, if he thinks I'll be listening to his hate-spreading Volksempfänger for one second more . . .' She marched over and grabbed the radio. A spark flew from the wall as the cable was ripped from the socket. She threw it to the floor and proceeded to stamp on it. The thin, wooden frame collapsed easily under her weight. Josef pushed himself up and joined her, and between the two of them they ground the box into the rug.

Hannah watched in surreal fascination as they jumped and stamped, and she couldn't help but think that, for something with the potential to destroy so many lives, it really was quite weak. There was little more to it than dead wood and empty space.

When all that had ever existed of the radio lay trampled and broken on the parlour floor, Hannah realised – there was somebody missing. 'Where is Frau Meinhardt? What happened to her?'

Aunt Maud snapped her head up at Hannah. Then at Josef. She grabbed him by the shoulders. 'Josef! Where is Frau Meinhardt? Did they shoot her, too?'

Josef shook his head. 'No. She wasn't there.'

SIXTY-FOUR

Hannah felt the final strands of hope seep out of her. If the woman with the bright blue eyes and the constant smile had betrayed them, then all hope was lost. They may as well surrender now.

Could Frau Meinhardt really be working with the Oberstleutnant? The thought cut deep. Hannah asked Josef to tell her everything he knew about her. But she had arrived in the village just after the Oberstleutnant, he said. The previous teacher had left one day and never come back. Frau Meinhardt had just stepped into her place.

They went to the Oberstleutnant's room to check for clues, but it had been cleared out of personal items. Everything now rested on George.

The village children had all returned to their homes, carrying the order from the Oberstleutnant. The village would comply, Hannah knew. They would all, at six o'clock, turn on their Volksempfängers. And they would listen. Out of fear of the consequences if they didn't.

Josef said he should go home, too. His mother and grandmother would be starting to worry. He said he would try to explain to them as best he could, but if they still chose to listen to the radio, he wouldn't stop them. But he would find a safe place to hide. Until the bombs struck the castle or, failing that, for when the soldiers came.

Hannah didn't want him to go. But of course, he needed to be with his family. As he hurried across the square, he stopped, turned his bruised face towards them, and waved. Then he was gone.

'He's a brave young boy,' said Aunt Maud. And Hannah had to agree. The bravest.

They brought George up to speed with the events of the afternoon. His mood, buoyant with purpose since the night before, dropped when they told him how their plan to hide the children had failed. That the headmaster had been shot and Frau Meinhardt had mysteriously left the school at lunchtime.

'So you think this teacher is working for the Oberstleutnant?' asked the airman.

'There's no other explanation,' said Hannah. 'The soldiers were waiting for them. They must have been told.'

George tutted. 'It's a dirty war. You can trust nobody.'

'Can we trust you, George?' asked Aunt Maud.

George nodded. 'But at seven o'clock, take cover. Stay away from windows. There are going to be a lot of explosions.'

Hannah had taken cover before. And look what good that had done her. This time, she wanted a front-row seat. This time, she was going to look out for those planes, and cheer when the night sky lit up.

SIXTY-FIVE

They sat side by side in Hannah's room, shoes and coats on, just in case . . . The fog was, as always, relentless. The square was a ghost of autumn past. The cat was perched high on the wardrobe in the window opposite, staring back at them.

Six o'clock came. In the houses around the village, radios were being turned on. People would be sitting down to listen, fearful of what they would hear. But even more fearful of not listening.

Six-thirty arrived, and the village wept silence.

The cat rolled onto its side.

They waited.

Six fifty-five.

The fog fell lower. The square had almost disappeared.

'Move away from the window,' said Aunt Maud.

Hannah pushed her chair back, but just a little. *Please don't miss the castle. But please keep Elias and the other village children safe.*

Seven o'clock.

Still silence.

Five-past.

The cat rolled onto its back and kept rolling.

Careful, puss, or you're going to . . .

It fell, landing on the sill, in the space between the wardrobe and the window. Hannah waited for it to find its legs. To shake itself off and pretend, with feline arrogance, that it had meant to do that.

But the cat just lay there.

Hannah yawned. 'Get up, kitty.' Another yawn. It had been a long day. She decided to let some fresh air in. What harm could it do? Where were those bombers? Had she missed the explosions? Surely not.

She pushed open the window.

From beside her came a snore. Hannah turned. Aunt Maud was low in her chair, head on her shoulder, arms limp at her sides.

Hannah felt like she could do the same. Should she? Why not? There was very little she could do from here but watch and wait. Let them come. Let it be over when she woke.

Something wasn't right! Hannah stared down at her body, slumped in her chair. To Aunt Maud, slumped in hers. The cat, dead to the world on the sill opposite. She tried to get back, but her body wasn't having any of it. This had happened one time before. On the night she had drifted up to her room and imagined the strange creature there.

She scanned every corner, but there was no sign of the creature tonight. She listened for footsteps on the floorboards outside, but still there was silence.

The open window.

Hannah floated.

Over to the cat. It wasn't dead. She could see its chest rising and falling. Shallow and rhythmic.

Along the street she drifted, down low, trying to find a window to look through. Half-a-dozen doors along she found a gap in the shutters. Bones hung from twine on the door. She peered through. Three people. A young woman, an old man, a girl. All asleep. The sound of a radio.

High above, a shadow. The only movement.

Hannah rose.

Into the fog.

Nothing.

Higher she went. Terrified.

White. Haunting. Empty.

Up.

She burst through, and there were the stars. So high above, twinkling in the clear sky.

Ahead of her, a hole. A place of no stars. Just darkness.

Below the hole hung a small, silver rectangle. And from that rectangle, a luminous fog spouted, billowed, spread and fell onto the village below. But it wasn't fog. Hannah knew that. The fog that hung over the village was still, dead, inanimate. This was bright, alive, searching.

It wasn't a hole in the sky. It was an airship, moving slowly, silently, over the village. And there were two more, further away, each of them carrying a small compartment throwing a steady jet onto the houses below.

Like a magician, I cannot expose all the tricks I have up my sleeve.

The final trick had been revealed. Gas. That was how the Oberstleutnant prepared the village for the message that would play out on the radio. First the gas sent them all to sleep. Then the Volksempfänger did its work.

From far below came that heart-stopping rumble of engines that filled Hannah's whole being with terror.

The soldiers had come early to take the children. To take her.

And still there was no sign of the bombers.

SIXTY-SIX

Soldiers leaped from the rear of each of the three trucks.

They spread out, heading for the doors where The Old Man's Bones hung. Doors behind which children slept.

'Hannah!'

She was pulled back up from the street, through the window and into her body. Somebody was shaking her. But it was no good. The gas had done its work. She could hear the voice, and heavy, raspy breaths, could feel the hands upon her. But she was unable to respond to any of it.

From somewhere close by, a burst of gunfire. Shouts.

Panic flooded her body. Helping her to surface.

She was being moved.

More gunfire.

'Sofia!'

It was difficult to breathe. There was something on her face.

She embraced the panic. Used it to wake up.

Hannah opened her eyes. The first thing she saw was the face of that creature, huge insect eyes, the snout of a pig, smooth white head. It hadn't been a dream. And it was back. She pushed away, hearing her own gravelly breath in her ears, but those huge hands held onto her. She kicked her legs, but the creature took no notice. Her vision was beginning to mist up. A sickly smell. She reached up to wipe at her eyes. Her hand hit something hard.

A flash of light. Outside. An explosion. Large enough to make the house shake and the window rattle. A blast of warm air entered the room.

'Sofia ...'

The creature holding her stared back, eyes wide and pleading. But it wasn't a creature. It was just a man. A man in a gasmask. She felt around her own face again. She had one on, too.

Any other houses these children may have visited will also be searched. That was what the Oberstleutnant had said. It had been a soldier in a gasmask on the night Elias went missing, looking to remove any sign that Elias had been in her room. It had been so quick, and she had been blinded by his torch.

The gunfire outside was constant now. As if . . . as if there were two sides fighting.

She stared into the brown eyes behind the glass. There was something familiar. Pupils of different sizes . . .

'Pieter?' The word echoed in her head. What was he doing here? She reached for her mask, but his hands stopped her.

'Breathe slow and steady.'

She did as he said and lowered her hand.

'You're okay.' Pieter's eyes smiled. That big, bear-like smile. Even with his mask on, she recognised it.

She nodded. The mask was uncomfortable, the smell awful, but she was getting used to breathing.

Aunt Maud was still in the chair, sound asleep. Pieter stood, and Hannah could see a rifle hanging from his shoulder. There was a revolver at his hip and small pouches around his waist. And he looked to be dressed in white uniform, so far removed from the mild-mannered man who had brought her to Felshoven. She remembered the look on his face when he had spoken of the German soldiers. Was he here to save the village? Had George called him in?

'What are you . . .?'

Downstairs, the front door flew open.

'I'll explain later,' said Pieter. 'You need to hide.'

She tamped down the terror and focused her mind. The wardrobe? Under the bed? No. She knew just the place. 'The dumb waiter. Out in the hall. But Aunt Maud . . .'

Outside, gunfire. Shouts. An explosion. The sound of an engine starting. What was going on?

Pieter helped her to her feet. 'She'll be okay.'

Of course, it was the children they wanted. She wobbled, and he steadied her. They made their way out into the hall. Footsteps at the bottom of the stairs.

'Get in,' whispered Pieter. He pulled the door open and helped her climb inside, then took the revolver from his belt and handed it to her. It felt heavy. He placed a hand on her shoulder. 'If you need to use it, just point and pull the trigger.' He closed the door, and she heard his footsteps recede along the hall.

Hannah sat in the darkness and listened.

Distant gunfire from outside. Her own breath heavy and deep inside the mask. She concentrated on getting it under control, on not losing the tiny amount of composure she was trying so hard to hold on to. What had just happened? What was happening now? Pieter! From the noises coming from outside, it sounded like he wasn't alone. Whose side was he on? Was he British, too, like George? There were too many questions. And too much noise.

Whatever the Oberstleutnant had been planning, she was sure it hadn't been this. Despite the mayhem that was going on, she took more than a small amount of satisfaction from knowing that, whatever happened to her tonight, they had disrupted the man's plans.

The shots from downstairs made her jump. She heard a man yell, but she didn't know whether it was Pieter or one of the soldiers. She decided to move. George would be able to help. If they were all fighting the Oberstleutnant and his soldiers, they all had to be on the same side, didn't they?

Perhaps they had already bombed the castle. Was that the explosion she had heard? She hadn't heard the planes. But she had fallen asleep. Or been forced to.

From downstairs, two more quick shots. Something fell over. A door slammed. Another shot and a shout. '*Come out, traitor!*'

Pieter was still alive!

She placed the revolver on her lap as the house fell into near silence. Mingling with the rasp of her own breath, attenuated by the mask, she could hear the distant sound of the radio voice. Which was strange. Josef and Aunt Maud had smashed the Volksempfänger to pieces. She tilted her head, trying to work out whether it was coming from above or below.

More gunshots from downstairs got her moving. Hannah pulled on the rope. The brickwork dropped away and disappeared. She passed the second floor and cursed the bell that gave away her location. Worried that one of the soldiers would tear open the door and pull her from the lift, she hurried her ascent. A huge explosion tore through the night.

A blast of air from above or below and debris, broken bricks, perhaps half the chimney rained down onto the roof of the box. She felt the lift drop and her hands burn as the rope was torn from her grip. It finally stopped, the compartment crashing against the side of the shaft. Hannah forced a scream to stay inside while praying the rope wouldn't snap. Perhaps *that* had been the castle. If so, nobody up there could have survived, surely.

Not even if they were in the dungeons. *Oh, Elias!*

Up she went again, into the attic, and now she could hear the radio more clearly. It was the man's voice, slow, steady, almost calm. The one she had heard the night she had drifted off from her body.

What was it doing playing in the attic?

She pulled to a stop and listened. Perhaps she should stay in the lift. It was as good a place to hide as any. She wondered where Josef would be hiding. Everybody she knew was in danger.

The gunfire outside had slowed to short bursts. There was a square of light now around the door. Every other time she had visited, the room had been in darkness. She leaned forward, her mask up against the crack in the door, and stared through.

The room was just as she had seen it before, but the curtain had been pulled back and an electric lamp was strung up to a beam. George sat in a chair, facing away from her. He was wearing a gasmask, too, and headphones. In front of him, on a desk, was a box with switches and dials and beside it another with two circles that rotated round and round. The voice was coming from that box.

Something Heinz had said came back to her. *They would need somewhere high to transmit. Somewhere in sight of the whole village.*

But it couldn't be the castle, she realised now. That couldn't be seen from Frau Lister's cottage. And she listened to the radio all the time. There was only one place that could be seen from the whole village.

George continued to press buttons and turn dials. Then he spoke. But he no longer had that British taint to his accent. His voice was now pure, perfect German. 'I believe we've lost several men, Oberstleutnant. I no longer have radio contact. Two vehicles have been destroyed. Should I stop the transmission?' A few seconds of silence, all the time George staring at the box in front of him. 'Oberstleutnant? Oberstleutnant Kessler?'

George! No! He had betrayed them all. Not Frau Meinhardt. There were no planes coming to save them. There never had been. So what was happening out there? What were all the explosions? Who was shooting at who? And Pieter . . .

To her left, out of sight, there was a rattling on the door. 'Sofia, are you up here?'

George snapped his head around. He tore the headphones away and slid open a drawer, muttering a curse. He stood up and turned. George was no longer the dirty, ragged British airman. He was dressed in full SS uniform, stiff and black. His hair was combed back, glistening in the light from the bare lamp that was still swinging from the last explosion.

'Sofia!' Pieter wanted her to answer.

The soldier edged towards the door.

'Sofia! Are you in there?' repeated Pieter.

George's head spun towards her. Despite the lift door being closed, she felt fully exposed, as if he could see right through the wooden panel. He began to creep towards her. Hannah reached down and picked up the gun. Her vision was misting.

Just point and pull the trigger.

'Sofia? Are you in there?' mimicked George. His voice was quiet. Calm. But with an icy edge. His eyes flicked back to the door keeping Pieter out. He was trying to work something out, she could tell.

The mystery of why the Oberstleutnant regularly stayed here had finally been answered.

Another step closer.

'Tell me,' he said, 'how you remembered your friend.'

There is one. But we are looking into it. That person will be dealt with. She had thought the Oberstleutnant was talking about Heinz, but could he have known that she remembered Elias all this time?

'Sofia! Are you all right?'

A flick of the man's eyes back towards the door. 'Let me deal with your friend first. Then I'll be back for some answers. And be assured, if there is one thing I'm good at, it's getting answers out of people.'

'I'm coming in, Sofia. Move away from the door!'

'Come in, my traitor friend. I'm waiting,' whispered the soldier. He raised his gun and stepped out of sight.

The door from the stairwell flew inwards. At the same time, Hannah kicked the lift door as hard as she could. It was enough to put George off. He began to turn towards her. But then he thought better of it. He pointed his gun back at Pieter and fired.

Hannah fired, too. She was flung backwards, the revolver tumbling from her grip and falling into the shadows below. The bullet hit the man in the leg. He fell to a sitting position and turned to face Hannah. He brought his gun up. She ripped the mask from her face, no longer caring about the gas. She wanted him to see her. Who she truly was. There was hatred in his eyes, two black pits of fury, and she wondered how she hadn't seen it before. There was nothing she could do, nowhere to go. She closed her eyes.

Hannah screamed as the shot rang out. But she felt no pain, no impact. Still, she stayed there, expecting to feel warm blood seeping through a hole in her dress and pooling onto the floor of the compartment. When there was nothing, she slowly opened her eyes. The man was there, just as he had been, staring back at her from behind his mask. A dark spot had appeared at the top of it. It glistened. A trickle of blood oozed down over the glass. The gun fell from his fingers. His hand dropped. His head drooped forward.

And there he stayed.

Hannah put her hands on the edge of the lift and leaned out. Pieter was there, his rifle still raised. A red rose was blooming at his right shoulder.

'You've been shot,' said Hannah.

Pieter went to wipe at his nose, but his mask was in the way. 'So has he,' he said, nodding at the dead soldier. 'But I'm going to live to tell the tale.' He paused. 'You're still awake.'

For a moment, she wondered what he meant. He removed his own mask and sniffed at the air. 'It's safe.'

'What are you doing here, Pieter? What is happening out there?'

He dropped his head. Held it there. Then looked up. He looked sad. Tired.

'I . . .' he stumbled. 'We, the fighters outside, have all lost somebody because of this damned war. We've seen what our country is doing to its people. To the world.' His eyes shone, and Hannah wondered whose memory lived inside his mind.

He slung the rifle onto his back, skirted around the body and over to the radio. His eyes traced a cable running up the wall. He grabbed it and tugged. The cable came away, sparks flew, the reels stopped rotating and the voice became a slow drawl and then ceased completely.

'Come on.'

With a palm pressed hard against his shoulder, he staggered over to Hannah. He held one huge arm out to her. She took it and stepped out into the attic.

'You saved my life, Sofia,' he said.

'And you saved mine.'

Now they had to go and save some more.

SIXTY-SEVEN

Aunt Maud was beginning to come around, murmuring and fluttering her eyelids. Pieter helped her out of the chair and down the stairs until she was able to stand by herself. A pair of booted feet stuck out from the kitchen doorway at an unnatural angle, and Hannah gasped at the carnage that had obviously been caused by Pieter and whoever had broken in. There were holes in walls, splinters and dust all over the floor that Aunt Maud worked so hard to keep clean. And blood. Lots of it. She had seen the devastation caused by bombs in Stuttgart. But never the bodies. And to see it here, so far away from any city, proved to her that nowhere and nobody was safe.

Josef. Elias. Frau Meinhardt. Frau Lister. The whole village. She didn't want to step outside.

Her worst fears were realised. It was an alien land. Hissing chunks of metal smouldered in the melting snow. She had seen Stuttgart's ruins from a distance, but here she was amongst it. Uniformed bodies lay sprawled against walls and across pavements, streams of crimson flowing out from beneath them. But it only flowed so far. The night was cold enough to freeze blood the moment it stopped pumping.

The lady in pin-curls on the train had been wrong. The mountains could be touched by war.

So many dead. She didn't want to look. But she had to. To see if there were any villagers amongst them. Anybody she knew. But no. Not as far as she could tell.

A few fighters moved among them, dressed in the same white camouflage as Pieter. They were checking each body. But not to save them, Hannah could see. They were making sure the soldiers were dead.

In the middle of the square, two fires raged. A truck was on its side, another leaning back onto an axle that had lost its wheels. She saw one of the wheels in the frozen trough. But the strangest sight of all was the heavy black cloth draped like a giant slug over two houses on the opposite side of the square. On the cobblestones below it, a burning silver box. Even as she watched there was a huge explosion. She bent and turned away, Pieter shielding her and Aunt Maud with his bulk. After a few seconds, he straightened up and all three of them stared at the carnage that had been the village square.

The air was acrid, the smoke unlike that which usually filled the village. Burning metal and rubber. And something else, putrid and sickly. To the left of the square sat the only truck remaining intact, some fighters beside it, rifles raised and pointing off into the fog and smoke.

'What in God's name?' asked Aunt Maud. She had finally returned.

'Try not to look,' Pieter said.

Hannah knew what he meant. The bodies.

They made their way over to the truck, Hannah and Aunt Maud holding on to each other.

People began to emerge from doorways. Villagers. Woken from their induced slumber. Telling children to remain inside. Hannah glanced up and saw the cat arch its back and leap down from the sill.

Pieter turned to a man crouched over a radio. 'What's the situation at the castle?'

The man repeated the question over the airwaves. A woman's voice came back. Hannah was unable to hear the words.

'We are in,' said the man. 'Six prisoners captured. One principal amongst them. One friendly. But we have losses.'

Pieter nodded, sadly.

Losses, thought Hannah. *So many losses.* She felt Aunt Maud squeeze her hand.

'Have you found any children?' asked Hannah. 'A small boy? About eight? Is that who the friendly is?'

'Children?' asked Pieter. 'What children?'

'The Oberstleutnant, he . . .'

Pieter shook his head. 'Which Oberstleutnant? I don't know what you're talking about, Sofia.'

She had expected him to know what she knew. Had thought that was why he was here. But now . . .

'The soldiers have been taking children. From the village,' said Aunt Maud.

'One of them was my friend,' added Hannah.

Pieter breathed deeply. He leaned back against the side of the truck, and stayed that way for a while. Then he straightened himself and cupped his hands over his mouth. 'Okay, everybody, we're moving out! The village is secure!'

The fighters slung their rifles over their shoulders and climbed up into the truck. They smelled of sweat, oil and smoke. They looked tired.

'Climb in,' said Pieter.

'Are we coming with you? To the castle?' Hannah wanted to go. But she hadn't expected him to offer.

Pieter gave a brief laugh. 'I left you here once before, and look what happened. You're coming with us.'

It was an attempt at lightheartedness, she knew. Once more, she felt protected by this huge, gentle man.

'And besides, it sounds like you two know more about this than we do. Up you get.'

Hannah climbed in. Pieter helped Aunt Maud up and then hoisted himself in beside Hannah.

'Sofia!'

Hannah stared past Pieter. 'Josef!' He was safe! Racing towards her, slipping in the snow, falling and finding his feet again. Joy filled her heart.

'A friend of yours?' asked Pieter.

'The best. He needs to come with us.'

Josef took Pieter's offered hand and was pulled up and in. Hannah wrapped her arms around him.

'You'd better hug her back,' said Pieter. 'She's happy to see you.'

Josef did as he was told.

'Have we stopped them?' asked Josef, pulling away.

'I think so. But we need to find Elias and the others.'

He clasped her hand. She squeezed back.

'Let's go!' yelled Pieter.

A thump on the back of the cab and they were away.

The gates of the castle hung from the stone walls like half-pulled teeth. A fighter ushered them through and then turned back to stand guard as the truck rumbled into the courtyard.

They pulled to a stop.

'Stay here,' said Pieter.

Hannah went to protest.

'Just for a moment,' he insisted. He jumped down. The other fighters followed.

Hannah sat there with Josef and Aunt Maud. She could hear voices outside. A man talking quietly. Then Pieter. And silence.

A loud thump on the side of the truck made them all jump. Hannah stood.

'He said to stay,' began Aunt Maud, but Hannah was out onto the cobbled floor before she could protest any further.

She stepped away from the truck. The courtyard was eerily empty. Pieter stood with his head against the canopy, his fist clenched from where he had just punched it. Another fighter, presumably the man he had been talking to, was walking away.

'They've gone,' she said, continuing to gaze around her. 'All of them.'

Pieter straightened. For the first time since she had met him, he looked defeated, crushed. 'They made their escape when we began our attack.'

'Shouldn't you go after them?' asked Josef. He had appeared beside her.

Pieter shook his head. 'There's no point. We came on foot. Twenty-two of us. Some to the village, most straight here. All we have is that truck. We'd never catch them.'

'Do you know who was here, Pieter?' Hannah asked. She couldn't believe they had let them escape.

His eyes drilled into hers. 'I know who was here, Sofia.'

She felt the anger rising up in her. 'So why haven't you caught them? They were all here. Together. Why come to the village when you could have come here and –?'

'Because I only just found out. None of us knew. They tried, Sofia. They really did. Look around you.'

Hannah stepped forward and took in the scene. She hadn't noticed before. The outfits the fighters wore were white for a reason. They were barely visible. Only the red streaks from the fallen bodies gave them away. Hannah counted half-a-dozen corpses on the snowy floor, arms and legs splayed where they had fallen. People who had given their lives to stop the Oberstleutnant's insidious plan. Up on the balcony she could make out the bodies of the soldiers they had been fighting, some draped over the low stone wall, others in the frozen garden beds.

'There were too many soldiers, Sofia. They fought us. While the people they were protecting escaped. Because they are cowards. They run when they're the ones whose lives are at risk.'

Her anger turned to remorse. And guilt. So many had died.

The fighters from the truck were heading up the steps towards the castle.

'We should go inside,' said Pieter. 'Question the prisoners.'

'We need to find Elias,' said Hannah. 'And the other children.'

'And Heinz Schundel,' added Josef.

Pieter frowned at the boy. 'Heinz Schundel? You know him?'

Josef shrugged. 'Well, not really. He used to hang around our school. Sofia knows him better than me. She's been talking to him.'

The big man raised his eyebrows. 'You've seen Heinz? Recently?'

Hannah nodded. 'It's complicated. I've been talking to him. Do you know him?'

Pieter stared off into the distance. 'I came here to Felshoven with him many years ago, after the last war. I helped him build his house. And without him, we may not be here now. Let's get inside. There's somebody else you might want to see.'

SIXTY-EIGHT

Hannah was so busy trying to not see the scene around her that she didn't see the woman approach from the main entrance.

'Hello, Sofia.'

She looked up. Like the other fighters, this woman was dressed in a dirty white outfit with a rifle slung over her shoulder. It took Hannah a few seconds. Last time she had seen that face, the hair had been hidden by a clean, white hat with a red cross on the front. Her lipstick had been immaculate and her skin fair. Now, her hair hung lank around her shoulders, and her face was smeared with whatever was on her coat.

'Marianne . . . what are you doing here?' Hannah ran to Marianne and hugged her. She caught a whiff of smoke and something metallic. But underneath, there was still that perfumed comfort.

'The same as Pieter.' She straightened and turned to a man who had walked out to greet them. Hannah recognised him, too.

'Hi, Hugo,' said Hannah. His long hair was gone. It was now shaved close to his scalp.

'Hello, Sofia. It's good to see you safe and well.'

Marianne glanced beyond her. 'You must be Maud Meyer.'

Hannah turned. Aunt Maud was standing hand in hand with Josef.

'It's nice to finally meet you. And thank you for all you've done for Sofia.'

For the first time ever, as far as Hannah knew, Aunt Maud blushed.

'It's Hannah,' she replied. She would no longer hide her true self from her friends.

'Sofia's not your real name?' asked Josef.

A part of her felt guilty. For keeping such a big secret from her best friend. She shook her head. 'Hannah Ginsberg,' she said.

'Isn't that a –?'

'Jewish name, yes.' She let him take this in. 'Marianne, this is Josef. My best friend. He helped me when nobody . . .'

She regretted what she had been about to say, but Aunt Maud finished her sentence for her. 'When nobody else believed her. Including me.'

'Believed her about what?' asked Marianne.

'Let's all get inside,' said Pieter. 'It's cold and we need to swap stories. Put everything together and see what we've got.'

'Believed me about Elias and the other missing children,' said Hannah to Marianne.

'Missing children?' asked Marianne. 'What children?'

'We think they're here. We need to find them.'

The stairwell wound round, deep down into the bowels of the earth. It was cold down here, so cold that Hannah's teeth began to chatter and her ears turn numb. It was dark, too.

A man she didn't know led the way, his rifle raised, followed by Pieter, whose shoulder had now been cleaned and bandaged. Then came Hannah, Josef, Hugo and Marianne at the rear. Aunt Maud had stayed behind. She was still feeling drowsy and said that her tumbling to her death down a steep flight of stairs wouldn't help anybody.

They went softly, in case any soldiers had been left behind. They finally reached the bottom where a great wooden door with thick steel hinges blocked their way.

'Let's hope one of these works.' Pieter jangled a ring of keys and started trying them in the lock. Hannah willed the door to open. On the fourth attempt, she heard the latch turn. Pieter ushered them all back with his hand. He nodded to the other man. Whisper-counted to three.

He turned the handle and the two of them burst through, guns raised.

Nothing.

Darkness.

Silence.

Somewhere, a groan.

Then voices. Children's voices.

Hannah couldn't wait any longer.

'Elias!' She burst through the doorway, past the two men, hearing her name called from behind but ignoring it. She heard footsteps following.

And then Josef calling, too. 'Elias!'

And the sweetest sound coming back.

'Sofia? Josef?'

Her shadow raced on ahead of her and she heard everybody running to catch up. The light of a torch found a pair of eyes shivering behind thick, metal bars, and there he was, the sweet boy who had done nothing to deserve this, blinking at the brightness that had been stolen from him for so long.

He was so thin. And white, against the shadows. She remembered how his cheeks used to glow red in the cold. Not here.

And he was crying. She was, too. And Josef.

'Move back, Hannah,' Pieter sniffed. 'We need to get them out.'

The man she didn't know tried one key after the other.

'Please,' came other voices from behind doors. 'Please let us out.' Thin hands upon the bars.

The lock turned and Elias rushed out to Hannah, wrapping his arms around her, almost tumbling her over. He buried his head against her chest, and she dropped hers onto his thin, dirty hair.

They stayed there like that while the other doors were unlocked, the children released and every cell in those cold dungeons searched. Hannah recognised Boris. Karl, Ingrid and Felix from the drawings Josef had held up. There were two others. But no sign of Matilda.

'Ava! Matteus!' shouted Josef. The two children who had disappeared before Heinz had set to work drawing them all.

It seemed that everybody was hugging everybody. They made their way back out and up the stairs, and all the while Elias hung on to her.

And she hung on to him.

Tightly.

SIXTY-NINE

The great hall no longer looked great. There were bloodstains across a muddy floor. Shards of ornaments and chunks of statues lay here and there, and oil paintings were ripped to shreds by bullets. Over in a corner, two rows of bodies were being covered with sheets.

The friendly they had captured was Matilda, now reunited with her brother. While Josef took Elias to be checked by the medics, Hannah told everybody what she knew. Pieter filled in some of the gaps, starting with the day he had brought Hannah to the village. He had stayed with Heinz that night. His friend had warned him about some unusual activity at the castle. Then more news of sinister goings-on had come through their network of underground fighters from across Germany. People who had lost loved ones, who wanted something better for the country. Large generators had been moved up the mountain several months earlier, along with huge reels of electrical cable and, most alarming of all, canisters of gas. They kept eyes on the only road up the mountain. A road that was usually clogged with heavy drifts of snow but was now being kept clear. When the Zeppelins were seen being taken out of retirement, and flown up the mountain, they knew something big was being planned. They just didn't know what.

And then, a few days ago, a name from somebody on the inside. Operation Schwarzberg. A date. Today. An experiment. At Felshoven.

Then silence. Their communication channel was shut down. Their spy vanished. Probably captured.

The information had been enough for them to act. And they had arrived just in time to save the village.

But not in time to end all of the horror for good, thought Hannah. If only they had known who was here.

Pieter's eyes caught Hannah's, betraying the same thoughts running through his head.

The Oberstleutnant, his wife and two children made up four of the prisoners. It seemed the Führer had been less than impressed with the failure of his plan and had ordered them to stay behind while he himself fled, with the threat of them all being shot if they tried to follow.

The fifth prisoner was Frau Meinhardt. She had refused to leave the Oberstleutnant's side.

They were being kept in a well-guarded room towards the rear of the castle. When Pieter told the group that he intended to question them all together, Hannah demanded to be present. She deserved to be. They wouldn't be here without her.

Marianne tried to talk her out of it, but Hannah remained steadfast. And she needed to see Frau Meinhardt. To know exactly what role she had played in all of this. And Josef and Aunt Maud should be there to hear it all, too, Hannah insisted.

At first, Pieter refused. 'It's no place for children.'

The absurdity of this wasn't lost on Hannah. 'The world is no place for children at the moment, Pieter. I have seen things I never should have seen. Lost people I never should have lost. I deserve some answers. Maybe more than anybody else in this room.'

'Hannah's right,' said Marianne. And then, 'Whatever happened to that frightened little girl I met in the hospital?'

Hannah wondered about that, too.

SEVENTY

The Oberstleutnant did not appear frightened. Nor did his wife and son. They all sat upright, staring long and hard at Hannah and her friends when they entered. Ursula, on the other hand, looked terrified, though none of her family seemed interested in comforting her. Frau Meinhardt sat to the side of them, head bowed to the floor.

Hannah was surprised by how calm she felt. But the power had shifted. She was no longer the one feeling threatened. And she was surrounded by friends. Friends strong in body and spirit. And integrity. There was a certain resilience gained from being on the right side of morality.

When everybody was seated, Pieter asked, 'What are your names?'

'I am Oberstleutnant Erwin Kessler of the SS. This is my wife . . .'

'Let her say it,' said Marianne. 'You, what's your name?'

The woman spat the words. 'Frieda Kessler.' Hannah could hear the hate in them. She and her husband were two of a kind.

'You.' To the girl. Her eyes were red, and she struggled to get her name out from between her quivering lips. Hannah couldn't help but feel pity for her. Was it her fault her father was a murderer, a supporter of the monster that ruled over their country with his madness?

'Ursula . . . Ursula Kessler.'

The boy didn't need any prompting. 'Fredrik Kessler.' He raised his hand, straight and fast. 'Heil Hitler!'

Hannah felt no pity for him. He had already made his choice.

A sneer appeared on the Oberstleutnant's face. Was it hate Hannah felt for him at that moment? She didn't know, but if she could have wished for the world to open up and swallow him whole, she would have.

Pieter returned to the Oberstleutnant. 'Oberstleutnant Kessler. You murdered some families in the village. For not listening to a radio.'

'The women were traitors. They helped hide a British spy,' replied the Oberstleutnant.

'He was one of yours,' said Aunt Maud, calmly.

The Oberstleutnant curled up one side of his mouth. 'They didn't know that. And neither did you.'

'But you did,' said Hannah. 'The same as you knew that the Dittmars had never received a leaflet. And yet you shot them.'

'I should have shot you, too,' sneered the Oberstleutnant.

She wasn't surprised by his words. Not after all she had seen, all she had heard. 'So why didn't you?'

He chewed at his lip, stared up at the corner of the room, and then back at Hannah. 'Because I liked you.'

How could that be true? And was that all it came down to? One person's choice of who they did or didn't like?

Pieter placed a hand on Hannah's. She took it as a sign to let the Oberstleutnant's words go. 'You abducted some children from the village, and you planned to abduct the rest of them tonight. Is this correct?'

The Oberstleutnant cleared his throat. 'Some children accompanied my soldiers back to the castle … as an experiment.'

Fredrik's face was half smile, half sneer. His head was high, his neck taut. His sister, on the other hand, had hung her head and, every few seconds, wiped at her nose and sniffled. Again, Hannah felt that tug of sorrow for her.

'We found them,' said Hannah.

'Sofia helped us rescue them from the dungeons,' Marianne said.

Hannah glanced from the Oberstleutnant to Marianne, and back. 'Actually, my name is Hannah,' she said. 'Hannah Ginsberg.'

The Oberstleutnant's face darkened. His teeth clenched. 'I *should* have shot you.'

'And that just proves that we're no different,' she said, the absurdity of his hatred empowering her. 'You need those yellow stars to tell us apart from your so-called master race. Without them, we're all the same.'

And he looked away. Just like that, she had beaten him.

'There is no master race.' Frau Meinhardt's voice wavered. 'There are people who embrace differences. And there are people who fear them. You, Oberstleutnant, are the latter.'

The teacher slowly raised her head. She looked older. There were grey streaks running through her hair and lines on her face that Hannah had never noticed before. But still those bright blue eyes.

'Susan Meinhardt,' she said to Pieter. 'I'm a teacher at the school.'

'She's working with them,' said Josef. 'She told the Oberstleutnant we were going to hide in the tunnels.'

'Is this true, Frau Meinhardt?'

'No.'

Those blue eyes pleaded with Hannah to believe her. Then she dropped her head again, as though the weight of it were too much.

'It was George,' said Hannah. 'Or whatever he was called. We told George about our escape. And George told him.' She nodded towards the Oberstleutnant, who still had a look of superiority on his face. 'Before I shot him.' That look dissolved. She felt empowered.

'But she didn't come with us,' said Josef. 'She came here instead.'

Frau Meinhardt looked up. 'I'll tell you everything. And you'd better let me do it quick, as I don't have much time.'

Hannah gasped. The teacher's hair was almost grey throughout. Deep creases ran from each of her eyes, and the skin around her mouth was dry and wrinkled. Her neck sagged as she spoke. Her hands were broken by tight tendons and heavy veins. Liver spots speckled her wrists. Even her voice, normally smooth and soft, now sounded old and cracked.

But her blue eyes continued to shine.

Nobody spoke. Marianne was shaking her head. Aunt Maud had covered her mouth with one hand. Even the Oberstleutnant was leaning away, wide eyed.

'I come from a village in the Black Forest. There's a special type of storyteller there. And I'm one of them.' She gave a cough and pointed a crooked finger at Hannah. 'Hannah, do you remember asking me if I knew the tale of Edgar and Otto?'

Hannah nodded and flicked her head at the Oberstleutnant. 'He told it to us.'

'I lied. I know that tale very well.'

'Is this relevant?' asked Pieter. 'Are you all right, Frau Meinhardt?'

'No, I'm not all right. But all the more reason for me to continue,' said Frau Meinhardt. 'Was that tale what gave you the idea, Oberstleutnant? Did you fancy yourself as the Magician?'

'It is just a story.' But the way he looked at her rapidly ageing face indicated that he believed something else entirely.

'You come from Schwarzberg, don't you?' said Hannah. She was beginning to understand what was happening. Although it was hard to believe. For to believe this would mean to believe every fairytale ever told. And that would be both beautiful and terrifying.

Frau Meinhardt nodded. 'You remember Schwarzberg, don't you, Oberstleutnant?'

He didn't reply, but flicked his eyes towards her and back again.

'Schwarzberg remembers you. What you did.'

'There's truth in every tale,' whispered Hannah.

'Precisely,' said Frau Meinhardt. 'There's truth in every tale, Oberstleutnant. You know that. You were searching for that truth, weren't you? You knew it was somewhere in there. Perhaps you thought it *was* that tale. Is that why you told it to Josef and Hannah? But the tale changes every time, Oberstleutnant. And it was never supposed to be used for evil. Quite the opposite, in fact. We have a way, my people, of looking into the eyes of a child and seeing what they will become. If only we had met your Führer when he had been a child. Think of all the lives we could have saved.'

What *was* Frau Meinhardt saying? That she could see the futures of these children? Know, before it happened, which side of good and evil would win out in a person's future?

'But it comes at a great cost to the storyteller,' the teacher carried on while continuing to age before their very eyes. 'Your Führer is so interested in mysticism and magic. He loves those tales of Grimm. But our tales aren't in that book. They aren't in any book. People have tried, but . . .' she gave a great, hacking cough, '. . . if you were to try to write one down, it would erase itself before you got to the end. Just like it erases the lives of those children who hear it.'

'You told them one, didn't you?' said Hannah. She began to walk towards Frau Meinhardt. The closer she got to the teacher, the more she could see the lines deepening across her face, the veins breaking out on her skin.

'They take away all the innocents. And they raise monsters of their own. Like these two beside me. I have looked into their eyes, and I see the darkness that will engulf them.'

Hannah glanced at Ursula, who let out a small sob. Surely, there was still good in her. Her brother, on the other hand . . . even Hannah could see that he had already given himself to the darkness.

The Oberstleutnant refused to meet Frau Meinhardt's gaze.

'You won't remember my children, Oberstleutnant, that you took when you were in Schwarzberg. You have taken so many. Very soon, you won't even remember your own.'

Taken her children? Had he done this before? Or was it something different that time?

The Oberstleutnant squeezed his eyes closed. 'Is that what this is about? Revenge?'

A humourless laugh. 'Of course. What else is there when everything you had has been ripped away from you? I was waiting for your children to be brought here. But it wasn't happening. Then, Hannah, when you said they were all here with their children, the opportunity was too good to miss. And Josef, you were right. I came here to the castle.

But I didn't tell them of the escape. I rode Gretel up here and told the guard I was a teacher from the school. That the Oberstleutnant had sent for me. To keep the children entertained while the important work was taking place. I was to report to Frau Kessler.' Her blue eyes flicked to the Oberstleutnant's wife, who stared back, both fear and venom in her eyes. 'I couldn't believe my luck. She was more than happy to see me. We teachers carry great influence. And what better person to take *all* their children into a room and tell them a story while the grown-ups were busy.'

'I don't understand!' cried Frau Kessler.

Hannah took hold of one of Frau Meinhardt's hands. It was dry and cold.

'No! No! No!' shrieked the Oberstleutnant. He began to hit his forehead with the palm of his hand. Under other circumstances it would have looked funny.

His daughter's head shot up at the sound of her father's distress. Hannah guessed that she had never heard him like this. 'What is it, Papa?' She was bright red, round-eyed.

Fredrik, on the other hand, had turned pale. His smile, his sneer, whatever it had been, had disappeared. His face had sunk, and his skin was the same colour as the world outside.

'Take a good look at your children, Oberstleutnant. Study their faces. For soon my heart will take its last beat. And when it does, they will be forgotten by everybody here, including you. As will the other children who heard my story today. And not in the way some hypnotic radio broadcast fools everybody. They will cease to exist in the minds and the memories of the world, leaving nothing but a vacuum, which time itself will fill.'

'Take it back,' pleaded the Oberstleutnant. 'There must be a way.'

'Is there a way to bring *my* children back?' fumed Frau Meinhardt.

'The poor woman,' said Aunt Maud. And then, louder, to the Oberstleutnant. 'What did you do to them?'

It was Frau Meinhardt who answered. 'They're gone. That's all I'll ever know.'

'If I didn't see what was happening to her, I wouldn't believe it,' said Pieter.

'Did you enjoy the story, children?' Frau Meinhardt asked Ursula and Fredrik.

Ursula flicked her eyes to Frau Meinhardt as she spoke, but then returned them to her father. Her cheeks shone and her eyes glistened. Her voice was high and desperate. 'She told us a story, Papa. We ... we were in it. Me, Fredrik, all the children at the party ... we all disappeared at the end of it. What ... what does that mean?'

Hannah's mind was racing. 'The story the Magician told Otto was a story of him disappearing, wasn't it?'

'A story within a story,' croaked Frau Meinhardt. 'But you need to know exactly how to tell it. Every word in the right place, every syllable pronounced just so, every sentence rendered with belief. You have to be a true story-teller, raised and taught in the village of Schwarzberg. And you, Oberstleutnant, are not.' She tried to clear her throat and was racked by a long series of coughs.

'What's happening to you?' asked Josef.

'Well, Josef. That's the thing about most defence mechanisms. Think of the tale as the sting of a bee.' More coughs. 'It takes a lot out of you.' She laughed. 'In all those famous fairytales, even the one of Edgar and Otto, magic always makes the magician younger. If only I could have drunk their youth, instead of using up my remaining years. But it's good that it works this way. Otherwise, just think what men like him could do with it.'

'Are you saying these two children are just going to ... cease to exist?' asked Pieter.

Frau Meinhardt nodded. 'Part of me wishes that, when it happens, he'll be able to remember them. At least that way he would share in my agony. But no. Him, her, all the others ... tomorrow their lives will continue as though their children had never been born. But things will be better for the rest of you. I am sure of it.'

'Don't let us just disappear, Papa!'

At first, Hannah thought the high-pitched sob was from Ursula, but when she looked it was Fredrik who was pleading. Frau Kessler had thrown herself forward, her head in her hands.

Frau Meinhardt's blue eyes faded, and she let out her last, silent breath. One final beat of her heart.

When Hannah looked up, the Oberstleutnant and his wife were staring at two empty chairs. After a few seconds, a mist of confusion cleared from their faces, and they sat up straight, gazing ahead.

'Will that be all?' asked the Oberstleutnant. 'My wife and I have had a long day.'

Hannah picked up the hand of the old woman who had, until earlier that day, been a young teacher. What had just happened? There had been magic, she knew, but for the life of her she didn't know how or why. Or what that magic had achieved.

And, by the expressions on everybody else's faces, neither did they.

Hannah, Josef and Aunt Maud accompanied Elias back to his grandmother's cottage. The other children were returned to their homes by Pieter and the other fighters. The fog was thick, but Hannah knew the stars still twinkled in the sky as brightly as ever, just as they had when she couldn't see them from the Meyers' basement. Whatever happened upon this Earth, Hannah took comfort in knowing that those stars would always be there, shining down upon it.

Frau Lister saw them coming from her window. She had been waiting. Elias ran into her hug and stayed there.

Hannah, Josef and Aunt Maud left the young boy with his grandmother to be fed and hugged and pampered and be given the love that all children deserve, while they returned to the lodge. Home.

SEVENTY-ONE

They sat around the kitchen table. Hannah, Josef, Aunt Maud. Pieter, Marianne, Hugo. Outside, a clean-up was taking place. The first thing the villagers had done was to pile every single Volksempfänger in the centre of the square, ready to be set alight.

Aunt Maud had brewed some coffee. She went around the table, pouring it into cups.

'Everything from last night seems like the fog outside our door.'

'Do you think it was the gas?' asked Josef.

Pieter took a sip of his coffee. 'I think it's a mixture of a lot of things.' He placed the cup down and heaved a deep sigh. 'We found somebody, Hannah. A friend of yours. And mine.'

It took her a few seconds. 'Heinz? You found Heinz? Where is he? Is he okay?'

Pieter shook his head. 'He's gone, Hannah. They got to him. He's been dead for over a week.'

That couldn't be right. 'No. He can't be. I was talking to him only . . .' She suddenly understood. Their souls had met. But only one of them had had a body to return to. And what had Heinz said? *I got away. I'm somewhere they'll never find me.* 'It doesn't matter. I must have gotten it wrong. So much has happened.' She closed her eyes. So many people had died. But how many had they saved? If the Oberstleutnant's plan had worked . . .

'What will happen to the Oberstleutnant?' she asked.

There was a long silence, as if nobody knew how to answer.

'Our people will question him some more,' said Hugo, eventually. 'And, after we've gleaned all we can from him . . .' He shrugged, letting the sentence hang there.

She knew what the unspoken words meant. The world was better off without men like him.

'And Frau Kessler?' asked Hannah.

'We'll let her go,' said Marianne. 'She won't be living the high life anymore. She's probably already had her house taken back by the SS and all her belongings removed. She'll be the same as the rest of the German people now. Struggling to find food and comfort as the war rages on.'

'How long will that be?' asked Josef.

'As long as it takes for everybody to stand up to men like him,' replied Aunt Maud. 'Like you and Hannah did.'

Was that what they had done? Whatever it was, Hannah knew they hadn't done it alone. They had had help from friends. Some were here today. Some were gone forever.

Hannah wondered if, when it was finally over, people would learn from it. And if the countless lives sacrificed would be remembered. Or would they all be forgotten, as though they had never existed?

They sat silently, sipping coffee and disappearing into their own thoughts. A ray of sun broke through the fog and lit up the room. Somewhere, a radio began to play. Music. Soft and gentle.

'So tell us,' said Josef.

Hannah looked at her best friend. 'Tell you what?'

'Tell us about Hannah Ginsberg.'

Cups went down on the table. All eyes were upon her.

'I'd like to hear about her, too,' said Aunt Maud.

Hannah felt her heart rise into her mouth. Was she ready to tell all? To return to the person she really was? She glanced at each of them in turn.

Hugo. Marianne. Pieter. Aunt Maud. Josef.

Yes, Hitler was still in power. The war wasn't over. But here, at this kitchen table, in this lodge in Felshoven, right now, she was surrounded by friends.

She relaxed her shoulders, breathed out.

'I am Hannah Ginsberg. A Jew *and* a German citizen. I was born in Stuttgart on the fifteenth of May 1930. A few years before that, my grandparents decided to leave Poland for a better life . . .'

And, for the first time since the bomb fell on the Meyers' house, Hannah spoke of her parents.

Of how they had loved her, cared for her, protected her right up to the moment they were taken from this world.

She could finally speak the truth.

AUTHOR'S NOTE

I started writing *One by One They Disappear* under the working title *Forgotten*. It all came about when I had a fairy-tale style idea of a small mountain village where, on a certain day of the year, it was said that any child who should leave their footprints in the snow would be stolen away from their home and disappear from the memory of their family, friends and the world forever.

It soon became a tale based in World War II Germany and took on a more serious, sinister tone, requiring more extensive research and historical veracity. As such, I would like to make particular note of aspects of the story that I have fictionalised. Firstly, Stuttgart was not bombed by the Allies in September 1942. But there were over fifty raids on the city during the war, and more than four thousand people lost their lives. I chose this city due to its position relative to the mountainous regions of The Black Forest and the Alps. There are no such villages as Felshoven, Kalterfluss or Schwarzberg, as far as I know.

Operation Schwarzberg, and Oberstleutnant Kessler and his family, are fictional.

One truth that this story picks up on is that Adolf Hitler was keen to place a copy of *The Tales of the Brothers Grimm* in every German household. This may have had something to do with the fact that, throughout these tales, the characters who are physically or emotionally different from what the Nazis deemed as the norm were portrayed as evil or unintelligent. Some of the tales were certainly based in antisemitism, and the collection, as it stood, was used as a symbol of German Nationalism and racial superiority.

Another fact is that Joseph Goebbels, the Nazi Minister of Propaganda, saw the power the radio had for spreading Hitler's despicable message to the masses. World War II was one which saw this new wave of communication technology used to its full extent. Goebbels produced the Volksempfänger, a cheap radio that was affordable to most households, and it was said at the Nuremberg trials that, through this radio, '80 million people were deprived of independent thought'.

With all this in mind, this story, and the ones within it, are obviously tales of fiction. Any inaccuracies, errors or omissions are either here for the sake of the story, or because I, as the writer, have made a mistake.

There is truth in every tale, but no matter what horror this story evokes, it is nothing compared to what the millions of victims of the heinous Nazi regime suffered between 1933 and 1945.

ACKNOWLEDGEMENTS

First and foremost, I need to thank Niki from Penguin Random House Australia. This book would not exist, as it is now, without you. There were a lot of mistakes made in my initial draft – both historical, and when it came to capturing modern attitudes and acceptances. The dilemma was – how to write a book based in a time when, and a world where, these attitudes were so different to those that are acceptable in much of the world now. I feel that this final edition, in a large part thanks to you, strikes the balance right. But, to everybody out there reading this, if there are any instances where I haven't got it quite right, it is down to me.

Also, a huge thank you to Zoe for accepting the manuscript and for your valuable feedback throughout the process. And to everybody from Penguin Random House Australia who was involved in the production, and distribution, of this book.

Thanks, as always, to Dyan Blacklock, for believing in this story from the beginning. For your honesty and, let's be blunt, bluntness when things don't go quite as expected.

To Christa Moffitt of Christabella Design, once more, for capturing the essence of the book so perfectly with the cover.

To my fellow creators within the South Australian Kid Lit community, and others outside of it, for your friendship, encouragement and support.

To booksellers around Australia. I know what a great job you do, how it's much more than the simplification of the word itself. You are educators, informers, consultants, agents of change, entertainers and, sometimes, even counsellors. Thank you for your support of *What We All Saw*. I hope you enjoy selling *One by One They Disappear*.

Which leads me onto bookseller extraordinaire, ABA Children's Bookseller of the Year 2022, Literary Booking Agent, first reader, best friend and wonderful wife, Becky. I couldn't have done it without you.

And a very furry thank you to 19-year-old Morgan, who spent much of his time with me during the writing of this, often stretched out on the table in the sun, or walking across the keyboard. He may have contributed to some of the earlier edits.

And finally to you, the reader, for not only following Hannah's journey, but also for taking a moment to understand some of the elements that have gone into creating this book. A writer may work alone, but a finished book takes a team of people.

If I have forgotten anybody, please be assured you do exist in my mind and my heart. But sometimes those pages get stuck together so hard.